Boo'd Up with a St. Louis Goon

TaugJaye

D0681688

Copyright © 2018 TaugJaye
Published by Lucinda John Presents
All rights reserved. No part of this book may be reproduced in any form without written consent of the publisher, except brief quotes used in reviews.

This is a work of fiction. Any references or similarities to actual events, real people, living or dead, or to real locals are intended to give the novel a sense of reality. Any similarity in other names, characters, places, and incidents are entirely coincidental.

Chapter One

Tears trickled down Falcon's eyes as the incense burned in the air, creating a white, smoky, thick, fog that surrounded her son's casket. She held on to his lifeless hand praying to God that this all was just a dream; that the tears running down her cheeks were a figment of her imagination, and that she wasn't seconds away from burying her youngest son, Akil.

How could this have happened? Family was their number one emblem. Protect the family. Love the family. Honor the family. Bring no harm to the family. Nothing about Akil's murder had stemmed from the values and morals that the Platinum Kingdom was built off of.

She jumped when she felt a hand rest upon the nape of her back; she was lost in the sorrows that had disconnected her from the world surrounding her, minus her son. Falcon looked up and noticed the grey eyes of her salt and pepper bearded husband, Osiris. His face was like stone, but beyond his pupils laid the same hurt and pain that was consuming her.

"How could this have happened, Si? I just don't understand. . ." she wept in agony before her cries finally escaped her lips while she rested her head upon his strong chest.

Osiris held his wife close. Falcon had been out of character for the last year, ever since their beef with the Kamikazes was ignited. He rubbed her beautiful jet-black hair that fell down her back before he lifted her chin and kissed her lips. Falcon knew that one single kiss meant that her husband would handle their troubles and soon, so she straightened up her face and stood tall.

She eyed her dearest Akil resting peacefully one last time before her middle son, Jediah, approached the casket. He'd cut his thirty-inch hair down to a low fade out of respect for the passing of his baby brother. Jediah eyed the tattoo of the falcon symbol on the surface of Akil's left hand before he looked down at the same one along his very own. They've been separated by hate, but nothing could ever kill nor diminish the love and loyalty that would forever keep them bonded.

"We need to go."

The deep baritone in Osiris' voice always had the power to make Jediah and his mother cringe a bit. It was a dominate impact that Jediah hoped to have the moment he was coined with the crown to run the Platinum dynasty that he knew was soon to come. Falcon shielded her face with the large bubble framed shades to hide her swollen eyes as their family got ready to make their exit.

She hated to have so many eyes on her in this time of grieving, but she was the queen to a king who ruled the world, and she had to play her position like she has for the last thirty years.

The commotion, gasps, and sudden chattering from the crowd disturbing the peace that once controlled the atmosphere made Falcon, her husband, and son all turn around to see why the fuck their family and friends had disrespected Akil's burial. Homecomings were the times of peace. It was a sacred time where the soul had its last encounter on earth before it soared into the skies to reunite with the rest of their risen angels.

Falcon dropped her belongings and let her mouth hit the floor as well when she saw the image of the six-foot-four caramel skinned man approaching them.

"Seth. . ."

She couldn't believe her eyes. Her husband and son stood back as she began to meet him halfway. When she approached him, he bowed his head in respect before he dropped down to his knees and threw his arms around her waist. Falcon's emotions were taking control of her. She held the back of her son's head and kissed his cheeks in disbelief.

"What are you doing here? How did you—"

Seth held onto his mother's wrist as he gazed into her eyes, prompting her to cut her inquires short. He was her first born. He was supposed to have taken his father's place a year ago, but he was arrested while on a trip down in Mexico and was thrown in their prison to await a trial that he was sure he'd never see.

"Let me pay my respects to Akil first."

With a teary-eyed smile, Falcon nodded her head up and down, giving him the permission to once again rise to his feet. He straightened the black suit jacket along his stocky frame and adjusted his tie before he stood face to face with his father. Seth placed his left hand along his old man's right shoulder as Osiris placed his right hand along his son's left shoulder. While holding on to each other with both hands now, they pressed their foreheads together and said a silent prayer before they released.

Seth next stood face to face with Jediah. His younger brother was astonished to see him, but Seth was hollow. Jediah went to reach for his brother's left shoulder to show him respect, but Seth brushed his hand away and walked around him, not giving him the honor nor gratification for being in his presence.

The crowd sighed once more from his contempt. Seth was never the man to hide his feelings or put on a front before anyone. Not their family, not their father, nor their mother. He didn't give a damn. Family always came first, even if they were their own enemies, but Seth would never let that same family take him out of character. He honored the man he was, and his Geminis nature wouldn't allow him to bow heads with his brother knowing he wanted his blood.

The tears raced to the surface of Seth's eyes unlike any other moment in his life. His long thirty-inch curly hair hung over him as he bowed his head praying over Akil, and his unfortunate departure. When Seth got locked up he made Akil promise him that he'd take care of himself, their mother and father, and not let their dynasty crumble at the greed and deceit of Jediah's tyrant mind that no one other than him could see.

Akil was young, but he had heart. He was a Platinum man. Their blood ran through his veins, and Seth knew his brother had it in him to be a boss like him and Osiris, but it was Jediah's amiable nature and conniving tactics that always got Akil swept up in his grasp, which often held him back.

Seth remembered as the words *I promise* left his brothers lips from the last time he saw him, just as Akil managed to get away. Moments later, after holding up as a decoy for as long as he could to assure his brother's escape, he was surrounded by the police and taken into custody.

Akil's death confirmed every twisted thought that had ever entered his head in association with Jediah; not even prison could hold him back. Mexico would have to cross the border to take him down. Seth was at the point of no return, and he was ready to go to war with who ever had gotten in his path when it got down to the wire. Even if it was his family.

T

"Stop it! Stop iiiiit! Seth, get off of him!"

"Falcon, no! I said NO WOMAN! Calm the fuck down right now!" Osiris growled as he held his frantic wife by the waist.

She kicked and screamed, trying her best to break away from him so she could attempt to pull her sons from off of each other again. Seth was now on top of Jediah with one hand around his neck while his right fist continued to come down hard on his brother's eye. Jediah reached for Seth's neck, but he wasn't physically stronger than his brother. They used to have the same build until Seth got put in the pin and push-ups became his best friend.

Seth couldn't control the rage that was running through him. Blood splattered everywhere, and he wouldn't let up until the sound of a machine gun blasting in the air made him turn his head to see his grandfather holding an assault rifle in his hand.

"That's enough."

Nabawi's voice was low and rasp as his chest heaved up and down, fighting to inhale as much air as he could from the nasal cannula that was attached to his portable oxygen tank. Seth was so focused on his grandfather who was seconds away from an asthma attack, that he didn't see it coming when Jediah's knuckles made one with his mouth.

Fed up, Seth pulled the Desert Eagle from out of his suit jacket and blasted a single barrel in Jediah's chest; a reflex their father had instilled in them all when they were younger, giving him

8

a flesh wound. Once again, Seth had spared his life, but he knew the day would come when it was time for him and his brother to go heads up for real. This was nothing but a spur of the moment ordeal.

"JEDIAH!!!!" Falcon screamed at the top of her lungs.

She'd just buried one son, and she couldn't take the fiasco that was consuming their home just minutes later.

Seth rose to his feet and spat the blood out his mouth onto his brother who was holding his hand over the hole in his chest.

"What is your problem, Seth!" His mother continued to scream.

"My problem?" His voice was calm as he pushed his hair out of his face, so he could have a clear view as he looked at his elders before he continued. "If you don't know what the problem is, then we don't have shit to talk about," he hissed as his hand clutched the gun even tighter.

"You still think I was the one who got yo' bitch ass locked up! You fucked up, son! You dropped the ball on that bullshit! You the one who almost cost Akil his life *then*! If it wasn't for me coming to get his ass from the border he would've *been dead*!" Jediah roared as he struggled to stand to his feet.

He was a Platinum. Sure, he may have had a bullet in his chest, but they were built tough like oxen.

"Akil survived because I made it happen for him to escape! How the fuck did MPD know exactly when—"

"Fluke on yo' end bitch!" His brother angrily cut him off. "I told you that team you had with you wasn't loyal!"

Seth cocked his hand back and knocked Jediah out cold with the butt of his gun. He was tired of him still tryna fuck with his intelligence like he didn't know about the sketchy shit he had pulled. Jediah's body hit the floor, and his head slumped over while blood dripped from out his busted mouth.

"Get a fucking nurse in here, Osiris! Where the fuck is Luna!"

Their maid frantically ran in the living room from hiding behind the walls of the kitchen with a first aid kit in hand once she heard Falcon's inquire about her whereabouts. She pulled out all of her surgical tools, gloved up, and got to work immediately on Jediah's wound.

"If you came here to start some shit, Seth, then you can take your ass right the fuck back to prison! I'm not having this shit under any fucking circumstances! Your ass is seconds away from me busting one in your fucking head right now! Osiris, let me go!" Falcon was mortified.

"I see he dun' already got y'all caught up in his whim," Seth chuckled as he ran his hand through his hair. "Shit's funny." He continued.

"Seth, in my office. Now." His father commanded.

"I'm tired of speaking in private. That's how we got here. I was locked up for a year, and ain't nobody come after me? Everybody so fucking stunned to see me, but where the fuck was y'all at when them bitch ass niggas put me away!

"No fucking where! I had already been planning my escape, but when word about Akil got around, it should've been known that y'all was gon' see me again, and soon!" Their son barked.

"You took that shit upon yo' self to head out there on unmarked territory, Seth! And, you knew that shit with the Kamikazes wouldn't take nothing but a grain of salt to tip the scale, yet you pushed it anyway!" His father argued.

"Everything was straight with the Kamikazes until his son got murked! I told y'all to fall back on the Desoto invasion before we made it back in town! See, that's the problem, Si! Everybody gets thrown off track once Jediah gets to whispering in ya damn ear about this and that, when I've already laid shit down!

"I respect yo' hustle, Si! I always have, and I swore to God that I always would! I respect what you built for us, but you was supposed to trust me! Especially while we were in the transition of handing the dynasty over to my command! How the fuck you gon' trust a nigga to lead yo' army, but don't listen to shit he got to say, or pay attention to the moves he be making!"

"Kamikaze's son was murdered after you got locked up! You knew them muthafuckas thought the Platinum name was all over that shit!"

"No! Kamikaze's son was killed before that happened! I walked into a fucking set up when I got out there to meet up with Juno! Surprise muthafucka! That's why the fucking beef started because they think Akil was the muthafucka who murked his ass on some sneaky shit since he got away! And you would've known that had you come after me whether I was on unmarked territory or not!

"MPD kept me alive because they knew it was a high bid out on my name, and they was waiting on whoever to come and get me! Did you forget that we were still left undecided with Mexico too! You could've posted that mil on my name with no problem and signed an alliance, but you was too busy riding this nigga's dick on some bullshit! They was gon' hand me off to the first muthafucka who jumped fence, then choose a side, and they didn't care who came first!"

"Then why let you sit for a year Seth! Huh!!!" Osiris protested, ignoring his son's explanation.

He knew good and damn well that Mexico would let Seth sit until someone came after him, but he didn't want to jeopardize the start of an early war with the Kamikazes if they bailed him out.

Bailing Seth out would've coined their involvement with Juno's death, and he didn't wanna risk it, so he let his son sit. They had to take an "L" somewhere.

"Are you going against the grain of this family and saying that Jediah was the one behind the setup, P1? Huh?"

His mother's words were faint as she interrupted them. She had tears in her eyes. She couldn't believe that her son was disrespecting their emblem by pointing fingers at his own kind.

"What's said don't need to be understood. I don't show respect to no muthafucka that tried to cross me. Si is my father. I'll always owe him a sense of recognition because I came from him, but that's it. You made it clear who had your respect. You made it clear who you trusted. You made it clear that you chose Jediah to step up. My absence just picked up the tempo. You think I don't know how you move, Osiris?

"You only going after The Kamikaze's eye for and eye threat on some real shit now because Akil is dead. Then, you was

11

gon' step down, and hand the dynasty over to a nigga who don't even got y'all's best interest at heart. But because he's your "son" and you're letting your got-damn feelings interfere with business, you don't see that shit.

"A part of me believed that you was coming for me, but I see that shit with my own eyes now that you never intended on doing so. Now we wanna talk about upholding the family honor? Fuck out of here."

Osiris was boiling. Seth's blatant disrespect was unacceptable. His hand on the Glock 40 in his suit jacket was seconds away from putting one between his son's eyes, but Falcon had intervened, once again, when she stood in P1's face, blocking his target, and saving his life.

"Seth Shakur Platinum. I never thought I'd see the day when you betrayed your family, and out of spite? Get the fuck out of my house, and nigga you better pray that I don't send the army after yo' ass either."

Her son chuckled as he straightened his tie before he aimed his gun at the rear wall and emptied out the clip into their family portrait that came crashing down along the marble floor. He turned his back on each of them as his Valentino loafers click-clacked against the ground on his way out, with intentions on never looking back.

Chapter Two

Seth inhaled deeply from the Backwoods as the weed consumed his body. With one hand on the steering wheel he cruised down the freeway in his royal blue Maybach 6 convertible as some 3 Problems blasted in the air around him. His high was coming on instantly. A year away from his daily ritual cleared his head and made him aware of the things that he's been putting off for a while now. He thanked God for the enlightenment and the opportunity to take that time and get his mind right, but now he was back, and muthafuckas was gon' watch him put shit down like he never left.

The blue rays from his headlights lit up the highway until he exited off I-270 onto McDonnell and headed west until he crept upon Hazelwood county. The detour allowed him to take the city in and observe his surroundings. They were building up the area, but this was Saint Louis. Chaos roamed these streets no matter how good muthafuckas tried to make it look, and it would always be a death trap with or without new landscape.

Seth pulled up on the two-story home where a bunch of folks stood around chilling. It was August; the last few days of summer before the fall had hit the scene. It might've been nine at night, but the old heads had the music blasting, card tables were put up, and dominos and spades were being ran while the brightness from the installed field lights lit up the area.

Seth's potna Messiah had been living in this house since they were kids. When his folks passed away, they had left it to him, and in return, he turned it into the ultimate chill spot. Messiah was all about family as well, and even though his parents were gone, their relatives stayed coming over, cookouts were a weekly buzz, and they celebrated in their absence just like old times.

"Shoulda' known this nigga would pop out when he made it back to the states. Wassup young blood?"

"Fuck on with that young blood shit, Geno." Seth implored as he pounded his fist with his potna's crack head ass uncle.

"My fault. My fault. Young Crip. No disrespect. Aye, you got some shit?"

"You know I don't touch that shit. What you looking for? I'll have somebody pull up on you."

"Can you spot me this time?" he pleaded.

Geno looked like he was already wired. His junkie ass didn't need shit else before he got to tryna stick his little ass dick in every bitch he saw, regardless of relation.

"Fuck I look like, nigga? Product ain't free." Seth countered, disgruntled from the disrespect.

He was lucky he was his boy's uncle, or else he would've had his clip shoved down his throat lighting his stomach with bullet holes.

"A'ight. A'ight. I got five on it."

Seth shook his head as he kissed Aunt Boosie's forehead and slapped hands with the rest of the family.

"I ain't calling nobody out here for five punk ass dollars. When you ready to come at me correct, nigga you know where to find me."

"Damn, nephew? Don't do me like that!"

Seth kept making his way to the entrance as he grabbed one of the 16 oz. aluminum cans of the Bud Light Limes from out a trashcan filled to the brim with ice. He removed the cap and took a few deep swigs damn near downing the whole bottle.

"Hey, P1! You're back! Today is a muthafucking good day like my nigga Ice Cube says! How you doing, sexy?"

"Wassup, sweetheart?"

Seth threw his arms around Messiah's older cousin, Trudy, when she stood up to take a quick break from doing the white-blonde box braids on a shorty. She kissed his cheek before saying, "I'm good. Making this money like usual. Ya boy upstairs. He just made it in not too long ago."

"Bet."

"Damn girl who was that? With his fine ass. Look at all that fucking hair! Oh my God! Why you ain't introduce me!"

Seth could hear her client's statement as he began to climb the stairs while heading to the master bedroom. He pulled so many bitches that it didn't even faze him. He'd never came across a bitch who wasn't attracted to him, or one who didn't try to break her neck to get his attention in some way, shape, or form.

His native heritage is where he got his long, silky, and curly hair from. Standing six-four with a slim though stocky frame, anchor styled goatee, pantie dropping hazel eyes, and peanut butter skin, many women mistook him for the Atlanta model Shamoyy Persad who was featured on Nicki Minaj's verse in the "Do You Mind" music video.

It grinded his gears when he heard that shit. That wasn't a compliment in his eyes. Seth was a ruthless ass killer and knew he had nuts bigger than a punk ass model ever would. He was a businessman, a hustler, a fucking king; so, comparing him to a model was down-right disrespectful in his opinion.

He was a zaddy for real. His deep though mesmerizing voice when he spoke put bitches under a spell, just the way he liked it, and he was always fresh too.

Tonight, he kept it simple and was rocking a white t-shirt and dark Radburn distressed denim jeans with some olive-colored W SF Air Force Ones. A single snake link, gold chain hung around his neck corresponding the Rolex on his wrist while he wore his hair down his back.

Seth had a beautiful face; his acne free, smooth skin looked like the only thing he drunk was spring water. He appeared to be a pretty boy, but his body count was so high muthafuckas knew, from him, that looks were very deceiving.

When he approached the door to his potna's room, all he heard was ass smacking and the moans from a loud-mouthed chocolate chick.

Knock-Knock

"Come on!" Messiah hollered over the woman's moans, giving his potna the okay to enter. He was breaking her back in while her fat ass clapped against his thighs.

"Wassup, bruh," he greeted out of breath as he released one hand from her shoulder to pound his homie.

"Wassup wit' it?"

Seth headed straight to the joining bathroom to take a piss. Him and Messiah were dawgs. They'd been fucking bitches and running shit since the mid-2000's. A lot of females willingly gave themselves to the both of them.

They didn't even have to ask bitches for threesomes. Hoes spread their legs and got down on their knees without hesitating when they saw them. It wasn't no fun if the homie couldn't have none, right?

Seth had his dick in hand dripping it dry when the door opened. He looked back and saw the thick honey walk inside butt ass naked. When he turned around she was already kneeling in a praying position while pulling her hair up with a scrunchy.

He grabbed the bottom of her chin and let her mouth cover him. His dick grew quick. As if on cue, all ten inches of his fat brown dick tensed up, and he held onto the back of her head while his hips started moving forward and back.

Whoever shorty was, she was trill. She was taking the dick like a pro. Her mouth was wet and slippery. He couldn't help himself as he gripped her hair tighter while her saliva dripped along her chest as he fucked her face. I mean shorty was a monster. Most bitches couldn't fit more than half his dick in their mouth all at once. He had some work for a slim nigga, but he had to give chocolate drop her props.

Seth had been so focused on business that this was his first encounter with a woman since he'd been back in the states for the last couple of days. Before ole' girl knew it, he had one leg up on the tub, she had her hands on the toilet, and once he was strapped up he was pounding her shit. He had his hand around her neck while he watched her ass jiggle against him. There wasn't nothing like a big brown ass that drove Seth up a damn wall.

"Oh, fuck! Oh, shit! Aaaaaaaah! Ooooooh! Oh, my goood! Oh! Oh! Oh! Baby! Ooooh! Fuck me!"

Seth slapped her ass before gripping her neck tighter. Pussy was a spell a man just couldn't break free from until he got one off.

"I ain't yo' fucking baby, bitch," he grunted as he pulled her body back, away from the toilet, and bent her all the way over before he grabbed her by the waist and kept digging deeper in her guts.

Lil' chocolate drop was so lost in the sauce he could call her a million bitches and she wouldn't trip. A rough ass hood nigga made her pussy wet. That's what she liked.

Seth's dick was so fat her shit still felt tight even though the homie was fresh out her walls. When he felt himself about to let off, he pulled out, turned her around, and let his load off in her mouth, coating her Cardi B fat and long tongue. She sat like the ho she was and took his cum like it was second nature.

Seth washed himself off, dried his hands, and entered the room where Messiah sat in a pair of basketball shorts, smoking a fat ass Backwoods while rolling another.

"How we end up out the pin days apart my nigga?"

"On me," Seth responded as they slapped hands. "I heard you was in while I was jammed up. The fuck was that shit about?"

Messiah released the smoke through his lips as the woman exited out of the bathroom, got dressed, and quietly left.

"That was a fine piece of pussy my nigga. Might have to call shorty back. She get you right?" he grinned as he passed his dawg the blunt.

Seth laughed as they slapped hands while he inhaled deeply.

"But yeah," Messiah continued. "Back to that shit. That bitch ass nigga Jediah straight set me up, bruh. Had me going to pick up a "last minute" shipment, and the opps got me right after I had my semi loaded. The day we was supposed to hit up Mexico.

"If that shit wasn't sketchy, then tell me otherwise. It's like that when I see that nigga. I knew him and Osiris split us up for a reason. Killing two birds with one stone my ass. We the ones who got, got, my nigga."

Malice grazed over Seth's face when he thought back to the altercation from earlier.

"About that. We gon' handle that; like I should've done a long fucking time ago, but it's all good." His words were harsh.

"Niggas be faking, dawg. All they loyal to is the money, but I'mma be honest. Tito and the squad been laying low since we both got jammed up. He sent me a postcard in the mail from the Bahamas. I'm guessing they out there with Meme Aruba on the shore."

"Yeah, he sent me one too," Seth confirmed as he pushed his hair out his face. "I ain't even mad at that though. Them laying low after all the sketchy shit that's been going on with the dynasty was a smart move."

"I heard the Platinums sent squads looking for 'em. Fifty deep, each. Thought they was shacked up on one of the estates. They sent armies out to each territory on some backdoor bullshit tryna make sure everybody from our crew got smashed. I couldn't believe that shit when word got to me. I could only do so much; they had me in Riker's."

"That's yo' second home, fam."

"Bruh, for real. Lame ass fucking charge. They got me for sixty ki's too. Lil' shorty who just left? Her brother the new DA. She say lil' bro got in touch with her a couple days before we got out once he found some background info on somebody useful we knew. He saw she was some kin to the Fords who know us well, wired the money, and it was that. Shorty helped him get something together with her brother then the next thing I knew, I was out.

"I knew it was something about her that would pay off in due time. When Prodigy got involved that's how I got word out to you. We wasn't even gon' fall for that ransom bullshit. The Kamikazes was waiting on a muthafucka to come get you. We figured you'd pull sum' off once you heard about lil' bro. He said he last saw Akil three days before word got around that he got murked."

Messiah stopped in the middle of his explanation to bow his head in respect for his potna's loss before he continued.

"Peep this though. That nigga J4 helped O and JD set us up too. Jediah brided him to be his right hand man once we got taken out," he explained, referring to one of their potnas that they thought they could trust.

"That shit crazy, man. You can't trust nobody these days. Every important piece on the board dun' crossed us on some ho shit. I can't believe this shit. Tell me J4 dun' been bodied."

Messiah nodded his head in agreement.

"Akil and Prodigy took care of it the night they was together. Shits fucked up, man. They straight had us in a tight lil' bind for a minute. I just got back from doing a year my damn self before they got me out. I want a muthafucka to come after me. I ain't hiding from no muthfucking body. They know where the fuck to find me."

Seth didn't respond. Hearing about Akil was heartbreaking. The death of his baby brother was hurting like something he'd never felt before, and he couldn't explain it. This beef that sparked with their ally had him so discombobulated, he could admit that he didn't even know where to start.

He was jammed up, his potna was jammed up, his crew had to lay low to stay alive, and if the Kamikazes would've caught anyone tryna head to Mexico from their team, they were slaughtering shit.

He understood why his father hadn't come after him in one light. The heat was hot. Bailing him out would've sparked a hotter flame, but Si didn't even attempt to do so. He didn't even send a law team on Seth's behalf like he wasn't his son.

Osiris was the fucking king. Nothing moved in these waters without his consent, so he could've worked something out with the team they had in Cuba on some lay low shit. Everybody knew somebody who knew somebody.

The Platinum's name held rank. High rank. Their family was the most notorious cartel around besides the Kamikazes. If it wasn't owned by the Kazes, then it was Platinum territory. Period. They'd been on the fence for years, waiting on the ball to drop.

But, before Seth could finally get the peace going between them so they could really get down and start working on tighter international connects, he got locked up, and somebody had to go and murk Juno before they could even make shit happen.

"Where the fuck that nigga been at?" Seth questioned while rolling another blunt.

"Who Prodigy? You know that nigga been out filming in third-world countries and shit. He said he was gon' meet up with us as soon as he was done filming this movie for Netflix though. Ready for another plot twist?

"J4 ain't tell him shit about us being jammed up until *this summer*. A whole fucking year later thinking Prodigy wasn't gon' do shit because he be so busy with his career and got out the game years ago. I never liked that nigga J4. It was always something about him that I couldn't rock with. Why all these niggas moving so foul bruh? Shit's crazy."

Prodigy was one of the only solid niggas that Seth and Messiah fucked with outside of family. They all built a brothership running the streets. Prodigy was more into school when they were younger once he realized that he wanted to do more than sell dope, but his potnas respected that. It was reluctant to know that they still had some niggas on their team who still shared the same definition of loyalty.

"I knew it would come down to this," Seth finally responded.

"What? Making the fam choose between you and JD?" Messiah questioned, referring to Jediah.

Seth let the smoke release through his nose before he looked at his potna with hollow eyes.

"It's either they with me, or they not. We'll see how loyal a hungry dog is once the shit gets down to the nitty gritty, and soon my nigga. Real soon."

Chapter Three

"You say you gotta giiiiiirl,
Now you want me,
How you want me when you gotta girl. . ."

Sza's erotic smash hit "The Weekend" filled the air as Nasir's body flowed across the dance floor. No, she wasn't a stripper. Nasir was a dance instructor. With her eyes closed, her arms flowed like pastel water watercolors along an empty canvas to create a beautiful picture. Sza's words consumed her in a way that she couldn't control, and it made her connect with her inner self unlike she's ever done before.

Plie'. Round de jambo. Leap Leap. Swoosh, swoosh, swoosh!

Her arms moved in rapid movements.

Annnnnnd on those tippy toes, Nas. Gracefully make those feet flutter, then jump! Land lightly. Self-control. Discipline. But be delicate girl, and not too sexy. You're still on the job, but this is your shit. Sza did her thang, didn't she, bitch?

Laughter escaped Nas' lips as she opened her eyes and glanced at herself in the mirror. Her hair was pulled back into a tight French bun, and her lash tensions were bold amongst her face full of freckles. Nas hated looking in the mirror, so she closed her eyes once more and kept twirling around the dance floor until one of her students yelled, "WALL! Ms. Valentine! Ooooh!"

Smack!

Nas' eyes opened when her gut made one with the ballet bar before she fell back on her ass.

"Ooooouch!" she laughed as she flopped back in a supine position.

It felt so good to laugh. She hadn't remembered the last time when she had laughed so hard that tears fell down her face.

"I tried to warn you."

Nas opened her eyes when she heard her student approach her.

"Get up Ms. V, hurry up. You not supposed to be down there that long. Don't let people see you on the floor!"

Nas continued to laugh as Tiri helped her stand to her feet.

"Thanks, girlie."

She looked in the mirror as she wiped the dust from off the back of her leggings.

"No problem. Why do you do that?"

"Do what?" Nas questioned puzzled.

"Dance with your eyes closed? You always tell us to look in the mirror when we dance, but you do the opposite every time you freestyle."

Nas smiled as she used the remote to silence the surround sound system.

"I don't follow the rules, do I?" She smiled.

"But you're so good. I don't get it. Why wouldn't you want to look at yourself? You're so pretty. I mean, I'mma be honest; you pretty damn fine Ms. V, and that's woman to woman."

"Woman to woman? Didn't you just turn seventeen, talking some woman-to-woman?" Nasir giggled as they exited the dance floor.

"I'm for real." The teenager argued.

"What are you still doing here lil' momma? It's 3:30. School let out an hour ago."

Tiri playfully rolled her eyes, knowing her instructor was trying to ignore her question.

"I'm waiting on my big brother to get here. He's always late. Can't stand his ass. Every damn day I'm waiting in him for at least an hour. I can't wait until I get my license, but he's gotta finish teaching me how to drive first. That's fucking pathetic. I'm seventeen and I can't even drive. Ooooh, my bad, Ms. V." She caught herself with the fowl mouth.

"You better get that tongue in order. I know I'm not old, but *damn*."

"Okay, Ms. V!"

Their laughter filled the air. Nasir cut the lights out then locked the door to her studio behind her.

"Come on. I'll wait with you."

"You don't have to." Tiri assured.

"But I will. Come on, let's stop at the smoothie counter. Drinks on me."

"Well, yes ma'am. I won't turn down nothing free."

Nasir loved her job. She'd danced at performing arts schools up until she had gotten her diploma, she danced for Cocoa, and even went to UMKC where she graduated at twenty-two and received her license to teach.

She'd been an instructor at the new performing arts school ever since Saint Louis City had opened it three years ago. Eloquent VPA was her baby, and she loved all her babies from the ones who were new on the team, to her graduates and upper-class alumni.

"How's the school year treating you, miss lady?" Nas asked as they both sipped on their pineapple-mango smoothies while they exited the double glass doors.

The new school was beautiful. It was located on Vandeventer in the Central West Inn where a car wash used to sit, right across from the new IKEA store. It was a great location, the building was huge, and it held twelve hundred students.

Nasir was impressed with Saint Louis' output with the construction. She had never seen a city school so beautiful. It had Career Academy High, the latest school to be renovated in years, beat by a long shot, landscape and size wise.

"I'm doing okay. I'm not really the popular kinda girl. Everybody in my family is popular. My brother gets all the women, and my cousins are so hip and known throughout town. Then, there's me. Quiet, little Tiri."

"Oh no baby girl. Let me tell you something. Don't be that girl."

"But—"

"No buts, baby," she interrupted. "I was that way in high school, and it hit my adult life hard. Have fun, make those friends, smile, join a team, hell, join two teams, keep your grades high, and get those scholarships. You never get your high school days back.

"I'm not saying get out here and be a lil' hot ass, but what I am saying is have fun. Don't think of what you're not. Think if who you are and who you wanna be and have fun. Life is what you make it."

Tiri smiled.

"My momma used to tell me that before she died a few years ago."

"Then do that. Make your mother proud. I'm more than one hundred percent positive that she wouldn't want you to be down and sheltered. You're beautiful, you're smart, and your dance skills are so dope. You've come a long way since freshman year. We gon' do some damage senior year. Just watch."

"You think so?" Tiri smiled as her brown cheeks turned rosy from blushing.

"Aren't you always front and center in every dance? Who did I just give a solo to that had people so salty. Y'all teenagers are so cutthroat."

"The S-Chicks was hella salty when you gave me that part, Ms. V," Tiri responded, referring to the most popular girls in school.

They always hated on her. Whenever she wore anything designer and came to school rocking some exclusive shit they swore it was fake. The shade these days was real.

"Don't let them get to you. They're always starting some shit around here, but you keep working hard. Hate is silent love. They're just jealous because you all that Tiri and, you're not boastful with it. You keep doing you. They're just pressed."

"Thanks, Ms. V, that really means a lot to me."

Nasir smiled.

"You're welcome."

The loud sound of 3 Problems' Freestyle to his "When I was Broke" track interrupted their conversation as the black Bentley truck pulled up on the curve before them.

"Oh my God. He's so damn ghetto. Why you always gotta be seen and heard, Messiah! You already that nigga!" Tiri laughed as her brother rolled down the passenger's side window to his whip.

"My fault, bae! Get in the back!" he yelled over the music.

"Be safe, baby girl. I'll see you Monday."

"See you later, Ms. V. Thanks for the smoothie!"

"You're welcome."

"Aye, who that, baby sus! She bad than a muthafucka!"

"Shut the hell up, Messiah! She don't want yo ass!" Tiri joked as she walked up to the truck.

Nasir put her large bubble shades on as she headed in the same direction to cross the street and start for her car that was parked in the parking lot about a block away.

Seth bobbed his head to the music as the smoke from the blunt released from his nose. The moment he glanced up from his phone, his eyes hit Nasir. Her image threw him back for a moment.

She was rocking some Nike leggings, and a pink razor back, displaying the black ink that covered both of her arms. Her glasses were blocking her face, and it frustrated him for a moment because he was interested in seeing what she looked like without them. Yet, he was confused as to why.

Nasir wasn't his type. Seth had a thing for a chocolate, slim bitch with a fat ass that was proper for her frame. He hated light skinned, sadity bitches to be honest, but there was something different about the woman before him.

Nasir was sculpted like the plus-sized version of Heather Sanders. Her stomach was almost nice and flat, and her thighs were thick for days. She didn't have the fattest ass, but she had a nice lil' arch in her frame. Her waist was sculpted nice and slim, and those titties were sitting up plump and real perky just the way he liked them.

Seth was a tittie man if he were to be forced to tell the truth. Hell, all men liked ass, but he'd suck on some titties all day long like a newborn baby until he fell asleep. Her skin was a bright yellow complexion like Lauren London's, but she reminded him a lot of Heather look-wise as well, except she had a stronger face.

Strong as is solemn and cocky; sis basically rocked a resting bitch face unlike the sweet and sassy smile that always stayed on Heather's. Nasir looked more like here sister, Kaleigh, but she was still just as beautiful.

"Ayyyyye! Big girls need love too! I'll bend yo' ass over and do you right, miss lady!" Messiah yelled as he stuck the shirtless, top half of his body out the window while yelling at Nasir who had begun to cross the street.

"Would you stop it! Don't embarrass me like that," Tiri shrieked as she stuck her head out the window. Her brother was a mess. "I'm sorry, Ms. V! Ignore him. Quit it, Messiah!" She griped as she pushed him in the head.

"Ayyyye! I'll beat that shit up!" he grinned, continuing to fuck with Nasir as she waved to Tiri who was waving goodbye to her.

He'd just finished a bottle of Hennessy, so he was feeling real good.

Seth's eyes hadn't left her as she continued on down the street. She had his mean ass mesmerized, and he couldn't believe it. Messiah's messy ass bucked a right and crept up along the sidewalk going five miles per hour while he had Seth's window raised back down.

"Yo', miss lady? You need a ride?"

Never has Messiah ever pushed so hard for a woman, even if he was just playing, but he's never fucked a curvy girl before, and she would be the perfect first. He heard their head was fire, and their pussy was like a big cotton candy cushion bouncing on their dick.

Nasir turned her head from looking down at her phone and removed the straw from her mouth. She smiled.

"No thank you. My car is only a block away. Thanks anyway, though."

"Hop in, ma," he insisted almost getting aggravated that she was being so fucking difficult. He was tryna fuck something.

"Messiah!" Tiri was so embarrassed.

"No, it's okay. I'm sure—shit, what is in my eye," Nasir mumbled more so to herself as she removed her shades to try and get what, she knew was a stubborn ass eyelash, out of her eye.

"Come here."

Seth had finally spoken.

Nasir looked over her shoulder, wondering who the hell he was talking to.

"Yeah, you. Ain't nobody else standing there is it? Come here like I said the first time."

Nas cocked her head back from his response.

"Excuse me?" She countered.

"You excused for being defiant with me for the second time now. Don't make me ask you again."

Nasir's feet started moving without her permission. She raised her perfectly arched eyebrow when she made it up to the window and eyed the lil' scrawny ass nigga sitting in the front seat. Yeah, he was long, physically stacked, and his muscle tone was chopped up nicely that his fitted white-t had displayed. Nasir had to admit that she liked skinny niggas, but she'd never tell him that.

"Don't do that, Seth. Y'all, she's my teacher. Would you please stop?" Tiri begged.

"You're rude," Nasir sassed while looking him up and down.

"Shit, you rude. The fuck you sizing me up like that for? You don't know me like that. You almost got yo' self kilt," he threatened while clutching the Lwrc sub gun sitting in his lap.

Nasir laughed.

"That's cute. Be safe, baby girl. I'll see you tomorrow."

"Ok Ms.—"

"Did I say you could walk away from me?" Seth interrupted.

"Nigga, watch me," Nas checked as she put her shades on and turned away from him.

Messiah pulled up on the curve blocking her from leaving. Seth hopped out the car with his gold-plated thumper in hand and approached her.

"Don't ever disrespect me like that. I don't think you know who the fuck you dealing with, but I don't fuck around with that disrespectful ass shit."

His words were like ice as he stood in her face.

"No, I don't think you know who you're dealing with. All this being hard shit with that punk ass gun ain't moving me, nigga. Get the hell up out my face before I call the—"

"Fuck the police," he interrupted. "I got police. You better educate yo' self, Ms. fucking lady. Ask about me, ma. Muthafuckas don't disrespect a Platinum and live to see the next day."

"Are you finished?"

Her smart-ass mouth made Seth clench his jaw. He didn't understand why bitches thought that shit was cute. Nobody wanted to be submissive. Every female swore she could hold it down, and he hated it.

That's why all he did was fuck majority of the bitches that he came across. They'd rather take cum in the face as an oath than to act like they had some fucking sense and listen to their man.

"Hey, is there a problem?"

Nasir looked back when she saw the police officer who had pulled up behind Messiah's illegally parked vehicle.

Seth didn't take his eyes from off her. Boldly he removed her shades and turned her face back towards him, forcing her to look him in the eye.

"Fuck that nigga. I'm talking to you, ain't I?"

"Ma'am, is there a problem?" The officer questioned again while reaching for his gun.

Messiah was now out the car with his Draco in hand while a blunt hung out the side of his mouth. They lived to pop the opps. That shit didn't faze them.

"No officer. There's no problem at all."

Nasir's words had escaped her lips, but her eyes hadn't left Seth who was staring so deeply into her soul that it started making her pussy wet. The nigga was mad crazy, but it turned her on.

"She said it wasn't no fucking problem, mane. Now get yo bitch ass back in the car you Uncle Sam ass nigga, or this gon' be yo last fucking day with air in yo lungs!" Messiah barked as he pulled back the chamber on his chopper.

The officer was shook. It was his first day on the job, and after this, it was surely gonna be his last. He turned around and hopped right back into his Tahoe truck so fast that all they heard were tires screeching when he pulled off.

"That's the second muthafucka that almost got kilt at yo expense. I told you to watch yo fucking mouth," Seth hissed, but as he licked his lips, he felt himself calm down a bit. She was so damn fine he couldn't believe she had him acting out like this.

All the while, Nasir hadn't moved, but she hadn't folded though either. He didn't sense fear coming for her, but her silence let him know that she got the fucking picture.

"Would y'all stop! I can't believe y'all! This is not funny!" Tiri was damn near in tears as she rolled her window down.

She knew not to get out the car. Her mouth would talk shit all day long because Messiah was her brother, and Seth was like an uncle to her, but she knew better than to try and beef up with them. Nasir was bold as fuck, and it scared the little girl. She knew what they did for a living, and she prayed they wouldn't do the same to her teacher.

"Roll the window back up, Tiri. It's cool." Messiah instructed with a chuckle.

"Baby T," Seth called out to her, causing her to leave the window down. "Make sure you educate yo teacher on who the fuck we are the next time you see her. Next time a muthafucka ain't gon' be nice. Luckily, we got shit to do, or she coulda' got this work."

Nasir raised her eyebrow at his response. This nigga was reaching, and she couldn't help but to burst out into laughter once she was able to force herself to breathe.

"Aaaaauah, shit. I ain't had a laugh like that in forever. Y'all niggas is funny. That was cute."

Nas was hollin'. Who the fuck did these niggas think they were?

"Did I say something funny?"

Seth's inability to faze this woman was grinding his gears, and if she *was* moved by him, but was using her stupidity to show it, then she was built pretty damn tough. But he didn't play that shit. He was a king and that's how bitches was gon' treat him.

"Come on, bruh. Shorty can't take a joke," Messiah laughed as he put his gun up on his shoulder.

"Obviously, she can since she so fucking entertained." Seth looked Nas up and down before he turned his back on her. "Don't end up like that, Tiri. Them the kind of women that only get fucked and be wondering why they be sitting at home every night alone crying because a nigga don't deal with they ass beyond a nut.

"Obedience, Baby T. Obedience will get you far. Not that bullshit. Today was her lucky fucking day. If you wasn't here, that shit would've been handled. Let's get the fuck out of here man," Seth countered as he closed the car door behind him.

Tiri stared out the window with tears falling down her eyes, waving goodbye to her teacher. The teenager had such an innocent soul. She mouthed the words *I'm sorry* hoping that she wouldn't take their actions out on her on Monday evening in class, but she managed to crack a slight smile when Nas had surprisingly smiled at her in return. She blew out a kiss and waved goodbye before she put her shades back on and kept on down the block as if nothing had happened.

T

It was eleven that night, and Nas was still shook up about the altercation from earlier in the day. By the time she made it to her car, she had started balling her eyes out, appalled by what the fuck had just happened to her. Did the police really leave her there?

She knew not to trust them anyway, but damn! Did that boisterous muthafucka really mouth off to her like that? Was she really so afraid that she felt her bladder leak a few times on her way home! Those niggas scared the piss out of her!

Her hand shook as she held the wine glass up to her lips. She figured that a nice nap would erase her memory, but she saw Seth's piercing hazel eyes in her dreams and woke up with more tears running down her face. She had never been so petrified.

The ringing of her phone made her jump so hard that she dropped her glass on the floor. It spilled all over her carpet.

"Fuck!" she yelled as she quickly ran to the kitchen and grabbed the blue bottle of Dawn dish detergent, and a hot rag to quickly scrub the stain out.

When the phone rang again, she reached for it on her nightstand before answering.

"Hello!" she yelled.

"Damn, bitch! Why you yelling! What the fuck! I ain't do shit to you!"

Nasir held her hand up to her nose and broke down. She couldn't help it, and her actions surprised herself, but she quickly swallowed her tears and got it together before saying, "Wassup, Alicia?"

"Wassup with me? Bitch, wassup with you? Open this damn door. Why you breaking down like that?"

Nasir got up off the floor and headed to the front of her apartment. She thought Alicia was bluffing, but there she was standing in her doorway, dressed and ready to go out on the town.

"What the fuck, Nas! You not dressed! Girl!" Alicia huffed aggravated as she closed the door behind her.

"Alicia, I don't have time for your shit tonight!" she spat as she wiped her tears away.

"Look, you need to go out, that's why you breaking down and shit. Get dressed. I don't wanna hear that shit. Come on. Put this ass," Alicia smacked her friend's bare butt in her thong. "In a dress or something and come on. Chop-chop. We can cry later. It's time to get drunk and enjoy this open bar all night. I heard the Platinums was gon' be in the building, and we ain't missing this."

Hearing that name made Nas' eyes widen.

"Hell no! I'm not going!" She screamed before she stomped all the way to her room and slammed the door behind her.

Alicia swung that bitch right back open.

"Don't slam no damn door in my face. What the fuck is wrong wit' chu? I do not have time for your fucking mood swings tonight. Put some clothes on and come the fuck on! I drove my ass all the way out here to Maryland Heights on expired plates, and bitch, I'm not going home until the morning!"

"Huuuuuuuuuuh!"

"Huuuuuuuuh, nothing! Put that same energy into putting on a damn outfit you sad ass lil' wanch, and come on!"

Chapter Four

An hour later Nas found herself out in Tower Grove against her will, walking down the street in her light pink and velvet thigh high open toe sandals trying to keep up with her hot ass friend. The bitch was switching her hips like she's never been around dick before. Nas rolled her eyes full of disgust.

Alicia was always talking her into some kind of crazy ass escapade that she always regretted. They always, always, always, went as simple as this: Alicia got pissy ass drunk, niggas were all over her, and she usually went home with one of them, leaving Nas alone looking dumb as fuck.

Thank God she had drove this time around because the moment Alicia got to getting on that bullshit she was bouncing, and the bitch could find her own ride home.

"Come on, Nas!"

"Don't fucking yell at me!" Nasir spat as she put a little pep in her step.

Shotta's in Tower Grove was alllllways popping. It was a new club owned by the Platinum territory. Nas never really cared to go because she knew it was expensive to get in the door; plus, she knew the Platinums were one of the most dangerous gangs in the region, and she didn't wanna be around that mess. But hot ass Alicia just wanted her a Platinum nigga so got damn bad that she'd do whatever she had to do and at any cost to get one.

"It's fifty dollars to get in." Alicia informed when Nasir had made it pass the long line of people who were waiting.

She didn't know how Alicia had pulled that off, but whatever.

"Fifty fucking dollars! Are you fucking high, or just desperate!" Nasir 'bout lost it.

"Quit being cheap!"

"Bitch, I'd be balling too if I was living on Section 8," Nas spat in her ear not to embarrass her wannabe bougie ass.

She had to bring this lil' hood rat back down to size. Alicia knew when Nas got buck that she better had watched out.

"Girl, come on! You need another fucking drink! Yo' bitch radar still off the fucking wall! Bitch, you capping tonight!"

Nas didn't know how she got caught up being Alicia's friend. Maybe it was because she had pulled her out her shell a few years ago when they met in California. She helped Nas save her social life by being the best friend she'd ever had.

The bitch was mad bossier than she was fun though, and her attitude was pure trash at times. Every female had a little fire in her pit, but Alicia went overboard with the shit, and Nas just didn't like it.

She wasn't sure if she felt like she owed Alicia something, but whatever it was, their friendship was only hanging on by a damn thread, and she didn't have too many more times to act crazy with Nas before she whooped her ass and quit fucking with her.

"Aye, ma,"

Nasir looked up as she pulled her money from out of her bra. The bouncer went in his pocket and pulled out a stack of bills. He placed fifty dollars into the door collection and gave her a special wrist band before he nodded his head at the entrance.

"Have fun. Fuck her, and after tonight, find a real friend."

Nasir was drained. She didn't have the energy to argue with him, nor force him to take her money. Hell, if anything, the nigga was right. She gave him a smile and thanked him before she walked inside behind Alicia who was already at the bar ordering drinks. *I hope he don't think he getting some ass all over fifty punk ass dollars*, Nas thought as she approached the bar.

"Fifteen dollas! We got here too late because you wanted to throw a fucking temper-tantrum and take all day to get dressed!" Alicia yelled as she threw her hand out.

Nas handed her the money, and in exchange, she was handed a Long Island with an extra shot in it.

"Woooo! This shit potent!"

Nasir made a sour face feeling that extra shot of Hennessy going down her throat.

"Drink up. We about to get lit, wit' yo' fine ass!"

Nas managed to laugh when Alicia smacked her butt before she guzzled the whole thing down. She needed to get drunk. It was the only thing that would keep her level-minded for the rest of the night if she was gonna have to put up with her crazy ass.

Nas felt someone tap her on her shoulder. When she turned around, the bartender handed her another drink, took her empty cup, and slid her money right into her cleavage that was showing, giving her her money back.

"I see the wrist band, miss lady! Enjoy yourself!"

She raised her cup to him with a smile. *So, that's what this is for*, she thought. Alicia surely didn't get one, and probably hadn't noticed it either since she had walked off on her.

"Thank yooooou!"

"Right on, sexy!"

"Come on! Let's go see if we can in get upstairs! I heard the Platinums are definitely in the building tonight!" Alicia yelled over the music while grabbing her friend by the hand and dragging her through the crowd until they made it to the circular steps that led to the second level.

T

Seth sat back puffing on a blunt while a bitch was on her knees at his booth slobbing him down. Some head always leveled him out. He had opened his club a week before he had gotten locked up but hadn't stepped foot in it not once until tonight. He was feeling generous.

He had an open bar until twelve am, and that's why they were busting heads at the door. People who wore a wristband obviously had to pay extra in order to drink more after hour once the special was over, and that was an extra fifty.

Shit, muthafuckas paid for what they wanted. Their liquor supply was ridiculous though. Between Seth and Messiah, they owned over a dozen liquor stores in town, so it was nothing to hold an open bar. Money was rolling in like crazy from the turnout. The line had been wrapped around the building for the longest, and they finally closed the doors once they had reached capacity.

Seth felt his dick go stiff after a good twenty minutes of her head game. He puffed hard on the blunt as his semen exited from his body. The nasty lil' bitch licked all that shit up too before he took his dick from her mouth and got up from the booth leaving her looking stupid.

It was a party. Yeah, he had beef. Yeah, he wanted Jediah's head. Yeah, the Kamikazes were on bullshit, but he was always war ready. Right now, though, he was enjoying himself. A muthafucka was deaf, blind, and slobber mouth stupid if they found the gal to step to him tonight. He was itching to light some shit up; all it took was one wrong move, and he would shut the city down.

When J. Cole's "Power Trip" spun, the poles that were located throughout the entire club started to light up, and everyone knew what that meant. The first bitch to hop on got to do her thang and collect the money that started flying. This track was Seth's shit.

He wasn't a real sentimental ass nigga, but J. Cole spoke to him in ways that most rappers just couldn't. He bobbed his head to the beat letting the words flow through his mouth while he sipped on his drink. Nas had been on his mind all day, and he couldn't stand that shit.

A part of him wanted to fuck her ass like a rag dog for all the fucking hassle earlier when all he was trying to do was compliment her fine lil' thick ass, but she took him there, and he got to acting all crazy and shit. Other than his old bitch, no other woman had ever made him come out of character like that, and it was wild.

He stood up from leaning over the railing when his eyes came across a familiar face. It was her. Nasir was standing at the VIP entrance with that same ass smug ass look on her face while some lil' bitch she was with stood there arguing with the guard.

"Aye, send them up," he spoke into his head piece.

On cue, the guard opened the rope for them to enter.

"Girl, I didn't just argue with his ass for ten got-damn minutes for you to stand there looking stupid. Come on!"

"Bitch, you got one last time to talk to me like that, and I'ma buck yo' ass, you hear me!" Nasir threatened as she began to climb the steps behind her.

A guard led them through the booths until he approached Seth and Messiah, where a bunch of girls were dancing in little to no damn clothes while touching and rubbing all over each other.

The look that glazed over Nasir's face when she saw Seth made him double over in laughter. She looked like she was about to put one in his head, and he had to give it to shorty. She was tough as shit, and he could fuck with it.

"You came here to apologize for that shit you made me pull earlier," Seth yelled in her ear as he held her by the nape of her back.

He was a little drunk, and hell she was finnnnnnnne as fuck right now! Her thick ass could dress the fuck up! Nas was rocking the hell out of a white button down that was tied in a knot at her waist displaying her succulent breasts, with some distressed denim shorts that stopped above the stretchy thigh-high sandals she was rocking.

Her long black hair was parted down the middle and flat-ironed bone straight. He loved a classic bitch. The large bamboo earrings she was rocking, that he knew weren't real, gave him a 90's vibe to match the name necklace around her neck. The shit was too fucking appeasing right now.

And her face wasn't caked up in makeup. She kept it light, but her eye shadow was popping, and he liked her lil' style. She looked good enough to eat, and yeah, he was talking about putting his head between them thighs and chowing down on some thick girl pussy. Never has a curvy girl ever caught his attention, but she was so damn beautiful that he couldn't deny it.

He could just picture her full lips wrapped around his big dick, and hell, with the way he had been drinking, he'd suck and kiss all over them muthafuckas right along with those breasts that were begging for his attention.

That mean ass look on her face did nothing but make her look even sexier in his eyes right now. He was ready to put her over his shoulder and take her to a hotel with no more further discussions.

"Nasir?" He questioned as he read her necklace. "That's sexy, but hold the fuck up?" He turned his face up when he stepped back and really took a look at what the fuck she was wearing. "Why you got this come fuck me ass outfit on right now? I don't play that shit!" he was legit mad.

Is he really doing this right now? This nigga got some fucking nerve!

Nas was too outdone. This nigga really thought he was somebody like he didn't just have her balling her fucking eyes out an hour ago, and she was about to flip that script quick. She didn't even know this nigga! The nerve of him!

"Get out my face," she spat as she turned to walk away from him, but he grabbed her by the hand and pulled her back so quick that their lips were only meters away when she looked up into his eyes from facing him again.

"Don't fucking walk away from me. Do you not remember what the fuck happened earlier? You really wanna try me again?"

She gazed deeper into his eyes. Even in five-inch heels, he was still towering over her. Without them she was only five-three. He was like the physical version of Kovu from *The Lion King 2*; caramel, sexy, full of power, and he had her head in the clouds. His curly hair hung down the sides of his face in beautiful wavy curls like he braided the shit just to get the look.

And he smelled soooooo gooooood. A man in Gucci Guilty always made her knees buckle, and she couldn't move, nor say a peep. No matter how much she wanted to throw her drink in his face and snatch his hand away that wouldn't cease to roam her decent lil' booty, but mesmerizing hips, she just couldn't do shit right now. He had her stuck!

"Now, this is the Nasir that I was tryna step to earlier. This one right here. I can be honest."

He licked his succulent ass lips, and it made her legs tingle.

"Yeah, I got yo' ass, huh?" he teased as he went against the grain and kissed her.

His lips were so soft. . . they smothered hers just the way she liked it, and she was about to lose it.

"You don't got nothing," she hissed as she frowned up her face again.

He shoved her into the banister and pushed his body weight against her, pinning her down. Nasir tried to break away from him, but his skinny ass was holding some work. Physically and literally. *I know that is not his dick on my fucking stomach like that. . . Oh. . . my. . . God. . .*

"I'm always gon' win, so quit fucking playing with me, and get yo' act right. Don't make me embarrass yo' ass in front of all these damn people."

"Like, who the fuck are you talking to? Nigga, I don't even fucking know you, your name, your origin, what you do for a living, how often you wash yo' ass, or none of that! You gon' stop talking to me like—"

He grabbed her by the neck before he pulled her close and kissed her lips again. She couldn't believe it. For a minute, Nas totally just submitted to him and hung her head over to the side as their tongues overlapped on something serious.

Seth pinned his body closer to her. It scared the shit out of Nasir when he picked her up by the thighs and mounted her on top of the banister. Did he really just take over her body like that! A hunnid points for this nigga right here!

He stood between her legs with her now at his height and kissed her again. Bitches were mad! Wooooooooo! Seth was showing out! He was kissing a bitch in public, and she was plus-sized! A fine ass plus-sized woman at that!

Nasir was snatched, looking like she needed to be on the swim-suit cover for *Sports Illustrated*, and bitches couldn't even hate. His tongue was all down her mouth; shit, he might as well had pulled her on top of his dick at the rate they were going.

"UMMMM! IS THERE SOMETHING THAT YOU WANNA TELL ME, NASIR!!!"

The sound of Alicia's salty ass voice made her body cringe. She instantly pulled away from Seth, popping back into reality for a minute.

"She ain't got shit to tell you right now! Pick a nigga or sum', she busy! And interrupt me one more fucking time, and I'ma throw yo' country ass out!" Seth yelled over the music as he looked over his shoulder at Alicia.

She wasn't bad looking. Not bad at all, but she ain't spark no flames like her home gal' did.

"Bitch, do you not speak English!"

Seth turned around while pulling his Desert Eagle out.

"Don't do that," Nasir insisted as she pulled him back by the shoulder.

"So, this bitch yo' momma, or something? Nasir can't make no moves unless her lil' bitch say so!" he chuckled, but the frustration was written all over his face.

Nasir hopped down. She didn't have time for this. His statement embarrassed the hell out of her because hearing him say that made her realize that Alicia did have some kind of control over her.

If Alicia wanted the nigga, then he was always off limits; even if that nigga had wanted Nas instead of her. It made Nasir see red, making her now feel ten times as worse before he had made it clear to her.

"If I tell you not to walk away from me one more fucking time," he threatened as he held the gun up to her chin.

Nasir grabbed him by the nuts and looked him in the eye.

"Or, *what*," her voice had a bite to it as she put an extra sound on the letter "T".

Seth stared at her with a stone face for as long as he possibly could before he laughed and kissed her lips. She was something else; she was really taking advantage of him being on his level. Them 1942 shots wasn't no joke.

"You play too many damn games for me. Move, Mr. No Name!" she screamed frustrated.

Nas didn't like when she couldn't control herself, and at the rate things were going, she knew she needed to get away from this nigga and fast.

"I'm going to the bathroom, are you coming!" she screamed at Alicia over the music.

Alicia looked at her like she was crazy before shouting, "FUCK NO!"

Nas gave the bitch a puzzled look. Was she really that pressed over what had just happened?

"Oh, okay. I feel it," she spat with the roll of her eyes before she bumped pass them both and headed for the exit.

Seth watched her ass switch in her shorts, hypnotized. He couldn't believe it, but he started to go after her until Alicia stopped him and undid his zipper like she had been waiting on this moment all night.

Shit, he couldn't do nothing but look down and smile when the bitch hit her knees and got to sucking his dick in front of the whole VIP section, not giving a damn about her morals or her "friend's" feelings.

Chapter Five

Nasir looked at herself in the mirror the next morning after she had cried herself back to sleep. Alicia's actions didn't surprise her last night at all, but when she saw her down on her knees after that nigga had just had his tongue all down her throat, she knew then that the bitch wasn't shit but a rat and she would never change. How could she have ever called her a friend? Nasir tried to brush it off because it's not like she hasn't done a grimy thing or two in her past, but that was the *past*.

They were grown women now. Adults. Supposedly mature and aware of what the fuck was right from wrong. Shit happened in your teenaged years; hell, shit happened on the daily, but not shit like that. The longer she thought about it, the more it pissed her off.

Thank God she didn't waist her last hundred dollars at that damn club because mama needed some kind of therapy to calm her down. Eating was always an emotional outlet for Nasir, and that's what the fuck she did.

She got herself dressed and decided to head out to one of her favorite little spots in town: BrickTops. It wasn't too expensive, the food was filling, and the menu was delicious. The way she was throwing back shots of tequila last night once she made it home, she could feel the liquor in the pit of her stomach trying its best to digest without throwing it up.

She held the peach mimosa up to her lips as she sat alone skimming through some new costumes that she wanted to pick out for her dancers with the new budget she had this year. Dance was her life. She lived it, loved it, and breathed it.

It gave her a peace that she hadn't been able to receive from life in a long time, and it kept her sane. The incoming call from her mother made Nasir hit the green button that appeared on the screen of her iPhone 6S Plus.

"Hey, ma."

"Hey, daughter. What are you doing?"

"Nothing. Just having lunch at BrickTops."

"Oh, really? You should've told me. I would've came out there with you."

"I'm sorry. It was a last-minute thing."

"What's wrong?"

Her mother could sense her frustrations. One thing Nas couldn't do was hold her anger back. She wasn't gonna fold for anybody. If she was mad, she was mad, and she knew she needed to get a hold on that, but that bitch Alicia had pissed her off so bad she was fighting the tears racing for her eyes.

"Let's just say that you were right about Alicia after all." The comment made Nasir laugh. "I feel like a high school girl all over again. Mommas always know," she smiled.

"I told you that bitch was shady. What did that hood rat do now?"

"Suck the nigga's dick who was just all over me not even two minutes prior. In front of the whole VIP section."

The words flowed from Nas' mouth so fast that she hadn't even peeped how gutta it came out until she'd said it.

"WHAT! Are you serious, Nasir! Did you beat her ass?"

She sighed.

"I just walked away. The point I'm at right now, momma, I just don't even have it in me to fight."

"The hell with that! I know I always tell you kids not to resort to violence, but that bitch would've got her block knocked the fuck off that night! Girl you dun', oooooh. Where you at? BrickTops? I'm on my way."

"Ma, it's okay," Nas giggled.

"I'm on the way, Nasir. Give me twenty minutes."

"Okay. . ."

Nas smiled when she saw her beautiful mother walk through the door. Her old lady was the baddest forty-seven-year-old woman she'd ever seen. She favored Nicole Murphy to a "T", and she rocked that shit. She was flaunting a fitted black and white maxi dress with a pair of Marco Gianni bow-toed heels. Her short and funky hair was styled in lose curls that Nasir had done for her a few days back, and her flawless face didn't need much makeup at all.

Her outfit was simple, but her jewelry and her sex appeal alone made her look like a million fucking bucks. Nasir's mother was always the center of attention. Everywhere she went she received endless compliments on her beauty, and it always made Nas smile. She was truly blessed to be a queen's daughter.

"Hey, ma."

"Hey, boo. OMG!" Catori gasped when she laid eyes on her daughter once she stood up. "Hi, beautiful! Look at youuuu! You have lost so much weight; I'm so proud of you."

Nasir smiled trying her hardest not to blush. She was a solid 180 now, and never thought she'd see this day.

"Thanks, ma. I'm not where I want to be, but it's a great feeling to have a flat stomach after all of these years. I can't believe it."

"Believe it baby. You did it, and you are looking amazing. Look at them little ass shorts you got on."

Nasir laughed as they took a seat.

"I've never been here before. Everybody at work talks about this place. Is the food good?" Catori asked as she slid her glasses on to look over the menu.

"Yeah, they're real good."

"I know I need me a glass of wine after that shit you told me. What you drinking?" her mother insured as she read over the selections.

"A peach mimosa that I need a refill on. . ."

Once they had their orders placed, they picked back up on conversation.

"So where is the lil' bitch at now?"

Nas gave her mother the stink eye. Thinking about Alicia made her hot.

"Who knows. Her car is at my house, and it was still there when I left. She's probably somewhere laid up with a "Platinum nigga"," Nasir emphasized.

"A Platinum? The Platinum Dynasty? What Platinum were you tonguing down last night?"

Nas sighed.

"I don't even know if you want me to be honest."

Her mother laughed, trying so hard not to choke on her glass of wine.

"Nasir, oh my God!"

"What!"

The two women shared a laugh.

"Well, was he cute at least?"

Nas gazed off into her daydreams for a moment after her mother's comment. Remembering the way his lips felt against her, and the way he propped her up on top of the banister made her squeeze her thighs together. It sent a shock down her spine remembering how his hands caressed her body and the way his tongue felt against hers.

He was so damn fine. The dominance though mesmerizing allure in his voice, his facial hair, the way that gorgeous mane of hair on his head fell down his back, and oh my God, his beautiful, smooth, glowing skin against the red LED lights in the club had her hot and heavy. . .

"Nasir."

Hearing her mother's voice snapped her back into reality. She hadn't even realized that their waiter had dropped their meals off.

"Huh?"

Catori smiled.

"I know that look. He must be some man."

Nas tried her hardest not to smile, but it soon disappeared.

"No, he's not. Just another horny, paid ass nigga with nothing but a swinging dick to offer each woman that crosses his path. How are you?"

She changed the subject as she added black pepper to the cheesy shrimp and grits, and the side of fettuccine alfredo that was sitting before her.

"I'm good. Thanks for asking. Thanking God for an off day."

"I know right? I thought it was your Saturday to work?"

"No, my weekends have switched. I'm so excited for my trip to the Dominican Republic with Ray. I haven't been out the country since the 90's."

Nasir was happy for her mother. She'd met her new boo almost a year ago, and he was the sweetest. Catori was high maintenance, and she needed a man on her arm who could, not only keep up, but also check her when she got out of line too. Nasir's father left them when she was three, and she never got the chance to meet him.

Her older brother, Ali, had a different dad, but he was locked up for murder and was doing life. At the end of the day, Nas was just ecstatic that her mother was getting the love that she had always deserved.

"Have fun, and take pictures, momma. You don't never take any pictures. Tell Ray that's his job while y'all out there."

Catori laughed.

"I know. I will. I made sure his outfits matched mine too, so we have to get pictures."

"Y'all are too cute. I can't wait to hear all about it... Ali texted me this morning letting me know that him and Boo were safe. They're on the road to come and visit us. I'm so excited. I haven't seen them in months," Nas beamed referring to her older brother and niece.

"Yes, he told me this morning as well. Its about damn time he's came back out here. Gammy's baby is going to be five; she's getting so big. Oh, I pray to God they're safe on that road. There's always so much construction going on from here to Atlanta. Are you still thinking about moving out there with him?"

"I'm pondering it. You know my lease is up in February. I want to. I just gotta get this credit together and try to get me a new car. It's always something."

"Don't stress, baby. God will bless you when he thinks you're ready."

"Well, I'm ready. I swear I take two steps forward and get pushed ten steps back. I'm just over it."

"You're not having faith in Him, Nasir. That's why your blessings have been prolonged. Faith without deeds is dead, and you know that."

"*I know*," Nas rolled her eyes. Her mom always had something smart to say, and she was always right. "I'ma do better. I promise."

"Positive thoughts, young lady. Your spirit has to match the universe in order to receive the energy that you're looking for."

"Yes, ma'am." She sassed, over the conversation.

"Look, you onion head lil' girl. Don't pout at me."

They shared a laugh.

"Do you have everything you need for your trip, Ms. Glamourous?"

"Girl, I'm glad you said something. We should head right over to the mall once we're done. I've gotta pick up some shoes I ordered. . ."

An hour later, they were across the way at Neiman Marcus where her mother worked as a manager. The prices on the shit in this store were making Nas' head hurt. *Must be nice*, she thought as she eyed the thousand-dollar Louboutin shoes before she walked away. She continued to admire the other merchandise they had while her mother conversed with a coworker.

Nasir was off in her own world. Her head was so far in the clouds that she didn't notice the two men coming up on the escalator behind her. Seth noticed her hips the moment his eyes changed from his phone to her direction. It was something about Nasir that he just couldn't get a grasp on.

The whole time he had Alicia bent over, the only image in his head was Nas' hips in that fucking outfit that pissed him off each time he thought about it, and she was about to get her ass handled again.

The black long sleeved Fashion Nova Team Player romper she was rocking looked painted on her body, it fit her so well. It made her butt look fuller, and all the sexy tattoos gracing her legs that he couldn't see last night were showing.

The feathered red Nike slides she made herself were under her feet, and she wore her hair high in a bun. Seth headed in her direction instead of following the sales woman he typically shopped with to where his belongings were waiting for him to look through.

It was crazy that he could already smell the Versus by Versace fragrance drifting from her body. They didn't even make that shit anymore, but the fragrance was one he could never forget from the first time he smelled it penetrating through her pores. His eyes were glued to her ass, hips, and nice thick thighs.

Nas could feel someone approaching her from behind, so off instinct, she turned around. It threw her back a bit when she laid her eyes upon Seth. He had an evil glare in his eyes, and she returned the same look picturing him with Alicia.

"What the fuck did I tell you about dressing like this?" he spat as he approached her.

"What the fuck did I tell you about talking to me like that? Go on about your day. Why the fuck are you approaching me? Shouldn't you be with the bitch that had your dick in her mouth not even three seconds after I walked away last night?"

"What the fuck do that got to do with this lil' tight ass shit that you got on, Nasir? We ain't discussing shit but you right now."

"I don't like your tone," she shot pissed to the max.

He grabbed her by the hand and pulled her close. The look in his hazel eyes was so meek that they started to glow in a demonic way. Uncomfortable with how he was tryna size her up, she pushed him off of her.

"Don't touch me. You don't have shit to say to me and keep your fucking hands to yourself!"

"Aye—"

He tried to reach for her, but Nasir was quick when she had stormed off and headed to the escalator. *Fuck that bitch. I ain't got time for this shit,* he thought T'ed off as he redirected his attention to the reason why he had come to the mall in the first damn place.

He and Messiah were making a trip down to the Bahamas to go pick up their squad before they got back to business, but the man had to go in style. Thug or not, he lived to get fly. Dressing was a hobby to him, and he had to have all of the latest threads.

"Aye, where you take that lil' bitch from last night when you dropped her off?" Seth questioned Messiah who was trying on a short-sleeved Burberry button down.

"Shit, somewhere out in Maryland Heights where she said her car was. Off of, uuuuuh, 270 and Dorsett. I think she said it was her home girl spot. I wasn't paying too much attention to where though.

"I was tryna get that bitch the fuck up out my whip. She kept gagging and shit like she was gon' throw up in my shit. I was seconds away from throwing her ass out. I had to pull over and get that bitch a plastic bag or sum'."

"I told you to call that bitch a UBER. Her pussy wasn't even good enough for you to be tripping off how the fuck she got home."

Seth shook his head as he shot his private investigator a text. He received an instant phone call in return.

"Dome was stupid though," Messiah laughed as he put the straw Fedora on top of his head.

"Yeah, I'll give the bitch that. She could take cock too." Seth agreed.

"Hello, Mr. Platinum," the man answered when their call connected.

"Aye, find out everything you can on a Nasir Valentine, a'ight?"

"Yes, sir. I'll have your information for you shortly."

Seth hung up the phone as he walked over to the window and caught a glance of her crossing the street. *She so fucking extra dawg*, he thought as he couldn't help but to stare at her. He laughed out loud when he saw her approach a black Dodge Avenger. It was about to be 2017, and she was rolling around in one of them trash ass whips?

The front grill was cracked in half, barely hanging on by a thread, her front window was cracked, and there was just too much other damage done to the body to even explain. *That's why she got a fucking attitude. Hell, I would be bent about that shit too,* he thought amused as he watched her pull off.

T

Sometimes more liquor was the best solution to a broken heart. After driving around town and clearing her head with a few blunts for an hour or two, Nasir finally made it back home with a fifth of Hennessy as a souvenir. She didn't know why she was allowing this nigga who she'd barely even known to get up under her skin like she was his bitch in the first damn place. Aggravated, she slammed the car door and headed to her apartment.

"Nas."

She turned around and mugged the fuck out of Alicia as she noticed her making her way down the stairs.

"Where you been? I've been here waiting for over an hour, and my phone is dead. I left my charger. Girl, I need to lay down; I don't think I can drive home. I can hardly stay awake," she whined as she started to gag.

"Call the nigga you was with last night and ask him to drop you off. Get the fuck out my face!"

Alicia stood up from doubling over and vomiting in the grass.

"What the fuck is your problem, Nas! You've been on bullshit for the longest and I'm tired of this shit with you!"

"You're my problem! Point, fucking, blank, period! You can be a nasty ass bitch all you want to, but you not gon' do that shit to me no more. *I'm* tired of it. Granted, I don't even know the nigga, but that shit that you pulled was whack as fuck, not to mention it was ratchet as hell, and it just went to show the little to no respect that you have for me.

"I bet you fucked that nigga and his friend all night too, didn't you? So why don't you give him a call and ask him to drop you off at home. Oh, wait. He didn't leave a number or even take you to his spot, did he? Now I'm ya friend when you need something? Bitch please."

Alicia was so stunned she couldn't even respond right away. When Nas got buck, she took it there, and she always succeeded at making Alicia feel like shit. But she was not going out like that.

"Bitch, if it wasn't for me, you wouldn't even have the little bit of confidence that you do now. You was dressed in baggy clothes and tennis shoes, and only wore hats until I crossed paths with yo sad, depressed, and mad at the world ass.

"If it wasn't for me, you wouldn't have even tried to lose the fucking weight in the first place. Bitch you owe this lil' funky ass brand new ego you got to me. Niggas won't even check for you unless you with me, so get yo shit right, and come at me correct!"

Nas took the bottle of Hennessy in her hand and busted the bitch's mouth open.

"Nah, ho! That's what I've owed your hating ass for years now! A fucking ass whooping! Fuck that nigga! It's about the disrespect, and yo dusty, dirty ass thinking you could get away with murder just because you was a quote-unquote "bad bitch"! Pay yo bills first bitch! Get yo plates first bitch! I might not be balling, or the smallest bitch out here, but my shit straight!

"I bet that woke your ass up! Now get the fuck off my got damn property and pray that I don't send Maryland Heights to tail them expired ass plates you got! Dusty ass bitch, get yo life up before you think a muthafucka owe you something! Bitch, I don't need you! You ain't fucking me, you ain't paying no bills, so you can shake with that shit!"

Nas stormed off like the girl didn't have blood rushing out her mouth at her expense. She could give two fucks if the bitch had up and collapsed right then and there from the excitement. She'd wanted to do that shit for so long, and she thanked the little devil that was sitting on her shoulder for pushing her to finally swing on the bitch. Most of the time her sweet side managed to talk her out of doing something crazy, but today she was being rebellious.

Nas was shaking. She paced her apartment back and forth a few times then swung the door open before she went back up to the main level, and just as she thought, the bitch was gone. Alicia thought she was tough shit, but she knew she really couldn't fuck with Nas.

She could deep throat that nigga's dick her damn self for pointing that bitch out to her. She didn't feel sorry for her, she didn't regret her actions, or none of that. Alicia had fucked over the last one, and Nas would go heads up with the bitch again if she had to.

Chapter Six

It was going on eight that night, and Nasir was finishing up on her dinner. She felt so bad for eating out earlier that she refused to eat for the rest of the day until she could no longer withstand the emptiness and the sound of her loud stomach growling.

Sinead Harnett's "If You Let Me" was playing through her Mega Boom speaker as she chopped up the last sweet potato. Her house was smelling so good that her stomach wasn't fighting fair, but the frozen lemonade margarita she was sipping on was holding her off.

Just as she washed her hands she could make out a knock from her front door. *What the hell? Who is that,* she thought as she wiped her hands dry. It was so stupid of her to unlock the door without looking out the peephole first.

For all she knew, one of those killer clowns who had been roaming the streets and were being caught on Channel 2, could be at her front waiting to chop her up. When she opened it, her feet melted into the floor. She stood puzzled. Her body was shaking uncontrollably, and she couldn't move.

Seth's rude ass walked passed her as he cut his eyes, entering her home without her permission. Nasir closed the door and turned the music down low before she turned around and looked at him.

He was silent. He casually leaned up against the wall with a toothpick hanging out the side of his mouth, looking fine as hell with his hair pulled up high in a bushy bun. He was just as mesmerized by her.

She had on some itty-bitty red shorts that her ass swallowed up, and a crop top with no bra, displaying her nipple rings. Nasir was cute in her Armani prescription glasses with a bun high on her head as well.

Seth was a man. Woman was his type. A snatched waist, hips, thighs, and titties was his type; that was the kind of shit that Nasir did to him after two fucking days, and he thought his damn head would explode.

"What the fuck are you doing at my house?"

"You mean yo shack?" he chuckled as he tucked his hands underneath his arms.

"Oh, sorry I'm not sorry that I'm not a billionaire, Mr. Big Shot."

"Yo attitude? Kill it, before I fuck you up."

"Nigga I'm still untouched ain't I?"

His jaw clenched. If she were any other bitch he would've smacked the shit out her ass.

"You a hot mouth ass muthfucka, mane."

"And you're not?" she retorted.

"I'm the fucking man, Nasir. I run this town. I walk, talk, and move how the fuck I want. So, watch yo tone, and watch what the fuck you say to me. You this close to—"

"Goodbye."

She waved him off as she went back into the kitchen and rinsed off the sweet potatoes before adding cinnamon, brown sugar, white sugar, vanilla, a little bit of water, and a heaping of honey to make sure they got nice and sticky. She covered them and put the heat on medium.

> *"This what happens when I think 'bout you,*
> *I get in my feelings, yeah,*
> *I start reminiscing yeah. . .*
> *Lord please save him for me. . ."*

Nasir sang out loud, adding a slight remix to Bryson Tiller's lyrics, with the radio, as she moved around the kitchen, forgetting that Seth was still there. The sight was something he had never seen before. Yeah, his mother cooked when she felt like it, and the maid used to keep their meals coming like clockwork, but he'd never seen a woman in action around her home cooking and doing her thing.

His eyes couldn't leave the *Nasir* that was tattooed on the right cheek of her ass that was peeking out of her shorts. He could tell she didn't have any panties on. With less clothes she looked smaller, she was badder, and he could only imagine what she looked like raw.

"You're still here, Mr. Big Shot? Doesn't the nigga who runs this town have better things to do than be a fucking creep, and pop up at a woman's house that you don't even know?"

Seth walked up on her and twisted the arm she wasn't using behind her back while he pressed up against her, leaning her into the stove. Nas forced her weight against him and pushed him back into the sink while turning around to face him, but he moved so fast that he spun her around until she was against the counter. He picked her body up and laid her back flat against the surface while holding her arms above her head.

"I'm starting to think that you like this shit," he growled as he gave her that demonic ass look again from earlier.

Nas stared him in the eye until a smile spread across her face.

"Can you please let me go?" Her words were sincere, but he wouldn't let up.

He continued to hold her down while gazing at her until he decided when he wanted to let her go and walked out the front door. Nas hadn't even realized that she was still laying on top of the counter until she felt the cold water that had splashed from the sink against her back.

"Shit!"

She was soaking wet. Her kitchen wasn't big at all. You turned around and you were back in the same damn spot. She hopped up and removed her shirt before going to find another. *That nigga plays too many damn games, and how did he find out where the fuck I lived at,* she thought in disbelief before she slid on another crop top.

Nasir's body was banging, and she hated clothes. Even when she was heavier she used to walk around the crib in the same attire. This was the norm for her. She reentered the kitchen and flipped her potatoes over, making sure none would stick to the bottom of the pan. The sound of her front door opening and closing made her jump.

"Would you stop that! Damn! Scared the fuck out of me, and you don't live here! Get out!" She shrieked as she held onto her chest.

"Shut the fuck up, Nasir." He stated as he took a seat on her vintage couch.

He inhaled deeply before he ran his hand over his face. He was trip-ping in her presence, and he couldn't fathom it.

"Seth," he spoke aloud.

"What?" She asked as she pressed pause.

"Seth Platinum." He introduced himself.

She walked over into the living room where he was and stood in front of him with her arms crossed. *This girl.* He shook his head from the sight of her breasts being pushed up higher.

"Well, I'm sure I don't have to introduce myself, being that you know where I stay. Guess the bitch ran her mouth about me last night, huh?"

"That bitch got fucked last night, shorty. You think you was on her mind?"

His words made her eyes widen.

"The ho a rat. Why you fuck with that girl? She ain't shit but a lame ass lil' hating ass bitch anyway. I could see that shit the way she interrupted us. She had her lil' five minutes of fame and got ran by some real niggas. I'ma just put it out there."

"You are so fucking ignorant," she shook her head. "And, why are you here?" She snapped.

"Obviously, because I wanted to see you. You got any more of them smart mouthed ass questions, or is you gon' chill the fuck out? I'm this close to saying fuck yo ass. This hard to get shit ain't cute, and it's gon' make me do some shit to you that I've been forcing myself not to do since day one. What you cooking? That shit smell good as fuck; I ain't ate all day."

Nasir laughed. Never had she ever met such a reaching ass nigga, but at the same time, she had liked it. She'd known the Platinums from their reputation as notorious drug lords, their property management businesses, and the lethal ways they kept that shit afloat. Seth wore his reputation well.

She should've been dead considering all the shit she's talked to his ass. The deaths associated with the Platinums stayed on the news, but Saint Louis was owned by them. They knew too many people, they had too many legal ties, and so much power that no one but themselves and the enemy could stop or go up against them.

Seth was a king of the streets. There was so much pussy out there that she knew he played into it, so she just couldn't understand why he was so infatuated with her. Whatever the case might have been, that still didn't stop her from talking shit.

"Food," she responded with a smart tone.

"Nasir."

The way he said her name all zaddish and shit like he was checking her made her heart stop. She walked away from him to go reunite with her margarita. This was too much for her right now. Nas had been invisible for so long that she held it up well, so receiving so much attention, and especially from an obscure and powerful man, had her damn head through the roof.

She remained silent as she stood with her back to him. She had to take a few deep breaths. A part of her was nervous as fuck. She was half naked in front of this man, and his fine ass had her pressed. Period. Her heart raced when she felt him grab her from behind. He couldn't fight the urge to wrap his arms around her.

"Look, I ain't even gon' flex. You taking a man like me out of character. I don't do shit like this, a'ight? So, you gotta drop this funky ass lil' attitude and try to meet me halfway. Don't stunt like this ain't what you want."

Nasir giggled when she felt his soft lips brush against her neck.

"Now, be a good lil' shorty and tell me what you cooking because my trust ain't the easiest, especially with food, but you got this muthafucka smelling good. And what's this lil' shit you drinking?"

"It's called a frozen margarita, sir."

She looked up into his eyes. He held her chin up and kissed her lips. You probably wouldn't believe it, but this nigga hated kissing. It was never his thing. His lips would kiss a bottle before he swapped spit with a woman, so Nasir was very naïve to what she did to him.

"Some crockpot BBQ chicken breast, sweet potatoes, oven baked macaroni, green beans sautéed in minced garlic and tomatoes, and corn bread."

He smacked her on the ass before he headed back to the living room.

"Fix daddy a plate. I don't want that lil' girlie ass drink either. What you got straight?"

His cocky ass, she thought with the roll of her eyes.

"Tequila. Wait, I got some Hennessy left, I think."

She stood up on her toes and reached inside of the cabinet. She was pissed she wasted her whole fucking bottle on that broke bitch, but it was so worth it.

"I'll take the Henny."

When she wasn't all attitudinal, Seth could infer from her actions that she came off like a good woman. When he made it back from washing his hands in the bathroom, she had a little China town decorated folding table set up for him with his drink and dish ready. All the utensils he needed were there, and she even had seasonings and napkins.

"I knew that attitude was just a front. And you better act right from here on out."

"I better?" She questioned as she popped in *Safe House* with Denzel Washington and Ryan Reynolds; one of her favorite movies.

Before he could respond after blessing his food that he prayed to God wasn't trash, he was interrupted by the ringing of his phone.

"Hello. . . a'ight. . . bet."

When he hung up the iPhone X that hadn't even hit the stores yet, he received a call from the iPhone 8 Plus that was buzzing in his pocket.

"P1."

He hung up after hearing the caller's code. Shit was looking all good with his territories, so now he could really kick back, and relax for a damn change. Nasir was highly impressed. Seth did not *appear* to be a thug, but she could sense that shit, and she knew she was fucking with a boss. Was it safe to say that so soon?

Seth was done with his plate before she even had the chance to sit down and dig into her own food. She giggled at the empty China in front of him. *I guess it was good*, she thought as she crossed her legs and sat her plate on the arm of the couch. As long as her drink had a stationary place to sit then she was good.

She didn't need a table or anything. She was a homebody and she wasn't gonna front for him. Hell, he was the one who popped up uninvited. She honestly didn't even think the nigga was checking for her like that, but whatever. She'd probably never see his ass again after tonight anyway, so she shrugged it off.

"I won't even flex, that shit was fire. Had a nigga nervous for a minute. Mommas don't teach they daughters shit but how to take cock these days, and half them bitches can't even do that."

She laughed as she sipped her drink.

"You just let anything come out your mouth."

He glanced over at her. He admired her comfort. She was grounded to herself, and that was something he could respect.

"I'm me. I ain't gon' sugar coat shit."

"Trust me, I know."

The ringing of her phone made Nas put her plate down; she went to get it from off of the counter.

"Hello?"

"Nubia Valentine. Why did you leave me?"

She busted out in laughter.

"Ma, that was over seven hours ago. Did you just now notice that I was gone?"

Her mother laughed.

"I just made it home and decided to call you. What happened?"

Nas was surprised when she felt Seth pull her into his lap on her way back to the couch. Her heart was racing; she'd break his skinny ass in half, but he was all for her curves.

"I'm alright. I had gotten a little—" She pushed his head away; his succulent lips were placing kisses to her neck. "Frustrated. . . Stop it," She whispered to him.

"Girl, what are you doing?"

"Sorry, ma," her daughter giggled as he continued to torment her.

"Well, don't forget your brother should be here shortly. They'll be staying here at my house for the night. Their hotel room won't be ready until tomorrow around noon."

"Okay. I'll come over in the morning. Maybe we can do breakfast or something—stop,"

His tongue traveled over that part of her neck that she couldn't resist.

"I'ma call you right back, ma."

Nas hung up the phone and was greeted by him wrapping his arms around her waist while his tongue continued.

"This couldn't have waited," she tried to fight him off.

"I like that," he whispered as he kept attacking her.

"Like what. . ."

She tried so hard not to moan, but he was making her body shutter from the pleasure.

"How important family is to you. That's our family emblem. At least it was."

"It's bittersweet. They'll be the first ones to do ya dirty. I learned that early on," she referred to the absence of her father.

He looked up at her.

"I don't think you know how beautiful you are, ma. Real shit."

His voice was soft. Nas couldn't help but smile.

"So, you're not an asshole around the clock? Just most of the time, huh?"

His smile made her insides tingle. His big, juicy, pink lips were begging to be sucked on, and Nas almost couldn't help herself.

"I'ma have to lock yo ass away somewhere. I can't have mu'fuckas seeing how nice you got me. I'm a heartless, nigga, ma. I'ma keep it one hunnid."

"Being who you are you have to be. A leader has to spark fear no matter how good they are at what they do. It's a respect thing."

He licked his lips.

"What you know about honoring code, and the chain of command, ma? You ain't no thug. Ain't been in the streets a day in yo life."

"You don't know what I've done, nor what I've experienced." She raised her eyebrow.

"I see I'ma have to put yo smart mouth ass in yo place."

"Seth, listen. A woman will be submissive if she has the right man to be submissive to, but that does not mean that I'm stripped of having an opinion, a voice, nor my independence. And when I say independence, I speak on my womanhood, and my right to stand my ground. Who wants a weak woman? And if you can't handle me speaking my mind, then the door is right there."

Tired of hearing her mouth he grabbed her by the hair and pulled her head back before he leaned over and kissed her. She may have had a point or two, or maybe even three, but right now he had to have her.

His free hand ran up and down her thighs as their heads swayed back and forth. It continued to roam her body until he made his way up to her breasts. He lifted her shirt and let them spill before his tongue glided over her nipple as he held her plump breasts steady.

Sometimes, Nasir couldn't feel it when she got her titties sucked, but he had her body under some kind of spell. His tongue felt amazing. The flicking and sucking and kissing and tugging sent her head through the roof. Nas had to chill.

She knew her shorts were getting wet because her clit was pulsating on high. Using her free hand, Nasir reached back and pulled the drawer open on the end table. She pulled the blunt she had rolled up out. Nas wasn't on her level. . . yet. The two margaritas in her system had her loose, but she wanted to be in the clouds.

Nasir inhaled deeply from the Backwoods as he inhaled from her breasts like he was waiting on milk to release. Seth's ass was gone. He'd been drinking all day, and that last glass of Hennessy got him right. He looked up at Nasir as she inhaled from the blunt once more.

He leaned in close to her as she blew the smoke into his mouth before their tongues began to overlap once again. His dick was so hard that muthafucka started to throb. He had to get in her thighs. He cradled her body and led her back to the bedroom.

Nasir blinked, and he had her butt ass naked with her back against the sheets. She laid against the pillow with the blunt up to her lips as she watched him remove his shirt. *Ooh shit. . .* she bit her lip trying not to smirk at the way he was sculpted: six abs, the swimmer "V", and the curvature of his stacked arms drove her wild. With his shoes off, but jeans still on that sagged below the large bulge in his boxer-briefs, he climbed in bed and got on his knees in between her legs.

He ran his hands down her thighs as she put the blunt in his mouth. Nasir was so fucking beautiful. Tattoos were everywhere. She was tatted like Kat from *Black Ink:Chicago,* and that shit made his dick grow harder. He looked down when she used both of her hands to lower his Versace threads, releasing his monster. Nas' eyes glowed. He had one of those thick, brown Porn Hub dicks, and her mouth started to water.

She sat up and stroked it a few times before she stared him in the eye as she took him into her mouth. Seth removed the blunt from his lips unable to control the groan that had escaped as her warm mouth continued to inch him further down her throat.

She released him slowly before she let her tongue twirl around the tip, never breaking eye contact with him. Nas was on her shit tonight. Her right hand stroked while her mouth went to work. He ran his free hand through her hair until he found the perfect grip. She was bobbing so damn good he didn't even need to guide her.

Nas knew when to suck it, how hard to stoke it, when to spit on it, lick on it, then deep throat it again, and all that shit. The man lost it when she took his sack in her mouth and let her thumb play with the opening of his dick.

"Damn girl," he mumbled while taking another pull from the blunt.

Nas' forehead made one with his stomach after she inhaled all of him. He held onto the back of her head and rotated his hips. She gagged, but that shit was sexy as fuck to him right now. She held her mouth open and let him stoke at his leisure. Nasir looked so fucking sexy with his dick in her mouth. He was wrapped up in her head like he'd never had any before.

"I dare you to put another nigga dick in yo mouth, Nas, I'll kill you," he groaned as she continued to bob up and down.

Seth slowly pulled her head back feeling himself getting too excited. He hated a bitch who could make him bust so quick from brain. That shit fucked up his rep, and he couldn't go out like that. He put the blunt in her lips before he grabbed her by the thighs and made her head hit the pillow again. With her pelvis in the air, he put her legs on his shoulders.

Seth pulled her fat pussy lips back and felt his dick jump when he saw her hood jewelry. His mouth was like a vacuum on that muthafucka. He couldn't believe this shit. He barely knew her, and she had his head between her legs like it was normal.

Eating pussy just wasn't him; his ex-girl had to beg him to lick the clit, but this woman right here. . . she could get whatever the fuck her heart had desired. He shook his head back and forth making a fluttering sound against her flesh. Seth didn't even get mad when she grabbed the top of his head. She pushed his face in further, and he kept licking that shit at full speed. Her vibrator in the damn drawer was jealous as hell!

"Ooooooh. . . ooooh my God. . ."

She finally let the words escape from her lips; she could no longer fight it. The nigga she had been fucking for years had always laid her with some good dick, but she never got her pussy licked, like NEVER, so not only was she surprised, but she was enjoying the fuck out of his head. She hated hearing stories about when somebody's man had them climbing the walls when she'd never experienced that kind of pleasure before, that is, until Mr. Platinum took a dive in.

He had her body back on the bed with his arms around her thighs while his mouth kept going to work. He wanted her to cum. He wanted to keep hearing her moans escape through her lips. He wanted to lick all that shit up. She kept trying to inch away from him, but Seth held that ass still and went to work. Nas was whimpering like she was under some kind of spell, and the shit had precum dripping from his dick.

"Seth. . . oooooh my God, I'm cumming! I'm cumming! I'mmmm, aaaaaaah!"

Nasir's heart stopped when she felt her juices trickle everywhere. *Did I just squirt,* she thought in disbelief with her mouth wide open. She couldn't believe this shit. When he lifted his head up, the man's face looked like that meme from off Facebook of the nigga eating that bowl of cereal with milk dripping from his beard.

She grabbed him by the face and pulled him on top of her. She wanted to taste herself, so she threw her arm around his back and kissed him with nothing but fire and desire. He slid his hand between her legs and stuck his fingers in her milky slit, digging for gold. He finger-fucked her for a minute before he pulled his fingers out and slid them down her throat, testing how freaky she really was.

Nasir licked that shit up while looking him in the eye. Seth chuckled before he licked her tongue that she stuck out for him before he sucked on it. Play time was over. He removed the rest of his clothes then got back in bed before he held her legs in the air.

This girl just got her pussy ate by him. Fuck what she thought; he was going up in her shit raw. Her pussy was so tight, it took a minute before he was able to slide inside of her walls.

You would've thought the nigga popped an X pill the way everything froze around him when his dick felt her flesh. Stars were dancing around her damn head like a Snap Chat filter as Seth looked down at her biting her lip. His hands grabbed a hold of her breasts as his hips started moving forward and back.

Seth took it slow for a bit, letting his dick hit each and every angle of her walls. He chuckled as he watched her lick the tip of her fingers before she started rubbing on her clit. Yeah, she was a freak. He was gonna enjoy having her nasty ass around.

He held her legs up higher wrapping his arms around her thighs and started pounding her shit. He owed her shit talking ass nothing but hard strokes. His nuts clapped against her ass while he kept hitting that shit, but that didn't last long. He had to kiss her lips.

He laid on top of her while pinning her arms above her head and put his tongue in her mouth while he stroked her at a moderate pace. She moaned between each kiss. It was like they were using the his and hers KY jelly she was so fucking aroused.

"I knew his pussy was good. That's why yo ass was tripping because you already knew once a real nigga got up in them thighs he was gon' have that ass," he groaned before she sucked on his tongue.

Nas' fingers were digging in his back. Normally, he hated that shit, but it was making him stroke her deeper. This girl was throwing him so far off his rocker he 'bout ran out the door on her ass. Seth had to let his alter ego take over.

He couldn't take it a second longer. He flipped her over and positioned her with her face down. The sight of her ass in the air made him shake his head in disbelief. Her pussy was looking so good bent over he had to eat it.

With both hands on her butt, he put his face in it, and smacked his lips against her flesh. Nasir had the fucking sauce man. She was gon' have him out here killing niggas for just tryna look her way. This shit was crazy. She held onto his chin while he licked up her silky love. He might've been a Platinum, but she had some platinum fucking pussy, and he wouldn't dare flex.

Nas' chin was in the air when he grabbed her by the hair after he slid in her from behind. The way her ass rippled with each stroke while she backed up against him drove the man insane. He couldn't hold his groans back. She was throwing it back better than a skinny bitch.

Most women held still because his dick was so damn fat, and when he hit deep, it caved their chest in so bad it felt more like painful anal. Hell, Nasir took the dick like that too. He slid his dick in her butt and she kept her ass tooted up begging for more.

"Fuck me Seth! Oh my God, just like that!"

Her damn head was spinning.

"Like that, mama? Hmm?" he grunted as he stroked her hard for a few moments before his dick slid out.

He took his meat and rubbed the tip against her clit before he slid back in that crack addict pussy of hers.

"Aaaaaaaah fuck, Nasir! Shit!"

He stroked her fast while holding onto her waist with both hands before he let go and smacked her ass, watching it jiggle. He smacked it again, and again, and again, then threw that same hand around and tickled her sore clit, but she wanted more. She wanted all that he had to give her and some.

"Ride this dick 'til you cum," he commanded as he took a seat.

She had sweat dripping down his forehead. He thought she was gon' be on some shy shit and get to whining and griping because she was a thicker girl. Shit skinny bitches hated to get on top too; plus, it wasn't one of his favorite positions, but he needed a damn break.

Nas took his dick back into her mouth for a while. She cleared all of her juices from off of him before she climbed on top and stuffed her pussy with his fat dick. She planted her hands on his rock-hard abs while her body bounced up and down. He had to admit it; she was impressing the fuck out of him.

She wasn't rocking back and forth on that lazy shit, but she was actually riding his dick like a porn star, and he couldn't fight the feeling. Seth sat up, threw his arms around her waist, and pulled her close as his mouth inhaled her bouncing breasts.

"Naaaaasiiiir, fuck girl," he groaned as he held his head against her chest.

She was making a bitch out of him. She was screaming, he was groaning, the headboard was knocking, and his dick was running in and out of her as he held her body still while he started beating that shit up. She grabbed him by the face and put her tongue in his mouth.

"Make this pussy cum again, Seth. Make this pussy cum again, baby, aaaaah, yes..."

"You gon' cum on daddy dick? Hmmmm?" He groaned as he kissed her lips.

She nodded her head up and down while he placed a smack to her ass. Seth gave up man. He leaned back against the headboard and let her ride the town until he felt his dick tense up.

He held onto her hips and busted a nut so fat, he wasn't sure if he had lifted her from off of him soon enough. Nas sat back and rubbed along her clit while he stroked the rest of his semen out of his dick with his head back and his mouth open.

"Oh! Ooooh my God I'm about to cum!"

She was rubbing herself so hard she was bound to come any second, and she knew from the build-up within the pit of her stomach, that it was gonna be another good one. Seth pulled her on top of him and laid on his back while letting her mount his face.

He had to let her get hers off too. She held onto his head and rode his mouth until she felt her vagina contract. She screamed his name at the top of her lungs before she felt her body tap out. Nas climbed from off of him and laid beside him.

They both were panting, gasping for the air their lungs had been fighting for, for a while now. He moved her hair out of her face and ran his thumb across her cheek. Breathless, she held onto his hand and kissed it. She had a good heart. He could sense it. The way she looked lying there all red in the face with her eyes closed made him chuckle. He pulled her body close and laid his head on her chest after lying between her legs.

Nas' chest heaved up and down as she ran her fingers through his wild hair. Both of their hair had unraveled in the mist of their steamy escapade. Between that one hand in his head and the finger-tips of her other rubbing up and down his back, Seth's ass had fallen asleep before he could even wrap the shit around his brain how a curvy girl had the best pussy that he's ever stuck his dick in.

Chapter Seven

The ringing of Nas' phone made her shoot her head up from off the pillow. Once she realized that it wasn't in her room, she hopped out of bed and ran into the kitchen.

"Sus, I swear to God if you ain't answer the phone this time I was gon' pull up on yo ass, and kick the fucking door in."

Nasir laughed as she put her hand on her head.

"Hey, Ali. I'm sorry. I didn't hear my phone ring."

"I know you didn't. Yo ass always sleep. Meet me and moms at that lil' brunch spot in Saint Charles that we always used to go to in about an hour, a'ight?"

"Okay."

"Don't fall back asleep, nigga!" He joked.

"I won't! I'm up! Jeez!"

He chuckled at her cute little high-pitched voice.

"A'ight, sus. I'll see you in a minute."

"Alright. Bet."

She hung up the phone and looked around the house. When she realized that there were two plates left out in the living room from dinner last night, she ran back to her room to find an empty bed. Her heart dropped at the sight. *So much for wishful thinking,* she thought sadly as she went to pee.

Nas' poor coochie was throbbing. She remembered falling asleep, then waking up to a hard dick in her guts three other random times that night. She saw why bitches went crazy over him. That nigga *was* the man. He'd given her so many orgasms with his dick that she was ready to hold his hood ass down. Thoughts of him stroking her wet pussy until she came had her fingers rubbing her clit to yet another climax before she washed the night's mind-tingling events away.

After taking a nice long shower, she exited the bathroom, but frowned when she noticed the black card sitting on her nightstand once she reentered her bedroom. *Dubai First Royalty MasterCard, Seth Platinum!* She looked down at the note that was left next to it. She opened it and smiled when she saw the inside.

I'mma be out the country for a few days.
Have fun on me.
Talk to you soon.
-Seth.

For him to be so fucking heartless and not trusting, he leaves a fucking black card. What the fuck. . .

𝒯

Seth's Gucci flip flops left a trail in the sand as he and Messiah headed up to the sidewalk that led to Meme Aruba's beach house. The sun beamed down against his bare chest while he rocked an unbuttoned white mesh shirt and Gucci shorts. Every time he visited the islands it put him at peace.

His father's family was originally from Hawaii, but his great grandmother moved to the Bahamas forty years ago when she married her second husband, who was native to the land. Whenever he saw sand, it was home sweet home, and one day soon, he'd be purchasing his own cribs both in Hawaii and the Bahamas.

"Look at my baby! You are so handsooooome, ka mo'opuna nui!"

That was Hawaiian for great grandson.

"Aloha, Keanu." He placed a kiss to her forehead as she wrapped her arms around his waist. "How you doing beautiful? You don't age, kapunawahine *great grandma*, do you?" He smiled as he looked into her beautiful eyes.

Keanu would be ninety this year, but she was aging gracefully.

"Aaaaw, you're so sweet. My Lord, you're covered in hickeys, child. And you got gold teeth? Are they permanent? And scratches? Good Lord, you surely enjoyed yourself before you came out here, didn't you?"

Seth smiled as she embraced Messiah.

"Wassup, GG?"

"Hey, Messiah, baby. You are just as handsome as well my chocolate drop. Is that a man bun? Good Lord, the styles have definitely changed."

The Michael B. Jordan look-alike laughed as she tugged on his hair.

"What you cooking girl? Smell good." He sniffed as he and Seth followed behind her into the house once they removed their shoes at the door.

"I've got some lomi-lomi salmon, some pineapples that just came off the grill, some poi, and poke. Y'all hungry? Your henchmen have been eating me out a house and a damn home." She joked as she wiped the beads of sweat from off her forehead.

"You heard from Osiris?"

Keanu could sense the seriousness in her great grandson's tone.

"No. You know about the noncommunication with me and that negro. He came out some time ago last year. It was right after you got locked up. He had an army with him. I had to have your team hide in the cellar for two days. He was around here looking around and things, and it really pissed me off.

"You know I keep a couple of tricks up my sleeve. I had a feeling you were in trouble before I got word about it. The cellar is new, so he wasn't able to find them. Now, what's this all about Seth? Why are you and the ohana not at peace with one another? I don't like that."

Seth took a sip of the 1942 as he looked into her eyes. He could never lie to her. She and Falcon were the only women to hold his heart, but it was fucking with his head how one of those women had decided to betray him when he had needed her the most.

"Some shady stuff been going on, GG. I'ma keep it a hunnid. My squad wouldn't still be out here, and he wouldn't have had a search team if it wasn't serious."

"Now, Seth. Have I crossed you? Now, granted I apologize for not being able to do anything about you being in prison. I tried to reach out to our people in Cuba myself after Prodigy called me seeing if we could make that happen, but your father had given them strict orders not to intervene. What is going on?

"I've never known Osiris to be so dark and hateful; especially to his boys. Now, I know that what I say won't change your mind, and it won't stop you from this foolishness, and these drugs and all that, but your GG cares so much about you, and I don't wanna lose another great grandson."

She held on to his face.

"My heart has been hurting since you got locked up, I've been torn to pieces since Akil was murdered, and I'm in agony knowing that y'all are not one; especially during such a hard time like this. But the spirits baby? They've been talking to me. Something bad is about to unfold. Something really bad. I love all of you, but the spirits are not happy with your brother and father. They aren't."

Keanu was deep into Hawaiian voodoo. She believed in it all. There was a bad spirit that leveled out the good. Seth never really got into all that shit. He knew who he served, and that was God, but he never spoke down on his great grandmother. Whenever she had a feeling or claimed a spirit had talked to her, nine times out of ten, she was never wrong.

The winds blew hard around the mansion causing the lights to flicker. The shit always sent a chill down his damn spine. He gripped his Desert Eagle tight in his pants as he looked around.

"I just pray for you, baby. I really do. You know Keanu is here for you no matter what. And I mean that. Your men have been safe here. They respect this home, they respect Darcy and I, and most importantly, they respect *you*. Not the Platinum dynasty, not your father, but you and your origins. I don't feel it in my heart that those men did anything that interfered with your arrest. It's that brother of yours that you need to watch. You hear me?"

Seth kissed her forehead as he threw his arm around her.

"Mahalo, GG. Aloha Ah Ia 'Oe."

"I love you too, baby. Now go ahead. They're all down in the basement waiting on you two. You wanna take a plate with you?"

"I will, G."

Seth laughed at Messiah's always hungry ass with a shake of his head.

"I already had your plate made, Messiah. I knew you would be hungry. Here you go. Let me refill your drink before you go too. It's plenty if you change your mind, baby."

"A'ight, GG. 'Preciate it."

The duo both climbed down the stairs, and were greeted to their squad of thirty, all awaiting on their arrival. Seth appreciated Keanu for letting them live in her guest home until he had his shit straight. He and GG always had a special connection, and he knew with all his heart that she would never fold on him.

"Look who dun' popped out?"

Prodigy chuckled following Seth's response as they slapped hands and embraced. The last time the infamous trio had linked up, they were out in Maui for Seth's twenty-sixth birthday turning the fuck up, right before he got put in the jam.

"On me. You know how shit go. Ain't shit changed." Their potna responded.

Seth nor Messiah had to verbally explain the reluctance they felt to know that Prodigy was present. He may have been busy with his career but the fact that he'd been down and assisting Akil to connect the dots, before he was hated on, said more than words verbally could express.

They were brothers. Different by blood but loyalty was the DNA that kept them intertwined. Knowing they had solidarity within him during these trying times no matter what his schedule looked like is why their bond would always be unbreakable.

Niggas tried to turn their potna against them by keeping him out of the mix and taking advantage of his distance via his Hollywood setting, but you couldn't intercept what was meant. Jediah and J4 tried it, but Prodigy was as real as they came.

Tito, the head of their defense crew, approached Seth and Messiah after their heart to heart with Prodigy. With his arms behind his back he bowed his head in respect, and the rest of the men followed suit.

The room was quiet for a moment. Seth said a silent prayer over him and his men before he picked his head back up. He took a seat inside of the recliner that was near, then everyone else sat after him.

"Catch me up to speed," he commanded.

Tito cleared his voice before he began.

"Osiris was going on and on about how it was time to go on with the Desoto invasion to claim the new territory. As you know they still were left undecided on who's side they were gonna choose, and he was getting tired of waiting. Before that, we already had an understanding that we would be heading down to Mexico with you to handle the Juno case, but Jediah put a lock on the safe house before we could even make it out.

"That's why you ended up meeting a different squad at the border before you crossed over. You know we ain't with the funny shit. By the time we had put two and two together, they sent a squad in after us. As you can see everybody didn't make it out alive, but enough of us did. And you know Meme Aruba got a way with them spirits. I don't question it.

"We managed to escape through the tunnel that cuts through the Desoto territory, and she had a travel bus waiting for us by the time we made it down to St. Clair. We took that to the border while they were still in Desoto and caught a flight out here."

"So, Desoto is Platinum territory now?" Messiah countered.

"Yeah." Tito confirmed.

"So, if they were in Desoto, then how the fuck did Jediah make it all the way to the border to get Akil?" The shit wasn't adding up in Messiah's head.

"That's 'cuz he already figured that some of them would shake the safe house, but he thought they was gon' head out to me in Mexico. Ain't nobody ponder the Bahamas until they realized they couldn't find them." Seth inferred.

"This whole lil' ordeal was a set-up. Muthafuckas ain't think I was gon' make it back from Mexico alive, so incarceration was the perfect trade off. It still ain't adding up why Akil was the one who got murked though."

It was like a knife had been driven through his heart when the words left Seth's mouth. That shit was so fresh on his chest, he thought he'd snap at the thought of it.

"We gotta get back to the states. Fuck all these shrouds, and this laying low shit. Si and Jediah on some old foo-foo ass shit together, and Falcon right in the middle of it. Moms ain't never been no advocate to no bullshit, but it's a'ight though. Meet us at the dock at eight in the morning for departure. I'm about to show these muthafuckas that they could never be bigger than me without me."

T

"Tee-Tee, Nas!"

"Hi, Booooooo!"

Nasir's beautiful niece jumped into her arms when she saw her approach the table. It's been months since she's last seen her, and she missed her little chicken nugget so much.

"You're getting so big! Hi beautiful!"

"Hi, Tee-Tee! You're not fluffy anymore, Tee-Tee Nas! What happened!"

Nasir laughed as she put Shanice aka Boo back on her feet.

"Tee-Tee lost some weight baby girl."

"Well you look beautiful, Tee-Tee. I almost didn't know it was you! Hey, you've got more tattoos! I likey!"

"Too many damn tattoos to count."

Nas looked up at her brother.

"Shut up, Smiley. Wassup, bruh!"

She jumped into her brother's arms as he placed a kiss to her cheek

"Wassup, sus. Damn you beautiful. You always have been, but I'm happy you finally did this for yourself."

"Thank you. You look good, and stress-free, pimp. I see the co-parenting with Yoni is working out."

He laughed.

"She know better. She thought a nigga was bullshitting when I said I was moving down there. She wasn't taking my daughter away from me. Fuck that shit."

"Watch your mouth around my grand baby, Ali." Catori griped as she slapped the back of his head.

"Hey, ma."

"Hey, beautiful."

Nas and her mother embraced.

"I hope there's room for one more."

Nasir's eyes bucked when she laid them upon her favorite cousin who peeked her head around Ali from hiding.

"Riley!!! What!!! What are you doing here!"

"Naaaaaaaaas, baby, you look amazing !!!!!"

Riley jumped up and wrapped her legs around Nas' waist as if she were her long- lost prison bound husband. They grew up together. Identical hair styles, identical 90's gear, identical smiles, and all. Nas and Riley were the only girls growing up. They had a family full of all boys until those boys started getting their bitches knocked up, and they all began having girls.

Riley was beautiful. Nas swore on everything she loved that her cousin looked just like Morgan Westbrooks. People called them the double mint twins. Two bright yellow, full body tatted, full lip having, and now they both were slim, bad bitches.

"I see y'all missed each other," Ali chuckled as he took a seat.

"I have!"

Nas had tears running down her eyes, and when she put Riley down, she saw her tears running as well.

"Ooooh, best friend!" Nas cried as she wiped her tears away. "What's wrong? I'm crying because I'm happy to see you, but I see hurt in your eyes. What happened now?"

Riley managed to laugh as she wiped Nas' face too.

"Girl." She dropped her head, but Nas raised it back up.

"What the fuck that nigga do now?"

Riley smiled.

"We're getting a divorce. It's gonna be finalized this weekend when I go and get the rest of my stuff." She whispered.

"What!!!!"

"Yeah. Ali had to come over the house and beat his ass. He had jumped on me, and. . ."

"Riley! What!!! Why didn't you call me!"

Nas was screaming so loud everyone in the outside section was staring and whispering amongst themselves about the commotion.

"You two have a seat. Come on." Catori insisted.

Nas was seeing red. She couldn't believe her ears.

"I'm okay. I'm gon' be okay. I know God got me," Riley smiled as she took a sip of the water that sat before her.

"So, everybody at this table knew but me?" Nas questioned with the raise of her eyebrow.

"Don't blame them. It's my fault that I haven't said anything to you yet. It's just been so hard, and I know you've been stressed a lot lately, Nas."

"That's beside the point. Y'all know I'ma be there ten toes down for any of y'all."

"We know, sus. Trust, we know. Everything happened so damn fast, we just wanted to make sure that she got back to Saint Louis safely. That nigga was on some other shit, and I almost put one in that nigga's head," Ali retorted.

"That bit—" Nas caught herself before dropping the bitch-bomb in front of her niece. "I can't believe this. So, you're moving back?"

Riley nodded her head in agreement.

"Yes."

"Well, where are you staying?"

"I... don't know yet. I didn't wanna go with granny, but I just had to get out that city, and fast."

"Well, you're moving in with me."

"Nas."

"Riley. Get a storage and move all you can in. We'll figure it out. Hell, nah you ain't going with granny. It's too much going on over there. I'm single, and there's no traffic coming in and out of my house, so it's cool. You're moving in, and that's that."

Nas played no games about her cousin.

"According to those hickeys all over your neck, I don't know if I believe that single comment."

Nasir's face turned red from her snide remark. She had her hair down, and she was just sure that her full bouncy curls would hide them once her hair had dried from her shower.

"Damn, sus. You fucking with a vampire? Y'all have fun? Shit!"

"Ali Chambers!" Catori gasped.

"Daddy always cusses, gammy. It's okay," Boo cheered as she continued to color in her princess coloring book.

"I'ma fuck you up," Catori hissed through grit teeth.

"Gammy, you just said the f-word!" Boo gasped.

"I'm sorry baby. Look at what you made me do!" Catori laughed as she threw a napkin at her son.

"I ain't make you say that. Tell gammy she gotta take responsibility for her own actions, Boo." Ali teased.

"I'm not saying that to gammy, daddy. I'm more scared of her than you."

"Yooooooo! You foul, baby girl! It's like that? It looks like you gon' be washing dishes to pay for yo food, lil' momma," he teased.

"Nooooo, daddy! I don't like dishes."

"You gon' like 'em today," He laughed.

"Well, it's true, daddy. You say not to lie, I mean tell a story, so I didn't wanna tell a story. Please don't make me wash the dishes. I'm sorry."

They all shared a laugh as she got up and ran into his arms.

"Back to you though, cousin. You're glowing." Riley teased as she squeezed Nas' thighs that were showing in her t-shirt dress.

"I'm not glowing," she insisted with a smile so wide that her dimples showed.

"But you are. I see why you didn't call me back last night."

Nasir laughed at her mother's comment.

"Get off me. This ain't about me."

"He was hitting that shit huh, sus? Look, can't even stop smiling."

"I hate you, Ali! Oh my God!" She was filled with laughter.

Family was everything to Nas. This little circle surrounding her was her world, and she hated that her cousin was going through such difficulties, but she was ecstatic to hear that she was moving back. She's been living in Atlanta for the last seven years, then when Ali moved out there three years ago, she felt completely alone.

She promised herself that she would remain close with her mother because that's all she had, and Alicia might not have been the best friend with her lil' rat ass, but with Nasir being single for over four years, she held onto the people she had around her. . .

"What if I break my lease?"

Nasir looked over at Riley as she sat in the passenger's seat of her cousin's 2016 5.0 mustang. It felt good to ride shotgun for a change.

"Don't do that. Ain't that shit like fifteen hunnid at Haven?" Riley obliged.

"Yeah, but so what. We can move to one of those townhomes right off of Olive. The ones right behind the AMC where uncle Vic used to stay at."

"Those are dope." Riley agreed. "They have one available?"

"Bitch, yes. Immediate move in. They want a deposit and first month's rent."

"How much is the deposit?"

"Fifteen hunnid."

"And how much is rent?"

"Fifteen hunnid."

"Nas! Who the fuck got forty-five hunnid, shit more than that because we gon' need help moving all of that shit. I'ma be honest, I don't have it right now. Maybe we should just wait until your lease is up instead of breaking it.

"That's gon' save us fifteen hunnid that we both could use in our pockets. We can definitely stack some shit by then. I'm transferring to a gym out here, and I have new clients lined up already starting next week, so my payroll hasn't stopped."

"Look, Riley. You wanna move, or nah?" Nas questioned with the raise of her eye brow as she passed her the blunt.

"Bitch, you got five thousand dollars? Did you get that high ass electric bill paid? I thought you still needed help with that."

"I paid it today, and yes I have five thousand dollars, so you wanna go look at that muthafucka, or nah?"

"Bitch we wreak of weed, and hold the fuck up, where did you get five grand from?"

"You ask too many damn questions. Make a right, right here. We going."

"First, you gon' tell me where you got this money from. You hit the Missouri Lottery or something?"

Nas laughed.

"Bitch, something like that. He'll probably kill me, but—"

"Bitch whooooo! You blushinnnnnnng! The nigga that put these hickeys on yo neck! I seen some on them thighs too!"

"You didn't!"

"I just did! Who is this nigga!"

Nas blushed.

"Girl, it just happened out of fucking nowhere. Long story short, I've only known this nigga for three days tops; we went four rounds last night, and he left me his black card while he's out of town."

"Yoooooooo! Whaaaaaat! Stop fucking playing! Nasir gots the fucking juice, bruh! You gave him some of that Karrine, super-head, didn't you! Didn't you!"

They were cracking up.

"So, who is he?"

"He's a Platinum."

"Bitch what? Platinum, like Platinum dynasty, bitch!"

If you were from the Lou, then you've heard of Seth and his family.

"Girl, yes. I can't fucking believe it."

Nas quickly filled her in on how they met and explained to her about the whole Alicia situation. Before they knew it, they had pulled up at the apartment complex.

"We gon' beat that bitch ass. I always knew that bitch was a rat. She straight did that shit, Nas?"

"Girl I'm kinda glad I had that bottle because if I would've put my hands on her I would've killed her."

"Wait, bitch, wait. Spray some of this on you."

Riley reached in the backseat and grabbed the bottle of Unstoppables Febreeze.

"Girl, this ain't gon' do shit for us. Light this Black for a minute. At least it'll take that weed smell away some."

"Cousin, you gon' have us smelling like old heads on a Friday fish fry. I be tryna stop smoking these, but they remind of a hooka, and I love the taste."

Riley took a deep pull before she passed it back.

"I know right. Come on."

Nas was surprised to see the high ratio of black staff in the office that day. They only had one apartment available, and after she and Riley got the tour, they had to claim it as their's. It was so decked out, and the new renovation, plus all the three levels of space they would have, sold them instantly.

"We'll be giving you two a call as soon as your applications clear, and we'll need to verify your income. It takes less than twenty-four hours, so you should be hearing from us soon. Lastly, we will need the fifteen-hundred-dollar deposit to hold the apartment if you are approved."

"Damn."

Nas laughed at Riley's inability to hold her thoughts back.

"I've missed you," she giggled as she handed the black card over to the manager.

When the woman took a look at the name on the card, her eyes widened.

"Excuse me one moment."

Nasir thought the damn lady had seen a ghost.

"Aaaah, shit. I ain't like that look. Bitch why didn't you just go and get a money order?"

"Can you take money off of a black card? Hell, I didn't know. They said they take cards."

"Yeah, but bitch, yo name ain't on that card."

"So?"

"You gon' get us locked up."

Nas laughed.

"Wouldn't be the first time we went to the jam together."

"You know what, Nas? We swore to never speak on that. I just got off papers fucking with yo ass."

"Me! I told you to throw the bag out the window, but yo scary ass wouldn't do it."

They held their laughter in when the manager came back.

"Ms. Valentine, Mrs. Heights. You two have been approved for the apartment. Just give me a few moments to gather up all of your paperwork, and we can get everything signed, and your keys in hand within the next thirty minutes. Your deposit, moving fees, and first month's rent have all been waived as well, so there is no need for any payments. Here is your card back, Ms. Valentine. I'll be back shortly."

Nas and her cousin looked at each other like two deer in headlights.

"Bitch, what the fuck just happened!" Riley shrieked.

"I don't know. I—"

The sound of Nas' text message ringer went off. Hurriedly, she pulled her phone out. She didn't even know she had the nigga's number, but when the name *Seth* appeared on her phone, her heart dropped. All he sent was an emoji smiley face with that cheesy ass "aw yeah" smirk on its face.

"What does this mean?" She handed the phone over to Riley.

"It's just a smil—oh, this is from big daddy. That means this must be Platinum territory. Now bitch, whatever you did to him last night, I need to be taking notes because yaaaaaas best friend. How else do you explain us getting a three-thousand-dollar fee waived?

"Don't nobody play about three stacks. Especially out here in Creve Coure. She must've saw his name on the card and called that nigga. You didn't tell me if he had a friend yet because it sounds like I need to join this circle!"

"Biiiiitch," Nas shrieked.

"Ladies? Your paperwork is ready. Can you please join me in my office?"

Chapter Eight

Seth sat up on the side of the bed and ran his hands through his hair. His nerves wouldn't let up. It wasn't fear; fear never bothered him, but he could admit that the meeting with the Platinum dynasty earlier in the morning had him on edge. All he's ever known was family. All he's ever sworn to do was honor and protect the family, but now those were his very enemies.

He reached over on the nightstand and grabbed the bottle of Hennessy. He'd been slamming in pussy all night, but he just couldn't find that same sense of calm and satisfaction like he did a few days ago when he was laid up with Nas.

Seth stood to his feet with the bottle up to his lips and headed over to the floor-ceiling windows. Resting his arm above his head, he took another swig while his mind raced.

Ever since he made it in from the Bahamas he's gripped his gun more times than he could remember. Everybody was the fucking enemy. But for his own mother and father to betray him... his heart was heavy.

The shit didn't surprise him coming from Jediah. Ever since they were younger he knew the nigga wasn't shit, but Falcon and Osiris' actions had him so disgruntled that he couldn't even think straight.

Looking down at his phone he hit the call button, hoping the person on the other end of it would answer.

"Hello?"

The sound of her groggy voice slapped a smile on his face that he couldn't hide.

"Wassup, mama."

"Hey." Nasir yawned as she turned over in bed to look at the clock that read 4 am. "Everything okay?" She asked with another yawn.

Nas tried to be calm, but her heart was racing. She hadn't heard from him since that text message two days ago. She just knew she'd hear from his ass about that shit from the apartment complex, and the fifteen hundred dollars that made her cringe when her old apartments swiped his card. Hell, she had charged her four-hundred-dollar electric bill to that bitch too, but she had yet to have heard from him until now.

"I'm straight. I just had to hear yo voice."

She smiled so hard she knew he could see it through the phone.

"At four in the morning, Seth?"

"I know what time it is. I don't give a damn if it was every hour on the hour no matter how early it is. If I wanna call and hear your voice, then that should be no problem, a'ight?"

"Yes, daddy," she taunted.

He chuckled.

"I know it's been a few days. I'm just taking care of some shit right now."

"I didn't say nothing," she insisted as she pulled the covers up over her shoulder. The air was on freezing just the way she had liked it.

"I don't wanna hear that shit. Yo ass been flipping yo damn wig. I'm already hip."

Nasir laughed.

"I figured you'd call eventually. So, it's cool."

"Aw yeah? I guess I gotta give it a few more months or so before I see you get to spazzing out on a nigga. This lil' calm ass act I'm not buying."

Nasir giggled.

"Seth, you're not my—"

"Don't say that bullshit to me."

"What!" she gasped.

"I already know what yo smart mouth ass tryna say. I don't wanna hear that shit. What I tell you about coming at me correct?"

"And what I tell you about talking to me like that?"

He took another swig from the bottle. In his head, his hand was around her neck, and his tongue was down her throat while his other hand was playing in that fire ass pussy that he couldn't keep his mind off of. Seth couldn't believe this shit. He wasn't a phone talker, and from the way he kept smiling, he knew this girl was gonna be a problem.

"I'ma see you tomorrow, a'ight?"

"Tomorrow as in later on today, or tomorrow as in Wednesday?"

"Why you always gotta question what the fuck I say?"

"I'm just tryna make sure I got the day right, nigga. Calm down, would you?" She smirked.

He didn't want to, but he chuckled.

"I'll give you that one. I just got a lot of shit on my mind right now, mama. My fault."

Sometimes the man didn't even know how stressed he was until nights like this hit him and he couldn't sleep.

"If you can't control it right then and there, then stop tripping. The morning will be here before you know it. Handle whatever it is when it can be handled. That's why yo ass be so damn mad at the world; your mind is always occupied. Turn that damn brain off for a minute and just relax."

Shorty was making a lot of sense. Seth wasn't the one for the correct criticism. The shit kind of made his teeth grind, but he couldn't argue with her because she was right. Plus, she did something to him that he couldn't explain. Seth was growing to like that shit. A lot. And he hated it.

"I'ma call you, a'ight? Soon."

He could sense her smile, and it gave him the relaxation that he knew he'd receive from her even if the call had only lasted a few minutes.

"Okay."

Click.

"You must really like her."

Seth looked over his shoulder at Kelani who was sitting up in bed with the sheets wrapped around her.

"I don't think I've ever heard such a gentle tone come out of your mouth. She must really be something."

"Look, I don't wanna hear that shit right now."

That quick he went from zero to one hunnid. Women talked shit all fucking day. That shit must've been programmed in their fucking DNA, but Kelani always said some shit that instantly made him mad.

He'd been kicking it with her for a few years now. Somehow, he ended up falling for her fine, Tika Sumpter, looking ass. She held him down and he could admit that, but when he got jammed up he saw her true colors.

Granted she still held a place in his heart, but he knew that he couldn't trust the bitch, and if he couldn't trust you, then he had no business associating with you. Period. But just like it was something about Nas, it was something about Kelani too that he just couldn't get both of his feet out the door right now.

"And you think I wanted to sit here and hear that shit? The least you could have done was went in the fucking bathroom like you're not in my bedroom, in my house, and haven't been fucking me all night."

He sat on the edge of the bed after picking his shirt up off the floor and slid it on. He had too much other shit to be tripping off of, and her bitch fit wasn't one of them.

"So, you gon' leave? Go ahead. Go. Go to your lil' ho like I haven't been your bitch for almost three years now. You come home from the pen and now you don't know nobody. Get the fuck out of here."

When she pushed him in the back of the head, he stood up and walked around to her side of the bed. He grabbed her by the throat and hemmed her up against the wall.

"You think muthafuckas wasn't watching yo ass the whole time I was locked up bitch? The moment I bounced you was out here acting like a wild bitch off a leash. So, don't step to me with that bullshit. I got eyes and ears everywhere, and you know that shit. Fuck with me if you want to. You know I don't play that shit."

He let her neck go and watched her slide down to the floor while gasping for air.

"Gon' come to me about what the fuck I'm doing. Bitch I'm me. Shit was one hunnid until you got ran by the same niggas I was breaking bread with. How the fuck you expect me to hold down the same bitch that dun' fucked my whole team? You trash now ho. I told you to watch yo fucking mouth, but you always think a nigga playing."

He slid his pants back on and grabbed the keys to his whip along with the last of the Hennessy that disappeared between his lips. The loud sound of the glass crashing against the floor on his way out the door left Kelani empty. She knew she had lost her man, and way faster than it took her to get him.

𝒯

"Si, does it really have to come down to this?"

Osiris finished pouring himself a glass of scotch before he looked up at his wife. Often, Falcon pushed him to the point where he had to remind her who the fuck he was, but he let the liquor slide down his throat and put him at ease for the moment.

"Doesn't that look like what the fuck it's come down to Falcon?"

"Watch you're fucking mouth! Don't get all snippy with me because I'm worried about the welfare of my husband and his sons!" She snapped.

He downed the rest of his drink before he picked the crystal glass back up and fixed him another.

"You're a little too late for that, Falcon. A year too late. You've known what the fuck has been going on since day one, so don't come at me with this white flag bullshit. If Seth wants to disrespect this family and go against honor, then I'ma let his ass do what the fuck he gon' do. Niggas ain't siding with him without me. They ain't stupid."

"Have you forgotten that your son has helped this dynasty evolve to where it is this very fucking day, Osiris? What the fuck has gotten into you? Did we not just bury Akil? Did we not almost lose Seth last year because you held out on him at the last minute?"

Falcon's choppy bob swung in the air once the back of Osiris' hand made one with her face.

"Watch what the fuck you say to me! I'm yo husband! You married me! You swore an oath to me! So whatever fucking decision I make, shut yo got-damn mouth and follow suit! You hear me!"

Falcon cut her eyes at her husband so hard, it made a vein pop out his bald head, pushing him over the edge. He grabbed her by the throat and hemmed her up against the fireplace while looking into her eyes.

"Self-con-trol." He hissed. "Be my wife. Don't let your obedience run astray. I know you all fucked up about Akil, but you gotta stay in line. You hear me?"

His tone softened up when tears started trickling down her eyes. Osiris grabbed his wife by the back of her head and put his mouth over hers. They kissed sloppily. Tears continued to run down Falcon's face as she felt her husband penetrate her walls. He hiked her leg up around his waist, and their bodies started moving as one.

"I'ma take care of this shit alright. . ." he grunted as he pulled her hair back and let his tongue glide over her neck. "Do you trust me? Have I ever failed you? Huh?"

"No. I trust you, Si. I'm sorry. . . ummm," she grunted loudly when his penis hit her spot.

After thirty years of marriage, they knew how to get each other off quick, yet with the same sense of pleasure from a night of endless love making. Falcon held onto the back of her husband's head as her chest heaved up and down.

She was so torn between what she knew was about to come, but like her husband had said, she made an oath to honor him through sickness and health, life and death, right and wrong. He placed a kiss to her cheek before he put her leg down and got himself back together.

"You coming, or what?"

He looked down at her as he fastened his belt. Falcon looked up into her husband's eyes as she pulled her skirt down and ran her fingers through her hair.

"Yes." . . .

The Prada Monk Strap shoes click clacked against the marble stone pavement as Seth strode through the courtyard of the Platinum Dynasty's mansion. The look amongst his face was grim as his suit jacket lightly blew in the wind. Messiah was to his right, Tito was to his left, and his mob was behind them as they crept upon the large double doors where his mother and father, Jediah, and the entire army all stood awaiting his arrival.

Osiris' smile faded when he saw the army behind his son. Even Jediah was puzzled to see the very men whom he'd searched high and low for this last year, appear in broad daylight as if the Platinum's team wasn't excellent in search and seizure. Seth chuckled when he approached his father. Their courtyard looked as if they were lining up for a funeral instead of preparing for the biggest split in the Platinum dynasty history.

"This is your last chance, Seth. In front of everybody. Bow down to me, and apologize for disrespecting this family, apologize to your mother, and this throne, and just admit that you were wrong. And if I were you, I'd choose wisely."

Seth chuckled from his father's comment.

"My decision has already been made, Si. It's time to let the army choose."

Fire burned in Osiris' eyes as his son stared at him with that cunning ass smile slapped upon his face that he wanted to knock off. Falcon tried her hardest not to crack. Never had she ever dreamed of the day to come when she would have to choose between her oldest son and her husband, and it broke her heart.

"So be it." Si countered with the shake of his head.

Seth and his father both stepped forward and stood a few feet away from one another. Osiris was so naive to the fact that Seth had so much of him running through his veins that he honestly thought his son would back down. He had his cockiness honest.

The Platinum dynasty had been split once before, and it was when Osiris' father, Nabawi, had ran the throne, and he had to choose between Si and his other son, Titus, whom Osiris ended up murdering after everything was all said and done. He never thought he'd be back in this same predicament up against his own son, but sometimes that's how the ball bounced.

"I advise all of you men to choose wisely. From this day forward, your fate, your welfare, your success, your power, and your sanity solely rely within the hands of the man that you choose to honor. As stated before, all Platinum territory will be divided.

Seth has earned the rights to all of his properties, *for now. . .* Jediah."

Seth stared his brother in the eye as he approached his father and stood by his side.

"With your deceit, fickle disrespect, and the inability to honor the code of this family, P1, your brother has been appointed to take your spot. I told you this wasn't what you wanted."

"Nah, I told y'all this ain't what the fuck y'all wanted. Enough with all this petty shit. It's P1 or Si. Once you cross over, you cross over. So, like he said, choose wisely."

Seth's heart was racing one hundred miles per hour, but he'd never let that shit show. No one had moved for a few moments, but when the first soldier made their move, everyone stood in silence.

It was the manager who had ownership over the dynasty's lending platform. A number of cartels borrowed from their company, and over the last three years, they've brought in billions after configuring revenue, interest, and paybacks. Their company launch was so popular that it was even open to the public.

Osiris underestimated his son. When Seth graduated from college, he and the owner had launched the program, and it was one of the Platinum's highest sources of income. Fifty-year-old, Christian Saints, placed his right hand on Seth's shoulder and bowed his head in respect before greeting Messiah, and standing beside them.

Henchmen from the army began to cross over, manufacture owners crossed over, three of the four armorers, plus one of the two ordinance conductors for their weapons of mass destruction team, bowed his head before Seth choosing whom he was destined to honor from this day forward.

Like Seth had pictured it, the dynasty was split right down the middle, but he was honestly surprised at how many alumni had chosen against his father. Osiris' head was stuck so far up his ass that he hadn't even paid attention to the way his son had been moving, the ties he'd made, the bridges he'd built, the wealth he'd established, and all that good shit.

"Then it's done."

Falcon's words were soft as she stood in the middle as a signal to the end, and the finalization of their crossover. She looked her son in the eye. She could see his pain; she could see his fallen heart that had shattered all over the floor knowing that her husband, and his father, had come between them. Seth's eyes watered as she turned her back to him and stood next to Osiris.

"So be it then."

His voice was condescending as he and his father stared one another in the eye.

"You're no longer welcomed on this property, or any other Platinum platform that isn't within your ownership. Now get the fuck out my house before I'm forced to light that ass up."

Seth rubbed his chin as a chuckle seeped through his lips before he presented Osiris with his last statement that would forever divide them.

"Welcome to the crossover."

Chapter Nine

"*All* these fucking boxes. I just can't. I'm stressed."
Nas sighed as she plopped down on the couch.

She and Riley were all moved into their new home, but now was the hard part. Unpacking.

"It's actually not that bad. Once we get all these empty boxes out of here, it should start to turn around. Chin up buttercup."

Nas smiled when Riley grabbed her by the chin after she plopped down next to her.

"I'm just hungry as fuck. I haven't eaten all day." Nasir pouted.

"I told you to stop doing that. That shit's not healthy. What do you wanna eat?"

"Well, I can tell you one thing. We ain't cooking shit. I don't even know where the plates are." Nas giggled.

"I wasn't even gonna go that route. We can hardly get in the damn kitchen it's so much shit in there. But I do wanna say thank you. You didn't have to do this you know."

Nasir smiled.

"Thanks was all I needed, Ry. We both need a break. Life's been coming down so fucking hard on us both. We deserve this. Now, I can save some damn money and get this car traded in."

"You better swipe that damn card and pay that muthafucka off. He said have fun."

"I am not putting five grand on that card. It gives me a heart attack just knowing that I have it. What about some Wingstop?"

"Nas, I swear to God I was sitting here daydreaming about some lemon pepper wings."

"With five boneless hot wings and dip them lemon peppers in the sauce. Oh my God I haven't had any in hellas. I deserve a cheat day."

"You deserve to relax. You know I know exactly how you feel. We've both dealt with them heavy days, but you gotta treat yo self or else you gon' binge. Just relax."

The sound of one of their phones ringing interrupted their conversation.

"Is that you, or me?" Nas asked.

"That's you."

She hopped up quick, tripping over a giant box with cleaning supplies inside of it on her way to the phone that was plugged into the wall.

"Ouch! Shit!" She laughed as she rolled over on the floor.

"Clumsy ass. Big daddy can wait a few more seconds."

"How you know it's him?"

"The way yo ass was running."

Nasir laughed before she answered the phone.

"Hello?"

"Yo, mama. What you doing?"

"Nothing. Taking a break from this unpacking to decide what we're gonna eat. I never got the chance to say thank you. I really appreciated that."

"Don't sweat it. She tell you yo rent was waived?"

Nas damn near shit on herself.

"Huh?"

Seth laughed.

"You fucking with a real nigga, ma. You think I'ma help you get yo foot in the door, then leave you hanging? As long as you fucking with me then you ain't got shit to worry about. Now put some clothes on. I'ma send a ride to get you."

Nas' head was so far in the damn clouds it took her a minute to respond.

"Ummm, my cousin is here. We live together now, you know? I'm not leaving her."

"I'm good, Nas. I'ma just chill and unpack some more."

"Nah she ain't unpacking shit. Tell her ass she coming too. I'ma put my potna on her."

"Your potna who? The one in the Bentley? Tiri's brother?" she asked.

"Yeah. Him."

"Nah, she's good."

"Yo, don't be like that. Shit went wild that day, and I'm tryna make it up to you. Messiah a good dude. Now get dressed like I said. The driver gon' be there in an hour and be mindful of what the fuck you put on."

Click.

Nasir raised her eyebrows as she looked down at the phone.

"Where y'all going?" Riley asked as she dug her hand into the large bag of peanut M&Ms.

"Ummm. *We,* as in you and I, are getting dressed, and a car is coming to get us. He has a friend for you."

"Nas, no. I just got out that shit with Tevin."

"Girl, I didn't say go marry the nigga. You just heard me say I wasn't going without you. I know this nigga isn't bullshitting so you going. You ain't leaving me hanging."

"Nas, wait!" Riley ran after her as she ran downstairs to her room. "I don't even know how to date anymore." She protested as she stepped over a large duffle bag that Nasir was digging around in.

"Hell, and I do? I've been single for four years. The most excitement I get is from when Richard comes in town every blue moon, and all we do is fuck, then he's out the door. So we both in the same boat."

"What does this friend look like? You know how I feel about blind dates. You remember Dermy?"

Nas busted out in laughter. Back in high school she was dating this guy named Sean, and he told her to bring her cousin because he had a cousin too. Well, when Nas and Riley pulled up, the blackest, skeet twisty having, crater face acne having ass nigga was sitting on the porch. He looked like a hood Winslow from *Family Matters.* Riley didn't talk to Nas for two whole days she was so pissed off.

"And that nigga had the nerve to think that I was gon' fuck his ugly ass? I get pissed off every time I think back to that shit."

Nas was hollin' as Riley grabbed her by the back of her neck with both hands.

"Well, this is no Dermy. I promise. So are you coming?"

"I mean, I guess. If this Seth is giving out black cards, then I need to see what this friend is about. I could use a new "friend"."

"Okkkkkay! Time to go be hoes." Nasir cheered in excitement.

"Oh gosh. The last time we were hoes we got locked up. I'm not sure if I'm down for this."

"Well, let's make it another night to remember. We just can't get too drunk. I gotta work in the morning."

T

Nas' heart was pounding. She couldn't sit still. This shit just wasn't real. She'd never even had a dude pick her up and give her a ride anywhere, like ever, and now she was sitting on leather seats inside of a Maybach limo. She kept pinching herself. Man, she was begging God to wake her up. The shit was happening so fast, and she's barely even known this man for a week.

"Yo cousin, you cool?"

Nas looked over at Riley and smiled nervously.

"Girl this is. . . have you ever been in a Maybach before?"

"Bitch, I've never been in a limo. The fuck?"

They shared a laugh.

"I take that back. I rode in one on our wedding day. Maybe I shouldn't have come. With me and Tevin signing papers this weekend I'm just—"

"Nope, baby girl. None of that. Tevin fucked up. He had a good one, and he lost out on you. Fuck him. Here. Take this last shot."

She handed her the glass of 1942.

"This shit is nasty, Nas. I'm not doing it."

"Just take it. On three. One."

"Two." Riley mumbled while holding her nose.

"Three!" *Gulp.* "Yuuuuck!" Nas gagged damn near throwing it back up.

"I feel it already," Riley gagged as well. "Hurry up and light the new blunt, bitch, hurry up! Shit we pulling up. You get out first, Nas."

"Me! Why me!"

"Because he's your man, bitch!"

"He's not my man!"

"Not yet he isn't. Come on. Put them cakes on display. You looking extra fine tonight. Where are we anyway cousin? I see the Platinums got the city on lock..."

When the driver opened the door, Ms. Nasir Valentine stepped out shutting it down. She was rocking a fitted mauve colored, latex, thin strapped, and backless dress from Fashion Nova, a pink French beret to match, and pink furry chunky heels that strapped around her ankles.

Her long natural thirty-inch hair was bone straight of course. It was her signature style, and at the last minute, she cut her some long choppy Chinese bangs. A sparkly gold clutch from Aldo hung on her shoulder and last, her lips were painted in a deep matte nude from the NYX line. Nas was tired of hiding underneath big and baggy clothes; it was her time to shine.

Riley was show stopping as well. The white bandeau, low-rise white skinny jeans, and the teal pointy toe pumps looked good on her slim thick frame. Her hair was styled in a long blunt cut bob, and just like her cousin, tattoos covered her body. Her full lips were painted in a shade of Sin lipstick to match the bottom of her pumps, and the Furla purse she had on her arm.

A crowd of people surrounded The Flamingo bar/pool hall, and it recently had a shooting range added that was located on the new top level. *Damn, Seth is that nigga,* Nas thought in disbelief that this was actually her life right now.

"Nasir?" A rather large guard asked her as she approached the door.

"Yeah?"

"Come right on in, ma. You ladies enjoy yourselves."

"Thank you."

"Damn, Nas, is that Seth with all the hair? He fine as fuck," Riley whispered in her ear as another guard led them over to where he was sitting with Messiah and the men from his crew.

Seth removed the blunt from his lips when he laid eyes on Nas. The way she made his dick hard should've been a fucking crime, and an immediate file for sexual harassment.

It's like she controlled the muthafucka when he got around her. She and her girl were definitely the center of attention. Messiah put his arm around Seth's shoulders as they slapped hands.

"Bruh, that's the cousin! My nigga always come thru! Oh yay!"

Messiah's silly ass was always pumped.

"Aye, be nice to her man. Don't fuck this one up. Shorty off limits."

"So that's you?"

Seth's eyes hadn't left Nasir as she had gotten closer and closer to him.

"Damn fucking right. She *off limits*. We can't share her bruh. That's why I told her to bring her girl."

Nas held the glass of 1942 up to her lips as she finally made it over to him; she was so nervous. She made a face so sour after it went down that Seth couldn't help but laugh.

"Tryna be hard and shit. You want me to get you one of them sugary ass drinks you be sipping on, mama?"

"Damn right," she gasped as she patted her mouth dry.

Seth smiled as he pulled her close. Being careful not to burn her with the blunt between his fingers, he grabbed her by the waist and placed a kiss to her lips. He'd missed these lips. He'd missed wrapping his arms around her waist. He'd missed her presence.

"Hold the fuck up." He countered as he spun her around.

His eyes bucked when he saw her round ass, and her back covered in black ink that her dress displayed. Seth pulled her close so she could feel his monster sitting right on her back.

"Yeah, you like fucking with me. I should choke the shit out yo' ass." He licked her ear.

"As long as that dick is in me when you do it then, I don't see the problem."

Nas was lit. Their pregame was a success.

"Aw yeah?" he grinned as he wrapped his arms around her. Their lips met again.

"Okay cousin! I see you girrrrrl! Yaaaaas, thick fine ass! Get yo' man!"

The smile on Nas' face couldn't be hidden.

"My bad, girl. Seth, this is my cousin, Riley. She fine as fuck ain't she?"

"You gorgeous, mama. Nice to meet you. Seth."

"Nice to meet you, Mr. Seth."

"This my potna, Messiah. He gon' keep you company tonight and make sure you a'ight." He introduced them.

Riley had to give Nas her props. She came through this time, unlike the last one, and she almost stopped being her damn cousin because that blow was so low. Messiah was fine as fuck. Because the braided man bun, his panty dropping smile, and the denim button down along with the black Radburn jeans and Balenciaga sneakers he was rocking surely took her mind off all of her troubles.

"Wassup, mama. Damn. My nigga don't never let a lie come out his mouth. Yes, you are fine as fuck."

Riley blushed as he grabbed her by the hand and kissed it. His cheesy actions tickled her pink, but she kinda liked it.

"Thank you, handsome. Is the kitchen open? I'm starving; we been drinking and smoking all night, and I need something to eat."

He laughed.

"Yeah, I can fuck wit' you mama. A woman with an appetite right up my alley. What you want? I got some wings and Bud Lights at the table now. They fresh."

"Bud Light Lime?"

"Them the only ones I drink, ma. Come on now?"

She laughed.

"I'm just making sure. You gon' fix me a plate? Don't be skeet either."

He grabbed her by the hand and led her over to the leather booth. He boldly sat her in his lap and handed her a drink before he fixed a plate on the table sitting before them.

"So y'all gon' show up to a bowling alley in heels and shit?"

Nas looked back at Seth while she sat in his lap.

"You did not tell me where we were going. You just said to get dressed. I'd rather be over dressed than under dressed."

He kissed her lips before he popped the cap on the beer for her.

"Mo' like dressed to kill because that's what I almost did to you when I saw yo' ass. Look at you. You look cute in yo' lil' French hat and shit."

Nas was bugging up.

"Save this space right here for my name, a'ight?" He ordered as his finger glided along her breast above the abstract tattoo of the Capricorn goat she had.

"If yes is what you wanna hear then, I'll play into that tonight. You probably won't be able to stand me a few months from now."

Seth's smile made the insides of her legs tingle. Nas didn't know if she liked it better when he wore his hair up, or down, but his blow-out hanging down his back with the front pulled back was too sexy on him right now.

She hated niggas with hair until she met Seth. Nas could see herself fucking around and giving him a silk press to see how long it really got.

"You're in a good mood," she smirked as she put her arm around his shoulders.

"A real good mood, mama. Business going good, billions coming in like clock- work, and I finally got the chance to see you again. I thought I told you to have fun. I ain't get that many notifications on my phone about no purchases. Paying bills ain't what I meant."

"Paying bills is fun. Especially when you have the money to pay them all? And have money left over? That's a fucking celebration."

He admired her honesty and the simplistic beauty that coined her personality.

"I feel it, mama. I can't say I understand where you coming from because this has always been my life. So I admire you for staying grounded to who you are, but like I said the first time. I want you to enjoy yourself.

"So tomorrow after the gig, if Messiah don't sweep ya girl off her feet, and they don't disappear somewhere, y'all kick it. And if you worried about maxing it out, then you really got sum' coming fucking with me. Money is not an issue and it never will be, so spend at your leisure. First things first though, we gotta get you out that beat up ass whip. I know that."

Nas laughed so hard she had to hold her chest.

"Don't talk about Esteban. That's been my Rollie for five years now."

"I see that. Very Clear. You need to get rid of that mug. A-muthafucking-sap."

"I will get rid of my car when I can afford to do so, okay?"

"Don't disrespect me like that," he raised his eyebrow as he put his hand on her thigh.

"I'm not disrespecting you. You not about to buy me no expensive ass car that I can't keep up with. That would be dumb on my part, and how do I know that you gon' be around long?"

He leaned into her and kissed her lips again. She gave him the sudden urge to do so whenever she licked them.

"Worry about today. That's why y'all females be so damn stressed; overthinking and shit. What I tell you earlier? I see you don't like to listen."

"Seth—"

"Nasir. Just shut the fuck up, a'ight?"

She smiled.

"You gon' bowl in heels?" He questioned as he looked down at her pedicured feet.

"And kill myself? I think not. You gon' get me some shoes?"

"So you *can* do more than sit here and look cute?"

She playfully hit him on his chest.

"I'm just saying, mama." He chuckled.

"I'm not the best bowler, but I will play. Now pool, that's more up my alley. I was always good in physics."

"And anatomy. You gotta A+ in that mu'fucka," he teased as he squeezed her butt.

"Would you stop?" she blushed as she reached over on the table and stole a wing from off of Riley's plate.

He couldn't resist smacking her ass that was in his face. Her confidence was sexy as fuck. He never thought he'd be so attracted to a curvy woman. She was stacked just right, and he loved that shit.

Seth and Messiah both kicked back and watched the ladies do their thing. The positive energy that vibrated from how Nas and her cousin fed off each other was something else. They bowled, they shot pool, fucked up the darts section, but now it was time for the real fun.

Seth held onto Nas' ass while he led her to the door that had the shooting range behind it. Nas' eyes glowed. It was like home seeing this place.

When Ali lived in town, he used to get a lot of burners dirty, and he always let her pop rounds. She had some experience unlike Riley who'd never even shot a real gun before.

"I don't know how I feel about this," Riley panicked a bit as she sat her glass down.

Messiah grabbed her by the hand before he led her over to a spot where a nine, an automatic shotgun, and a line of different Mac models sat lined up.

"We gon' start you off with sum' simple. This a nine. What hand you write with?" He asked as he stood behind her.

"The left."

"Here. Hold it, now put yo' right hand at the base for support."

"Like this?" she looked back at him.

He was so damn fine, and the liquor in her system had her ready to jump all over his tall ass, but she had to remain calm. Riley couldn't be throwing her damn panties after just a few hours.

Messiah licked his lips. Hot yellow wasn't usually his type, but he was just as attracted to her, and it was unlike him to not have already gotten some head from a bitch.

But his boy told him to be nice. Plus, Riley was a cool ass lil' chick. He liked her lil' hip though girly ass. He could fuck with it.

"Yeah, just like that."

Click-clank. BOW!

Click-clank. BOW!

Click-clank. BOW!

"You show off!" Riley laughed as she looked over at Nas who was letting off rounds from the Remington Tatical Shotgun like a damn pro.

"Don't be scared, girl! Make that gun go—"

BOW!

Riley laughed before she looked out at her target and shot the gun. She didn't even hit the board.

"Don't sweat it, mama. You a beginner. Try it again," Messiah chuckled as he held her by the waist.

Riley stuck her tongue out and let the gun go off until all she heard was the empty clip clicking. She'd hit the target this time, and it gave her a rush unlike anything she'd ever felt. She was ready to reload and try again.

"Let me see you work." She smiled as she looked up at the man whose cologne was hypnotizing her.

Messiah took a swig of the beer before he picked up the Desert Eagle. With one arm still around her waist, he emptied out the entire clip into the bull's eye.

"Okay, I see you. You pretty dope with that. Can we smoke up here?" She held the Backwoods in her lips as she searched for her lighter.

Siah lit a flame for her and stared into her eyes as the blunt burned. He could see pain, but she wore it well. For the first time in a while he was thinking with his head and not his dick.

Messiah fucked with her vibe. Hard. Something in that moment had him wanting to sit back with her in his lap and just rap over more Backwoods. Just on some chill shit.

"You should fuck with me tonight."

Riley smiled.

"Negative," she automatically shot down.

He chuckled.

"You didn't hear what I said. I said you should fuck *with* me. Not fuck me. Trust me, ma, if I wanted to fuck you, I would've already been and done that two hours ago."

She raised her brow.

"Aw yeah?"

Messiah licked his lips.

"You want me to be honest, or what? You just seem like you got a lot on yo mind, and I wanna kick back wit' you. I mean, but shit, I can fix that too if you want me to, mama," he joked.

It felt good to smile. Riley had been drowning in endless tears for months now considering the back and forth with Tevin. So, being around a bubbly personality versus the controlling and antagonizing bully she'd been cooped up with was a breath of fresh air.

"I think I'd like that."

"A'ight then. So let yo' guard down, and fuck with me."

Chapter Ten

"**You** bet not be tryna low-key kidnap me, nigga. You saw how I was working that clip back there. I got skills."

Messiah and Riley shared a laugh as he opened the gate to the elevator before they stepped off. Riley had stumbled for the umpteenth time that night. Her feet were not her friends after all of the liquor she's had.

Yet she refused to be dirty and take her heels off. In one swift motion, Messiah swept her off her feet and cradled her body as he continued for the door to his penthouse.

"I'm fiiiiiiine," she laughed as she laid her head on his shoulder.

"Yeah, ok, mama. I hear ya."

When they entered his home, the fresh smell of Bora-Bora Febreeze plug-ins hit her nose. One flick and the movie theater dimmed lights lit the enormous opening that joined the dining room, the kitchen, and the living room.

"Damn, this is dope." She smiled before a yawn escaped her lips.

Messiah laid her body down on the suede, smoky grey, pit styled sectional that looked more like a bed than a couch.

"You need anything? You good?"

His voice was soft as she looked into his eyes, never letting her arms release from around his neck.

"Some water would be nice, and maybe a few Tylenol, or whatever you have."

"A'ight, bet, but you gotta let me go first, mama."

"Oh! I'm sorry."

Messiah chuckled as he went off to grant her request. Riley laid her head against the mountain of pillows behind her and gazed out of the floor-length windows to her left. So much was going through her head. From Tevin and her divorce to her sudden move and the amount she had drank that night, she just couldn't find any peace.

"You a'ight, mama? You ain't gon' pass out on me, are you?"

Riley opened her eyes when she heard Messiah's voice. She smiled when she locked eyes with him. He was sitting by her feet with a bottle of Eternal water in his hand, and a few Advil pills on a napkin.

"No. I won't. Thank you."

He handed her the opened water after she put the pills in her mouth then, removed her shoes admiring the art work that covered both of her feet.

"My old lady used to say a woman covered in tattoos got a heart of steel. She can withstand a lot of shit, and she's often stronger than most women."

Riley smiled.

"She was right. It's not even a painful experience at this point. I'm like numb to it. I'll just sit there now and let my mind race, and it'll all be over before I know it."

"How many you got?"

"I've lost count after about fifty."

They shared a laugh.

"Like, real shit. I'm surprised my whole body isn't covered yet. I'm tryna catch up to Nas. Mommy is tatted yo. That's my boo. I just love her. She's really been keeping my head afloat these last few days considering all that's been happening."

"Happening with what?"

He was now lying beside her with a lighter up to a Backwoods. He inhaled it a few times before he put it up to her lips. Riley closed her eyes and inhaled until her lungs couldn't stand it. It was quiet for a moment before she looked over at him.

"I'm finalizing my divorce from a husband of seven years this weekend. We've been separated for a year now, but still."

"Damn. That's fucked up."

"Yeah, it is. We met in college, got married two years later at twenty, and it's just been one hell of a ride up until now. To make a long story short I have PCOS, and we've been trying to have kids for a while now, but God's just been like nope."

She looked down at her feet that were freezing. When he noticed her shivering, he grabbed the fleece blanket hanging over the arm of the couch that was near him and covered her.

"Thanks."

"Don't sweat it. So that's why y'all divorcing?"

She looked over at him.

"Yes. He. . . just doesn't love me anymore, and it's not like I haven't seen the signs, and it's not like I haven't known about the cheating, and it's not like I haven't noticed the way he's talked to me, the way he's been degrading me, and how he blamed it on my health and all that shit. I used to be heavy. I was a hundred pounds heavier when we met.

"I was heavy for a while actually, I just lost all of the weight within these last three years right before I became a personal trainer. Some doctors were like if you lose the weight it'll help with conceiving. Well I lost it, but nothing happened. I've been to so many fertility doctors and gynecologist that it just got mentally exhausting, and I gave up. Then, he gave up on me."

Messiah wiped the tears away that had fallen down her eyes.

"I'm sorry. I should go."

"Aye," he grabbed her by the waist when she tried to get up.

Feeling his arms around her had Riley's head through the roof. She couldn't even tell you the last time she's had a man's arms around her. She and her husband had been sleeping in different rooms for years now. Even after the separation they continued to live together because her name was on the house as well. It was just so much.

"Messiah," she sobbed with tears steadily trickling down her face.

He turned her chin towards him and swept them away.

"Look at me."

Riley opened her eyes embarrassed that she had cracked in front of him.

"I haven't shed a tear the whole time I've been here then, boom. It just hit me."

She cracked a smile and it made him smile as well.

"Listen to me, ma. Don't let that nigga fuck up yo head because of something you can't control. I've known hella women who have PCOS, and they got hella lil' bad asses out this world. Don't put that shit on yo self.

"And if that nigga can't stay by yo side through shit like this then what he around for? If a muthafucka wanna leave, then let 'em. I mean yeah, I see y'all was married and shit, but if that nigga tryna destroy you and shit like that, and y'all get to—"

"Sleeping in separate rooms, and all of the fighting, and screaming, and arguing, and him holding you down forcing you to look at pictures of all the pregnant women who were never you, and all of the little babies you wish you could've had running around the house. Then, the thought of all the mental catastrophes that he's casted upon you?

"It's too much. I'm only human. I won't fold under a lot but this? Messiah, I can't take this. I just can't." She wiped her eyes before she took the blunt from him. "This is horrible chill talk, man. I'm sorry," she laughed.

Messiah had to admit that he admired her strengths. Maybe he was just drunk. Maybe he was just faded, but she had his head on ten and he tried his hardest to shake it. Him and the sympathy thing just didn't click. After raising his baby sister for the last few years though, he's learned to be more open and mindful, but to a bitch he was fucking? That shit just didn't matter to him.

He didn't give a fuck about this or that, he didn't wanna get to know you, he didn't care about ya childhood, or none of that. As long as that mouth could open, and the pussy got wet, that's all that had mattered. Now he saw what Nas was doing to his potna. He swore Seth had already married the woman in his head before his mouth could even make the damn proposal, and he couldn't see how or why his nigga was geeking up until now.

Some women had that kryptonite, and he wasn't sure if he was up for this. Messiah was a lady's man. Fucking bitches was his motto but lying here with Riley right now was cool. It was something he could see himself doing if the woman was worth it. It's like she was whispering a bunch of sweet nothings in his ear, and he was game right now.

"Oooooh my head. Damn," she sighed as she put her hands on her forehead.

"You got so much shit on yo mind, mama. Relax."

Riley smiled when he pulled her closer to him. He stretched his arm out around the back of the couch as she laid her head on his chest.

"Can you put on some music or something? This silence is killing me."

He chuckled as he reached for the remote.

"Come here," he instructed as he sat back.

She got up and climbed in between his legs, resting her back against his chest. When the seventy-inch Samsung flat screen came on, he flipped through the channels until something caught her eye.

"This my shit. This is a classic. Who doesn't like *The Chronicles of Riddick?*" She smiled as she wrapped the cover around her.

"That third one go harder though," he countered.

"I mean, I liked it. The storyline just fell flat for me. It was cool."

He chuckled.

"What's your favorite movie?" she asked.

"Ummm, shit. That's a good question."

"Everybody's got a favorite movie. I know I can watch *Players Club* all day; like, all day."

"*In the nude. Titties! Ass. For free. . . Wasn't no shame in them walking around, bucky naked,*" he quoted from the classic scene.

They shared a laugh.

"RIP to the king man. That's my shit," she smiled.

"I'm hip. If I had to narrow it down though, I would say the whole *Friday* series."

"Nah, you gotta pick one."

He laughed.

"That ain't fair though, mama. You got Smoke Dog acting a fool in the first one, and Mike Epps just set the mood for the last two."

"Dun, dun, dun, duuuuun. A damn snitch."

"Top flight security, Craig."

They shared a laugh.

"You gotta ashtray?" she asked as she held the end of the blunt with her nails.

"Yeah, over there."

"I'll get it."

When she got up, Messiah's eyes roamed her frame. Riley was bad as fuck. Her ass was looking good in them jeans, and he was trying to be cool, but he wanted her so fucking bad.

"Where's the bathroom?" She asked as she looked around his house.

It was so big she could've put her entire home in Atlanta on the first level alone.

"Down the hall and to the left."

When the door closed behind her, Messiah hopped up and fixed himself a drink. He had to chill. Sometimes, a drunk Messiah was more calm and content than a sober Messiah. He took a swig from the Don Julio before he cracked open a beer and headed back to the couch.

He was leaned against the frame flipping through Netflix until he noticed Riley approach him. He removed the drink from his lips when he noticed that she didn't have any pants on.

The way her panties sat up on her waist and how sexy her hips were covered in tattoos, he had to admit that it was a pressure that he couldn't withstand. Riley was a size six, and she was stacked just like a Coke bottle now.

"I changed my mind. I do want you to fix it for me. Please?"

She climbed on the couch and mounted him. He sat back with the beer up to his lips as she removed her bandeau, letting her succulent breasts spill out.

"I may be a little drunk, but I do want you, Messiah. The way that dick's been getting hard all night, you can't flex like you don't want me too."

Riley took the beer from him and downed the rest while he inhaled her breasts. With them both in his hands, his mouth devoured her nipples as his dick started to grow. Riley could feel it up against her, and she couldn't control herself. She looked him in the eyes as she unbuttoned his shirt.

"I love a man that takes care of his body. That shit is so sexy to me," she smirked as she removed the shirt completely then ran her hands along his muscular chest.

In one swift motion, Messiah had her back against the couch and was holding himself over her while they engaged in a nice tongue down as if they were counting sheep to help the time fly by. Riley was feeling things that she hadn't felt since she and Tevin first met. The way his tongue felt against her neck drove her so far up a damn wall she could've came right then and there.

She giggled when he climbed off of the couch and pulled her pelvis to the edge. It happened so fast she hadn't even realized that he had one leg wrapped around his neck and the other pushed up in the air while she sat in a sitting position, until his tongue started flickering across her love button.

Messiah had a mouth like the gods. Eating pussy was his specialty. If the bitch was clean and he felt like she was worth it, he was going down on her. No questions asked about that shit. He hiked her right leg up further so his mouth could cover all of her flesh. His tongue swept back and forth like a figure-eight, and Riley couldn't stand it.

She held onto the back of his head and started rocking her hips. His tongue felt so good she could cry from the level of ecstasy he had her body venturing to. He had his head between her legs like he was tryna answer the *'How many licks does it take to get to the center of the Tootsie Pop'* riddle.

"Messiah!" She whimpered out of her control while her free hand roamed her breasts.

His mouth made sounds against her flesh, and his moans while he licked up every drop of her cream put her up under a love spell that she never wanted to be removed. She was in love.

"Stand up," he commanded as he sat on the edge.

Riley did as she was told and stood between his legs. To an imaginary beat she started shaking her ass. Young Blacksta's "Booty" was playing in her head, and she had her ass bouncing like it was Cancer season, and her birthday was near.

Messiah laid back for a minute and stroked his dick that he pulled out while the other hand smacked her on the ass. Riley was a freak on the dick. She held onto his knees and started throwing that ass in circles.

"I wanna see you do that shit on this dick, you hear me?" He commanded as he bent her over and made her touch her toes before he buried his face in her butt.

Messiah was a freak. Like he said before, if she was clean, and he was drunk enough, he was going all the way. He slapped her ass while his tongue tormented her butt. Riley had never had her ass eaten before, and she was pissed off from what she had been missing! One of his hands was rubbing on her clit while he shook his head back and forth before his tongue traveled to her creamy pussy lips.

"Oh my God! Oh my God! Oh my God! Uuuuuuum!" Her words seeped through her lips at the speed of light.

Bitches would be pressed from the way Riley's moans filled the air if they could hear her. She was going wild sounding like Jada Fire in one of her flicks. Messiah's dick jumped when he felt her wrap her hand around it.

It was so thick, and the sight of it was making her pussy cream in overtime. She stroked his meat getting hungrier for him by the second, but the way her vagina contracted, she had to let go and scream for dear life while her juices trickled from her body.

"Messiah! Messiah! Messsssiiiiiah! Ooooh, shit!"

She was exhausted, and she hadn't even done anything yet. He gave her pussy one last lick before he sat up and smacked her ass. Riley stumbled as she stood to her feet, causing him to laugh.

If she thought his head was something, then she was in for a treat once he got that ten-inch dick in her walls.

He removed the rest of his clothes and sat with his legs open steadily stroking himself while she fired up another blunt she had already rolled up. *Yeah, I fucks with her*, he thought as she walked over to him with it in her mouth.

She put her ass back in his face before she climbed on top of him from behind and mounted her feet on the couch. With his dick in her hand, she rotated her hips until she felt him break through her tight slit.

"Daymn!" She cooed as she inched more of him inside of her.

She thought Tevin's dick was big, but Messiah had a fucking monster between his legs. He put the blunt in his mouth that she passed to him before he grabbed her by the waist and pulled her down on top of him. She reached back and held onto his neck before her body started moving up and down. Her breasts bounced from her speed, and her head was in the clouds as his free hand tickled her clit.

He removed the blunt from his lips and stuck his tongue in her mouth. Her pussy was so tight it was like he was fucking a virgin. She wasn't lying when she said she hadn't been touched in a while, and he was about to give it to her. He rolled her over and laid her flat on her stomach with her legs closed.

He let his dick slide in and out of her ass cheeks for a second while he puffed hard on the gas before he put it out. Her back arched when the tip of his dick found the opening to her slit. Messiah was hitting every angle of her vagina, and she couldn't fight the feeling.

"Damn, this some good ass pussy, ma," he groaned while his tongue flicked over her earlobe.

"And this is some good ass dick, daddy," she laughed before their lips met.

Messiah shoved all of himself inside of her and rotated his hips while their tongues continued to tango. She was so warm and so wet he didn't wanna pull out. She felt him all the way in her cervix, his dick was in her so deep. Now she knew what Trey Songz meant by pain and pleasure.

"How you want it? Hmmm?" He asked between kisses as his hips started moving forward and back again.

The feeling of his dick in her pussy was hypnotizing him. Thoughts of a condom wouldn't do nothing but fuck up his mood because her shit felt like heaven.

"Baby. . . you can have me anyway you want me. . ." she groaned.

"All night?" He questioned as their tongues continued to torment one another.

"All night, baby. . . all fucking night. . ."

Chapter Eleven

"*Riley* be careful!" Nas shrieked, trying her hardest not to laugh at her cousin tripping over her feet while Messiah walked her up to the passenger's side of his ride.

"Shut the fuck up, bitch! You didn't see that! Wait, gimme some suga', lil' momma."

Nas ran on her tippy toes and held onto the door of the car before they kissed each other's cheek.

"Be safe. Messiah, you better be nice to my cousin," Nas teased as she closed the door behind her.

"I been nice to her all evening, mama. I thought I apologized about the other day?" He chuckled as he put his arms around Nas' shoulders.

"Yeah, okay. You saw me with that Remington and them .45's back there. I don't miss nigga." She giggled.

"Where you get her trill ass from, dawg! Damn! We gon' have to give her a position with the squad or sum'," Messiah joked as he and Seth slapped hands.

"Y'all be safe, man," Seth laughed as his potna hopped in his whip.

"On me. Malama pono, my nigga."

"Malama pono, bruh."

"Malama pono? What's that?" Nas asked as Seth walked over to her and grabbed her by the nape of her back.

"That's Hawaiian for take care and be right."

"Ooooh. So papi is from Hawaii? That's interesting," she teased before she kissed his lips.

"Yeah. Osiris is Hawaiian."

"Your father?"

"Yeah."

"Now, that's something I have to put on my bucket list. A visit to all five islands, and some Hawaiian cuisine."

"It's actually eight islands, but there are five main tourist locations. I'mma have to take you to meet Meme Aruba. She lives in the Bahamas now after my great grandfather passed, with her new husband. Nobody's hands throw down on some Hawaiian cuisine like Keanu."

"Things just get even more exciting with you as the days go by, Mr. Platinum." She twirled her finger in his hair while looking in his eyes.

"You know you almost got fucked in front of yo' girl, right?" His voice was low as he licked his lips.

Nasir laughed, but before she could respond, the valet driver pulled up with a Kawasaki Ninja motorcycle.

"Word? Is there two?" she gasped, glad she still had her heels off.

Seth had taken the socks off his feet and given them to her because she just couldn't do another minute in her shoes. Hell, Nas wasn't gonna kill herself tryna uphold her balance in no heels when she knew she couldn't. She'd broken an ankle before trying to be cute, and swore she'd never let that happen again.

"What you mean? You ride?" He inquired with the raise of an eyebrow.

"Yes, I ride!"

"Aye, I think you had too much to drink, mama." He laughed as he wrapped his arms around her.

"No, Seth, I'm dead ass serious. I got my license when I was living in California for a while. Back when me and that bitch Alicia met, we were determined to get a bike and learn how to ride. I sold my Suzuki because I needed the money, but yes, I can ride."

"Bullshit?"

She looked up into his eyes.

"No bullshit, baby."

Their lips met.

"Yo', pull Messiah's bike around here too," he directed to the valet driver.

"Yes, sir."

Moments later, the man pulled up with an identical ride.

"Mama, you sure you know how to ride?" He asked nervously.

Nas ignored him as she mounted the bike. Seth raised his eyebrow at the sight of Nasir's dress barely covering her ass. She put her purse around her neck before she put the helmet on and gave it some gas.

She dead ass fucking serious, he thought in amazement as he hopped on his bike and took off.

Nas was right behind him. They shot down Washington Street until they got to Jefferson, bucked a quick left, then flew down the road until they hit Highway Forty and headed west.

Nasir had to be the most interesting woman he'd ever met. He looked over to his right at this girl, and she had the bike in the air popping a sit-down wheelie.

Before he knew it, she had her legs sprawled out, hitting a no footer like the shit was no problem. He didn't know whether to be impressed or pissed because that damn dress she had on was hiked up, and all he saw was the Nasir on her damn ass.

This girl man, he chuckled as she sat back down and fixed her dress.

"I'mma let you get that off!" he yelled, even though he knew she couldn't hear him.

Seth had to give her a show back. Once he found the perfect speed he hopped up, planted his feet on the seat, and spread his arms like an eagle.

He dabbed on her a few times and let the bike cruise for a minute before he sat back down and cranked up the speed. He threw the bike into the air until the front tire was at the perfect vertical angle in the sky.

Seth looked over his shoulder when he heard her engine roar and saw Nas hitting the same stunt. He couldn't remember the last time he enjoyed himself with a woman like this outside of sex.

Shit Seth loved sex. A woman was God's greatest gift to earth, but one who came with this many different qualities, traits, and such a spontaneous personality? That was a blessing all in itself.

Nas followed him down the highway until they entered Chesterfield. She slowed her bike down a bit when they entered the mile-long driveway before her eyes laid upon the largest home she'd ever seen in person. Her mind was blown when she took her helmet off.

"Is this your house?" she gasped as he removed his helmet.

"Naaaaaah, mama. We just came here for a lil' rest stop."

"Okay, smart-ass," she laughed as she hopped off the bike.

"I give you yo' props, ma. You the shit. You was cold with that shit too. That's wassup. You dope." He admired.

With her hat in hand she followed him as he headed to the door.

"Thanks. Wait for me," Nas was full of giggles as she hopped on his back.

Seth held onto her legs that she wrapped around his waist before he opened the door and disengaged the alarm. Nas couldn't breathe. It reminded her of those extravagant homes from that old television show *MTV Cribs*.

The pure luxury, and the marble floors; the gold fixtures, the sparkling chandeliers, the symmetrical stairway, and the large window frame before her where the living room sat was absolutely breathtaking.

"Seth, this place is so fucking amazing!" she gasped as she slowly turned her head back and forth, observing her surroundings.

She was like a kid in the candy store her mind was so blown. Seth gave her a quick tour of the main level, then climbed on the elevator and showed her around the top floor before he entered the master bedroom.

"The paint still smells new," she gasped as she laid her head on his shoulder.

"I'm hip. I just moved in last week. It turned out pretty dope."

"You had this built from the ground up!" She exclaimed.

"Three-year project. 14,000 square feet, river view in the back yard, movie theater, pool hall, two pools, one indoor, and one out, a jacuzzi, and too much other shit to even list right now. It's a lower level where all that's located at."

"That sounds fun," she smiled as she looked over his shoulder into his eyes.

"What?"

"The jacuzzi. You got some bubbles?"

He laughed.

"Does it look like I keep bubbles, mama?"

"Look. You're lucky you're so fucking handsome and that shit you talk is kinda of sexy, Seth." she raised her brow as she wrapped her arms around his neck a little tighter.

"You wanna take a bubble bath with daddy?" He kissed her lips.

She nodded her head yes as their tongues overlapped for the umpteenth time that night. . .

"Are you sure Riley is okay?" Nasir questioned a little worried as Seth poured her a glass of champagne.

"Mama, she's a'ight. She's a big girl, and Messiah gon' make sure she's safe. That nigga might be crazy as hell, but he ain't gon' let nothing happen to her. I promise. That's been my nigga since the tenth grade. He's solid."

Nas looked back as she sat in his lap. The water from the jacuzzi felt so good against her skin and it felt better to be in his arms.

She turned around and mounted him so that they were face to face. They each took a swig from their drinks as bubbles from the mini bottle of Beautiful Day body wash that she found in her purse, surrounded them.

"I can't keep you up too much longer. Don't you got class in the am?"

Her eyes bucked.

"I do! What time is it?"

"Like, three sum'."

"Oh my God. I'm gonna be exhausted," she laughed as she slapped her forehead.

"So what do you teach?"

"I am a dance instructor. I've been teaching it for the last three years. I love it."

"What did you do before you started teaching?"

Nasir sighed.

"I was living in Cali for a few years. I just *knew* that I was destoned to be that plus sized back up dancer. I was like eighty pounds heavier back then though. Now a bitch is snatched."

He chuckled.

"But, yeah, I was out there living my life, auditioning for every music video they were filming in town, but... no luck. 'Great dancer', they'd always say, but... I just didn't have 'the look'.

"That's how I met Alicia. She's done dozens of videos, and that's how I met a lot of interesting people in the entertainment world because they knew her, and she always brought me on set with her when they filmed.

"It was quite an experience. I don't regret it though because being told no a million and one times made me go harder and realize how much I really wanted to make a difference in the world of dance, and it pushed me to lose weight, so in all reality, I did win."

"That's wassup. I'mma have to come check out one of your shows this school year. I won't even flex, I kind of underestimated you, mama. I gotta apologize."

Nas smiled.

"What made you underestimate me?"

Seth finished his glass.

"I just don't do this shit. I told you that. My last relationship wasn't nothing like this. I mean, I fucked with shorty, but let me put it like this. She just didn't bring out this side of me, and I can admit that shit."

Nas smiled.

"I understand, and hey, you've learned things about me in a week that some men haven't even noticed in years of knowing me, so I guess this is a bunch of firsts for the both of us." She sighed. "It's like so hard to believe, Seth, that you noticed quiet little me."

"Real shit, I was surprised that I was attracted to you. No disrespect, mama. You're a beautiful ass woman—"

"But we all have our types. I understand. There's no need to explain."

He wrapped his arms around her.

"How you do that shit?" His voice was soft.

"Do what?"

Seth kissed her lips.

"Just keep a nigga so fucking content and shit. I've been dealing with a lot lately, especially with me just getting out the pen and," he sighed. "All this crazy shit with my family. I just find peace with you, Nasir."

"Energy is everything. Whether you call it a vibe or science, the shit is real. I wasn't always this content. My head can be through the roof sometimes, but lately it's just been like if I can't control it then fuck it.

"And if I can then, do it. Annnnd..." she shrugged her shoulders. "I don't know. You just get tired of the negatives, and the best thing to do is just drop it and let shit be."

"Yeah, I feel it. Doing what I do though, it's a lil' mo' complicated than that, sweetheart."

"What do you do? Is that safe to ask?"

He smiled.

"I used to run the Platinum cartel with my old man, but a lot of sketchy shit's been happening, and now we're at war with one another. All our property has been split, our team's been split, and it's me against my whole family."

"Damn," she uttered.

"Yeah. That's it in a nutshell, but money still gotta be made, I gotta keep my buyers happy, I gotta keep my product rolling, and all that good shit. Civil conflict don't stop shit."

"How old are you?"

"Twenty-seven."

"Me too, well, will be in December." She corrected.

"December what?"

"30th."

"Mines the 2nd."

"Of December, or January?"

"June."

Nas playfully pushed him in the shoulder.

"You said that like it was close to mines. That's why you're so fucking mean and indecisive with your heart. Confused ass, bat-shit crazy, Gemini," she giggled.

"I ain't alone. Yo' hot shit ass mouth be on one, mama. Mean ass Capricorn."

"I can admit I get a little out of control sometimes. I can admit that." She ran her hands up and down his muscular arms while his hands rested on her butt. "Please don't break my heart, Seth," she whispered.

"What made you say that?"

Nasir looked up into his eyes.

"Everything's just moving so fast, and I don't wanna jump ahead of myself and—"

"Aye," he cut her off with a kiss. "How 'bout this? We just take this shit one day at a time how we been doing it. There's no rule book to this shit, mama. Hell, this shit different for me like I've said, but I wouldn't have done none of this shit if I didn't want to. Trust me, you would've known if you was just a fuck.

"I would've took you home that day in the Central West Inn before we even had the opportunity to meet up again at Shottas, fucked you, then you never would've heard from me again, nor saw me.

"A'ight, that shit was fucked up what I did at the club wit' that lil' ho and what not. It was. But you know what though? Her pussy was so fucking whack, I had to think about you to even nut."

Nas held her hand up to her lips as she tried not to laugh.

"Talk about embarrassing. That bitch swore she had the sauce. Ran through ass. I'm glad I got rid of her. Hell, *I* wanted to suck your dick for that shit. Thank you."

He laughed.

"Yeah, my first impression wasn't the best," he licked his lips.

"It wasn't. A bit zaddy-ish once I stopped crying and thought about it, but it really wasn't."

"You cried?" he laughed.

"I did! Y'all scared the shit out of me. Then, those little hateful ass beady eyes with that evil ass glare you get was all in my dreams. I was devastated."

They shared a laugh.

"Damn, mama. I see I gotta make up for that. That's fucked up."

"You already have. What made you give me your credit card?"

He chuckled.

"It's just money. We've already had this conversation."

"Do you give all your—"

"Don't be worried about a bitch who ain't you. Never, and that's the end of that. A bitch ain't never had it if that makes you feel special, though."

She held the bottle up to her lips and took a swig with a devious look in her eye. Seth couldn't figure this woman out. She was the definition of ambivalence, but he had liked it.

Nasir seemed like she had the key to unlock a better him, and at the rate they were going, she'd be his queen way before she could even wrap her head around how sprung he was off her already. But it would be a while before he'd ever admit that to her face.

Chapter Twelve

"*Here*, baby. Let me change that bandage for you."

Kelani sat on the edge of the bed with all the supplies she needed and a bucket of water filled with a remedy her mother taught her when she was a little girl.

"What the fuck is that shit? That shit stink! Get that shit the fuck away from me, bruh. I swear you always be tryna blow my got-damn high," Jediah griped as he turned his nose from the horrid smell.

Kelani smiled.

"Shut up. You're a big ass baby. Now, let me change it."

He shook his head as he put his blunt out. He'd just have to finish that muthafucka when she was done doing her thing because the smell was making his stomach hit all kinds of flips. The bullet Seth put to his chest was more than a damn flesh wound. The hollow points he had his gun loaded with almost went through his chest and exited out of his back. Hell, it would've been better if it had done just that because now Jediah's been down longer than he thought he'd be.

Ever since they were younger there was something about Seth that didn't sit right with him. He thought his brother was a backdoor ass nigga to be honest. Yeah, Seth had a nasty ass attitude too, but the way he moved was too damn dexterous and swift. People loved his mean ass. Seth barely cracked a fucking smile, yet everyone respected and protected him.

He'd fuck a bitch, her cousin, her sister, and their mother, and all four hoes would still try to be on his team after he did them dirty. Jediah played by all the fucking rules. He was humble, he didn't treat bitches like shit, and he was a fine ass O'Ryan Granberry replica that all the bitches loved. Jediah was fine as fuck, but because he was the younger brother, the only person bitches saw was Seth because he was the oldest. Akil even had all the hoes when he was alive because he was the baby.

It was like Jediah had gotten kicked *"To the left. To the left"* because he was the middle child, and he grew tired of the bullshit. He was always a cool guy, but jealousy lived in his blood, and he could never hide the thirst he had to be on top. Tradition didn't mean shit to him. Yeah, he respected family honor and all of that shit, but just because Seth was the oldest didn't mean he was entitled to everything. This wasn't 1418 or the fucking century of the medieval legislation.

It was 2016 and if anything, Osiris should've divided everything equally between him and his brothers and kept them all game, but he didn't so Jediah had to plant his own seeds to reach success and so far, so good. He was now in Seth's place, but this was only the beginning. Seth's army might not had been as high numbered as Jediah's, but he had a bunch of key players on his squad, and that's what had put Si's territory at a disadvantage.

"Did he say anything about Mexico and what he had going?" Jediah questioned Kelani as she removed the gauze that was packed inside of the hole in his chest to keep it from infecting while it was healing.

"He didn't say anything. All he said was his dick was hard, and we fucked."

Jediah grabbed her by the throat but quickly released her when the pain from his chest struck him like a lightning bolt.

"Fuck!" He roared as his back made one with the headboard again.

"That's what the fuck your ass gets! Damn! I already got hemmed up by him; I don't need this shit from you too!" Kelani spazzed as she got up and walked away with her arms folded underneath her breasts.

She was devastated about the way Seth had treated her. Kelani could do nothing put replay his conversation over and over in her head from that night when he was talking to whoever the bitch was on the phone like she wasn't lying right there. Kelani loved Seth.

She saw the potential he had inside of him to be a good man. There was just so much hate in his heart because of the back and forth with Jediah and all the backdoor bullshit he knew was going on, but he just couldn't figure it out a year ago because he was so busy tryna make other shit happen.

She rode for Seth through everything, and even though he fucked with her, she always felt like she didn't shine bright enough in his life. Maybe it was horrible timing for him to try the relationship thing. But he took care of her, he was there for her, he wasn't the most intimate, but that phone conversation confirmed everything that he'd been holding back from their relationship and she just couldn't believe it.

Kelani had him... in the palms of her hands. She'd given him all of her unconditionally, yet that still wasn't enough. All Kelani wanted was the affection that he wasn't giving her. When he got locked up it hit the core of her heart. She'd sucked the soul out of Osiris' dick and begged him to get Seth out of prison, but all he did was nut in her mouth and put her out his house. She was devastated, and all she needed was someone to hold her, so she started fucking the people closest to him to feel closer to his heart in his absence.

Hell, it made all the sense to her. She knew good and damn well that Messiah wouldn't be down for that shit. Him, Tito, or Prodigy, but a handful of his boys were, and it surprised the fuck out of her. But karma was one hell of a pay back. Most of the niggas she had fucked didn't make it out the safe house invasion alive, and the ones who did, she was almost sure that Seth had taken care of them since he knew about her sex parade.

Kelani was just hurt and lost, and she wasn't thinking right, but when Jediah approached her it was like love by first contact. All he wanted to do was make her smile. He wanted to go out on cute little cheesy dates, he loved taking selfies with her, he loved to kiss, he rubbed her toes, and all. And she didn't have to beg him to eat her pussy. Everything Seth wouldn't do Jediah did times ten, and she couldn't help the way she fell in love with him. When he held her it just felt right; he was the missing piece to her broken heart.

He couldn't lay the pipe down like Seth could because let's just face the fact that Seth had a dick from the gods. When he got his dick in her walls, it was like she had been injected with dope and it had her seeing all kinds of weird colors like that boat scene off of *Willy Wonka and the Chocolate Factory.* His dick would change a bitch's life even if he didn't enjoy the shit, but the head Jediah had though? The man had a tongue that would have her cumming back to back and quick, so it made up for his lack of dick sleighing skills.

Seth wouldn't even kiss Kelani. She didn't know why he did her so wrong or refused to go all the way with her when she knew she had deserved his heart. Everything was such a fucking mess. She loved Jediah, she loved Seth, but Jediah was more active. Yet, Seth held her heart, and she thought her damn head would explode. Seth would kill her the moment he found out she was fucking his brother, and if he had already known, then she knew she didn't have much longer to live.

Kelani had JD move her into a new loft purposely to stay away clean out of dodge once Seth made his return, but she didn't even let the phone ring more than a second after she saw his name pop up on her screen. Before Kelani knew it, Seth was at her house blowing her damn back out the way she'd always remembered him doing. Now she was caught up in the middle of this shit, and she just didn't know what to do.

"Come here."

Kelani turned around and faced Jediah when she heard his voice. Tears had stained her cheeks, and he hated to see her cry. She'd cried enough because Seth had done her so fucking dirty, and he promised her that he would try his best to never make her hurt like his brother did.

"Come here, sweetie. Come to daddy."

Kelani walked over to him trying to wipe her tears away, but there was no luck. She was so shook, and she couldn't control it. Jediah pulled her in his lap and placed a kiss to her lips. He continued to do so until she began to kiss him back.

"I'm sorry," he whispered as he wrapped his arms around her.

"I'm sorry too. I didn't mean to react like that. I know I have to watch what I say, but there was no other explanation to that."

Jediah looked into her eyes and smiled. She was such a beautiful woman.

"I swear on my life, Lani. All I wanna do is make you happy. It's gon' be a lil' rough right now, but I need you to stay solid because once this shit is all over and we handle that bitch ass nigga, we gon' get married, and you gon' rule this dynasty with me and hopefully, our son."

He rubbed her belly with his eleven-week fetus inside of it. He couldn't wait until the next breed of the dynasty had touched down. He was gonna teach his son everything he needed to know so he'd be a boss just like his daddy.

"You gon' have so much love and happiness at your fingertips, that you won't even know what tears are anymore, but you have to trust me, ma. You love me right?"

Kelani nodded her head yes before he kissed her lips again.

"Alright, so we gotta remember that love when it comes to this shit. That's the mold that's gon' keep us together, but you can't fold. You don't think I feel some type of way about you still having to fuck with that nigga so we don't throw him off? That shit makes me hot, mama, and I overreacted when I grabbed you. You my bitch right?"

"Right," she smiled.

"Alright then. We just gotta hurry up and get this shit taken care of, but you gotta be on yo shit though, and stay solid. I'll let you know when to go after him again, a'ight? But first we gotta find this bitch he been fucking with. We gotta use every outlet he got against him."

That shit made her eyes glow. She'd had thoughts about how she was gonna put a hole in whoever the bitch's head was for days now. Jediah knew just what to say to cheer her up, and she was so happy to have the man she knew she had always deserved.

"I love you, baby." Her voice was soft as she threw her arms around him.

"I love you too, mama. Now come on so you can patch me up and ride this dick. You gon' get nasty for daddy?"

She kissed his lips.

"Real nasty for you daddy. Just the way you like it. . ."

T

Maybe Kelani should get Jediah worked up more often. Even with a chest wound he fucked her brains out like never before. Those ecstasy pills were starting to work in his favor because she didn't want him to leave, but she knew that he had to go and make shit happen for their future. That still didn't take her eyes off the prize though. Her adrenaline was pumping to get to know who this bitch was that Seth was all geeked over, but it still broke her heart.

He was so sweet, so loving, so sincere, and passionate while still exercising that Platinum Dynasty thug that ran through his veins when she overheard his conversation. It was heartbreaking, but sexy at the same time, and she could only imagine how he was making that bitch feel if she had felt some type of way when he wasn't even talking to her.

Kelani sat at the bar at the Flamingo rocking a Fashion Nova tube dress that barely covered her ass and some heels with her hair pulled back into a ponytail. She heard Seth had shut the spot down a couple of weeks ago because him and Messiah had some bitches here, but wasn't nobody giving out any info, and she was getting pissed off.

She knew she should've jumped on that shit when she first heard about it. Now she was looking stupid. His crew was acting like she didn't used to be his bitch and were treating her like these groupie hoes who jocked his property, waiting on him to arrive one night just to have their little five minutes of fame. Kelani didn't know how to swallow that, so she kept taking shots of Crown Royal until this loud-mouthed light skinned chick on the other end of the bar had caught her attention.

"If it wasn't for me, that bitch wouldn't even be who she is! Because if she was still as big as a fucking house like she used to be, a fucking *Platinum* wouldn't have even looked her way! And then, she gets the oldest brother! The fuck! Like, who doesn't want Seth's fine ass! I had him; I was this fucking close! I mean so close!"

"Girl you ain't have him," her friend rolled her eyes in jealousy as she sipped her martini.

"Bitch, shut your fucking mouth because I did! Him and his best friend." Alicia stuck her tongue out while having flashbacks to the night they put that good dope dick on her.

Kelani swallowed her last shot before she walked over to the woman and slid in next to her and a chocolate chick. One thing she wasn't was a scary bitch. All one hundred and twenty pounds of her would fight a lion if she had the right gun to do so.

"So, I overheard you talking about Seth and Messiah."

"So?" Alicia rolled her eyes as she sipped on her Long Island.

"Well, Seth is my man, bitch, so that's why I approached you."

"If he's *your* man then, why was he fucking *me*, and whyyyyy do fat bitches got his muthafucking attention?" Alicia gave her a quick scan before continuing. "You bad as fuck though, and I am too. And shit, I won't stunt, Nasir fine as fuck too yo! I've eaten her pussy a couple of times, so I know he's going crazy over her."

"Nasir? You talking about Nas? The one who holds the adult dance classes over on the south side?" Kelani gasped.

"Duuuuuuh." Alicia turned around and looked Kelani up and down, this time a little more thorough before she smiled. "You heeeeeeella fine. I mean, bad as fuck. What's yo name again?" She licked her lips. All the liquor in her system was doing the talking at that hour.

Alicia was definitely bisexual. Bitches turned her on just as much as niggas did; especially a bitch who would let her lick the clit while they got dicked down together. Kelani slid in between her legs and grabbed her by the face before she stuck her tongue in her mouth. She was just as drunk as that bitch was, but she had to admit that Alicia was a baddie too looking like Masika Kalysha from *Love and Hip-Hop*. Plus, if she had known Nas personally, then why not get all she could've out of the equation?

"Let's get a room," Kelani smirked as Alicia slid her hand up her dress.

"Bet. What's in it for me?" She licked her lips.

"More than you'll ever know. A little bit of this, a little bit of that, and a few manipulating schemes we can come up with together after we get finished cumming together."

Alicia laughed out loud with a devilish though sexy grin along her face.

"Bet that shit. I'm right behind you, boo."

Chapter Thirteen

"*Ry*, you should've let me come out there with you."

"No, Nas. I gotta do this shit on my own."

"I know, but with the heat still being so hot with y'all right now I should have. You've been freaking out ever since he pushed the finalization back two weeks ago. I know you, Ry. You're probably sitting in front of that house right now tryna go in there and get your last word in before y'all even meet up with the lawyer."

Riley rolled her eyes as she inhaled from the Black and Mild. Her cousin knew her all too well, and sometimes she couldn't stand it.

"I'mma call you when we leave the office, okay?"

Nasir sighed. She had a gut feeling that things were gonna go left, but she held her tongue and let her be. Riley was grown, plus her mind was already made up.

"Okay. Just be safe."

"I will."

Riley hung up the phone and took a deep breath. Her nerves were all over the place. Her stomach was choppy, and she was drunk as can be like their meeting wasn't in an hour.

"Nah, Tevin got me fucked up. I gave him seven years of my got-damn life. He gon' hear what the fuck I got to say. Fuck that shit."

She shoved the door to her rental open and took one last swig from the pint of Remy Martin before she walked up to the door. This nigga had changed his number, and all of their assets were frozen. Riley wasn't going out like no bitch.

"So the dumb ass didn't change the locks yet?" she mumbled as she unlocked the front door.

Her heart was racing so fast she thought she'd hit the floor because she knew that nigga was crazy, but she was already in there now, and there was no turning back. The little feet running from down the hall made her stop in her tracks when the little boy in a Polo outfit, who couldn't be no more than two, ran into the living room where she was standing in the doorway.

"Hi!" He smiled while throwing his arms in the air. "Mommy! Mommy! Mommy!"

"TJ! TJ! TJ! What big boy—"

The woman froze solid when she exited the bedroom and laid her eyes upon Riley. She'd recognized her from the photographs that used to be hung up in the home that she and her son had moved into. Tears trickled down Riley's cheeks at the sight of her big round belly as she waddled in her direction.

"We didn't want you to find out like this."

The woman's voice was low as she stood before Riley with tears in her eyes as well.

"Is there a better way?" Riley chuckled as she forced herself to smile. "How long have you been messing with him? From the looks of your son, it's been a while."

She felt like she'd been hit by a damn truck after those words left her mouth.

"Three years," she honestly confessed.

"Wait, you're the secretary from the bank when we got the loan on our home. Aren't you?" Her voice cracked.

"I'm so sorry. It just happened. Riley, I never meant for it to turn to this. I'm—"

"What the fuck are you doing here! Huh!"

Riley and his new fiancé, Jessica, both jumped from the sound of Tevin's voice as he entered the garage door.

"I haven't even been gone nothing but two weeks and you've moved her. . . no, them in? Already? Youuuuu, were that pressed, that you had a whole family on me because of something that I couldn't control?"

Riley's words were barely above a whisper.

"You've got two minutes to get the fuck out of my house, or Georgia police will be here to drag yo ass away!"

"Tevin—"

"Shut the fuck up, Jessica! This ain't got shit to do with you!" he screamed.

Riley laughed when Jessica looked down at the floor and did as she was told to do.

"Even after the infidelity, and your son, and your child to come, you're still an asshole?" she shook her head. "Tevin, you ain't shit, and you know what? I'm glad I came here today. You really are a lame ass nigga who just needs the right bitch to submit to your whack ass because you know a real woman wouldn't put up with that shit."

Whack!

The back of his hand made one with Riley's face so fast that it startled her when he grabbed her by the neck and shoved her into the wall.

"Daddddddy!" Tevin Junior broke out in tears instantly as his mother swooped him up in her arms and ran for the bedroom where she hid behind the door.

"Bitch I'm tired of yo shit!" He threatened through clenched teeth with his hands still around her neck.

Riley couldn't breathe a lick, but a thought had crossed her mind telling her to headbutt his ass, and that's exactly what she did since he was holding her so close. Her body hit the floor while she tried to gasp for air, but he grabbed her by the hair and started to drag her around the house, ramming her body into every piece of furniture in his path.

"You should've took your dumb ass up to the fucking office and left this fucking relationship exactly with what you came with bitch! Shit! You couldn't contribute shit! You wasn't paying for shit! You couldn't even give a nigga a son yet you pressed about a bitch who could do what you'll never be able to do!

I already let yo ass keep the fucking car, but you had to play hard, huh!" He roared as he threw her body into the glass living room table, causing it to shatter. "Alright bitch, if this the game that you wanna play," he spat as he removed his suit jacket and undid the sleeves of his button-down, ready to square up with her like she was a nigga.

Riley rolled over with all her might as if glass wasn't all in her back. She grabbed the handle from the broken table and swung it so hard after she stood to her feet, that all she saw was the blood that flew out his mouth. She hit his ass like a professional baseball league batter.

"On the floor, now! Police! On the floor! Drop your weapon!"

Everything moved in slow motion when officers swarmed in the house with their guns aimed. How the fuck was she gonna get out of this shit now?

Chapter Fourteen

"*I'm* gonna kill him," Nas mumbled as she started transferring the dinner she cooked over into the Pyrex glass bowls.

She picked up her phone and held it up to her ear as she called him again.

"Seth."

"I know mama. I know. I'm 'bout to pull up now. Did you know you needed four tires too? I told you to get rid of this muthafucka, man."

Nasir laughed as she put the spoon down.

"I told you I would've taken it to get all that done because I knew you weren't gonna do nothing but talk shit about my damn car. You so foul man, but how close are you though, babe? You know my class starts at 8:30, and it's 7:50. I've gotta get all the way to the south side."

"I told yo ass I was pulling up, mama. Why you ain't just take my whip like it's not sitting outside?"

"Because I'm not driving no damn Vision 6 Maybach, or whatever the hell it is. I can't even tell you the name of it, and you want me to drive it? I'm good. Just bring me my car please."

"I'm coming down the street right now. Chill yo ass out. Did you cook?"

"Yes, I cooked. There's plenty here, and come inside when you get here. I need help with all this stuff."

"You make enough for two, sus!"

She laughed at Messiah in the background.

"You think I wanted to hear your mouth about not having enough for you, Messiah?"

"Long as you know, ma!" he joked.

"Y'all just hurry up."

"Bring yo ass outside, man."

"Okay. The doors' open. Everything's at the stairs."

Nas put her phone in her jacket pocket and closed the bowls before she grabbed her purse from off the kitchen table and headed down the steps. Tonight was Saturday. Every other Saturday night, she held her adult dance class and she was always extra. She brought bottles of champagne, fresh sliced fruit, champagne glasses, decor, prizes, dancing props, and she even had a set of disco ball stage lights that she set up for them to dance to. She went all out.

When she first started the business, it was hard getting clients, but once her views started picking up on social media she was surprised at how many women started to support and attend the class. The more women who supported her, the more often she could hold the sessions because sometimes she didn't have an extra hundred-something dollars every other week to rent out the studio and buy all of the goodies. Her finances were tight, but Seth never asked for his black card back, and shit, as long as he wasn't asking for it then, she wasn't offering it. Was she wrong? No, she didn't think so either.

Nasir was bent over picking up one of the three boxes she was taking with her when the front door opened. The slap to her ass was none other than a greeting from her man.

"Just gimmie five minutes up in this shit, mama," he whispered as he held her close.

She smiled.

"Maybe if you would've showed up on time then I could've granted that wish for you. But you didn't. I've still gotta set up the studio, sir. I'm not messing wit' you until class is over."

"See, all that shit wasn't even called for, Nas. I should've just stuck my dick right in yo shit but be like that then wit' yo mean ass."

"*That's* rape."

"Not when you fuck with somebody."

"Whatever. I just need help with those last two boxes right there."

Seth took the box out of her hands as Messiah entered the house.

"Damn girl, it smell good up in here. What you fix?"

"Pepper steak and basmati rice, now grab a box, hungry. Is the trunk open?"

"Yeah. Go 'head."

Seth let Nasir leave out the door by herself. *Three, two, one. . .*

"Oh my Goooooooood! Noooooooooo!"

He and his potna walked out to see her holding her hands in her face while bent over in disbelief.

"What is this!" She sobbed as she removed her hands just to quickly shut her eyes again at the truck parked in front of her apartment.

"Thought I was coming back with that bullshit, didn't you?"

"A fucking Range Rover, Seth!" She just couldn't believe it. "Is this a joke? Where is my car?" she gasped.

"At the fucking junk yard where that muthafucka belong."

Nas stood there with her hand on her forehead.

"I think I'm gonna be sick."

"Surprised me too, mama. You ain't the only one. I see you be putting that pussy on a nigga real good, huh?" Messiah teased as he closed the trunk.

"Shut up, Messiah," she countered with a real attitude. This was unbelievable.

"Don't you got somewhere to be? Now you ain't in no rush to shake like you ain't been blowing my shit up all evening?"

Nas looked over at Seth. She wanted to smack that silly ass grin off his face as he stood before her with one hand inside the other, just staring at her. She was so speechless she couldn't do anything but throw her arms around his neck.

"That's more like it. You so fucking hard to please sometimes, bruh. I swear."

He wrapped his arms around her waist before he reached down and grabbed a handful of that ass.

"And you don't listen. I told you not to do this."

"A'ight. I guess I'll just take it to my side bitch then. I bet *she* appreciate it."

Nasir pushed him away from her.

"Don't get your ass whooped, nigga."

"Then quit saying dumb shit. Gon' and head out. Facetime me them tears while I'm fixing me a plate."

She smiled before he kissed her lips.

"Thank you. . ." Her voice was soft.

Nasir was truly astonished. He could see it in her eyes. It's not that she wasn't excited because all she ever talked about was getting a new ride with the money she had been saving, but she'd been victimized for years by men who always expected her to open her legs.

Nas bent over backwards for every nigga that had crossed her path, but she'd never received not one birthday card, she'd never received a Valentine's Day gift, she'd never had her gas tank filled, or was just genuinely taken care of by a man like the women around her were.

All Seth wanted to do was make her happy. He knew off vibe that Nasir wasn't a sketchy ass woman. The night she looked into his eyes and basically begged him not to break her heart, he felt that shit. For the life of him he just couldn't bring himself to give Kelani his all, even after two years, but for Nas, he'd go through hell and high waters just to keep a smile on her face. How could he not?

She gave his crazy ass peace, and she was such an authentic woman who had honored to stay true to herself. That's why he jumped for her, that's why he fell for her, and that's why she had him wrapped around her damn finger. He'd never met such a beautiful soul, and to be honest she reminded him a lot of how Osiris used to court his mother when he was growing up.

Si's only mission besides upholding his dynasty and caring for his family was to keep his woman happy. Seth had rarely seen Falcon cry. Yeah, they argued, and they had their times when he could remember Si leaving and giving her a couple of weeks to herself, but overall, he remembered her happiness more than their troubles. His parents weren't perfect, but they held each other down.

Si might've fucked him a couple of bitches, but none of them had ever disrespected his mother; plus, they all were just fucks. He wasn't spending no time or dropping no money on a bitch who wasn't Falcon, and Seth couldn't even lie when he said that Nasir made him feel like that. Sometimes you just know when something is supposed to be, and that was him and Nas in a nut shell.

T

"Mommy I can't believe this!" Nasir squealed as she grabbed the last box from out of the trunk.

"Hell, I can't either. What's the fucking catch!" She laughed while eyeballing the black on black 2017 Land Rover with the matte black rims to match.

The plates read **4Nas** and she damn near fainted when she read the ownership papers and realized that the vehicle was in her name as well.

"What kind of tricks you doing for a one hundred and twenty-thousand dollar truck giiiiirl! His ass dun dropped cash on that muthafucka too! Oooooh weeee lil' freak!"

"Mommy!" Nasir gasped as they headed up the steps to the studio to hurry up with the set up.

They were cracking up as they quickly moved around the room hanging and arranging everything with only five minutes to spare before the ladies would begin to arrive.

"Hell, I'm serious. So you know I have to ask right?"

"Ask me what?" Nasir turned around and looked her mother in the eyes.

"How do you feel? Like, do you feel he's one of those undercover crazy ass men? Is he controlling? Does he spazz out on you? Like, it's barely been a month."

Her daughter sighed.

"I know. You think I'm not surprised either? This all new to me. I've been on one date in my whole entire life before I met Seth. Everything is just different with him. You know how you can feel it when someone's really not who they appear to be?"

"Yeah."

"I don't feel that with him. I'll be honest like, all BS aside, I don't think he's a bad guy. I mean he runs the damn city and some; like, he's a kingpin to narrow it down. Granted he's gonna have hoes; that comes with the territory. I know not to be all gullible about him.

"But some of the things, hell, most of the things that Seth does just don't seem like he's doing them for a lot of women. He's very self-centered. Not like selfish but he's aloof, you know? He doesn't like everybody in his business and his mean ass doesn't trust anyone. You get what I'm saying?"

Catori nodded her head in agreement.

"I get it. I just want you to be careful. It was like that with me and your dad, and you see how that ended. Not saying that Seth is like your father at all, but what I am saying is to just watch yourself baby."

"I know. I can only take things one day at a time, but I've just never met a man like him before." Nas sighed. "I don't know."

Catori could hear it in her daughter's voice. She was falling for Seth hard and fast. How could she not? He was crossing all of his t's and dotting his I's; I mean the man didn't skip a beat.

It was just a bit scary from a mother's point of view because she'd been down that road before. Nas' father Jamie-O was everything Catori could've ever imagined having in a man. He swept her off her feet, they got married after six months of dating, and life was like a dream.

Shopping sprees, traveling, romantic getaways, the sex was beyond this world, and in the end, they loved each other. It was tragic when Nas turned three and he up and left. She'd never seen nor heard from him another day in her life.

No rumors about him being in jail, going missing, since he was a drug dealer, or even being dead had ever gotten back to Catori. That happened twenty-four years ago. To this day she sometimes wondered what she did that was so wrong that would make a man just up and walk away from his family.

Leaving or falling out of love with her was one thing, but to neglect Nas was another. No matter how much Catori wanted to see her daughter happy she couldn't help but to be alarmed because it all was Deja vu to her.

All she could do was pray that God ordered her daughter's steps on this new-found journey with Seth. She prayed that his intentions were pure as well. The last thing on her to do list was to go to prison for killing a Platinum, but if he broke her daughter's heart that was one risk that she was willing to take.

"So, when will I get to meet him?" Catori smiled.

She could sense Nas' mood change, and the last thing she wanted to do was bump heads with her baby.

Nasir smiled a bit.

"I'll talk to him. I'm sure that won't be a problem..."

Nas' head was spinning. She knew her mother meant well, but now she had her head racing and she couldn't get their conversation from earlier off her mind no matter how exciting tonight's class had been. She was rinsing the champagne glasses out after the last woman left when Catori approached her with her purse on her arm.

"You okay?"

Nas looked into her mother's eyes and smiled.

"I'm alright. Just a little tired. What a session tonight?"

"I know! That was so much fun. I can't believe I can still move like that. I've got me some moves for Ray when we leave town next week!"

Nas couldn't control the laughter that escaped her lips.

"OMG, mommy! You are so silly! Tell him to record it. I've gotta see it. And you know you've gotta get all Ciara and Future on him and have a cute little outfit on too."

"Girl, I already bought one. You think I'm playing?"

Their laughter filled the air.

"This I have to see." Nas grinned.

"You sure you don't need any help? I'm more than happy to help you load the car up."

"No, I've got it. It's late. I should be out of here in the next twenty minutes. Let me know when you make it home."

Catori kissed her daughter's cheek before she wrapped her arms around her.

"I will. I love you baby."

"Love you too, ma. Be safe."

"You too."

When the door closed behind her mother, Nas placed all of the clean glasses inside of the box before she shut out the lights. She then flipped the switch on the stage lights and watched them bounce around the room until the melody from K Young's "Lay You Down" filled the air.

She removed her hair from the bun on top of her head and ran her hands through her gorgeous, thick, and full mane while staring at herself in the mirror. All she wore was an off-shoulder leotard, an off-shoulder, oversized sweater cut into a crop top, and thigh high socks.

K Young's voice hypnotized her as her body began to glide across the dance floor. She was so lost in her own world that she hadn't made out the image standing by the doorway. Freely, Nas continued to dance along the floor until she hit a backwards roll and landed in a split. Nas knew dancing with her eyes closed was risky, but she loved the way she pictured herself in her mind versus the mirror.

Seth stood back with his arms crossed watching her work the floor then the chair in the center of the room that he swore she would trip over, but Nas had learned the studio by now. Her movements were graceful, dainty, seductive, and mind stimulating.

He wondered what was going through her head. She'd smile, then she'd bite her bottom lip as her hands caressed her curves with each move. She'd smile again, then sing a few lines, run her tongue along her lips before pursing them, then smile once more.

The look of love was along her face as her body kept moving. Seth put his phone and his keys down before he walked over to her. The music was so loud he was sure that she couldn't hear his footsteps against the floor.

The song was on repeat, and Nas had yet to stop her body from flowing, so he took a huge risk and sat in the chair knowing that she'd be using it again as a prop. He ran his hand down his beard as she stood before him, eyes still closed, throwing her body, swaying her hips, and admiring her curves.

He watched her slide down to the ground until she did the same move once again where she hit a backwards roll, hoping to land in the chair. Nas damn near passed out when she felt her body fall on top of someone instead of the seat she knew was waiting for her.

"Oh my God!" she gasped terrified.

Seth laughed as he caught her in his arms before she could hit the floor; she'd jumped when she finally opened her eyes and saw him.

"You are such a creeeeeep!" she shrieked as she hid her face.

"I dun' stood there and watched you dance with yo' damn eyes closed for hellas waiting on yo' ass to fall or trip over something." He laughed.

She looked back at him and they made eye contact. Nas didn't care what her mother had said. Seth was the shit to her in every way, shape, and form, and she fucked with her man. The long way.

"What are you doing here?" Nasir smiled as he held her close.

She'd picked up her phone that was underneath the chair and turned the music down so they could hear themselves talk.

"It's late, and I knew yo' stubborn ass wasn't gon' have nobody here to walk out with you."

She smiled.

"You don't know me, Seth."

"On the contrary, mama, I do. A nigga's day be busy from start to finish, yet he still makes time to see ya smile and talk to ya. Even if it's only for a lil' minute."

The way he licked his lips mixed with his eyes piercing through her gave her butterflies.

"Where you about to go?" She asked with the raise of an eyebrow.

He laughed.

"I gotta meeting in the AM with a team from some new territory. I should be back in a few days."

"I knew it was something. I guess you can go," she joked.

"Aw, you guess I can go, huh? I'mma let you think you run shit, Nasir, but we both know the truth. Ride daddy's dick right quick before we bounce. I got a few more minutes to spare before I gotta be at the airport."

"Right here?" She whispered as if someone else were there.

"If you don't get yo' ass up and ride this dick. I been too nice to yo' ass."

Nas laughed as she stood up and unbuttoned her leotard.

"The owner should be here in like ten minutes to lock up behind me..."

Her words got faint at the sight of his hard dick sitting straight up in the air. Seth pulled the chamber back on the Glock 40 with the extendo clip loaded.

"Ask me if I give a fuck."

Nasir looked into his eyes as she mounted him. Seth rested his elbow on the back of the chair, never breaking eye contact or releasing the gun. Their eyes were glued to one another as her body moved up and down. Every time she got around Seth he put her body up under a spell, and all she wanted to do was... make love to him.

It was never a case of casual sex to Nasir. Seth did things to her body that she couldn't even explain. Her pussy did a lot of talking for her, and it honestly left her perplexed.

Was the sex the mold that held them together, or did he really like her? Nas was head over hills for this man. She could lay in bed and stare at the goatee that surrounded his mesmerizing lips and listen to him talk all day.

All it took was for her to cook dinner, then sit up and chill with him. He'd be screaming at the damn TV with his head set on talking big shit to Messiah, and her legs would dangle off his shoulders while she switched back and forth between scrolling through social media and choreography videos.

They had a lot of sex, but they also connected on a level where they were still getting to know one another and enjoy their presence. Nas couldn't get him to talk much about his mother because of the current situation he was battling with the split of their empire. She could tell that was a sensitive subject for him.

Nasir remembered questioning him about the falcon symbol he had tattooed on his hand, and it damn near brought tears to his eyes. He had to get up and walk the shit off at 3 am with a blunt, it altered his mood so much. She knew Seth was harboring a bunch of feelings that he couldn't address right now, but she also wondered why.

Sometimes he'd be as open as the deep blue sea with her, and their conversations would last for hours. Then there were the days where she couldn't get a peep out him because of his aggravation.

Seth wasn't perfect, but she could admit that he was a man who didn't fold. When he felt something, he'd express it. It might not be the explanation or the actions that Nasir might have been looking for, but he either nipped it in the bud and let her know up front that he'd address it, or if they should drop it.

It was a bit challenging dealing with a headstrong man when her head was just as big. He taught her a lot about herself that she'd never noticed before. This journey with Seth was mind boggling, yet so satisfying...

Nasir was going crazy as she grinded against him while biting her lip; watching him bite his own with a smirk along his face that she couldn't resist. It made her body shutter. The way he continued to gaze into her eyes made her pussy tingle. She was about to climax and hard.

Seth smacked her on the ass with his free hand, prompting her to increase her speed. Nas threw her arm around his neck and kissed his lips. This man never fought fair when it came to sex. His dick was so big and filling, and the way he tickled her cervix while hitting her g-spot all at the same damn time was embarrassing.

For a woman who never received a vaginal climax from a penis in all her years except maybe once or twice, he had her cumming all over the place. It's like he had control over her body in a way that she had no say so against. Seth grunted loudly when he felt his soldier tense up.

"Seth wait... baby wait!"

He ignored her groans and held her body close while he started to stroke her quicker.

"Seth pull out, pleaseeeeeeeeeee! Oooooooh my God!"

With a handful of her hair he pulled her head back and caressed her neck in that enticing spot until he felt himself shoot his load off into her walls. Nas panted out of her control as her juices trickled all over him.

"Oh my God..." she gasped unable to breathe. "I'm gonna kill you. Stop doing that." She had the hardest time catching her breath as she climbed from off of him.

"Damn girl," he sighed as he looked down at his defeated soldier.

Nas could make him bust a nut so fat he had no choice but to go limp sometimes.

"I think you're purposely trying to get me pregnant, Seth," she griped as she jumped up and down after cleaning herself up, getting the Fashion Nova jeans over her butt that was lifting quite nicely.

Between working with Riley in the gym and daddy's deep doggy strokes, her ass was coming to life. Seth stared at her as she removed the leotard and slid into a white camisole she wore above her belly ring.

She was ten pounds smaller than she was when they met. Her shape was curving out like Instagram plus-sized model Lolli Cakes now, rocking a size 10.

Nas always had a small waist, but her torso was slimming out and her hips were more prominent on her shape. She was still stacked in those thighs though. That was Seth's favorite part about her. A bottom-heavy woman was sexy as fuck to him, but he could honestly admit that he didn't want her to lose another inch.

Nasir stood out from her curvy frame. She set a different tempo for him. Bitches hated all day long that he was fucking with a curvy woman, and he liked that shit. It boosted her confidence, and it made him feel like there was more substance to him as a man.

He couldn't tell you how many times he'd caught niggas eyeing her whenever she came around, even niggas from his squad. She was beautiful in the face and her body made the most arrogant niggas look her way. Shorty was the shit.

"Aye, you can't lose no more weight," he commanded as he picked up most of her belongings.

"You not my daddy."

"I am, and you heard what the fuck I said. You already gotta big ass head."

"Shut the fuck up, Seth," she giggled as she closed the door behind her before they headed down to her truck.

"Umm-umm. Where you going?" he asked with a frown while she sat in the front seat, sliding her feet into the suede, wine colored pumps.

"Don't you have a flight to catch, sir?"

"You about to catch these damn hands, Nasir."

She looked up at him and laughed.

"Boy, would you go on about your night. I'm about to go grab me a drink and something to eat. I've been craving some wings from Exotic, and they have a show tonight so, I'mma step out for a minute."

Exotic Bottles and Mommies was the best strip club "in town". It was located in East Saint St. Louis, forty-five minutes outside of the city, but it was worth the drive.

The food was great, and the atmosphere was dope. Pure luxury for a price that didn't put too bad of a hurting on ya pockets when you had the money.

"Don't play with me, Nasir."

Seth knew all about EBM. It was his favorite spot. He knew how it got down in there, and all he could think about was a nigga or one of them pussy licking ass bitches tryna snatch her up. That muthafucka was a breeding ground for ballers. That's where he'd met Kelani at a couple of years ago.

"I'm not gonna stay long...Sike." She smirked as she threw her arms around his neck.

By the look on his face she could tell he wasn't with that shit, but she didn't care.

"Be in there showing yo' ass, a'ight?"

"I gotta do a little dance," she teased. "Don't pull no gun out on me. The fuck is your problem? Enjoy your trip, be safe, and let me know once you've made it in."

Nasir kissed his lips not giving him the chance to respond as she hopped in the truck and pulled off. She did that shit so fast, Seth just stood in the middle of the street watching her merge into traffic, looking stupid.

"A'ight. That's the game she wanna play."

He sent a quick text as the door to his black Maserati Gran Turismo flew ajar before he hopped inside. The Mas was a classic; it was one of his favs when he wanted to move around a little more low-key yet still in luxury.

Seth bucked a U-turn and merged into traffic, smiling from his army's reply. Nas had him fucked up if she thought she was going to the damn strip club without his eyes and ears on the set. He didn't play them kind of games.

Chapter Fifteen

The D'USSE had Nas on her level. She threw her hips to Jeezy's "SupaFreak" with a blunt up to her lips. Charm wouldn't leave her alone. She was a stripper at the club who's had her eye on Nas for a long time. Nasir used to get herself into some shit back in the day.

Alicia had her in all kinds of scenes, and she just didn't have the time to sit back and explain to you the crazy ass missions they've been on. She'd always knew Alicia was bisexual... let's just say that for right now.

So, she had a lot of home-girls who liked girls, and a lot of those girls took a liking and fond interest in Nas. She was a redbone for crying out loud, and even when she was heavier, she was still bad when she took her hair out of a cap and slapped some lipstick on with a cute lil' fit.

Charm spotted Nasir the moment she entered the club. They were good friends, but she wanted her as more than a damn friend, and she wished her thick ass would quit playing and just take it there with her.

Charm's big ass rippled in Nas' face as she threw ones at her. Hell, the woman liked to have fun. Who didn't? She wasn't with the bi-shit though. Two threesomes was enough experience that she'd ever need.

If she could erase the shit from her memory she would; that bitch Alicia was toxic. Birds of a feather flock together was always some bullshit until they started hanging out, and all Nasir could do was shake her head at the thought.

"You should come to the back with me," Charm leaned over and whispered in her ear once she turned around to look at Nas' fine ass.

She had a pint of D'USSE up to her lips as Charm tried to kiss her neck.

"Mommy," she smiled as she pushed her away but not making it too obvious that she had dissed her invite. "Dance only."

Nasir raised her eyebrow signaling for that bitch to fall the fuck back before she put the paws on her. Everybody knew she had hands, and that's one fight no one ever wanted to get into.

"You gon' quit fronting on me one day, sexy. You hear me? I just wanna eat that pussy one last time." Charm smirked as she licked her lips while eyeing Nas' succulent breasts.

"And you gon' get punched one more time too," Nas placed a smack to her ass after sliding a Benjamin in her g-string for her dance. "Now carry on."

Nasir stood up and walked off not giving her the opportunity to respond. She was so tipsy it didn't make any sense, and she needed to get out of there before her drunk ass told the bitch yes. Drinking was the devil.

"Hiiiiiiii, Nas, baby!"

"Hiiiiiiii, Tila!" Nasir beamed as she and the owner threw their arms around one another.

"You are so fucking bad girl! Look at you!" Tila complimented as she scoped her fine ass friend out.

"Thank you! Look at you! You performing tonight?" Nas asked before she took another swig from the bottle.

"I already did. I opened the show. I'mma have to do a little dance for you girl. Who you here with? Alicia?"

Nas looked Tila up and down like the bitch had HIV or sum'.

"Well damn, girl. I'm sorry." She giggled.

Nasir smiled realizing how rude her actions were.

"Sorry, girl. I just don't fuck with that bitch anymore."

"I don't blame you. I heard she's been salty, honey. We all know you fucking with Seth, mama, and bitches are pressed," she grinned.

That was one of the perks from fucking with him that she didn't like. Nas was low-key. She hated people in her business, but the hype was inevitable when you were fucking the kingpin of the city.

"She said you stole him from her," Tila continued.

Nas laughed so hard tears came out her eyes.

"That's funny. That's so fucking funny that I have to pee, it's so fucking funny."

Her drunkenness was consuming her for sure.

"She's just mad because after she got ran he didn't want her dusty ass. And news flash, I knew that nigga before she had her mouth wrapped around his dick; ole' nasty ass slut. Tell that bitch to get her facts straight if she gon' throw some muthafucking shots. Because she can get these fucking hands for real this time!"

Yeah, it was time for Nas to go home. That shit sent her head through the roof. She placed a kiss to Tila's cheek before she headed to the restroom. She had to get the piss out of her bladder within the next six seconds or else it wasn't gonna be pretty.

Bang! Bang! Bang! Bang! Bang!

"Hold the fuck up! Don't you see this fucking toilet is occupied, bitch!" Nasir screamed as she stood up from squatting and fixed her clothes.

When she opened the door, she was greeted with a punch to her mouth, causing her to fall back onto the toilet. The bitch sucker punched her ass.

The woman then ran into the stall and grabbed Nas by the neck with her bare hands and tried to choke the life out of her. Nas grabbed her by the wrists and shoved her so hard into the door that she had locked behind her, that they busted through it.

She kept pushing the woman until she was able to throw her ass off of her and into the mirror behind the sink, causing it to shatter.

Bloop!

There goes another punch to Nas' mouth.

"ALICIA!" She screamed once she was able to stop seeing double.

"So you gon' give me the hands bitch!" Alicia yelled amp.

And that Nas did. Her punches swung in combinations getting all face shots until Alicia grabbed her by the hair and bent her over. She rammed Nas into the wall and managed to light her head up with a few good licks until Nasir gave her a good blow to the stomach, knocking the wind out of her. Alicia hit the floor instantly, then Nas stomped her ass out; heels and all.

Kelani hopped up from the sink after she shook her dizziness off and ran for Nas, but shorty was quick. She grabbed Kelani by the shirt and started punching her in the mouth non-stop until she got short of breath, but she wasn't done yet. She rammed the bitch's head into the bathroom stall just minutes before security came in and pulled them off of each other.

"Put me down!" Nasir shrieked as the seven-foot guard picked her up. "Them bitches got me fucked up, B! Bitch get up and finish getting yo' ass whooped! You ain't learn from the first time! You tripping off a nigga that was never yours! Are you serious!"

The laughter that started to escape Nas' lips made her sound like a lunatic.

"Sour ass bitch! And you gon' have the nerve to try and jump me! Should've had a whole fucking pack, bitch, to take me down, and y'all still would've got y'all's asses whooped!"

"What the fuck happened!" Tila yelled as she approached Nas once the guard put her back down on her feet.

She hadn't even been away from her two whole minutes.

Nasir had blood running down her lip, and all over her Cami.

"Who the fuck was that bitch with Alicia! I got something for that ass! That bitch don't know me! The fuck! Who is that Tila!" Nasir screamed as bouncers carried the unconscious chocolate woman out of the restroom.

Tila's eyes bucked when she recognized who it was.

"That's Seth's ex, Kelani."

T

Seth had his feet up sipping on a glass of Hennessy as his jet soared through the clouds. Shit just hasn't been sitting right with him ever since the crossover. Si was silent, Jediah was silent, and that shit made him uneasy. They were family.

No matter how fucked up it was that they had a line drawn between them, they still had the same blood. He could feel it in the air. He knew they were gonna be coming for him. Osiris wasn't sitting still knowing his son had the people on his team that he did. He knew that for a fact.

They were gonna try to take him out, so he had to act on that shit, and fast. Osiris got dirty. He got grimy. Seth watched his father sleigh his own army and kinfolk to be where he was today.

A lot of the hate in Seth's heart grew from walking in Osiris' shadow. He was a good father and husband, but one thing he wasn't was a good leader. The nigga was a tyrant. He'd cross anybody to get what he wanted, but Seth never fathomed that he would cross him.

After being prison bound he knew anything was game, and if niggas wanted to get down and dirty then he'd bring it too. He was headed out to Vegas to meet up with King Kamikaze. Seth knew that shit would rock the boat, and it wouldn't be easy getting on their territory considering their present beef.

But if Osiris would've taken the thong from out his ass and waited like Seth told him to, then this shit would've been and happened, and the beef would've been over. Shit was hot. Akil's death had him ready to shut their territory down, but he had to take his time with this shit.

He couldn't jump off impulse before he got his foot in the door, so he had to calm himself down and stay level-headed. That's why he was going alone.

Messiah was still in town handling business. He already knew if him and his boy would've stepped foot in Vegas together the shit would've lead to an instant war.

Messiah was hot-headed. Wasn't no talking in his eyes. That nigga jumped stupid, ready for whatever, with whoever, where ever. Seth was more level-headed; meaner, but more subtle.

Messiah was a savage and he fucked with him, but this situation had to be handled with care. This shit was fragile, and he couldn't allow his potna's temper to throw it off just yet.

The moment Seth dimmed the lights to catch some rest his phone rang. He started to ignore it, but when he saw Nas' name he answered.

"Wassup, mama?"

"Who the fuck is Kelani, Seth!"

It was like a molly had hit him. Everything around him moved in slow motion.

"What?"

"Nigga don't what me! Who the fuck is Kelani, and why is this bitch coming for me, Seth! You still fucking this bitch?"

Irritated by her yelling in his ear, he Facetimed her. When her face appeared on the screen and he saw the blood all over her and her hair a wild mess, he blew a fucking gasket.

"What the fuck happened, Nasir!" he yelled.

"How the fuck do I supposed to know! I'm tryna take a got damn piss, the bitch is banging on my stall, then the next thing I know, I'm being greeted to a fucking punch in my mouth! I knew your sneaky ass was up to something!"

"Yo', calm the fuck down, Nas! I don't wanna hear that shit right now! Stop talking that bullshit and explain to me what the fuck happened without all the extra shit! You better talk to me like you got some damn since!"

"Nigga you gon' hear it tonight! I don't give a fuck about your damn ego! There's only one reason that she would be coming for me, and it's you! You got bitches out here tryna jump me nigga! You got me fucked up! I'm not doing this shit with you, Seth! I can't believe yo' ass!

"I can't even look at yo' ass right now! And where ever yo' ass is headed, stay there and don't come back looking for me! And you ain't getting shit but yo' cap blown the fuck back if you come for me nigga, and that's on my fucking momma! Fuck you!"

"Nasir—"

She hung up on him. Seth tried to call her again, but it went straight to voicemail. She'd cut her phone off on his ass.

"This just what the fuck I need," he hissed as he dialed Messiah's number.

"Wassup, bro?"

"Bruh," Seth was so disgruntled he couldn't even think.

"The fuck is up, mane?"

"Maaaaaane," his explanation was stopped when his iPhone 8 started ringing. "Now these fucking niggas wanna call me. Hold up, bro... hello?"

"Yo', Kelani just jumped on ya girl with that whack ass lil' bitch Alicia."

"Who?" Seth spat.

"The bitch Nas used to roll with. The one from Shottas."

Seth ran his hand down his face, defeated. There was nothing he could physically do without being in town.

"Alright, man. I'mma handle that shit when I get back. Keep watch on Nas, and if that bitch Kelani get to popping off on some stupid shit before I touch back down, handle that shit. You hear me?"

"I gotchu."

"This bitch," he sighed as he put the other phone up to his ear that Messiah was on.

"Aye, I just got notice from the squad. The fuck is up with that shit man?" His potna questioned.

"I don't even know, man. Nas just called me going off and shit, and now a nigga gotta damn headache. I Facetime her ass, and shorty got blood everywhere."

"Damn, bruh."

"On me. Her lip was busted and shit, but you could tell from the amount and her lack of damage that it all ain't come from her. I knew that it was something sketchy about that lil' bitch," he scoffed in reference to Alicia.

"Yeah, that bitch ain't wrapped right. You want me to handle that?"

That's why he fucked with Messiah. He knew that nigga would hop out of bed in that moment and go fuck Kelani's ass up, but he wanted to do that shit personally.

"Nah, I'mma handle that shit when I get back. Just make sure Nas straight. She dun' cut her phone off on my ass."

Messiah chuckled.

"The fuck is funny, nigga? You amused?"

His brother from another mother continued to laugh.

"You man. I'mma keep it one hunnid. I ain't never seen you this pressed about a shorty. Not since high school when you was in love with Hannah."

Seth didn't want to, but he laughed thinking back to their high school days. Hannah was a bad ass chocolate cheerleader, and every nigga in school wanted her fine ass. She had Seth up under a got damn spell, he wanted her ass so bad.

"Dead that shit bro. You always bringing up old shit."

They shared a laugh.

"On one thousand though. Like bruh, you really feeling Nas?"

"What the fuck kind of question is that?"

"Mu'fucka you talking to me remember? Real shit. You dun' gave this girl ya black card after day two, or was it day three? She in ya complex on day four with free rent, then by week three, you dun bought this girl a whip. Some expensive shit too. You out of character man. You wasn't even geeked like this when you started fucking with that bitch Kelani."

Seth downed the rest if his drink. He often asked himself the same damn thing. A part of him was wondering if he was doing right by her because he knew he fucked Kelani over on some foul shit by staying disconnected from her no matter how hard she rode for him.

A part of him was wondering if it was the pussy that had him so gone. To be honest, he didn't know what it was but, he knew that he fucked with her though.

"On me man. It's crazy. Considering all that's been unfolding, it's hard to narrow that shit down. Nasir man," he sighed. "She just came and intercepted everything. On some real shit.

"Her vibe different; her demeanor different. And for real, for real, shorty just kind of opened my eyes to a lot. I don't know, she just made me realize how fucked up I been out here.

"It's like I wanna do right by her because I know she deserve it, plus I know I ain't been right in the past with all the bitches I was fucking with. You and me both know I wouldn't even be entertaining her if I really didn't want to."

"On me. I feel it. Just looking out for you, bro. Yo head be in the clouds and shit, and I gotta make sure you know what you getting yo self into. You falling my nigga. Real shit.

"Ain't been a bitch in how many years that we ain't shared? We ran Kelani the first night you met her before you threw that off-limits bullshit at me. A nigga ain't even get the chance to dip in them cakes Nasir got. No disrespect."

They shared a laugh.

"You gon' let a nigga fuck Riley?" Seth joked.

"See, mane, you-you can't even throw that out there now. That ain't 'em relevant no more." Messiah laughed.

"Then shut yo bitch ass up then. You can go fuck Kelani again, though, bro. That's free game."

"Don't nobody want that washed up ass bitch. Not even you."

Seth shook his head. Too much was going on right now and he just needed a break.

"I'm gon' kick back. I'mma hit you up when I make it to Vegas." He was calling it a night.

"Aight, bro. Malama pono."

"Malama pono, fam."

Chapter Sixteen

"*Please* pick up. Please pick up. God, please let this girl answer the phone this time. . ."

"Hello?"

"Oh my God, Nas. Thank you so much for answering the phone best friend, thank youuuuuuu."

Riley burst into tears once she heard her cousin's voice.

"Ry? What's wrong baby? What the fuck! Why are you calling me from jail?"

"Nas, can you please come and get me. Please, I swear to God, Nas, please. They knocked my bail down to five-grand from fifty. Can you please come and get me? I swear I will pay you back. I'll cash in my 401k as soon as we make it back to St. Louis just please." She couldn't stop crying.

"Where are you!"

"I'm at Fulton county jail."

"And I'm on the fucking way. Let me see when's the next flight out to—" An idea suddenly rang in her head, cutting her sentence short. "Fuck that, I'm on the way. I'll be there soon. Dry your face up baby. I'll see you in a minute, okay?"

"Thank you, Nas."

"I got you, baby. I'm on the way."

Nasir rolled out of bed and stumbled so hard she hit the floor. She was still way above the influence at five that morning, but she didn't give a damn. She hopped back up to her feet, slid into some Vicki Secret leggings, a hoodie, and slides, took another swig of the D'USSE on her dresser, then headed for the door.

"Oh shit my purse!" She shrieked, stopping midway up the steps before heading back down to her room. "And my keys. Lawd, get it together, baby girl."

Nas couldn't back her truck out fast enough and head for the main road. She hooked her phone up to the Bluetooth speaker as the call connected. Her fingers nervously tapped along the steering wheel before Seth finally answered on the last ring.

"Yo?"

His groggy voice indicated that he was sleeping, but she didn't give a fuck. He was lucky she'd called his ass in the first place. She was still on fire about that shit from a few hours ago.

"I need a flight out to Atlanta now. Send me the address to the Platinum airline and hurry the fuck up."

Click.

When Nas pulled up to the Platinum Hangar, she was blown away by the view. Three G5 jets were stationed on different docks, and the one waiting for her along with Messiah standing war ready with one of the biggest rifles she'd ever seen, was prepared for her to board. She took one last long hit from the Backwoods before she exited the car and walked over to him.

They greeted with a one-arm embrace and loaded the plane followed by a small army of five large men. Seth knew she couldn't have gotten herself into that much trouble, but he still wanted to make sure that she was safe.

"Drink?" Messiah asked as he fixed himself a glass of 1942.

Shit it was noon somewhere in the world right now.

"No. If I have one more drink I'll be throwing up everywhere. Is there something to eat on this damn thing?" She groaned as she placed her forehead in her knees that were pulled into her chest.

Her head was throbbing, her heart was racing, and no matter how swiftly the jet was soaring through the clouds her body felt like she was stuck in high tide at Hurricane Harbor.

"Yeah. What you want?"

"Anything. Some chicken strips, fries, a waffle, some grits; shit, tell them to bring out a full course."

Messiah chuckled as he placed a call back to the dining staff for her. Once Nas had some food in front of her she was able to think and wrap her brain around Riley being in jail.

"I knew I should've went down there with her. Something told me not to let her go out there alone. I swear to God I'mma beat the shit out of Tevin," she scolded with a quarter of the waffle in her mouth.

"I thought they finalized the divorce a couple weeks back?" Messiah asked as he put the hurting on the food sitting before him as well.

"His bitch ass moved it back two weeks for only God knows what. I knew Tevin wasn't shit the first time she called me and told me he hit her three years back. I kept telling Riley losing no amount of weight in the world was gonna change the way that nigga saw her unless he wanted it to happen.

"Kudos to her for trying to save their marriage, but I'm not dealing with no nigga that's gon' fuck up my mental like that. No amount of money or tainted love is worth that shit. It's too much dick out here to be keeping stupid ass niggas like Tevin around."

Nas was hot. She could only imagine what the fuck had happened, and they couldn't get there soon enough. It was tragic for the both of them growing up being heavy.

Nas was bullied in high school and so was Riley. Thank God they didn't grow up when social media was really dominating the world like it was today.

Even though they went to different schools it was like they fought the same battles. If the senior football players weren't dragging either of them because they both loved to dance, then they were getting dogged out by bitches.

Nas never knew how hateful people were until she stepped foot in high school. Fat people existed but you'd think the shit was the latest tea the way she used to walk home crying her eyes out from another day of torment.

It was already hard for them as kids because their mothers were so beautiful. Riley's mom Catrina was tall and slim with a caramel skin tone and men absolutely loved her. Now just imagine being two plump teenaged girls walking in the shadows of their beautiful mothers? People couldn't believe they were their children no matter how much either of them had resembled their moms.

Life had always been hard on them until Ry took control and showed Nas that losing weight was possible. Now they were banging, and couldn't nobody tell them shit, but Nas knew it was deeper than that when it came to Riley's argument.

She lost weight to keep her man. Tevin would threaten her on the daily about leaving her or finding him a new bitch and making her his side chick if she didn't get in shape.

Nasir couldn't count the nights she's sat on the phone and cried with her cousin because of her heartaches. Tevin has had mind control over Riley for a long time, and Nas couldn't wait until this divorce was over.

She was proud of her girl for stepping up and putting her foot down when it came to him. Tevin wasn't even all that cute if you asked her. His Future looking ass had to keep shades on in order for her to even compliment his big head ass.

The thought made her crack a smile as she took a sip of her mimosa. Yeah, Nas was that type. Her lips said one thing, but her mind forced her to do another like swallow that second drink.

"I fuck with how y'all ride for each other though, mama. That's wassup. I won't stunt, seeing you used to roll with that lil' sketchy bitch kinda had me eyeing you sideways until you cut her off. Then, seeing how you and Ry interact, and the way you got my bro's head in the clouds? You a cool ass lil' chick."

Nasir rolled her eyes in a joking like matter. Thinking about Seth right now made her head hurt.

"I'm sure you know about that shit that popped off," she insinuated with the raise of an eyebrow.

"Yeah, I heard. Them bitches is foul."

"So, what? They call themselves linking up to come for me? I ain't never seen Alicia with that bitch a day in my fucking life. For two years, I couldn't keep that bitch off me like flies on a shit pile, so I know who all she associates with.

"The whole fucking world knows; ole' loud mouth ass." Nas felt her lip where the cut from her being stole-on was located. It was still tender. "So, for her to pop up out of nowhere with his ex is really fucking bugging me right now."

"You gon' have to wrap with him about that shit, mama. I will say this. Kelani a lil' crazy ass bitch. She, she dirty, so I ain't surprised at how that shit popped off. She get down like that."

Nas rolled her eyes.

"No, that bitch thinks she's crazy. She ain't seen nothing yet, and I know you ain't gon' tell me shit. You'd die before you rat that nigga out. I guess I can respect y'all's lil' loyalty to one another or whatever the fuck you wanna call it."

He laughed.

"You sound a bit salty over there, ma," he joked. "Check it though. I don't question yo loyalty to ya girl. How the fuck you mad at my nigga, but demand that he sends you to Atlanta all first class and shit, but won't hear him out?"

"He did it, didn't he?"

They shared a laugh.

"I'll kill somebody over Riley. That's my lil' bae. Including you. Drop the ball you hear me?"

Messiah shook his head as he lit a blunt.

"We just chilling, mama. She got enough going on right now. I ain't even the relationship type to be honest. Don't get me wrong she hella chill. She's a dope ass woman, but between the havoc that's going on in her life right now and being who I am, I'm just doing my thing.

"And I know for a fact that Riley got too much on her mind to be thinking 'bout "us". Sometimes you just gotta let shit run its course. I ain't tryna slap no ring on that like Seth's ass tryna do with you."

"Shut up," she smirked.

It was all she could say right now because in her head she was preparing for their argument the moment his sneaky ass made it back in town, and she was sure that he wasn't gonna like what she had to say at all.

T

Seth threw the duffle bag along the dock before he climbed out of the water. He quickly removed the thermal protectant swimwear and changed into the Armani suit that was tailored perfectly for his frame.

He wrung his hair out and pulled it up high into a bun before tucking his gold-plated Desert Eagles in the back of his pants while loading and slapping a suppressor on the third and fourth ones he kept at his grasp. They each had a thirty-round loaded too.

Seth could've done things the easy way and let the Kamikaze mob kick his ass and drag him in like a prisoner, but he bowed before no one. Not even Osiris at this point. He had one of the best spies and CIA agents on his team, so he was able to board a private yacht and swim his way onto the multi-million-dollar mansion. It was located on a private estate that sat off of Colorado river, and you couldn't get within a certain mile radius without sparking heat.

"You got three boogies right outside the west wall where you're located, then a team of five on the level above."

"Bet," he spoke into the ear piece as he retracted the chambers.

Phew. Phew. Phew.

The guard's bodies twisted and hit the floor like dominos before they had the opportunity to realize that they'd been hit. Seth removed the keys from one of the guards before he grabbed the fire extinguisher that was hanging along the wall and took the elevator up to the next level. When the doors flew ajar the guards stationed all drew their weapons when they realized no one had made an exit.

The red tank hit the floor, then exploded when Seth put two rounds in it. Gunshots rang in the air until he was the last man standing. He dropped the body of one of the dead guards from the lower level that he used as a shield before he straightened his collar.

Two, four, then six more men ran from out a side door located at the furthest end of the hall with their assault rifles aimed. Don't let the hair fool ya. Seth was trill with that shit like Liam Neeson in *Taken*.

His straps let off rounds while he took niggas down with his hands too. His hands could crack a nigga's skull. They were like sledge hammers. Ask Jediah whose face was still healing from the fractures he put in the temporal, zygomatic, and ethmoid cavities of that cranium.

Seth was accustomed to pain. Osiris had beat his ass enough, a number of henchmen had brought him down to his knees through all his training, and he'd even survived a few rounds of police brutality to know how well pain felt in order to inflict it upon the next.

That classic Rocko "Squares Out Yo Circle" was on repeat in his head as he took niggas down left and right. This shit was like exercise to him.

That's all y'all got? He chuckled to himself at the thought.

"You've got two teams headed your way. Get your ass to the penthouse now."

Seth chuckled again at the spy's comment as he pulled the vent out and climbed inside.

"Location reached."

The message came in when he made it to his destination. He kicked the vent along the ceiling out then jumped through, landing on his feet, squatted down with both his arms extended as his second set of Desert Eagles were aimed and ready.

He was surrounded. Seth scanned the room and eyed the team of at least thirty men with guns aimed at him. He chuckled at King Kamikaze who had his feet propped up along his desk while puffing hard from a half-smoked Cuban cigar.

"Mr. Platinum. So, you're the one who's disturbing my peace? And... you managed to make it to my office. Bravo."

Seth watched as King K removed his legs from the desk and stood to his feet.

"You caught me at a bad time. I was just leaving for a round of golf my good man," he commented on his tan Brooks Brothers shorts and sky-blue polo shirt that both were ironed to perfection.

"Dead 'em."

"You sure about that?" Seth questioned as he dropped the gun in his left hand, letting it hang around his finger so he could flash a detonation device that was ready to blow this bitch to pieces.

King Kamikaze's eyes were malevolent, matching the glare written upon Seth's face. The beeping noises that filled the air sent a signal to King K that this man before him wasn't on bullshit, and he was more than ready to sacrifice himself along with his estate if he'd made the wrong move by attempting to kill him.

"Alright."

A smile swept across P1's face as he disengaged the alarm for the next five minutes. He rose to a standing position and fixed his collar not letting go of his burners.

"You've got a lot of nerve stepping foot on my property muthafucka," the fifty- year-old spat as his nose flared. "Tell me. What should I have engraved along your head stone following me watching you gasp for your last breath? I'll be sure to bury you right next to your brother," he threatened.

"And you'll watch me bury your wife and daughter right next to your son if you don't shut the fuck up with all that bullshit."

Seth hit another button along the detonator that brought up an image along the flat screen located on the wall behind the man's desk. King K turned around and gasped in fear when his eyes laid upon his family sitting at the kitchen table with duct tape around their mouths and arms while six huge men surrounded them with rifles.

"Start talking muthafucka! I'm seconds off invading every fucking strip of Platinum territory as we speak! You really wanna fuck with me right now!" King K's brown skin flushed red from his frustrations.

"Now that I've got yo fucking attention," Seth emphasized with a smirk. "Let me get you hip on what the fuck Juno and I were working on before he was killed."

"Bullshit!"

The look on Seth's face was everything but bullshit. Kamikaze's anger, his army, and him being outnumbered didn't faze him at all. He stood solid. He remained calm. He kept his head up. The man didn't crumble. Seth's durability was intimidating.

"All Platinum territory has been divided, and we've been living within the days of a crossover."

The King chuckled.

"You and your silly ass brother against who?"

"Them against me."

Kamikaze's smile faded. He'd heard about Seth. Seth had never been a threat to him. He always came off as a lame ass pretty boy whose only mission was to stunt for bitches, so to hear the truth behind the civil war was perplexing. The long-haired mutt had impressed him.

"MPD let you free because of the crossover?"

"What's done ain't gotta be explained. You see I'm out don't you, nigga? And you see clearly that MPD is still undecided territory, right?"

"The fuck does that have to do with me!"

"Everything. Because either you can hop on board, join Berkeley and we all can conquer MPD before we take over the rest of the Platinum territory, or you can wait for OP to come after yo ass," he imposed, referring to his father's squad.

Kamikaze was puzzled to hear Berkeley come out of Seth's mouth.

"Berkeley signed a treaty to remain out of US cartel associations. Why the fuck do you think we don't get our supply from them anymore—"

"Out of *your* cartel association. Out of Si's distribution, but guess whose territory that is now? Cash rules everything, bitch. So, if you need me to put that into prospective for you, nigga, you work for me if you plan on staying in business. You know I'll make sum' shake once I get that grade of snow in the states. Now what?"

King K's eyes widened. His trade and the Platinums may have been the biggest cartels in the states, but Berkeley was the direct source and location of the purest supply that sold cocaine. They moved millions of dollars' worth of dope in Central America.

The supply he purchased from in Cuba was some good shit, but Columbia was the heart of the Southern Hemisphere. Their product was 100 percent raw. Columbia was the birthplace of the dingiest and most potent supply anyone could get their hands on.

How the fuck did he manage to pull that shit off? Muthafuckas have been trying to get Berkley back on board with the US for years now.

"Why do you think he was meeting me in Mexico? Once Juno and I would've touched down in Columbia this shit would've been over, but we had a few interceptions."

"How the fuck did I know what the hell y'all were doing in Mexico? The fuck I'm worried about undecided territory for unless I wanna cease? That was stupid as fuck to meet on their terrain in the first damn place," Kamikaze argued.

"Yo son wasn't the brightest, but he was sure that he had some shit worked out with MDP. Let's just say there's always been a certain level of trust that was established between Juno and I even with the beef. Plus, that's y'all old niggas' problem. Y'all sweep shit under the rug until you're forced to deal with it.

"Imagine what would've happened if Mexico would've bought out Columbia before one of us, then what? Who was they coming for? The Kamikazes and Platinum territory muthafucka. But y'all niggas was so worried about going to war with one another that y'all ain't even let that shit cross y'all's mind. I see that old age and hair loss setting y'all niggas back."

"Watch your fucking mouth you hear me!"

Kamikaze was hot. He couldn't help it that he's been bald since his thirties.

"I ain't come here to play games with yo ass, Kamikaze. Take the proposition if you still wanna eat because you already know it's over."

King K grabbed the cigar and lit it once more. His mind was racing. He was getting old as fuck if shit like that had never dawned over him. The reason why the Kamikazes and the Platinums had been beefing for years was because they had the same cocaine supply in Cuba. So, sales were based solely off of contracts with other smaller cartels and territory.

That's why he had Juno taking over in the first place. His head wasn't where it used to be. Ever since he found out he was diagnosed with an early case of memory loss, he hasn't been himself. He was the king, and he always would be, but the fine details were something he couldn't keep up with. That's why he appointed his nephew to take over once his son was murdered.

"Send in Rocky," King spoke over the phone to his secretary in reference to his nephew.

Seth chuckled when the door behind him opened. The cigar from Kamikaze's hand hit the floor when his crying secretary walked inside the room with a glass case that had his nephew's decapitated head inside.

"Looking for him?" Seth questioned with a chuckle. "I owed you that. It's white flag right now considering Akil's death, but—"

"Akil's death ain't have shit to do with the Kamikaze mob! I ain't that fucking sloppy! So, this is what this shit is about! Offing Juno was low, but if you thought I was gon' wait a year to clap back on you muthafuckas then you got another thing coming my nigga!

"I hit y'all muthafuckas where it hurts! Ya pockets nigga! Ask Si why it took him a year to get his head out the fucking waters! Wasn't shit but Kamikaze product moving in these streets because I bought out so much product from Cuba, keeping him out of shop!"

Damn, Si been broke? The fuck been going on this last year man? Seth pondered.

"He ain't get shit from Cuba until word got out that Akil was murdered, and Pedro felt sorry for the bitch ass nigga! I don't know what kind of fluke ass shit y'all got going on in St. Louis, but one thing my old bald head ass know how to do is stack my fucking money and never fall off! I'm warning you Seth!"

The beeping noise to blow the building cut his argument short.

"So what the fuck it's gon' be? Hurry up and make a fucking decision, or neither of us will live to see the outcome."

Steam was rising from Kamikaze's head as Seth's hand rested on the button.

"Six months, bitch. You got six months to make this shit happen, then after that, it's me and you. And the last muthafucka left standing takes it all. Six fucking months max and not a day later."

P1 disengaged the alarm with a smirk along his face.

"Then it's said. Six months it's is, old man. That's my word."

Chapter Seventeen

"Riley Stuart. You're out."

Hearing her maiden name made her heart race.

The fuck, she thought in disbelief as the guard opened her cell.

"Your belongings, Ms. Stuart. We'll need you to sign these papers as well that were handed over by Attorney Black. They are the finalization of your divorce, but Mr. Heights refuses to see you in person," the clerk explained.

Riley scribbled her name so fast on those papers she threw them back at that damn lady. Fuck Tevin, fuck that house, and fuck everything! If pride was the only thing she had to walk out her marriage with, then so fucking be it.

He could have it all. She had her car and that's all that mattered. Praise God they got it in her name in the first damn place. He hadn't paid the note on it in six months anyway, so that was her shit.

"Riley!"

"Nas!"

A mixture of happiness and sadness swept over Riley when her cousin jumped in her arms. She was defeated. Before she knew it, her knees had hit the ground and they were in the middle of the Fulton County Jail's lobby crying their eyes out with one another.

"You ladies have to get out of here. Now."

"Would you shut the fuck up! Didn't I just drop five stacks in this bitch?! You better mind yo got damn business and check a metal detector or something!" Nas spat as she held onto her cousin tighter.

"Ma'am—"

"Didn't she say shut the fuck up? Don't make me turn this muthafucka up. It won't be the first time."

The guard's eyes widened when he recognized Messiah. Messiah was a ball of fury known in every major city. He'd earned his title and respect from the way he'd make a gun clap, invade a city, from frugally fucking the kingpin's bitch's lights out knowing niggas weren't dumb enough to step to him, and from his hands. The officer stood back as Messiah helped Riley up to her feet once Nasir stood up.

Holding her hand in his sent a feeling through him that he couldn't describe. The tears running down her cheeks mixed with the finger prints around her neck pissed him off so bad he was ready to swing on that nigga Tevin if he saw him right then and there. He wiped her eyes, dusted her shoulders off, and handed her the ice-cold bottle of Green Apple Gatorade he had waiting on her.

He didn't understand females and the whole Gatorade crave. Granted, she worked out a lot, but she drank that shit like water. Who was he to judge though? He knew it would put a smile on her face, and right then, seeing her crack even the slightest smile knocked his anger down a notch.

"Chin up, mama," he mumbled before raising it and placing a kiss to her lips.

Riley's body rekindled. She didn't expect him to be there, but it surely made her feel a thousand times better. When he put his arm around her to leave, he felt her body tense up and it made his eyes travel to where she was looking. It was a swollen-faced Tevin with four police officers and his attorney.

"Yo, muthafucka," Messiah held his tongue for no one.

He lifted his jeans as he headed for the group of men who were damn near running for the front door.

"Aye, bruh," Tito grabbed Messiah by the arm before he could make it out of the exit.

The man reached in his pocket like he had a gun. Tevin flinched so damn hard he tripped down the steps from paying attention to Messiah's crazy ass. Siah chuckled when he opened his arms, showing him that he wasn't strapped, but he soon held his hands up like he was holding a set of his trusty Glock 10's with the 30 clips.

The look in Messiah's eyes told Tevin that shit wasn't a front. When one of his guards whispered the name Platinum in his ear his whole mood changed. Riley was fucking with the mafia now? That's how she was doing it? And from the way Messiah had reacted, Tevin knew exactly who she was fucking too.

***

"Messiah, must you shop everywhere we go?" Nas joked once she realized that their car had pulled up in front of Lenox Square Mall.

"It's what I do, ma. Gon' and get out the car and let me talk to her for a minute before we head inside."

"Well excuse me, nigga. You ain't gotta tell me twice," she playfully rolled her eyes as she exited the car and closed the door behind her.

Messiah climbed over to the side of the limo where Riley was sitting and looked into her eyes. He'd been sitting across from her just staring; sipping his drink and admiring how beautiful she was laying with her head on Nas' chest with her feet kicked up. Even through all the pain, he saw such a beautiful woman.

Orange did her skin complexion wonders. The Champion t-shirt displaying those tattooed arms down to her fingertips, and the black spandex shorts that hugged her thick thighs drove him wild. And the curvature of her full lips. How sexy it was when she chewed on her bottom lip out of nervousness. He'd peeped the habit on their first date, and the shit made his dick hard.

And those eyes. The eyes that had roads for miles, and all of him wanted to travel down that interstate right to her heart. Messiah may have said one thing, but when he got around Riley it was a different story. Yeah, they were just chilling.

Yeah, she was a cool lil' chick, but she captivated him unlike anything he'd ever felt before, and he couldn't deny it. He was tired of seeing her cry. Her tears started to trickle down her face once again, and on cue his hands slid her shorts down.

He didn't care that she'd been locked up all night; he had to put his mouth to work. He pushed her knees in her chest and let his tongue do that thing she liked over her clit at full speed. Riley's pussy got so fucking wet the shit drove him wild.

One of her hands held onto the top of his head while her free hand pushed on the ceiling; he was attacking that shit so good. You'd think the clit was the person who had him so damn disgruntled; he was slamming that pearl with no mercy while her slit leaked juices that ran along his chin.

"Messiah. . ." she groaned as she rubbed his head.

Her body shuttered when his tongue slipped down to her butt. His thumb played with her pearl before he reached up and put it in her mouth. Her tongue attacked him wishing it was the bulge in his pants.

Messiah's life flashed before his eyes as he continued to chow down. This shit took him back to the first time he'd ever gone down on a woman. He was sixteen, and the lady was twenty-seven. He had a lil' part-time gig at Footlocker before he and Seth started slanging, and she used to beg him to fuck every day on the job.

Three kids, a husband, and all; she still wanted the kid. She taught him how to get nasty with that shit too, and after he got the hang of it, head was his specialty.

"Messiah! Oh, my Gooooood! Oh my God!"

Climax number two rushed out of her while he let his tongue take it all. No umbrella; he wanted all that rain to pour down.

"Whose pussy is this, mama? Hmmm?"

Her eyes crossed when he slurped on her clit. Her pelvis was lifting up off the seat, her sinuses had her congested, and it was getting hot up in that muthafucka with the sunroof open. Riley just knew the whole damn mall heard her cries because the nigga wouldn't let up.

"Messiah. . ." she finally answered, her voice barely above a whisper.

"Who?" he grunted as he slid his rock-hard soldier between her thighs after she climaxed a third time.

He felt his shirt lift in the back as her nails dug into his flesh. They had the back of that limousine rocking.

"Messiah, baby! Oh my God!"

When her mouth released from biting on his shoulder, he kissed her. Her tongue lapped up all of her juices that were left over from his three-course meal.

"This my pussy, huh? I don't hear you."

He stroked her deep with his knees planted on the floor while he held her by the shoulders. She threw her head back and moaned so loud, the only place it could go was out the sunroof.

"Messiah, this is your pussy! Oh my God this is your pussy! I'm cumming! Oh my God!"

"Say my name like this my pussy, Riley. Say my fucking name."

"Messiah! Messiah! Messiaaaaaaah!"

He grunted loudly as he pulled her closer then relocated his hands to her ass. He slammed her down hard on his dick with his name still exiting her mouth nonstop until he felt his soldiers shoot up her walls.

They fell back against the seat and sat there for a minute. Panting, barely breathing, sweating, wondering where the fuck the water was at, needing the a/c to be blaring on high instead of the heat waves from hell that were attacking them right now.

Messiah looked up at her. His dick was still inside her walls. Still throbbing, still tryna tense back up, but that pussy played no games.

She grabbed him by the sides of his face and kissed him. Their tongues overlapped until her jaw wouldn't let her continue.

"Thank you," she whispered with a smile, her hand rubbing his head and her eyes burning while looking into his.

"Don't sweat it, mama. Come on. A nigga need some Chick-Fil-A after that shit."

T

When Nas exited the car, her stomach dropped once she recognized Seth leaning against the limousine that was parked in front of the one that she'd arrived in. She rolled her eyes at him and headed for the mall entrance.

I thought he was in Vegas? She shook her head disappointed.

Nasir's body went flying when she felt him snatch her up by the elbow and shove her into the nearest wall.

"Yo', don't cut yo' fucking eyes at me, Nasir, and don't disrespect me like that. I don't give a fuck where we at; you will get yo' ass handled. And two, I told yo' ass not to go out to that damn club in the first place, but you did anyway!" He barked.

Nasir was stuck. She'd planned on being the person who would be doing all of the "going-in". Seth didn't know why she steadily liked to play with him.

She knew he hated being ignored. That shit drove him crazy, but little Nasir still liked to play with fire, and one day soon she'd get that ass burned.

"Get your damn hands off me! What the fuck I tell you about doing me like that! I'm a fucking woman, not some ho you just gon' push around! I'm the one who should be mad, nigga!"

"Lower- yo' fucking- voice," he hissed while pulling her closer and giving her that stare.

You know what stare I'm talking about. The one where his eyes got all demonic and put her in her place real quick.

"You're all pissed off at me when I'm the one who got jumped on by *your ex*, yet *I'm* in the wrong? Fuck you, Seth. I see how it is now," she spat with tears trickling down her face.

Nas shoved him off of her and continued on with her arms folded across her midsection. Seth rubbed his chin as he watched her short little legs shuffle back and forth as fast as she could to get away from him.

Short ass, he chuckled.

Seth looked over his shoulder and noticed Messiah pulling his shirt down. Riley was pulling on her damn clothes too, and all Seth could do was laugh as he and his potna slapped hands.

"What's wrong with my baby?" Riley gasped as she noticed Nas doing the quick walk. That walk was usually accompanied by tears, causing her to push Seth in the shoulder. "What did you do?"

He threw his hands up before she went after her cousin.

"Damn, bruh, you couldn't wait to handle that shit once we made it back to town?"

"I ain't got time for that attitude shit, man."

Seth waved it off.

"Aye, bruh, can you blame her? Security sent me the pics from the club this morning. That shit got wild."

Seth sighed. He scratched his head while they followed behind the women who were walking into Neiman Marcus.

"Bitch are you serious!" Riley gasped as she held Nas by the face to look at her lip.

She hadn't even noticed how swollen it was; Nasir had done such a good job at calming her down after she was released.

"And he wanna be mad at me talking some, *'I told yo ass not to go anyway.'*"

"That's besides the fucking point, nigga. Why the fuck was bitches jumping on you? Ooooh, I'm swinging on that bitch Alicia when we get back I swear."

Riley had her fist bald up ready to rock her ass to sleep. Nas wiped her eyes. She could be a big baby sometimes, but so what.

She was hurt more than anything. So many thoughts were swarming in her mind right now that she couldn't think straight.

"Do you think he was still messing with her?" Riley asked.

"I don't know," she pouted as she held onto her temples. "I just wanna go home. I don't wanna shut Atlanta down. I'm this close to swinging on his ass. Like you mad at me? What the fuck did I do?"

Riley rolled her eyes, equally irritated by her man's funky ass attitude too.

"Did y'all talk about it?"

"No. I was too pissed off to even hear him out. I know Alicia is sneaky but Seth's ex? How the fuck does that shit just happen? Something is going on, and I'mma get to the bottom of that shit. I know that— Damn, where the fuck is the staff?"

"We been in here for ten minutes and a bitch ain't introduced themselves or nothing," Nas snapped as she eyed a pair of bubblegum pink Yves Saint Laurent platform heels that she'd always wanted since the first time she saw them when she was twenty-two.

The sandal was a classic, and they debuted them every season like it was new. She rolled her eyes when she saw Seth and

Messiah approaching them with bags from Chick-fil-A in their hands.

"Me and Messiah just smashed a whole five-course meal on the way here. Got damn nigga. You still hungry?" Nas laughed out loud.

"He just ate from the thighs of heaven too. Baby boy gotta appetite out this world."

"Bitch, that's why you smiling and shit! Ooooh, lil' Michael B. Jordan made that pussy cum with that tongue, huh, mama!"

"Shree times bitch, before the dick," she imitated comedian Darren Fleet and the way he always placed an emphasis on the word three.

Their squeals couldn't be ignored. The staff looked over in their direction to put faces with the ghetto broads as if it weren't Neiman Marcus.

But when they noticed their men approaching them, three different sales women walked up with fake ass smiles along their faces to greet their fine asses.

"How are you fellas doing?" A short brown-skinned chick asked as she flipped her hair out of her face.

"Why the fuck they been standing in here for the longest, and y'all just now walking over here?" Messiah questioned as he took a seat along the plush couch.

The silly goose was so shocked from his response that she spit her words out in nothing but stutters.

"I-I-didn't notice them. I-I—"

"Ask them what they want, and how you can help them. We don't need yo explanation," Seth then ordered as he handed Nasir the frozen strawberry lemonade.

Now yo ass wanna be nice to me. Damn bi-polar ass Gemini. . .

Messiah and Seth sat back while their ladies tried on at least two dozen pairs of shoes and boots. They were like kids in a candy store laughing and giggling and dancing around while making love to the mirror with their phones out.

"Nah, you can't wear them, mama," Messiah shook his head as he shoved the rest of the chocolate chip cookie in his mouth.

"Aye, I agree with my dawg. Take them ratchet ass boots off, Nas."

"Boy stop," both women countered in sync as they stood in the mirror.

Riley was rocking a pair of those thigh-high, vibrant purple, Balenciaga pointed-toe stilettos. Nas was rocking a pair of orange Vera Wang snake skin, cut out stilettos that came up to the creases right beneath her ass. The adjustments were perfect for her frame.

She could tell her man's dick was hard from the look in his eyes as she glanced at him through the mirror, getting his facial expression for Snap Chat. And if she didn't want him to fuck her right then and there, she needed to slide them muthafuckas off now.

"Since you insist on getting them muthafuckas, model walk for me, mama," Seth commanded while finishing up his drink.

Women couldn't keep their eyes from out their direction. Shoe boxes were lined up everywhere, and it wasn't any cheap shit either. Nasir walked over to him and stood between his legs. He spun her around and slapped her ass, watching it jiggle. It was real fluffy now.

"I'mma fuck you with them bitches on before you wear 'em out. Help you break 'em in," he smirked. "Aye, y'all got these in any other color?" He asked the nosey ass sales woman who couldn't keep her eyes from off him when she wasn't rolling them at Nasir.

"Y-yes, sir. They, they also come in black and olive."

"Bring me out each in her size and leave 'em at the register. That should keep yo hating ass busy before she knock yo ass out if you eye-ball her one more time."

The woman's mouth dropped in embarrassment. Nasir raised her eyebrow and threw her dukes up like she was Angela from *Why Did I Get Married, Too* at the scene from the Bahamas, before her salty ass went away to grant his request.

Seth pulled his woman into his lap and let his hand slide in her pants to hold her butt. His dick jumped when he noticed she didn't have any panties on.

"And, you're supposed to be mean to them bitches; not me," she sassed as she finished the rest of her cold fries.

He chuckled.

"I told you I was mean from the jump."

"Not all the time, you're not. You be wanting to be nice to me, but yo lil' ugly ass just gotta hold onto your ego like treating me good is gonna weaken your clout as a kingpin."

"Damn, mama. Why you gotta be so foul with that shit?" He laughed.

She looked him in the eye while sipping her drink.

"Because Seth. You play too many damn games."

"Games?"

"Yes, games. Last night—"

"We'll talk about that when we make it back in town. Right now, ain't the time, Nasir. It's a time and place for everything. I said I was sorry."

"You didn't!" she yelped. "In your mind you might have, but you haven't said shit to me."

Seth grabbed her by the neck of her hoodie and pulled her close before he kissed her lips.

"Just tell daddy you missed him. You always get bent and shit when I'm gone like you don't know that I gotta keep our money flowing. You know I'm coming home to you."

Seth may have been the most honest right in this moment than he's ever been with a woman in his life. Nasir was speechless. She could feel the seriousness from his tone in the pit of her stomach.

"Here," He went in his pocket and handed her a roll of money so fat, she was surprised it couldn't be seen in his jeans. "Go get ya shit so we can head to another store."

Chapter Eighteen

"*I* can't believe this shit! Are you serious right now!"

Osiris screamed in rage while looking Jediah in the eye. "Berkley! This nigga bought out Berkley! Mutha-fucka!"

Glass shattered as he threw the crystal center-piece from his desk into the brick wall that surrounded his den. He ran his hands over his bald head before a roar escaped his lips. His desk flipped over so fast Jediah had to jump up from out of the chair that was in front of it to miss being knocked over his damn self.

"Do you know how many fucking years I've been tryna buy out Columbia? Huh! Them bitch ass niggas wouldn't even jump when I proposed that shit to them last year when Kamikaze pulled that bullshit with Cuba, and now this! I had to cash in our Bitcoin stocks just to stay afloat these last twelve months, and Seth out here crossing me like this all because of his fuck up!"

Jediah remained silent. He knew his father was on edge, and the wrong comment would lead to him being the one to suffer the consequences. His head and face were killing him. He was on IV Morphine and OxyContin pills, but the pain from his fractures still wouldn't ease up without a lil' sniff of some snow.

Jediah was contemplating on how to respond. He'd talked Osiris into the crossover, into Seth's arrest, into neglecting Seth; into it *all,* with hopes that his brother had been dead by now. They both underestimated P1.

They expected his loyalty to the family to never run astray no matter what he had to face. They all knew this game came with sacrifices, but Seth had always been the one who thought that shit didn't apply to him.

He thought like he was untouchable, and he moved with an invincibility that would force you to hate on the nigga. His cockiness was the base of his character, and that could either be his downfall or be used to his advantage.

With the way he was making moves though, if they didn't act on it quick, then he'd be the one with the last laugh, and this whole scheme would've been for nothing.

"He's still weak right now, Si. He doesn't have an army. He might've bought out Berkeley, but you know good and damn well them muthafuckas ain't crossing the border. Not even money could buy that."

Osiris inhaled the Cuban cigar, nodding his head in agreement.

"That is true," he responded while gazing out of the window.

The courtyard was being re-flourished with peach Begonias to his wife's liking. He could picture the sadness written along her face in his head nonstop since the day the crossover happened.

Falcon loved all of her sons. Through right and wrong, no matter what, they were her babies. She'd lost one to the grave, and one from a situation that could've been avoided if her husband hadn't been so greedy and eager for his own selfish reasons.

He'd barely get a sentence out of her in a day's timeframe. Falcon spent most of her day scribbling in her diary while lounging in the courtyard or out by the lake. She'd been going to see her father-in-law more as well.

To her dismay, he was now living in a nursing home because Osiris was over having too many fucking people in and out of his house. Nabawi was on hospice; his existence between life and heaven was thinning, and his son clearly didn't give a fuck.

Yet, Falcon was in a dark world, and Osiris knew that he was the one to blame. It hurt him not to see his wife smile, or to hear her singing off tune and off-beat to every song that came on the radio while she cleaned their palace despite the housekeepers that kept everything well intact.

Everything was spiraling out of control and fast ever since Seth made it back to the states. He was a fucking plague that Osiris was barely withstanding, and he had to take care of that shit by any means; even at the risk of his wife's heartbreak.

"Send that nigga a warning," He commanded as he turned to face Jediah. "First, you get my new fucking shipment in from Cuba and get that shit going. Get rid of it all before he has the opportunity to put Columbia product out. And you better pray to God, nigga, that he hasn't or else ..."

Osiris hit the button underneath his turned over desk and it made the fixture above the fire place turn around. A dead skull was sitting along the mantel like a deer's head. The initials *TP* had been carved along the forehead. Jediah recognized who it had belonged to instantly.

Osiris chuckled while he glanced at his brother's last remains. Often, he'd sit in his den with his feet propped up on his desk staring at it for insight, staring at it for motivation, staring at it as a reminder of who the fuck he was and what the fuck he was capable of doing if he was pushed to the edge.

"Yours will be to the right, and Seth's will be to the left if you don't get this shit under control. Do I make myself clear?"

Jediah bowed his head out of respect. Osiris' vibe was enough to know that he was down with whatever to make his way to the top like he's done before. Everything was perfect. Seth had Berkeley under his whim, and now, all they had to do was take him out to be blessed with keeping what they killed. Everyone in the game knew once you got rid of a kingpin, then whatever he owned became theirs, and it was only a matter of time before Jediah and Osiris had succeeded.

T

Falcon's eyes burned as she watched the nurse use the suction tube to clear Nabawi's throat so he could breathe and no longer suffer from aspirating. Nabawi meant the world to her. She'd been with Osiris since she was fifteen-years-old. Her mother married her off to him despite the opinion of society.

The Platinums had been known in St. Louis for years. Their last name was a brand all in itself. They'd been holding the cocaine game down solid since the 40's, and May made it her destiny to make sure that her daughter would coin their hood rich, well, hood *filthy* rich, status by marrying her off.

Osiris was ten years older than Falcon, but he liked them young. She was a hot beauty who every nigga wanted despite her family's tax bracket. Falcon grew up poor. She shared a small home over in the hood on the west side off of Hodiamont where she and her mother lived with her uncle Harry and Aunties Ferra and Georgia. A total of ten kids and four adults lived in the three bedroom and one and a half bathroom house.

Falcon could remember being a little girl walking down Skinker Boulevard. Not the beautiful end of Skinker in Forest Park with the rich folk, but the slums where people argued could either be the west side or Wellston depending on which direction you were headed.

She remembered the day she was carrying her school books pinned to her chest to hide the breasts her teenage body had finally began to sprout, and her backpack low over her nice little, though plump, butt.

Falcon hated when men looked at her. She was already walking through the hood, and even though she wasn't alone because she had enough cousins to back her up for days if some shit had ever popped off, she still felt like a target.

Falcon had always been the pretty girl. Her brown skin glowed like a shiny new penny, and she had beautiful long hair that she almost always wore half up in a ponytail and half down in curls. She was always best dressed too.

Falcon was her mother's only girl, so May had to make sure that her daughter was sharp. The white Levi jeans, colorful wind breaker jacket, clean all-white Reebok Classics that her mother had sucked two dicks at once for the money to get, and white beret on her head with her flawless curls falling down her back surely caught Osiris' eye one evening.

He was cruising down Skinker while she and a gang of her family were passing the Alfa Gardens Apartments. He'd fallen for the girl at first sight. Dressed fresh to death like he was the missing member from NWA with the chunky gold chain around his neck and his scrub cap cocked to the left, he was fine as hell looking like a young Boris Kodjoe, hanging out the driver's side calling after her.

She tried to ignore him out of nervousness and from being a timid girl, but he didn't like that shit. Osiris got whatever the fuck he wanted, and he made that shit known when he pulled his all black with the pimped-out rims to match, Classic 80 Cadillac up on the curve to block her and her crew from continuing on down the street. May knew from the moment when the car pulled up in front of the house and when her daughter exited the passenger's side that Falcon was their meal ticket out the hood.

Falcon's real father, Patrick, even popped up when he heard his daughter, that he's never given May more than fifty dollars total out of her fifteen years of raising their baby girl alone, was fucking a Platinum. Osiris changed her life around.

Falcon dropped out of school, married him three months later when she turned sixteen, being that her mother willingly handed her over, and all she knew from then was money. You take a girl whose eyes lit up when her mother gave her a dollar to go down to the candy store, and slap a stack of Benjamins in her face, she'd too submit to a nigga who was ten years older than her.

Shit, Osiris was that nigga. Him and his crew ran St. Louis. With that came a lot of heat, fist fights, and jealousy. Hoes in the Lou, whether they were old hoes or young hoes, stayed hating. Every girl wanted to be Falcon, and every nigga wished they made a quarter of what her man had raking in.

As long as she sucked his dick the way he liked it and fucked him whenever he wanted it without the attitude, he blessed her with whatever she fixed her lips to ask for. Things changed for the better when she married Si. It wasn't always peaches and cream, but she knew he loved her and she loved him.

Her uncle Harry wasn't shit but a drunk ass wino who was always asking for a damn Stag every time one of them had walked pass his door, so he showed her nothing about how a man was supposed to treat a woman in the absence of her father.

Her male cousins were all hoes too, so she was really misled by the true infrastructure of a man. Osiris took care of her, he loved her, protected her; he and his father. Her mother and aunts had convinced her at an early age that niggas weren't shit and wasn't worth a pretty bitch's time unless he had some money.

Well, Osiris was all that in a bag of chips and some. But as he got older, the high of being a kingpin got to his head, and he became more controlling as the years passed by. It's like he was afraid to lose their fortune and the static the Platinum name made, and he was stopping at nothing even at age fifty-five to make sure he held onto his dynasty.

Falcon dried her tears when the nurse raised Nabawi's head up further to a perfect 90-degree angle. He looked so weak. His long grey hair hung down his chest that heaved up and down heavily while he tried to breathe through the nasal canula as best as he could.

"You okay?" Her voice was soft as she placed her hand atop of his.

Nabawi nodded his head up and down, let out a few coughs, then finally spoke.

"I'm-alright. It's just-happening-a lot-faster-than-I could-ever imagine. . ." It took all of him to get his sentence out. "Baby," *gasp* "listen," *gasp*. I won't be alive-much longer,"

"Papa Nabawi."

"Falcon."

He may have been dying, but he still had that Platinum blood running through his veins. His tone silenced her; allowing him to continue.

"I need-to talk-to Seth. Immediately."

Her eyes widened in fear. If Osiris found out she'd spoken to him, he'd kill her without even thinking twice about it.

"I know-that's a lot-to ask of you, but it has to be done. Call Keanu and have her reach out to him. I know he's been communicating with her. The spirits have told me."

"Nabawi—"

"Do it. I know what your husband has said, and I know how my son moves. I raised him. Look at me!" He threw his hands up and shook his head in disgust. "A Platinum in a fucking nursing home? Osiris is possessed right now, and I need to speak with my grandson before-it's too late. Listen to me Falcon," He grabbed her by the arm with a nice grip. "That Jediah. . . he's got hate in his eyes."

"Noooo," she cried shaking her head, not wanting to believe what she knew was true.

"Falcon. Don't play games with me. You know me, and I know you. Very well. You've been my little princess since you were fifteen. I know your heart, sweetheart. Please do this for me. My time has come. I swore I'd outlive Meme Aruba, but that old bird's got me beat."

She lit up like a precious angel to see her father-in-law smile. He and Keanu haven't spoken in over twenty years. Once she found out that Nabawi had allowed Osiris to kill his younger brother, Titus, out of spite, hate, and greed, she never spoke to her son again.

Keanu had her ways with Osiris too. She only spoke to him because she loved the hell out of her great grand-children and Falcon, but she couldn't stand his ass either for daring to do such a deed. Who would betray their family by the base of a bullet?

"Please Falcon, please. Get my grandson out here to me. As fast as you can. You see my condition. I'm days away from heaven, so please. Send him to me."

Her lips quivered as he wiped her tears away. She nodded her head in agreement before he pulled her close and kissed her forehead.

"Aloha wau io 'oe. You hear me, maika'i?"

A cry managed to escape her lips before saying, "I love you too, Papa Nabawi. I'll call her as soon as I leave."

"Go. Now. We don't have much time."

She looked him in the eye and gave him one last smile before she kissed his forehead.

"I'll be back. Okay?"

"I'll be here."

Falcon shielded her eyes with the Chanel bubble frame shades and exited the room. Her heels click clacked against the wooden floors until she made it to the elevator and took it to the 4th floor. She'd never been so nervous before.

Like a long-haired stallion, Falcon moved swiftly knowing she only had five minutes to spare before their henchmen would come inside looking for her. She closed the door behind her and removed the shades once the six-foot man dressed in Brooks Brothers classic threads turned around.

"What the fuck are you doing here? Are you trying to get me killed? I said to meet me out in Wentzville. Do you know what the fuck you are doing by being here right now? It's Platinum men all over this fucking building," she spat, her voice barely above a whisper.

The man smiled as his eyes scanned the beautiful woman standing before him. Falcon was aging gracefully; still as beautiful as she was the day he laid eyes on her when she was twenty-two. At forty-six she was still gorgeous favoring Taraji P Henson.

"That means an old man still got it, huh? *You* arranged this meeting, sweetheart. Not I."

"Watch it," she threatened.

"Why am I here, Falcon? Why are you risking your life as well as your families to speak to me?" Kamikaze chuckled at her stupidity.

Bravery, but very stupid on her part. She loved playing with fire.

"Look. I'm going to keep this short. I've never asked you for anything—"

"So, what do you need now that I had to fly all the way out to St. Louis? You know this isn't my territory, and my life is just as much at risk as yours is for being here."

"This beef, Kamikaze? End it. Now."

He chuckled once more as he ran his hand down his salt and pepper beard.

"I'm afraid that can't happen, love. Anything else?"

One of her eyes 'bout popped out of her head.

"Bryan, listen to me. I understand that the Platinums and the Kamikazes have been at war for decades, but things have changed now. This shit is different than some back in the day beef. There are no boundaries in 2016."

"So talk to your husband."

"Muthafucka I'm talking to you!" She spat, ready to spazz out.

"I think you take advantage of the fact that I have a soft spot for you, Falcon. Don't insult my intelligence like that. I would've made this shit shake a long time ago if I didn't have respect for you, but you and I both know that this beef will never end until one cartel comes out on top."

"Look," her lips quivered as tears raced to the surface of her eyes. "I'm already on edge about the shit you pulled with Akil. I'm dying inside Kamikaze. Dying. I could kill you myself for that bullshit! So help me God you call this fucking war off for the sake of me not losing any more of my family over something so fucking petty or else—"

"Or else what?"

She gave him the most evil glare.

"At this point, a link with the Platinum dynasty is what you need, and you know that. You think Si isn't going to come after you for the shit you pulled with Cuba and cutting off his supply for a year?"

He laughed out loud, quite boisterous.

"That's how you hit a target. I've let go of that eye for an eye bullshit a long time ago, Falcon. Even though I'm still convinced that you all murdered Juno, I had to bring him down to his knees a little more crucial. I'll never stop the hunt for your husband. He's taken more from me than you could ever imagine, and in due time, he'll reap what he's sewn.

"Mark my words, but most importantly, why would I kill my own son? Huh? The difference between Osiris and I had always been simple. I'll never be a vulture to my own kind, and that's where you fucked up at when you declined my proposal in '93. You really think I'd sacrifice my own son even at the cost of my other one?"

Tears trickled down her face. Just staring at King Bryan Kamikaze brought her pain: he had the same brown eyes as her son, the same nose as her son, and with his appearance displayed the same secret that they've both kept for twenty-three long and trying years. It made her want to drive a knife through her own heart in this moment.

"You think about that, *Mrs. Platinum.* You're not the only person in this room who's lost something or someone. Yet you fix your lips to ask me about peace?" He spat with grueling anger. "At this point, the little common ground where that white flag has been waiving is officially destroyed.

"It went to the grave after whomever killed my son. You too will go down along with your husband, and I'm gonna make sure of it. You've taken enough away from me, but my pride and my cartel you will not. So tell your husband to bring it. Because this will not end pretty and, Falcon, that's a promise. . ."

Chapter Nineteen

Stress was a sickness to the body that could kill if you allowed it to, and that shit was winning the battle against Seth at this moment. Atlanta with his woman, his potna, and Riley was cool. It was relaxing, they ate some great food, did some great shopping, and made it back before Nas had to be at work the next morning.

That was a week ago, yet his head was still filled with anxiety, anger, sadness, and discombobulation. It's been over a month since he's talked to his mother, and the shit was eating him up inside.

Falcon was his queen. Every day he looked down at the falcon tattoo on his hand then her beautiful face along his forearm, and the shit turned his world black. He'd die for that woman. She was his heart.

Whenever his head got big, or if he got to tripping, Falcon knocked him back down to size, rearranged some shit in that brain of his, and Seth was good. He understood that she owed Osiris nothing but respect and an undeniable loyalty because that was her husband, but the way she did him, the way they both did him was vile, and it cut him deep.

Seth laid in Nasir's bed, balls out, the sheet barely covering his sack where one hand rested while the other held the Backwoods up to his lips. Nas had been trying to get him to talk to her about whatever it was that's been bothering him all week so he could attempt to clear his mind, but he just wasn't going for it.

He didn't wanna talk. Right now, he just didn't have the words, and all he could do was speak with his dick and release some pressure via smokes, alcohol, and a little lean here and there.

Sadly, the shit was running Nasir ragged. Disconnection was one of the worse feelings that she'd ever felt, and she wasn't happy with Seth being an asshole, extra mean, and all stand-off-ish just because he didn't wanna be an adult and communicate like normal people did when something was on their mind.

Nas was trying to avoid having the conversation that she'd been batting with herself about, in her head, for the last week now, but it was getting to the point where she could no longer withstand it.

Just let him finish his blunt, Nas, then say something. Maybe he'll actually listen to you once the weed really hits him, she hopefully thought with her own weed up to her lips as she stared at herself in the bathroom mirror. . .

"Hello?"

"Aloha, baby."

Seth smiled at the sound of Keanu's voice.

"Wassup, Meme Aruba. How you doing?"

"I'm okay, baby. You busy?"

"You know I always got a minute or two to spare for my favorite girl."

His comment made her laugh.

"Well good. I was calling because I wanted to talk to you about a few things."

"What's cracking?"

"Well. . . your mother called me."

It was quiet for a moment. A long moment. The sullenness made Keanu uneasy, so she cleared her throat to see if he was still with her.

"What that got to do with me?"

"Now Seth—"

"Keanu."

"Boy, you better watch your damn tone with me. I know that."

Seth sighed heavily. He knew he couldn't get that headstrong shit off with his OG; she'd put a round in his dome quicker than he could draw his shit from the waistline.

"Now, like I was trying to say. She called me, and she told me about your grandfather. I didn't know Nabawi was in an old folk's home?"

"What?" He raised his eyebrow with a smug ass look on his face. That shit she just broke him off with was disrespectful.

"So, this is news to you too? Your father put him out the house, took control over all of his assets, then threw him in a home because he's on hospice. He was tired of the traffic in the palace."

"Nabawi ain't dying, Keanu."

"He is baby."

The silence consumed them again.

"Did *you* talk to him?" He boldly asked with a tone that he knew wasn't permissible. Seth could see her sucking her teeth the moment his statement left his mouth.

"You little shit. I did, actually."

"Damn," he uttered as he took another pull from the blunt.

"I know. It's been almost, twenty-three years since I've spoken to my son and. . . it felt good to hear his voice. I hate to hear about his kidneys failing him and such. It's horrible, and I honestly do pray that he passes gracefully.

"We talked for a while, catching up and things, and he wanted me to reach out to you and tell you to come see him. He wants to talk to you face to face. That's all he said. He said you should understand what that meant, and I didn't get into all of that."

Seth nodded his head. He knew exactly what that meant, and to be honest, he wasn't sure if he was up for it. Right now just wasn't the time. Maybe if this would've happened before the crossover then he'd be in his whip at that moment headed to go pay his respects, but he put the thought in the back of his mind for the time being and was gonna get back to that shit later.

"You need something, maika'l *precious*? You good?"

"You know? You can be so sweet when you want to. You should try it more often," she grinned, commenting on him calling her precious in their native language. "Someone's got your heart. I can feel it," she teased.

His instant laughter told her all she needed to hear.

"You do that woman right, you hear me? Your great grandfather was a mean ass just like you are; hell, all of you

Platinum men are vile until the right woman crosses your path, and you better do her right.

"That nastiness is doing nothing but rotting your soul young man. You're twenty-seven, and you still keep all of your emotions bottled inside like someone is going to judge you. And I know what you're thinking, *get out my damn head Keanu.* Well, I won't."

Seth smirked. He couldn't stand her either. She knew him inside and out.

"Keanu loves you baby; with all her heart and all her soul, and always remember: *Kahuna Nui Hale Kealohalani Makua.*"

"Love all you see, including yourself," he repeated as he looked at the identical tattoo that was located above the falcon symbol on his hand. "I love you too, Keanu. You gon' meet me in Hawaii soon?"

She smiled.

"Just let me know, and I sure will. I haven't been home in, oh my God almighty, over forty years."

"It's long overdue for us all. I'mma give you a call real soon, a'ight? We gon' make sum' shake."

"Alright baby. It's a date. And please go see your grandfather. Check on your Ohana. GG feels it in the air." He was silent again. "Seth Shakur Platinum."

"A'ight, G, a'ight. I gotchu'," he chuckled, slightly putting her at ease. She knew his stubborn ass wasn't gonna act on it right away.

"Aloha, baby."

"Aloha, maika'i."

Click.

If the man wasn't already stressed, then he surely was now. He pulled the lap tray from off the top of the nightstand and started to roll him up another blunt when Nas finally exited the shower.

The smell of Coconut Lime Shae Body butter filled the air. She had a peach towel wrapped around her frame and an identical hand towel wrapped around her wet hair.

He glanced at the large CATORI tattooed across the back of her neck then the bed of smoky pink and purple peonies that stretched from shoulder to shoulder beneath it. There was also a large spinal cord that ran down her spine ending on top of her butt.

Seth thought that was one of the dopest tats she had. Those three were the largest images that could be made out between all of the shading and millions of quotes she had in the background.

Nas had something on her mind. She couldn't keep still. She rearranged everything on her dresser just to go in her top drawers and refold the already folded camisoles and leggings to buy her some time. She was trying her best to refrain from putting her foot in her mouth, but Seth knew when she was troubled.

"I think we should stop having sex for right now," Nasir finally blurted, her poor heart going 100 miles per hour, knowing he was about to blow up.

"What?" He scrunched up his face once more.

Nas turned around and looked at him. She couldn't let her name necklace go as she stared Seth in the eye more nervous than a virgin who was about to have her cherry popped.

"I said, I think we should stop having sex," she repeated this time in a lower tone.

"What is you on, Nasir? I don't have time for yo mind games today."

Here we go, she rolled her eyes.

"It's not a game, Seth. I've been thinking about this for a week now."

"All because of some shit that I couldn't control?" he barked, referring to the mishap at the strip club.

"No," she innocently groaned.

He raised his eyebrow at her knowing she was lying.

"Okay, maybe yes, but that's not the root cause of it though. I just," She put her hands on her head. "I just think we're moving too fast, Seth, like everything is just blowing my mind. I'm digging us, we do shit that most bitches can only dream about happening, and our vibe comes so easily that's it's almost scary.

"I just wanna make sure that we like one another for who we are and not all of the sex we have. That shit is easily mistaken and—see, this is why I feel like I can't never talk to you without you getting a fucking attitude. Where are you going?"

Seth didn't have time for this shit right now. He slid into his black denim jeans, black t-shirt, and black shell toe Adidas with the white stripes before grabbing his keys.

"That's the shit I'm talking about right there, Seth."

"Nah, you talking some bullshit, Nasir, and I ain't in the mood for it."

"Leaving just proves my point. If you ain't getting no pussy, then you ain't fucking with me. Whenever you don't get your way you get to acting like a damn child."

"So, I'm not fucking with you! Am I not stepping outside of my character for you! Am I not wit yo ass damn near every day! Do I not do for you beyond the physical! If I ain't give a fuck about yo ass you'd know it! What kinda nigga just moves you into a crib and pull up in Range Rovers for the hell of that shit, Nasir!"

"You didn't have to do any of those things!"

"I ain't have to do a lot of shit, but I did because obviously a nigga cares, but you so stuck on some stupid shit that you don't even know what the fuck is really going on in yo damn head! Have we not had this conversation before? The one about this shit being new to both of us, but you fix yo lips to say some dumb ass shit like, 'Oh, you only fuck with me because of the sex?'"

He inhaled deeply feeling himself about to lose control.

"If that's what you wanna do, then do it, ma. Find you a nigga that's gon' follow yo guidelines because you too damn insecure to realize when a muthafucka fucks wit' you. I ain't got time for this shit."

"All I said was that we should stop having sex for a while. You're the one who blew the shit way out of proportion like I asked you something that was so fucking out of pocket. So, it's like that? You gon' leave and break up with me because of something as simple as no sex? Really Seth?"

"Ain't that what it look like?"

The door slammed shut behind him before she could let out another word to try and plead her case.

T

Power Trip was Seth's go-to track. It calmed him and eased his mind; plus, it was the perfect beat for a nice fat chocolate ass to dance around the pole to. He sat leaned back against the plush booth with a blunt to his lips.

The group of six chocolate mommas throwing nothing but ass and succulent titties before him had his mind blown. He was already faded, and the bottle of 1942 at his lips made him feel as if he were floating on a cloud while bitches kept making their asses go 'round.

Seth tried to shake his emotions off. He tried to chill. He even tried to talk himself into some head from one of these fine ass bitches, but his heart wouldn't let him. The longer J. Cole's lyrics kept blasting out the speakers, the more it started to piss him off.

It did nothing but remind him of Nas and how fucking haywire she had him. This song reminded him of the night he saw her at Shottas looking fine as hell with that mystique glare in her eyes that enchanted him.

The way it felt to hold onto her thighs and prop her up so he could be eye level with her; their bodies merged as one while their heads swayed back and forth. It's barely been two months and she had his head through the fucking roof.

The indecisiveness was killing the man. He'd never wanted a woman the way he wanted Nas. He was used to bitches hopping on his dick because he was him, and the attention they knew they'd eventually receive from him always made those hoes stay in line.

He'd never had to work so damn hard for a bitch. As long as Seth kept throwing stacks at Kelani, she played her position. She played it so well that her proven loyalty had eventually forced him to sit back and realize that she was worth putting a little more personal time and effort into.

Nas was a different fucking story. She wasn't taking no bullshit; she wanted a man but didn't need a man, and that shit made him twitch. She could have two dollars to her name and would rather hold onto her pride and be broke until payday before she would ever let a man make her feel like if it wasn't for him she wouldn't have shit.

Her mentality was on a level he wasn't used to seeing, being that he'd only fucked with hoes who he could stick his dick in. Seth wasn't looking for love. Seth wasn't tryna wife a bitch up, or none of that.

He saw something in Kelani because she was this cool ass lil' chick he could slide on whenever he wanted some, and she'd give it to him however he wanted it. He'd gotten himself jammed up in some bullshit a few years back, and to his surprise she was one of the only muthafuckas who really had his back outside of his potnas.

Kelani jumped for Seth in a way that had impressed him. She had put a patent on her loyalty to him. It showed good signs of her character and made the man take a chance on the relationship shit. He was still fucking random hoes though. She was just his main.

But tryna keep her smiling and satisfied, like, truly satisfied mentally, physically, emotionally, spiritually, and with her health? His relationship with Nas had certainly surpassed his ego and jumped to a different level.

Seth was eager to work out wit with her when she went to the gym, he was eager to know about her day, and he was eager to know if she had smiled before she heard his voice. Nasir made him sit up straight and fix his collar when he got around her, and the shit was sick as fuck.

Nasir intimidated him. Point. Blank. Period. He shrunk down to that teenaged boy with his first case of puppy love in her presence, and it grinded his gears. Seth didn't even know that he could still channel those emotions, and the longer he thought about it the more it pissed him off.

With his bottle in hand he exited the private section and headed for the door. He needed some pussy. Some pussy he could slam in. Some pussy he could do some major damage to and have to make an insurance claim afterwards for sure. Like real shit.

Seth shook his head as he knocked on the door. He'd regret this night once sunrise hit but right now, Don Julio was wearing that black hood telling him to take that chance. He was single.

Kelani opened the door in nothing but a cami and a g-string with a toothbrush up to her mouth.

Seth lifted her off the ground by her thighs and wrapped her legs around his waist as he entered her house. Kelani's body shook like an earthquake had hit. She was so thrown off by his actions that it frightened her to the point where she wasn't sure if she should be smiling from ear to ear that he was there, or if she should be trying to run for cover.

He laid her down on the bed and unbuckled his jeans. Seth didn't even take his shirt or shoes off. He hadn't carried condoms in weeks since he'd only been sliding up in Nasir raw, but a G always came prepared.

Seth went into the empty wallet that carried one XL Magnum and nothing else for that sole purpose. He rolled that bitch on and flipped her over to mount her ass up.

Seth put his knees on the bed and positioned himself before he inserted her. Her body started jerking immediately. That nigga had a pussy tingling deep stroke, and when he hit it harder it filled a woman's walls in a way where she couldn't do anything but lay there and let him smash up.

He pulled her head back and held her with a mighty grip with his hand locked in her hair, while her ass clapped against him. At first, Kelani was into it, but as the seconds kept going by she started to feel uncomfortable. Seth was slamming her shit.

He was relieving every ounce of pressure that had been troubling him, and she couldn't take it. Her pelvis started to ache, her cervix was begging for mercy, and she thought her heart would explode the longer he kept going.

"Seth, please. . ." she whined, begging him to stop, but he gripped her harder and kept stroking.

He then eased up a bit and let a smirk cover his face when he saw the shadow climb in the bed. All he saw was another set of ass and titties, then thought to himself, damn fucking right. He was gon' blow both their backs out tonight.

The large curly red wig was covering the obscure woman's face, so he couldn't get a good look at her, but when he saw her kneel in front of Kelani and his ex started eating her pussy while she took the dick, he knew this shit was about to be clutch.

"You wanna come get some of this good dick, Alicia, baby? Hmmm? Taste my pussy on his dick. Aaaaah! Let me sit on your face! Please!"

The shit sounded sexy to two of the three freaks in the bed, but Kelani couldn't take the shit a second longer. Thoughts of her child were driving her insane, and she was about to lose it.

Alicia. . . Seth said the name to himself a few more times before he hopped up and cut the lights on.

His dick fell limp instantly when he saw that bitch's face. Alicia tried to run when she locked eyes with the rage brewing within his pupils, but his hand was already around her neck before she could move an inch.

"What kinda shit is you on bitch!"

He reached back and smacked the shit out of her. Thoughts of Nas being jumped at the club infested his mind, and he couldn't let that shit go. He grabbed Kelani by the throat after he threw Alicia into the headboard. Seth was like a tornado.

"Seth, please stop! I'm pregnant!" She screamed with her hand around his wrist while he held her body in a choke hold.

"Bitch, what!"

Seth threw her onto the bed as well as he placed his hands on his head. This was too much for him. He knew he shouldn't have come, but that shit from earlier had him so fucked up nothing he was thinking, saying, or doing was making sense right now.

"Bitch get up!" he yelled as he grabbed Kelani by the elbow.

"Where are you taking me!" She yelled as he damn-near drug her to the front door. Her feet were dangling.

"To get a fucking paternity test, bitch! I ain't got time to be playing wit' yo ass and no fucking baby! So shut the fuck up and get yo ass outside, or how bout we settle this shit right now!"

He snatched her up to a standing position and pressed the barrel of his gun into her stomach.

"It's not your baby! I swear it! I swear to God I'm pregnant by Jediah! It's not yours! I'm twelve weeks in, just please put the gun down, Seth, please! I'm sorry!"

He shoved her into the wall and snatched her head back by the hair so he could look her in the eye.

"Look at me, bitch!" His voice was so loud she was sure the neighbors could hear him. "What the fuck did you just say to me! You been fucking Jediah after all this fucking time!"

"Let her go!" Alicia yelled as she ran towards him.

Seth snatched her up by the neck so fucking fast she was seeing stars. He brought her down to her knees while clinching harder until she hit the floor completely. When his eyes reverted back to Kelani, she had fear oozing from her pores.

"I'm sorry Seth! It just happened! You weren't giving me what I wanted, and when you got locked up—"

Her head jerked to the left once he back handed her. He let her body hit the floor and slammed the door shut behind him. This shit wasn't real.

His foot plunged the gas on the 2017 Hell Cat Challenger, sending him floating down I-70. The chains blocking the River Front once he approached his destination made him illegally park the car and hop out.

Seth's roars filled the air as he held onto his head. Keeping shit bottled up was clearly an understatement for him. He'd been quiet for years. For years, he'd harbored everything and considering the recent shit that was piled on top of him, he could no longer take it.

Seth leaned up against the hood of the car and doubled over on his knees while taking deep breaths. His heart wanted to bleed dry of everything he was hiding but his mind wouldn't let him. Everything was just too much for a playa right now, and he didn't know what the fuck to do at this point.

𝒯

Tiri was gonna break her neck. Messiah stood off in the cut hiding behind the staircase trying his hardest to hold his laugher in as she tip-toed in the 5-inch sandals from Akira in West County Mall.

She was supposed to be out shopping for new clothes and shoes for school, but hell, when your brother gives you his black card, how could you not swipe it whenever you saw even the slightest thing that caught your eye?

"I just don't see how bitches do this shit. Aaaah!"

Tiri's ankle buckled and she fell head first into the couch.

"Messiah! What are you doing down here!" She panicked as she struggled to stand herself up when she heard his laughter.

"You not this mu'fucking funny, Tiri. What the fuck is you doing?"

She punched him so hard in his chest her feet buckled again, and she fell in his arms.

"Stop laughing at me! You so damn ignorant. I gotta learn how to be a woman someday! Every girl at homecoming gon' be wearing them stripper ass heels, and I'm not finna embarrass myself by tripping ooooooooveeeeer—"

He held her body steady when she felt her knees about to give out on her again.

"Baby girl. Baby girl. First of all, I'mma just let yo ass fall again if you don't sit down and take them damn shoes off. You gon' be at homecoming in a neckbrace and a cast at the rate you going."

"Shut up, dick slinger. You wouldn't know nothing about this," she pouted as she plopped down on the couch.

Tiri couldn't help it that she was seventeen-years-old and just started taking an interest in wearing heels. She was a tomboy for years until she realized that niggas only saw her as the cool chick, and no one wanted her to be their girl, so she had to step her game up.

Messiah sat next to her bashing a 20-piece lemon pepper combo from Wingstop before he broke things down for his baby sister.

"For one, the heel is too high. Two, it's too thin, and three, how the fuck you think you was gon' be able to sashay yo' lil uglass around here in some shoes you ain't even broke in yet?"

"Huh?" She looked at him confused.

"But I don't know what I'm talking about though?" He joked he as looked her in the eye. "I know you growing up and shit, Tiri. A nigga still can't believe you seventeen now. I still drive you everywhere man, but you gotta be smart, bae.

"Get you something you can work with first; something shorter and a thicker heel so you can learn how to shift ya body weight."

"How do you know? You wear heels when ain't nobody looking?"

"Yoooooo," he pulled his gun out. "Disrespect me again."

Tiri mushed him in the head before she stole one of his wings.

"What I tell you about that mouth?" he questioned while licking his fingers.

"Nigga, you my brother. I get a pass with you."

"That's that bullshit, Tiri," he chuckled while dunking a handful of fries into the large cheese cup.

"I just wanna be pretty at homecoming, Messiah," She pouted. "I'm tired of being the tomboy."

"You gon' kill that shit at homecoming, bae. I don't like all that low self-esteem shit you be talking. That shit pisses me off for real, for real. Mu'fuckas up at school fucking wit' you or something again?"

She eyed the big ass gun sitting on his lap knowing he'd use it on anybody.

"No. It's just how I feel. I'm tired of being the girl in sweats."

How could Messiah not go soft from always falling in the trap of her cute little puppy dog face when she was feeling down for the last few years? She was turning him into a sap, man.

"Well you shouldn't feel like that, bae," he lifted her chin.

Tiri really was a beautiful girl. Her chocolate skin, slim frame, and bright smile reminded anyone who crossed her of Justine Skye.

"You thought Mina was pretty right?"

"Hell yeah! Momma was beautiful! She went in a room and she lit that bitch up. I wanna be like her," she smiled, torn.

Tiri had such an innocent soul. She was truly a teenager at heart; not one of these hot ass lil' girls running around these days, and he loved that about her.

"You look just like Mina, Tiri. Real shit."

"No I don't."

Messiah pushed her into the couch, literally bodying her ass, causing the poor girl to roll onto the floor.

"Messiah!" She giggled.

"Shut the fuck up then, man. What big bro gotta do to make you feel better about yo' self? And don't sit here and tell me shit about no makeup and bundles and shit, like that's really gon' solve the problem."

"Them the kinda girls you always running up under," she rolled her neck in defense.

"I was just fucking them bitches, Tiri. You just wanna be fucked, and then a nigga forget about you until his dick get hard again?"

"Man, hell nah!"

"You been listening to that "Nann Nigga" shit with Trudy, ain't you? Sounding like Trina and shit."

She laughed.

"That's my song, but no I don't want to be treated like that."

"Then don't view the bitches you've seen me fucking as what *you* should appear to be. Which brings me to this. I wanna introduce you to somebody. I know you read vibes real good. I can admit it, I value yo opinion and shit."

"Who?!" She shrieked, raising her brow and flaring her nostrils too surprised.

Messiah smiled at her. Their mother used to make that face at least three times a day because George was a silly ass nigga and he always tormented her like Messiah did Tiri.

"Damn, baby sus, why you eyeing me like that?"

"Because I've never *actually* met a girl you were dealing with. I don't wanna meet no hoes."

"Aye, shut the fuck up, man." He threw his free arm around her neck. "Yo bro ain't like that. I ain't gon' introduce you to nobody who ain't worth it."

"So, what's her name?"

"Riley."

"I like unisex names. That's cute. Is she cute? Well," she slapped her forehead. "Duh! You always fucking with bad bitches. If you thought Ms. V was pretty, then I know you solid on how you choose your women."

He laughed thinking about the day him and Seth scared the shit out of Nas.

"She yo teacher's cousin."

"Really?! I'm so glad Seth ended up being nice to her. He got her so geeked, she's even dancing with her eyes open more now. I love Ms. V."

"She loves you too, and if you love her, then I'm sure you'll fuck with Riley."

"Do *you* fuck with her? I mean like, the long way?"

He stood up.

"I'm trying, mama. You know me and relationships ain't the perfect bond but... Come on. Meet her for ya' self."

"She's here?"

"Here you go with them dumb ass questions again," he chuckled as he climbed the stairs.

"Messiah wait— ahhh!" She tripped over her feet again, forgetting she still had the heels on.

"I told yo' goofy ass to take them damn shoes off! Now look at you! Feeling stupid!"

She threw one at his feet right before he made it out the door.

"Aye, square up Tiri! Right now!"

Tiri laughed as she climbed the steps. Her heart was racing, but she didn't know why. It's like she felt her brother's nervousness in her own chest. This was surely unlike him. He hated when she saw the bitches he had running in and out the house.

His greatest fear was for a nigga to take advantage of her the way he did hoes, but once Tiri really thought about it, she hadn't seen any women going in and out of their crib lately. Either he was being real slick, or he was really into this girl.

"Messiah, gone! These mines. I told you not to eat all yo food on the ride home. Now yo hungry ass mooching in our shit. And get out her food!"

Riley jumped at him as he stole a wing from out of both of their boxes.

"Damn, I should've just got us the hunnid piece."

He shook his head with a full mouth.

"I got something you can eat if you still hungry, my nigga," Riley joked as she twisted the cap on the apple juice she had in hand.

"You gon' sprinkle some lemon pepper on that shit so I can bash?"

Messiah stood behind her pulling her butt into his intersection.

"Nigga, that sound like it's gon' burn. Get yo goofy ass on somewhere. Shut the fuck up."

He coughed from laughing at her reaction with food going down his throat.

"Damn, ma, you tryna kill me?"

He coughed again before taking a gulp from her juice.

"Ugh! What I'mma do wit' you man. Get yo own!" She giggled as she snatched it from him.

"Hi."

Messiah and Riley turned around when they saw Tiri standing in the doorway of the basement.

Wow! She is pretty! Tiri thought in amazement.

Riley was tatted from underneath her chin to her toes, and Tiri liked how she was chill in some Nike shorts and a matching Tee with some slides on instead of the thirsty shit them other bitches wore when they got around Messiah. Tiri figured it out a long time ago that her brother must've had that dope dick the way bitches broke their necks to have even just a second with him.

Seeing Riley made her soften up about this meet and greet. Tiri was head over hills about her brother and she hated seeing him with hoes when she knew he could do better. Riley had that tomboy look, but she was sexy with it, and that really did something for Tiri.

"Mama, this my lil' bae, Tiri. Sus, this Riley."

"Hey, nice to meet you," Tiri smiled.

"You too. You are so pretty!" Riley beamed.

The girl turned red in the face. *Did Messiah tell her to say that?*

"Don't be shy. You really are. Own that shit, baby girl. Messiah!"

"A'ight. A'ight. I'm done," he laughed with a full mouth.

He'd just cleft two more wings from her.

Tiri laughed. Riley sounded just like her.

"Handle my light weight, sus."

"No can do. If you stop eating everybody's food, then you wouldn't get yo ass whooped. Man, Messiah, this don't look like a ten piece to me! Why you always eating all my stuff!" She spazzed as she looked in her box.

"A'ight, what? Y'all want me to go get some more?" He laughed.

"Well you ate everything, so I guess so. Matter fact, I'll go. Won't be shit left when you get back."

"I ain't even eat that much, man."

He threw his arms around Riley's waist and held her close.

"Don't be tryna butter up to me, nigga."

Messiah kissed her lips. They were in their own little world, and Tiri couldn't help but to stand back and watch. They were so cute, and her brother looked happy.

She didn't know how long they had been messing around, but she'd never seen him this way. He picked Riley up and wrapped her legs around his waist while she hugged him around the neck.

"Tiri, you should ride with Riley. I'mma go make a move right quick."

He'd almost forgotten about going to do his rounds and making collections from the safe houses in the three counties near him. Riley's had his head through the roof ever since the day he met her.

"I should make it back when y'all do. Don't be shy and shit, bae. I want y'all to get to know each other. Maybe she can help yo' clumsy ass learn how to walk in them damn heels."

"Messiah!" Tiri gasped embarrassed while holding her hands in her face.

"You gotta mouth on you. You so embarrassing, dawg." Riley pushed him in the head before she hopped down.

"Awww, bae, you know I be playing. Don't be like that."

He wrapped his arms around Tiri. She'd always been shy, even when she was a little girl. She couldn't help it.

"Get off me, Messiah," Tiri pouted.

"Aye, chin up, bae." He kissed her forehead. That always made her smile. "Spoiled ass. I be right back, a'ight?" He tossed Riley the keys to his car before heading out.

Riley's eyes bucked when she opened the garage and saw the black Continental GT Bentley.

"Yeah, bro likes you. He wouldn't even let our cousin Trudy drive this, and they go back to matching 90's outfits in baby pics," Tiri giggled as she climbed inside…

"So you dance at Eloquent? Messiah says you're pretty dope. I'm looking forward to y'all's Fall performance. Nas is really hype about it too."

"Who, Ms. V?" She questioned.

"That's right. You only know her by her last name."

"Nas. That's so cute. Y'all both got those unisex names. That's so attractive to me. Don't get me wrong I don't like girls or nothing, I just think it's cute when they have boy names."

Riley laughed.

"I getcha', lil' momma. I overheard y'all arguing about some heels down there," she referred to the two joking around in the basement.

"Oh no!" Tiri pulled her Polo cap down low over her eyes, embarrassed.

"I didn't start walking in heels until I was like twenty-four and I'm twenty-seven, so don't feel bad at all. That girl who was stumbling at all the formal events because she wanted to be cute but didn't know how to walk in heels was definitely me. You preaching to the choir."

"It's soooo hard! I've tried and tried," Tiri whined.

"It's nothing but practice. You won't get good at it unless you constantly do it. Plus, you have to find a heel that suits you too. I'm just now getting into stilettos. I'm more of a platform kinda girl."

"The ones with the chunkier toes, right?"

"Yeah. Once you master those then a thinner heel will come easier. What are you wearing?"

"OMG, I finally found the perfect dress from that guy Shane Justin off of Instagram. Messiah told me not to order it until he saw it though. I swear he wants me to look like a damn granny or something."

Riley was cracking up.

"Big brothers. They be on bullshit. I'm the only child, but Nas' big brother was like that with us when we were growing up. He wouldn't let us do shit."

"I know right? I mean I know he means well, but it's a tad bit annoying. I'm finally coming out of my shell, and the nigga just won't let me be great. I love sweats though. They are my life. Sweats and athletic gear."

Tiri couldn't believe how well their conversation was flowing. She was comfortable with her hair blowing in the wind while some Lil' Baby played low in the background.

"Who you telling? It's okay to be laid back." Riley agreed.

"I see. I always thought bro liked those stuck-up bitches. The ones who just gotta have the latest MCM bag or only wear Victoria's Secret, like, ugh. They irk. I mean material stuff is cool because I'll be honest I love Gucci. He's got me on this Gucci thing right now, but I'll throw on a white V-neck and some jeans before anything."

"And if you wanna feel girly, throw on some wedges or some cute heels, a nice shade of lipstick, and you good. Some chicks can't swing the tomboy look and still be chic without looking like a stud. And you got it, Tiri. Once you own that, it's gon' come so much easier."

"You can make that out from this," she shrieked about the Puma kapri leggings and cami she was rocking.

"Yes. You're already pretty. Once yo mind is right and your confidence peaks, you'll see what the people around you see."

"I wish it was that easy."

"It's not. Shit, I'mma be honest. I used to be heavy and people used to be like Riley you so pretty for a big girl, but I didn't used to think so. So, I started loving myself and I lost the weight and now can't nobody tell me shit. I love who I am. This sexy, simple woman got Messiah all goofy in the head, don't she?"

Tiri laughed.

"I like you. You ain't gon' switch up are you? I don't mean to come at you like that, but I just know how it be. Bitches is fake."

"They are, but I'm me. I'm just a chill lil' chick, and Nas can vouch for me. I know you really like her."

"Well you must be because I do. She's so down to earth. I wish I was a senior right now. They spend the most time in dance class. They do all the dope shit."

"Your time is coming. It'll be here before you know it."

"Hey, umm, can we stop at this lil' boutique right on Parker Road while we wait on our food? I wanna see if they got some heels I can actually try to walk in," Tiri blushed.

"Bet. Just tell me where to go..."

Chapter Twenty

"*Hey*, Bookie!"

"Hey, ma."

Riley wrapped her arms around her mother's shoulders as they embraced. She was in town visiting from Fort Lauderdale where she lived with her new husband.

"You look good, Bookie baby. Look at you. You lost weight, and I gained it."

"Awwww, ma you're still beautiful. The soul doesn't change, and this weight looks good on you."

"Well I appreciate it. Where's your granny?"

"Not here yet. She's coming from a late lunch with Barbra out in West County."

"Barbra? She don't even like Barbra," Catrina griped.

"That's what I thought."

"Chile' I don't know. You know how your granny is. So how have you been? I haven't heard from you since you moved back to town."

Riley took a seat in the wooden rocking chair that sat next to the front door on her grandmother's porch.

"I know. My divorce is finalized. I've been Riley Stuart for... today marks two weeks now."

Her smile was heart-warming. The thought to let those words come out her mouth feared her but hearing the confidence in her voice made her feel calm. It gave her serenity.

"Did he take everything?"

"Every last thing. I have my car and that's it. But I've gained so much more though. You know I don't really care for St. Louis, but just linking back up with Nas, and being around the family, and having a clear and unconscious mind for the first time in years is so satisfying. I haven't been this chill in a long, long time."

"I feel it. Your vibe is different. There's a certain energy about you now that tells me that my daughter is back."

Riley laughed a little.

"Yeah, ma. I lost my damn marbles in Atlanta. I'll admit that. But I'm getting them back. Slowly yet surely. I have a place to stay, a job that pays better, and… I can't complain right now."

"Well, I'm glad to hear that you're doing good. I've been praying for your recovery and I'm so glad you are still standing. That shit is not easy."

"No, it isn't. How have you been, though? I'm sorry, ma, I've been promising to come visit you and Luther."

"Girl you know I'm not tripping off that. You are grown; you have a life too. But we're good. You know you were my only child, so all these babies running around is something I'mma have to get used to."

"Babies?" Riley gasped.

"His oldest son lives with us, and he has three kids. They're eleven, seven, and four."

"Wow! That's a lot for you. You like your peace."

"Okay? Where is your granny at? We're gonna miss the show. Is Nas coming?"

"Nah. She's at home chilling. She decided to sit this one out. She's not feeling too good."

"Well I hope she's ok. I surely wanted to see her. Here your granny comes down the street. We'll take my car. I don't wanna hear her mouth…"

Forty-five minutes later they were downtown at a new jazz club. Local bands put on shows singing 80's Motown and soul, and tonight was its grand performance to welcome the fall.

Riley: I didn't know Gold Horns was Platinum territory? I see the cartel symbol on the building. Mommy says hi too.

Nas: Really? I feel bad. I should've come. Tell auntie I said heeey! I hate that he gets in my head like this. ☹

Riley: It's okay boo. I understand. Mommy and granny driving me crazy though. Smh.

Nas: □□aw shit. Granny turning up ain't she! I'm coming! I'm about to hurry up and slide a dress on!

Riley: You won't make it. It'll be over by time you get here. You know you take forever to get dressed.

Nas: Huuuh! Now I'm mad. Call me when you're on the way back. I'll put the food on. Deep fried tacos tonight biiiiitch!

Riley: Omm boo. I gotcha.

"Ms. Stuart?"

Riley looked over her shoulder and recognized Barley, one of the guards that worked for Messiah.

"And company. Right this way."

People started eyeballing them when the guard opened the velvet rope and escorted the women to the front.

"Right through here, ma. You look beautiful tonight."

"Awww. Thanks, Barley. I appreciate it."

They embraced before they headed inside.

"And what the hell is going on!" Her grandmother, Wilma, squealed as she fanned herself with the Chinese hand fan.

Riley laughed as they were led to a table down on the lower level right in front of the stage where the VIP members were being checked in at. They each took a seat while the waiter poured them all a glass of Icewine Riesling by Inniskillin.

"You wanna say something now! This is a sixty-dollar bottle of wine, girl!" Catrina grilled while eyeballing her daughter.

"These my peoples," Riley joked. "No, really though. I've been chilling with a guy who owns a lot of property here."

"You dating already? Hell, you young. Just make sure he's not like ya last one." Her grandmother looked over her shoulder at the waiters shuffling back and forth with bottles of wine and food trays. "Oooooh, this place is nice. Fancy," she continued.

"You didn't tell me you were seeing someone," her mother teased

Riley's smile was so big she had to literally slap it off her face.

"We just cool, ma. It's nothing like that."

"Yeah, okay. 'Just cool' doesn't get you in VIP, but I'mma let you have that."

Riley was a bit nervous and she almost couldn't handle her anxiety. Her stomach was hitting flips. She didn't know if it was because Messiah was clouding her thoughts or what. She knew they were just enjoying each other's company, but she was really starting to feel him.

They talked every day. Even if it was just them exchanging quotes from movies via text tryna see who made who laugh the hardest, the communication was constant.

Plus, with him introducing her to his baby sister? That's what was really killing her. Riley knew that she was probably overthinking everything, but Messiah was doing shit that most niggas just didn't do.

Meeting someone's family was a big deal in her eyes; especially sweet little Tiri, knowing how close to his heart he held her. She was basically all he had left from his close family once his parents died, so the whole ordeal had Riley feeling some type of way.

How could the woman not catch feelings! From all of the nights they spent with each other, to the early morning breakfast runs, the exotic sex, and the fact that they had personal toothbrushes at each other's cribs, you'd think she was his bitch.

He's warned her that he's not really the relationship type, but his actions spoke a different language. Riley knew not to go off of those actions, but she's always been told that *actions* spoke louder than words. She was torn. No matter how much she tried to convince herself that she didn't want Messiah, she knew that she did.

He's just a distraction from the shit that's going on with Tevin, Ry. Don't let him get in your head.

She sipped on the wine as the trumpet players started getting down. Riley loved Jazz music. She'd be there until closing and would make Nas come and get her if her grandmother wanted to shake early. Good music, good food, good company, and some St. Louis entertainment was all she'd been missing. The Melvin

Turnage Band featuring Tonya Poynter was her favorite and she'd held her pee up until the curtain closed after their show.

"I'm gonna go to the ladies room!" She yelled in her mother's ear over the nonstop clapping.

When she stood up all eyes reverted to her. Riley was so beautiful. She was a t-shirt, jeans, and sweat pants kind of girl. She was just laid back, and it was her go-to style, but when she cleaned up she was Halle Berry fine.

The bronze colored one shoulder, long sleeved dress stopped right below her knees and had a long drape on the right side. Her hair was flat ironed straight, and she wore long gold dangly earrings to match the gold heels that strapped up her ankles in a criss-cross style. Her shoes alone had cost Messiah a thousand dollars. They were Giuseppe Zanotti, and she wore high fashion well.

She was passing the entrance when the door opened and in walked none other than Messiah clean as can be, with a bitch on his arm. When he recognized her he stopped immediately. The woman along with him slid her hand between his arm and held onto him, wondering what the problem was. Her eyes changed to Riley, and she instantly copped an attitude.

"You know her or something? Who the fuck is that!" She spat while throwing her neck like she was about to make something shake.

Messiah grabbed the woman by the elbow and pulled her close. The look in his eye changed her body language at the drop of a hat. Her eyes widened like a little child. The man didn't even have to say shit. She knew his every thought off GP and walked away before he handled her ass. When she was out of sight, Messiah turned his attention back to where he'd first saw Riley standing but she wasn't there. He caught a glimpse of her disappearing down the steps that led to the restrooms, so he followed after her.

When Messiah barged through the French-styled doors, Riley was standing at the sink applying a new coat of lipstick. He walked over to her and put his hands in his pockets. He honestly didn't know what to say. He'd never been in such a fucked up situation before.

Kema, the bitch who had gotten him out of jail a few months back and was upstairs with an attitude, was just the chick he slid on the most outside of Riley. They went out on a few dates here and there, but it was nothing serious. He knew she was feeling him, but he also knew that he would never take it there with her either.

It was crazy how Riley had showed up out of nowhere and had him doing shit that even he couldn't believe. He just couldn't leave her alone. She had bitches questioning him day and night about having a girl the way he fucked with her.

He'd even gotten pictures of screen shots from Riley's Snap Chat sent to his phone and that's how he knew the shit was getting out of control. It's not like he didn't want to be seen with her or that he didn't fuck with her. That wasn't the case at all. He just moved too sneaky for his own damn good, and that shit led to this moment right here.

"Riley," He finally spoke.

Her silence was irritating him.

"Messiah?"

She didn't even look at his ass. She ran the mascara along her lash extensions without breaking her concentration.

"Look at me," he ordered.

"For what? You don't owe me anything. You don't owe me any explanations, or none of that. We just cool. We just fucking. You don't owe me the introduction of every bitch that's gon' be on yo arm. I'm good. Have a nice evening. I just hope you ain't introducing all them bitches to yo sister too. She don't need to be around all that."

"Yo, don't fucking walk away from me, and who the fuck you think you talking to?"

He grabbed her by the arm and pulled her back so he could look at her.

"Let me go, Messiah. Now."

Fear swept over her instantly just like the day when she saw Tevin once she was released from jail. In that moment he'd realized the physical and mental scars that nigga had left on her heart. Before today Messiah never had to put her in her place; he'd never had to interact with her like this, but to see her fold as if he was the one who had brought her to this state of mind made him feel like shit.

He'd fucked up bad. Out of everything he could've chosen to do that night it had to be somewhere he'd just known that he wouldn't walk into Riley at. He released her and listened to her heels click clack against the floor until she'd disappeared to the top level.

Messiah ran his hands down his face. That's why he moved the way he did. That's why he didn't date. That's why all he did was smash because it was too much having to be considerate about a muthafucka who wasn't him, his dawg, or his family.

T

Seth glided the microfiber towel along the driver's window of his Maserati, moving his hand in small circular motions to make sure he didn't leave any streaks. His hair hung over his face as sweat dripped down his forehead from the beaming sun.

85-degrees in October was a bit torturous in the Lou due to its high humidity and the games mother liked to play in the Midwest, but his mind was so boggled that the heat didn't even faze him. There was a light breeze, so the winds against his bare chest shined a bit of reluctance on his current state of mind.

The sun rays reflected off the glossy black paint-job on the body of his vehicle after the wax he'd applied dried, and he was impressed with his work. Normally, he'd pay the shop he owned to get his shit right but when his mind was blown, pertinent things like this calmed him, and he did a better job him damn self if he were to be honest.

"Fuck, where this streak come from?" He mumbled once he noticed the uneven layer of wax that was close to the back bumper.

That was nothing some detail spray couldn't fix though. He was buffing out the mark to make the finished job look even when a black Escalade pulled inside the parking lot where he was located, outside of an abandoned warehouse.

Seth kept minding his business; his brain was focused on making sure his job was done to perfection as the henchmen dragged the brutally beaten body of a fallen soldier in the dirt.

"Some niggas just don't understand what the fuck a crossover means," he chuckled, his eyes still fixated on his car.

When he was able to clearly see his reflection in the sun, he stood tall and used the rubber band he had around his wrist to pull his hair up high on his head and get it off his back. Seth then pulled the grey Gucci track sweats he was sporting up along his waist before he reached for the pliers lying on the ground next to his equipment and walked over to the body. He chuckled before he squatted down, now towering over the man's face.

"You not in good shape my nigga."

He was amused at the blood all over the man's clothing from his beating.

"I-Aaaaaaaah!"

Seth used the pliers to fish for his front tooth and he hit gold. The man's screams filled the air again as he squeezed his face tight to hold him still while he fished for the other. This tooth took a little bit more oomph from him, so when he pulled it out, blood splattered all over him.

"One mo', nigga? I was thinking so too."

Seth bit his bottom lip as he went in further and pulled one of his larger teeth from out the back.

"Aaaaaaaaah!!!!!"

The man's screams were music to Seth's ears. Disloyalty got you nothing but brutal resentment in return. He hated when niggas ran their mouths like some little bitty bitches. So that's how he had to treat them.

"Fuck all them screams and shit, nigga. When you made the decision to cross over and honor me, you also made the decision to leave that old shit behind you. So, communicating with men on Platinum territory that doesn't belong to me and Siah was something you should've taken more heed to.

"You should've kept yo' bitch ass with them, so now, I got more shit to clean up because you a snitching ass nigga. Snitches don't get stitches in my book, bitch," he used a metal clamp to pull his tongue out before he took the box cutter and removed it from his mouth in one swift motion. "They get kilt."

Blow!

The hollow pointed bullet from his Desert Eagle went through the man's temple and out the other before Seth stood to his feet and tossed the limp tongue on top of the corpse.

"Clean this shit up and send them niggas a message back since this the fucking game they wanna play with me. I'm feeling pretty tit for tat today," he instructed as he wiped his hands.

Rocking basketball shorts underneath ya bottoms was something all St. Louis men did. He removed the stained clothes and tossed them to the mob along with his sneakers for them to get rid of before he slid his slides on and rolled out.

Seth wasn't far from his crib that he hadn't been to since that night he and Nas chilled in the jacuzzi. Most of the time, he laid his head at his penthouse or at her crib, but for some strange reason it didn't feel right being there without her.

They shared his first night ever laying his head there together and it was like her presence was needed whenever he thought of going. But with them not speaking for a week now, he knew that wouldn't be happening any time soon.

The man showered then got himself dressed. He slid into a pair of black Prada straight leg slacks that stopped above his ankles and a dashiki ethnic print button down by Eric Dress.

Sometimes the simplest things caught Seth's eye; that's what made him stand out above a lot of men. He could dress down and make Champion look like Versace. Either you had it, or you didn't.

The Prada loafers with the no show socks, gold Cuban link wristlets on each arm, and his hair now lathered in coconut oil hanging down his back completed his look. Seth was a fine ass man and he knew it. He didn't have to be real flashy, but he definitely took pride in his appearance.

The melodies from that Musiq Soulchild "Halfcrazy" track playing in the background was killing him. If those lyrics didn't explain what Nasir was doing to him right now, then he didn't know what else did.

This shit was driving *him* half-crazy. One foot was out the door and the other was in. Maybe he was afraid of himself for possibly not being able to give her what she needed so that their relationship could continue to grow.

Maybe she was right, but maybe she was wrong. He wanted to get his dick wet just as much as he wanted to fuck *with* her. Her pussy was platinum! What the fuck did she expect when they'd been fucking raw since the day they've met?

The man was confused. Every time he found himself at the peak of some major transitions within his cartel, a woman popped up. But Nas just wasn't like them other bitches by all means.

Seth ran his hands down his face before he grabbed his car keys. He needed some clarity on if he was gonna close this door with Nas or not, and he was about to get that shit right now. So he hopped back in his coupe and headed out...

T

"Catori, your numbers for the day are through the fucking roof! Show these muthafucking white people you know how to finesse them out those coins, okay?"

Catori laughed at the young sales associate, Dayna. The green girls loved her. She was stylish, her aura was welcoming, and she stayed at the top of the sales charts.

"Okay? Somebody gotta do it. Are you ladies gonna be alright with that rush shipment coming in tonight? I don't mind coming back," she offered with her purse on her arm.

"We got it, miss lady. Enjoy some of this sunshine while it's still out— oh my Lord. It's Seth Platinum. His fine ass spends thousands on top of thousands of dollars every time he comes in here. Hey, Mr. Platinum!" Dayna waved her hand frantically as he headed over in their direction from the escalator.

This young man is handsome, Catori thought as he approached her.

"Mr. Platinum. How are you?"

Dayna slid in between them once he was in range.

"I came here to speak with, Ms. Rucker. Do you mind?" he countered with a condescending tone.

The look on her face was so perplexing that Catori couldn't hide her smirk. She saw why her daughter fell for his ass. He most definitely had swag.

"As you please."

Seth didn't lower his brow until the woman was out of his sight. He hated annoying ass bitches who broke their necks to get his attention. Thirsty asses.

"It's nice to finally meet you, Mr. Seth."

The raise of Catori's brow and her passive-aggressive tone made him chuckle.

Nasir get that shit from her, man.

"It's nice to meet you as well, Ms. Rucker. You have time for a drink?"

She smiled.

"I do. Where ever you choose is fine with me. Lead the way…"

𝑇

"Your Riesling, Ms. Rucker, and Mr. Platinum, your 1787."

"Appreciate it, man. Ms. Rucker, you want anything else? Entre? Appetizer? If so, order at your leisure."

Seth's demeanor reminded her so much of Jamie-O that he damn near had her hypnotized. She had to snap out of the charm from his boss mentality and the ability he had to sweep any woman off her feet, no matter what age she was, and focus. And no, Catori wasn't that kind of woman. Seth's presence was one you just could *not* get wrapped up into. That's all.

"I'd like to try your avocado rolls, actually," she informed the waiter.

"Of course. One of the most popular selections on our menu, ma'am. I'll have that for you momentarily. Anything for you, sir?"

"This is plenty."

"As you wish. I'll be back shortly."

When he walked away, Catori took a sip of her wine before jumping right into it. She was more eager for this conversation than he was.

"So, where do you see things going with you and my daughter?"

"Nasir is a piece of work," he immediately responded.

"She is. She's blunt, straight forward, and a bit indecisive at times, but for the most part, she knows what she wants and will not fold for anyone."

"The root of our every indifference," he chuckled.

"She's a lot like you. Isn't she? You see her, and strangely, even after just a few short months, you see a reflection of yourself in woman form."

Seth looked into her mother's eyes before he sipped his drink. She was dead ass on it, and she barely even knew the man.

"Look Seth, I know how this goes all too well. It was like this with me when I met her father. She's me all over again, except her head is on a lot better than mine was. I jumped right into things with Jamie-O, and yes, Nas has taken to you easily as well because the connection is obviously there.

"You care a lot about my daughter, Seth, and if you didn't, then we wouldn't be here. Nasir cares an awful lot about you too. I hear it in her voice, she stands up a little taller, she holds her head up higher, and that's the Nasir that I've been waiting on her to reunite with for a long time now.

"Nas is at the point of her life were she's finally discovered herself, and I'll give you your props. You complement her well; in a sense, you make her better. It's just that she's finally found that eternal peace she's been running from and she will not let anyone tear her down. She's been waiting on this.

"Nasir's just being cautious. She doesn't wanna play herself. Can you blame her? Out of the clear blue sky you walk into her life, and like that," she snapped her finger. "It changes drastically. Nas knows that she can lose you just as fast as she got you, so that big ass head of hers gets to working in overtime, and she can be a pill."

"She does have a big ass head, don't she?"

They shared a laugh.

"She needs a man in her life to make her smile, and I'm sure you do that a lot. Excuse me if I'm coming off strong, but I just know my daughter, Seth. No, her stubborn ass hasn't talked to me about anything. She respects you and y'all's relationship. But, she's my only daughter.

"I'm in tune with her heart, so I know when something is worrying her. I do appreciate you taking out the time to meet with me personally. It shows a lot about your character. And I can read bullshit from a mile away. You passed that test back at Neiman."

Seth chuckled as the waiter placed her dish in front of her.

"You want one?" She offered.

"Nah, I'm alright. I appreciate it though." He took another sip of his drink. "Tell me something, Ms. Rucker."

"Catori," she corrected.

"Tell me something, Catori. I'mma be honest right now, this situation with Nas is taking me through a loop. She just got me seeing things differently, acting differently—"

"Do you want to?"

"Excuse me?"

"I said do you want to be different? Not so much as lose yourself, but do you genuinely want to be the man that my daughter deserves?"

Her question hit him like a ton of bricks. It was a simple inquiry, but that was the million-dollar question that he'd had the toughest time matching the right answer to. That was the ultimate challenge.

"If I didn't want to be around your daughter, then I wouldn't be. Trust me, with all due respect, we wouldn't have made it this far."

"Then let things be."

It was quiet. Nas definitely got her personality from her mother. Catori had that same allure about herself that drew you in and made you want to pour your heart out like an open book. He couldn't wrap his head around how forthcoming he was with her mother; his woman had it honest.

"I learned from my first marriage, Seth, that a lot of times men put too much thought into the wrong things and not enough thought into the right things. I'm not saying turn into a sap ass nigga and recite poetry to my baby, but what I am saying is let your guard down, open up your heart, and take it there before you get to questioning yourself about walking away.

"Just because what you're enduring with Nas is different doesn't mean that it's a bad thing, or that it's toxic. And Nas has to learn that too. You're nothing like the trash ass men she's used to dealing with, thank the heavens, so you both have some walls to knock down if you two want to grow.

"She has to let go of the past and allow herself to trust you, and you have to give her the opportunity to show you that it isn't a mistake by listening to your heart. It's as simple as that. Sometimes we waste so much energy digging for clues and we're so strung out on finding enough evidence to support what's been right in our faces all along, that we fuck ourselves over and end up missing out on a good thing..."

T

Lil Baby's "My Dawg" blared throughout the speakers as Seth's whip flew down I-94. He bobbed his head up and down feeling the lyrics before he reached for the blunt Messiah had passed him. They both had shit on their minds.

Between Nas and the thoughts that were consuming Seth's head after wrapping with her mother, Messiah's lil' beef with Riley, and the ordeal with their cartel, they both had enough on their shoulders to make them crumble, but real niggas didn't get into that.

Seth had his lil' interventions, Messiah blew Kema's back out, with a condom of course; we don't need any more of those problems, and now they were back on their shit.

"Franklin county need to reup already," Messiah informed as he hung up the phone.

"Word?"

"On me. Check it."

Seth glanced over at his potna's phone looking at the $200,000 deposit they'd just received from a bank in New York.

"Bet that shit. King K say it's moving on the west coast like crazy too. I told them niggas not to fuck with us dawg." They chuckled as they slapped hands. "We gotta send another team down to Sycamore too now that I'm thinking about it." Seth then explained referring to the territory they owned.

It bordered the Desoto trade that was now Osiris' territory. That beef had occurred from the fallen soldier Seth had to make an example out of from earlier.

"I sent Tito and them down there for right now. They holding it down until the plane comes back with the mob from Vegas."

Messiah already had things taken care of. That's why they rocked so well together. An exchange of gunshots went down last night after that bitch ass nigga ran his mouth, and it left six of their soldiers murdered in cold blood. Osiris was tryna send him a warning, and now he had to clap back.

"Them muthafuckas must've gotten word about the shit with Berkeley. You know how long he been tryna make that shit shake? Why else would he try to come for me?" Seth shook his head.

"His ass should've listened to us from the fucking jump. O always tryna be scary when making a new move like we don't be knowing what the fuck we be talking about. He so comfortable with what he's been subjected to that he's been stagnant That's why our shit wasn't growing until the crossover happened, and now he on some stupid shit because he know he dun fucked up."

Seth nodded his head in agreement with his potna. He couldn't have said that shit any better himself.

"Fuck 'em," he hissed as he arrived at Haven Gardens where his grandfather was living at.

He then pulled up on the side of a large black Mercedes truck where a guard exited out the back and hopped into the driver's side of his car after he and Messiah exited. The car pulled off to circle around the block until they were finished with their visit while they entered the side dock.

Med resources usually did their drop-off's here, so the door was always open during the day. Sometimes Seth hated his name. He couldn't go anywhere without someone recognizing him, so he had to move swift and be as low-key as possible.

One thing Seth knew for a fact though was that Osiris wasn't going anywhere near a nursing home, and he also knew that he didn't have an army here with Nabawi either because he was cold like that.

Seth could've walked right through the front door if he wanted, but he was already hip about the secrecy that laid behind visiting Nabawi. That's why he had Keanu reach out to him instead of hitting him up directly. After he argued with himself for a few days, he finally chunked it up and made that move to go see him.

The situation had his blood boiling as he and Messiah headed down the halls. How could they not be noticed? CNA's were breaking their necks to see them. They stuck their heads out the doors, let go of mechanical lifts with patients halfway in the air, and had gloves on their hands when they all filled the halls to watch the two men head to the elevator like they were celebrities.

Seth's eyes burned when he entered the room and saw his grandfather hooked up to all kinds of tubes and shit. The one stemming from his stomach particularly had him seeing red.

"How long you been on a fucking feeding tube?" he spat as he gripped the Desert Eagle that was now hanging down by his side.

"For about a month now."

Nabawi's voice was low and rasp as he reached his hand out for his grandson. Seth couldn't handle this. That same pressure was coming back from the night he left Kelani's crib. His head was knocking, and his heart was working in overtime.

"Relax mo'opona **grandson**. Just relax."

Seth grabbed his hand, covered it with his other, and kneeled down before his grandfather. He inhaled deeply trying to calm himself. His hands trembled, and even though Nabawi was dying, the man still had a firm grip.

Nabawi held his grandson with one hand and Messiah, who was damn near blood as well, with the other. He too bowed his head while Nabawi let a native prayer escape his lips before they all got themselves together. Seth stood on his feet and crossed his hands underneath his arms never letting the gun go.

"Mahalo **thank you**, Seth, for coming to see me. I know we're living in trying times, and I know I won't be here much longer, but you two listen to me—Ummmmm!" Nabawi grunted loudly when a shock ran down his spine. Once the pain subsided he opened his eyes again. "You already know how fucked up your father is, and I'm already sure that you know that Jediah is behind all of this shit," he inhaled deeply.

"I need you two to go out to Sweden before I die. In Swedbank there is an account in your name, Seth. You've been a holder on my share since you were eighteen-years-old, and I figured now was the time to tell you.

"There's over four billion dollars inside, ownership to our land on all five of our islands in Hawaii, ownership papers to territories up north in St. Paul, and territory in Canada. Yeah, you didn't know I was rocking like that, huh? Now, you've got one more international spot to push ya supply in.

"As you can see I can't get out there myself due to my health reasons, and your father has been watching me closely. He knows nothing about this shit, but the moment I die it all will be at his grasp if you don't get a hold of my will before he does. I need you to get your hands on it before he takes anything else away from me.

"Away from this dynasty that he does not deserve. I'm sorry mo'opuna **grandson**. I know I haven't been the best, I know I've created that demon you call a father, and I know I shouldn't have made the decision with the first crossover and killed my other son.

"This shit is dangerous for the people who can't mentally handle it after a while. That's why I'm telling you to get yourself together, Seth. The fate of the Platinum family rests in your hands. You and Messiah. My boys. I trust y'all.

"I know y'all will run this shit right, and I don't give a fuck what you have to do to do it. Save this family from the wicked. Even if they are our own. At the rate Osiris is moving all that Akamu worked hard to build will vanish before you know it," he explained, referring to his dead father and Keanu's first husband.

"You already know it was Jediah who set you two up and got y'all arrested. I also wish that I had more information for you as far as the shit with Akil, but I don't. I do know this: your father is the one who had Juno killed when you two were headed down to MPD."

Seth looked over at Messiah. They had the same looks on their faces.

"He didn't want the link. His only mission was to lay low so he could get his money right and conquer the Kamikazes, and yes, mo'opuna *grandson*, he was willing to do it at your sacrifice. He knew you were up to something, and once he figured it out he shut it down. Here. Take this chain from around my neck."

Seth did as he was told to do. He'd never seen Nabawi without it. It was solid gold and had a key on the end of it.

"That key will get you in my vault in Sweden. Inside that vault is another key that will get you into each home on all the territories I just told you about. You do what you have to do mo'opuna *grandson*. You hear me? Protect my mother. Protect Falcon.

"Protect this family from your father and Jediah. I can't stress that enough. Promise me—" Nabawi coughed so hard tears ran down his eyes as his face flushed red. It was taking everything in Seth to stay strong while seeing his grandfather in this state of misery. "Promise me-you'll-handle- this..."

Seth bowed his head before him fighting hard to keep his emotions in line.

"Olelo wau *I promise*..."

Chapter Twenty-One

Nas didn't realize how in tune she was with Seth until he left her. Two long, exhausting, and emotional weeks had gone by since she last saw the door slam behind him. Her world had shattered.

She'd give anything to be around his mean ass; the days weren't the same without him. She kept trying to convince herself that she was surprised they lasted as long as they did in the first place.

Who the fuck falls for man in just two short months? Who really grows to truly feel for a person when they were strangers longer than they had known one another? I guess you could say the joke was on Nas because she had feelings in her heart for Seth that she couldn't fix her lips to deny.

Nasir ran the Swiffer along her dance floor with only minutes to spare as her seniors got dressed before the day was over. That Danity Kane "Sucka For Love" track spun on the radio and her hips started moving without her control.

Using the device as a prop her feet traveled swiftly, the pole twirled around her back, and she leapt in the air; spinning, jumping, throwing the pole under her legs. . . her body wouldn't stop.

She hit a back flip using her hands, then another one without touching the ground before she made it back up to her feet and noticed that her students were all standing around watching her.

Usually she'd stop, but the music had her possessed. Her eyes were open; wide open. Staring at herself in the mirror, her lips had formed into a smile for the first time all day. She felt relieved.

The pressure had let up a bit, and to her surprise she could relax. It wasn't until that song had gone off and J. Cole's voice filled the air when she finally stopped dancing. The sadness had automatically set in.

J. Cole was a binding force of she and Seth. They'd sit up and get so high and just let his albums play on shuffle, and the thought depressed her. She headed over to her phone and pushed pause, not being able to bare hearing his voice without seeing an image of Seth pop up in her head.

"Okay, Ms. Valentine! You killed that!"

Her seniors applauded as they approached her. Nas couldn't hide her smile. She knew they loved to see her freestyle.

"Thanks y'all."

"For real, Ms. V. That was dope. We should do like a freestyle night," Whitney, another student, advised.

"Oooooh, yeah! Like all the grades get together and we do a few songs a piece, and Ms. V hit a solo or sum'. Then, we all do a big dance at the end. That would be dope."

She raised her brow at her foreign exchange student, Irma's, suggestion.

"I like that. That would be dope. Y'all think the principal would approve it? We'd have to figure out how to turn it into something "educational and meaningful". Y'all know how y'all's principle is," Nas joked with a shake of her head.

"What if we did like a diversity and cultural awareness approach? We could invite other schools too, or how about Central VAP? Their a VPA school as well, and even though our school has been open for three years, we haven't had a welcome performance of our own. We could even invite the VPA middle school."

Nas high fived Pepsi.

"I like that Pep. Great idea. Let's get it all written up. I'll reach out to their instructors to see if they'll be down, and we can present it to Dr. Han next week. Sounds like a plan?"

They all agreed, eager to get their project started.

"We'll talk more on it Monday. And don't forget; your papers are due then too," Nas reminded.

"Dang, Ms. V! You gotta ruin our weekends like that!"

"Tylen, I've pushed this paper back twice already. And it better meet the word count. It's only a response paper, so two pages won't hurt you, sir!" She called after him as they all headed for the door.

"A'ight, Ms. V!"

"And don't copy and paste a sentence from all those different websites again like last year, you hear me!"

"You killing me, ma!"

Nas giggled as the text ring on her phone caught her attention. She walked over to the entertainment center and picked it up. Her heart dropped when she saw Seth's name appear.

Seth:

No ordinary love, Sade
Lady, D'Angelo
I can't Stop Loving U, Kem
Can You Stand The Rain, New Edition
On and On, Erykah Badu
 Half Crazy, Musiq Soulchild
Beauty, Dru hill.

The text made her smile. Nasir removed her phone from the aux cord and headed over to her desk. She pulled a notebook out of her oversized work bag and took a seat. Nas flipped the page until she found the words *What the Heart Wants*. She might not have seen or spoken to him, but every single day Seth sent her this one random text message. Days one through six consisted of the following:

Baked mac n cheese and Pancakes (mostly pancakes)
 Black
Blood and Bone
Micro management/not being in control
Loyalty
Dishonor...

It took her a minute to realize what he was doing, then it dawned on her that he was sending her random facts about himself: his likes and dislikes, favorites, and things of that nature. It took an entire day to figure out what the hell he meant by dishonor when he sent that, but then she realized that it was a fear of his. Loyalty was everything to Seth, so she understood his placement with that notion.

Nasir wrote the list of songs down before she locked up shop and headed home to get dressed and ready for a party she was throwing for her mother. Seth had her mind all over the place. He didn't want to talk to her or be around her, but he stuck his neck out to make sure she got those text messages.

Nas knew this was new to him, and that was okay. She felt the same way, but she'd been there and done that by moving too fast with the last guy she dealt with.

It turned out, Richard, her old flame, didn't even really like her. He thought she was cool, the sex was the shit, no man had ever talked trash on her pussy, and it was dope to sit up and smoke with her, but he didn't see her as anything more than a fuck.

That shit had happened to Nas twice before him, so meeting Seth and jumping right into a relationship had terrified her.

Nasir knew she was falling hard for Seth and she couldn't ignore it, but what had hurt the most were the thoughts of him not liking her for who she was. She didn't care what anyone had said. Niggas would lie through their fucking teeth for some pussy. Especially if it was some pussy that he really wanted and didn't want to let go of.

She was just tired of putting her heart on a platter praying that the next man would except all of her and not just what was between her legs. She didn't wanna piss Seth off, but she had to stand her ground and not be so naive.

Nasir had to love herself. If she didn't love herself then how could she allow anyone else to potentially love her in return or respect her?

That's where she was coming from when she proposed the no sex thing to him until she was sure that they were mentally on the same page. She wished she could explain that to him, but like the dozens of times before, all he did was let the phone ring until his voicemail picked up…

"Ms. Valentine! Are you the one who booked the party of twenty? Oh my God, you look amazing!"

Nasir smiled brightly as she put her brown Birkin bag along the counter while she searched for her wallet.

"Thank you, and yes, I did. Today is my mother's forty-eighth birthday, and I wanted to do a little something for her that I knew she'd enjoy. I'll be covering everything including everyone's dining expenses, so once the check is ready just hand it over to me."

"Sure thing, Ms. Valentine. Will Mr. Platinum be dining with you tonight?"

"No, it's just us ladies this time around. Has a Catori Rucker checked in yet?"

"No, ma'am. Not yet. I'll go make sure everything is prepared for your event. One moment, please."

"Okay."

The plan was for her mother to arrive before she did so she could be the one to choose the wine selections personally, but you know black people never showed up on time to anything. Not even their own birthday.

Blush was an extravagant and luxurious winery in Frontenac county. Nasir swore Seth owned every business in town, and if he didn't, then he knew the owners. Nas and her mother loved wine. They'd drink it all day if they could.

She and Catori would lay up in bed with their custom-made wine glasses sipping Riesling, eating homemade guacamole, and they'd watch one of their favorite movies, which often ended up being "The Proposal" with Sandra Bullock and Ryan Reynolds, together.

Nasir knew her mother had another trip planned for the following weekend, but she wanted to throw her a party today free of hassle, no worries about spending her own money, and she even bought her a Birkin bag for a gift. How could she not?

Seth had bought her two of the same bags, swearing he didn't buy her a brown one already, and ended up looking real stupid when she had it out waiting on him one day when he showed up at her house. So, she wanted to give it to her favorite girl.

Nas was so busy choosing ten different wines for the women who would be attending the party, to taste, that she didn't notice the woman who walked in the door behind her.

Falcon was going nuts. She had to get out of that house with her husband. As the days went by she swore she didn't even know the man any more. Out of thirty years of marriage she'd never wanted to be away from him so much, and it was tearing her apart.

"Mrs. Platinum! Hiiii!" The manager squealed as she ran over to her.

"Hello, Tina. How are you?"

"I'm great! How are you, Queen! You look amazing as always! Are you here for the Valentine party?"

"I'm sorry?" Falcon questioned confused.

"Your son's girlfriend is throwing a party here for her mother."

"My son's girl friend?" Falcon's heart had shattered.

Seth was in a relationship and she didn't know about it?

"Seth?" she asked, confirming that, that was who she was referring to.

"Yes, ma'am."

Falcon gave the woman a smile while batting her eyelashes.

"I didn't know my son was involved with anyone. This is news to me."

She looked around the room searching for who could possibly be lucky enough for Seth to be so open about dating. Her eyes danced around until they landed on the gorgeous smile of the stunning Nasir Valentine.

That's her, she thought while nodding her head.

Falcon could feel it. Nasir's appearance read Seth. She walked tall like Seth, she came off fearless, in control, and dominant like Seth, though poise like a woman.

Nasir looked amazing in the nude mesh blouse with two side splits and a black floral print base, black leather high waist leggings, and a pair of Tony Bianco Kiki Clear Vynalite heels.

Her hair was styled in a sleek ponytail high on her head that stopped below her breasts and four pairs of diamond earrings up each ear with that 90's flava, completed her look. Falcon was impressed.

First of all, she was a beautiful curvaceous woman, and she was shocked. Nasir definitely was not her son's type, but she could tell just from Nas' appearance that he really liked her.

How could he not? She stood out like a diamond amongst the caliber of women that were present, and the woman liked her already.

"What would you like to drink today, Mrs. Platinum? Riesling? Sangria? Something more robust, or a surprise?"

The waiter drew Falcon's eyes from staring at Nasir as if she were a piece of meat, to the tray he had in his hand.

"You have any 1787 handy?"

"Yes, ma'am. This glass right here."

"Thank you very much," she smiled.

"Would you like me to take your jacket?"

"Please. I appreciate it."

Falcon sipped her drink as she headed over to Nas. She was magnetically drawn to the woman. She could feel her son via her energy, and it brought tears to her eyes.

"Why, hello there, beautiful."

Nasir turned around and felt her pupils widen twice their normal size when her eyes fell upon Falcon. She'd noticed her from Seth's tattoo, and my, was she even more beautiful in person.

Her silk blouse hung off her shoulders displaying the 1/2 a million dollar diamond necklace resting on her neckline. The high waist wide leg slacks and pointy toe heels was flawless on her. She looked like royalty.

"Hi." Nasir smiled.

She didn't want to say the woman's name and feel out of place because technically, she didn't know her.

"Falcon. Seth's mother."

"Nasir. Seth's... girlfriend. Nice to meet you, Mrs. Platinum."

"The pleasure is all mine dear."

They stared one another in the eyes. Falcon wasn't doing such a good job at hiding her pain because tears started to cascade down her face.

"You are so beautiful," she sobbed as she wiped her cheeks. "And you, you just wreak of my son. I feel like I'm near him despite everything that's been going on. Please excuse me. I dearly apologize."

Nas handed her the napkin that was sitting on the countertop nearby.

"Thank you, baby. This is such a terrible way to meet. How is he? I miss him so much."

Nasir smiled trying her best not to cry her damn self. She was a sucker for a sob story.

"He's. . . okay."

Nas didn't want to lie to her, but then again, if he wasn't speaking to his mother, which she didn't know up until now, then there had to be some explanation as of why not. But she wasn't gonna go airing all of his business out either.

"You're so strong; so astute, Ms. Nasir. It took me until I was damn near in my thirties to learn how to speak to people when it came to addressing his father. Wow. My son is so blessed. I take it you're a wine drinker. This place is amazing isn't it?" She smiled brightly.

"It is. I fell in love with it when he brought me here last month. I'm throwing a birthday party for my mother actually. It'll be her first time attending."

"That's amazing! Happy birthday, momma! Is she here?"

"Not yet. She's about ten minutes away."

"How fun. I had all boys, so I can only imagine the things you and your mother get into. Wait, you say Seth brought you here? I didn't know he was a wine drinker. 1942 for sure, and maybe some Hennessy, but not wine!"

The two women shared a laugh as they each took a sip from their glass.

"Let's just say I wasn't the one walking out of here running into everything in my sight. I warned him that wine drunkenness is different than hard liquor."

The smile on his mother's face warmed Nas' heart. She could feel their energy as mother and son. She could tell that Falcon had really loved him, so it tore her apart as well to know that they were battling something so ugly that it kept them apart.

"My baby dun matured out here. Lord hammercy. When you see him baby... just... please... tell him I'm sorry, and I love him, and I miss him so much. I hate how things happened with the crossover and his father, then Nabawi just passed away, and then dealing with the death of Akil also is just so much."

"Seth loved his little brother, and I know that's what's been keeping him in such a dark place. I shouldn't have told you that. I'm sorry. The words just can't stop, the tears are draining me, my heart is in shambles, and—"

"Mrs. Platinum, it's okay," Nas smiled. "Sometimes, just getting those things off your chest is the best escape. I won't say anything. Trust me, I know how that grumpy lil' krabby patty is, so your secret is safe with me."

Falcon laughed.

"He hasn't been mean to you has he? That boy."

"He has his moments, but for the most part he's... everything a woman could ask for in a man..." Nas' voice soft as she realized what she'd just said.

She wanted to pull her phone out and call him right then and there, just to hear his voice. Nas wanted her man back.

"I know that look," Falcon smiled. "And I truly wish you two the best from the bottom of my heart."

Nasir blushed so hard it made them both laugh.

"Oh, my God! This place is amazing!"

Hearing her mother's voice made her eye change to the entrance. Nas could tell by the sound that she'd already been drinking as well.

"Mommy! Happy birthday!" Nasir squealed as she ran towards her.

"Thank you, daughter! So much! I can't believe you did this!"

"Anything for you!"

"Catori? Catori Rucker? Parkway West cheer captain of '86?"

"Falcon! Oh my God!"

Nasir stood back when they embraced one another.

"It's been, oh my fucking God, thirty years since I've seen you, Falcon!"

"I know! Look at you! You're so beautiful! Still so fucking beautiful! Nasir, oh my God, the jocks loooooved your mother in high school. I used to look up to her like, I want to be just like her when I grow up." Falcon gloated with the brightest smile.

"Noooo! You were so beautiful! Everybody wanted Falcon! Bitches used to be mad at us because all niggas did was stare when we came around! Shut up! It didn't even dawn on me when Nas told me she was dating a Platinum that you were his mother. How have you been! You look amazing! Please tell me you're here to celebrate with me!"

"I am now! I was just stopping by for a few glasses of wine and I ran into your daughter. She's so beautiful, Catori. It's such a pleasure meeting her. OMG, you ladies get anything you want. Everything is on me tonight! Ah-ah, Nasir, I know you said you were taking care of it, but I've got it. Waiter! We're gonna need more wine over here!"

Falcon couldn't remember the last time she'd enjoyed herself. Something told her to go up to Blush today and was she ecstatic that she'd followed her first mind instead of scribbling in her diary out in the courtyard another day. She needed this.

𝓣

"I hope our chicken ain't cold, Ms. V. They always leave us with some cold ass food."

"Pepsi!" Nas gasped as she pulled the key out to unlock the dance studio.

Mondays were always busy. Nas had forgotten about the field trip they had planned that day to take all the senior dancers to see a performance at Washington University. Her head had been in the clouds way too long, and all she wanted to do was sit down for a minute and just breathe.

"Well, it's true. I'm tired of that cold ass Popeyes they always get. How bout they bring us something like some Imo's, or WingStop, or some Qdoba, or something? We eat the same old stuff."

"Shut up, girl, damn. You been complaining all day."

"Tylen, be nice. Shit, let me get these lights on it's dark as hell in— oh, wow,"

Nas' body froze when she flipped the lights on and she saw her dance studio filled with pink and white roses from wall to wall. There was also a long picnic table set up with catered Qdoba, drinks, plates, and dessert.

"What the hell?" she gasped as they all entered the room.

"Ooooooh! Somebody's man loves her!"

"Shut your ass up, Pepsi!" Nas giggled as she put her purse down.

"Ayyyye, yooooo fam! Is this for us!" Tylen chanted, pumped as he rubbed his hands together, heading right for the food.

"I guess so. Wash y'all hands first. Have at it."

Nas was blown away. As her kids all stood around passing bottles of hand sanitizer back and forth, she noticed Seth enter the dance room with his phone in hand through the mirrors. She turned around afraid and nervous; butterflies were shuffling around in her stomach, causing her to stand before him with a vacant voice.

He was looking fine as hell in the black quarter-sleeve shirt, khaki, Mec straight leg jeans, and AF denim forces with his hair pulled up in a bun and a single gold chain around his neck. Seth was the only man she'd known who still wore that brand, and he rocked the hell out of whatever he threw on his body. He made the simplest attire look like it cost him a couple stacks, and she loved that about him.

Seth walked over to where Nas was until they were standing face to face with their lips just meters away. He stared into her eyes missing how lost he got inside of them. Seth ran his hand down his beard before he threw his arms around her waist and held her close.

Nasir buried her face in his chest, inhaling his scent that she hadn't been able to reconnect with in, what felt like, ages. She looked up into his eyes and felt her insides tingle when he pressed his lips against hers.

Bells rang, fireworks went off in her head, rice was thrown, hands were applauding, and a new flame was brewing as he held her close.

"You-betta-get-yo'-man-Ms. V! Yaaaaaaaaas!"

Laughter escaped Nas' lips the moment she broke their kiss.

"What am I gonna do with you, Pepsi!" she shrieked with a red face.

As you could see, her seniors gave her the most trouble.

"Hell, I don't know, but baby girl get 'em! He is fwine! And thank you, Mr. Boyfriend for our food because I know Dr. Han ain't pull no stings like this!"

Seth chuckled with the shake of his head as he returned a *you're welcome.*

"Eat your food, girl. Here, I need y'all to fill these papers out. It's front and back. Just some simple questions about the performance that I have to turn back in to the dance board."

Seth stood back and watched her ass jiggle in the denim, high-waisted pencil skirt while she passed the papers out. Yeah, he missed the fuck out of his woman, but he was fiending for that pussy too. After that night with Kelani that he'd low-key gotten away with, he realized that these hoes didn't have shit on the dark, slippery, and gushy cave Nas had between them thighs.

Bitches just didn't compare to her on any level. It was a long ass tempting two weeks without smashing some pussy, but if it wasn't his woman he just didn't want it. Seth was never the man to settle and he wasn't gonna start either just because he was all bent out of shape for the time being.

Nas fixed herself a plate once all the kids were done before she headed back over to Seth, who was sitting on top of the counter that boxed off the costume room.

"Thank you," she smiled as she sat her plate down.

He didn't respond. All he did was smirk at her, admiring how beautiful she was.

"I owe you an apology, mama," Seth sighed as he ran his hand down his beard again. "I be fucked up in the head sometimes. I can admit that. Yo' statement had just came at me so fucking sideways after the conversation I had with Meme Aruba, just minutes before you came out the shower, and it was like damn. Shit got hot for me quick, and after I thought about what you said I understood yo position and shit, but Nasir, I already told you what it was.

"I don't know why you like to make me repeat myself. If Seth say he got you, then, he got you. He got all of you; not just physically, but all the way. And I'mma need you to quit questioning that shit, first and foremost though, quit questioning me. You 'sposed to trust me, ma. We'll talk about this more later but—"

"I get it," she smiled. "I called you. I've been calling you."

He sighed.

"I'm already hip. It's just one thing after another... I want you to go to a funeral with me tomorrow morning. Don't sweat that nigga, Dr. Han. I already got yo' absence covered. I need you there with me. I know for a fact that I can't do it alone." His voice was soft.

Seth finally had his guard down.

"That's why I was calling. I heard about Nabawi, and I'm sorry for your loss."

He looked at her sideways, wondering how she knew who and what he was referring to.

"I wanna show you something." Nas pulled her phone out and scrolled down until she found the picture she was looking for. "Promise me you won't blow up."

He shook his head no.

"I can't promise that."

"Seth."

The sound of her voice shook him a bit. She had that Meme Aruba bite right now, and it kind of blew him back for a minute.

"Good," she smiled once she saw him raise his brow yet remain quiet.

Nasir handed him her phone and saw his eyes glow when he observed the picture. It was a photograph of her and his mother from Friday night at Blush. Nas was smiling so hard in the picture that her eyes were closed shut while Falcon held her arm around her shoulders, placing a big kiss to her cheek.

"We had an amazing time that night. Your mother is one hell of a woman. She and my mom went to high school together."

She scrolled over to show him the photo of their mothers. Two forty-fine ass women. Seth's stomach was choppy, but his soul was smiling. He scrolled back to the picture of Falcon and Nas and couldn't stop staring at it.

It was both of his girls. All that was missing was Meme Aruba, and he'd have his Holy Trinity in one photo. He pulled Nas over to him and made her stand between his legs with her back against him.

"When was this?"

"Friday night. I threw my mother a birthday party, and I didn't even know your mother was there until she approached me. I've never seen a woman tear up so much from the thoughts of her son."

Seth handed her the phone back, torn.

"She really misses you. I don't know what happened, and I'm sure you'll tell me when you're ready, but she said that she loves you, and that she's sorry. She never meant to hurt you. And if those words don't sell it to you, then the tears that couldn't stop falling down her eyes should."

He wrapped his arms around Nas and kissed her cheek. She knew a lot was on his mind right now, so she didn't bother to press the issue.

"I've gotta tell you something too," he confessed.

Her heart started racing.

"What?"

Seth laughed out loud.

"Calm yo' paranoid ass down, man. This ain't about another bitch. I met your moms a lil' minute ago. It was some time last week actually. I popped up on her at the gig and took her out. We rapped for a lil' minute. A good minute. Say, mama, I see where you get that bark and bite from. Catori a Pitbull, man. I swear she wouldn't let up."

They shared a laugh.

"She did not tell me that."

"She wasn't supposed to. You got a good moms, bae. She loves you too, and after rapping with her it kind of put a lot into perspective for me about us."

"Like what?"

"Like this is where I wanna be."

Nasir smiled.

"You forgive me?" He asked as he looked down at her.

Their eyes locked.

"I forgave you two weeks ago, Seth..."

He kissed her lips.

"Me too, mama," He sighed. "It's just been crazy."

"I know," she cooed, her voice soft and sensational as she held onto his arms around her. "I just wish you could clear your mind, babe; even if it was just for a day. I feel like I owe you that." She looked up into his eyes again. "You gonna let me do that for you? Hmmm?"

He chuckled.

"You gon' make sum' shake for, daddy?"

"Yes," she kissed his lips. "Mentally, and physically, Mr. Platinum. You need that."

Chapter Twenty-Two
Four nights ago. . .

Jediah slid in through the door at the loading dock that maintenance hadn't locked for the night and crept into Haven Gardens. He adjusted the cap on his head, dusted off the fake name tag, and grabbed the trash bin as if he were one of the other custodians on duty. His eyes were low, but the Sprite mixed with the codeine in his system kept him alert. He checked the notepad on the garbage cart to make sure he had the correct work order before proceeding to the 2nd floor.

The nurse at the nurse's station was laying with her head down; her big ass mouth was wide open with some obnoxious snores filling the air around her. He didn't see any aids in sight, so he crept down the hall until he reached room 209 with the initials NP along the door. Nabawi was never a hard sleeper but considering his health and the morphine he was on for pain, the neurons in his brain were firing at an all-time low, and he didn't budge when the door to his room opened.

Jediah was quick. He unhooked the bottle of Jevity 1.5 from the IV pole, opened it, then mixed the arsenic poison with the feeding. He gave the bottle a few good shakes praying to God that he wasn't too loud while mixing it up because it was half way empty. He increased the speed that monitored how fast the fluids pumped into the body before removing the band cutter from out his pocket.

When he went to reach for the gold necklace that he just knew was around Nabawi's neck, it was like a Xanax bar had finally set in his system.

The fuck?! He panicked as he started looking around the room, shuffling through the drawers hoping to find it, but he had no luck.

Jediah knew his grandfather. He knew it in the pit of his heart that the key around his neck meant something. Osiris never paid attention to the small details, but he observed everything.

He remembered when he was twelve and how Nabawi beat his ass with nothing but knuckles because he sold his chain to a corner boy for some weed that wasn't even worth rolling up. Talk about a spooked kid with blood down his shirt as his old man dragged him to the hood looking for the lil' niggas he'd sold it to.

Gunshots rang on the block that day. Jediah was young and naïve. He knew about the beef they had with the Kamikazes, but his only focus was getting his hands on a quarter ounce to bring the next day to school and stunt on the bus when he lit his blunt.

All he remembered was Nabawi letting his finger pull the trigger once and three bullets spit out the Barretta at the same damn time; all three of them hitting his target in the head before his body hit the ground in broad daylight.

They never spoke of that day once Nabawi had his chain back around his neck. Jediah was so shook he never even said shit to Seth about it. It was a secret he and his OG shared and swore in silence that they'd take to the grave.

It's all JD's been able to think about the last few days. He could only imagine what kind of doors that key unlocked, but the longer he searched and couldn't find it the more he started to sweat.

Nabawi never took that fucking necklace off! Who the fuck— *a thought suddenly hit him. Falcon was the only person who'd been coming to visit him every day.* ***Never would momma step in the middle of this shit. Nah dawg,*** *he thought in disbelief as he put his hands on his head.* ***Where the fuck could it be?***

"Looking for something?"

Nabawi's voice damn near scared the piss out of him, he had to hold his dick to keep it from dripping. Infuriated, Jediah grabbed his grandfather by the throat but quickly released him once he realized how tight his grip was, and how he didn't have on gloves to get away with the shit.

"We can do this shit the easy way, or the hard way," he threatened through clenched teeth as he pulled out his pistol with the silencer attached to it.

Nabawi smiled as he looked into his grandson's demonic eyes. He knew exactly why he was there, and at the nick of time, he'd caught a glimpse of him putting the empty bottle back in his pocket knowing he'd conjured up some kinda sketchy shit to speed up his death.

"Let's do it the easy way. You must've forgotten that I was allergic to metalloids and that's why I've only drank PH balanced water since I was five. So—" He inhaled deeply, feeling the instant build-up of pressure in his lungs from the drug. "Whatever you poisoned me with, I'll be dead—" He inhaled deeply once again. "Much faster than you planned. . ."

With malice in his eyes, Jediah grabbed the mattress that was ordered to be removed from the room and got the fuck out of dodge while Nabawi laid there staring into space. His body fought for forty-five slow, antagonizing, painful, and deadly ending minutes before his heart stopped.

If Seth would've waited just one more day before he finally decided to show up after he sent out the message to come and see him, then sneaky ass, deceiving ass, family code breaking, Jediah Platinum would've gotten away with it.

Nabawi knew that the karma for killing his own son would revert back to him before any natural disease ever would. He knew one day soon, once the crossover had been established, that he'd reap what he had sewn. . .

T

"Seth. Come here."

Irritated, he took a deep breath before he turned around and faced Nasir who'd just exited the passenger's side of the Bugatti. He had so many cars she honestly couldn't keep up.

"Nas, this ain't the—"

"Shut it up," she smirked as she straightened out his undone tie then, wrapped it around in the perfect loop before adjusting it. "I know you're uneasy about this, baby, but, take a deep breath and just count to ten or something. At the end of the day, you're here to pay your respects to your grandfather. Right?"

Seth didn't respond. He stood with his hands in his slacks ignoring her. The suppressor against his hand had him itching to walk through the door with his Desert Eagle aimed and let his thirty-clip loose on every muthafucka in sight.

"Hey," Nas' voice was soft as she grabbed him by his jacket with both hands and kissed his lips. "You're not alone."

He managed to smirk while looking down at his girl. She knew how to change his mood without putting up much effort to do so, and he appreciated that more than she'd ever know.

"Let me savor this moment because I know that smirk won't last for long. Maluhia, Mr. Platinum. Okay? At least for right now."

Seth didn't even have to voice it to her how agitated his family made him. His actions spoke for it, and she wasn't used to seeing him so uptight.

"Peace. Tranquility," He took a deep breath. "And contentment," he finished placing a definition to the Hawaiian phrase that meant harmony, when she basically told his hot-headed ass to calm down.

"Wassup, fam."

Seth looked over his shoulder as Messiah approached them. Nasir released him so he could slap hands with his dawg.

"Aye, don't be mugging me and shit, ma," Messiah smirked as he threw an arm around Nas.

Even through her shades he felt her cut her eyes at his ass like she was Salt Bae. He knew Riley told her about the mishap last week, and he still hadn't figured it out in his head how he was gonna apologize and make it up to her.

Nasir didn't want to, but she threw her arm around him and hugged him in return. The last thing her man needed was for her to be on bullshit and have a funky ass attitude on top of the way he was already feeling, so she let that shit slide until the moment the funeral was over.

"You ready?"

Seth nodded his head in agreement to his potna's question as he grabbed Nas by the hand and they headed for the entrance. . .

This muthafucka got a lot of nerve...

Osiris was hot when he saw the doors to the church open and in walked Seth and Messiah with company. Seth wasn't afraid of shit; if anything, he was afraid of himself and not being able to control his actions. That's why he needed Nas there. He could see the shit on the news already if only he and Messiah had popped out.

With all bullshit aside though, the rules to the Platinum dynasty were simple yet set in stone. Honor the family. Protect the family. And respect the homecomings no matter what the beef was. Seth had every right to be there as anyone else in that room did, and nothing was stopping him from paying his last respects to Nabawi.

Kelani's poor hand locked up when she felt Jediah tighten his grip. The animosity in the room was thick. Negativity coated the atmosphere, and even the people in the crowd knew something was out of line. And if that wasn't enough, she had to force herself to swallow the lump in her throat when she saw Nas on *her man's* arm.

Is he serious? Is he really bringing her here like he wasn't at my house a few weeks back? I know Seth don't love this bitch after two fucking months. Damn, she really is beautiful. . .

Kelani's heart was racing and so was Jediah's. He figured it was safe for him to bring her by since he knew Seth wouldn't step foot near the funeral, but that nigga hasn't been able to get shit right yet, and at this moment, the chess game between them wasn't in his favor.

The crowd gasped when Osiris grabbed the M4 he had stowed away underneath the podium and aimed it at his son. Funeral or not, him and Seth both would still get shit cracking. Messiah pulled out his two Desert Eagles the same time Seth removed both of his burners.

"You blaze, we blaze, muthafucka!" Jediah spat as his hands trembled while holding the Smith and Wesson.

"Is this yo' fucking property! Do you not understand what the fuck a crossover is!" Osiris' voice was so frightening that a few of the little kids in the crowd started to cry, and their mothers began to flee for the exit.

"I don't give a fuck about none of that shit right now. Don't stand here and act like you don't know what the fuck a homecoming means, nigga. Put the fucking gun down. Why don't you stop being a bitch for a damn change and act like a Platinum? Where's the honor and respect for yo' family in yo' actions right now?"

The calm in Seth's voice sent chills down everyone's spine. He was the only man making sense, even if he did have a gun at his grasp too. He had to stand his ground.

"You all can't even control yourselves at a funeral? What has gotten into you Osiris?"

Everyone looked back as the five-foot, tan colored woman with gray hair down to her knees approached the front of the room where her family was standing like they were at a war front.

"Put that fucking gun down. All of you. Now." No man had budged. "Am I speaking to the damn walls?"

Meme Aruba started chanting in her Hawaiian voodoo, and the lights began to flicker. You know good and damn well Seth lowered his guns. That spirit shit rubbed him the wrong way, and he wasn't fucking with it.

"Osiris." Falcon spat; embarrassed, irritated, disappointed, and full of tears.

His eyes glared at Seth before he lowered his weapon, but he kept his finger on the trigger as they all did.

"I believe this is a homecoming. Let's pay our respects, release the doves at the burial, and we all can go on our way."

Osiris waved Meme Aruba off as he turned his back on her. The looks on everyone's faces was equivalent; that may have been Osiris in the flesh, but spiritually it wasn't him.

A demon was hovering over his shoulders whispering dirty chants in his ear, and he danced like a cobra. It was heart breaking.

Tears rolled down Falcon's eyes, the chattering from the crowd grew louder, and even poor Keanu started to weep.

That really hit a nerve for Seth. Nobody made Meme Aruba cry. Nobody. She was his Keanu. Period.

"I'm okay, baby. I'm okay."

She tried to swallow her tears as Seth wrapped his arms around her, but she just couldn't believe how her family was acting. Her tears had Seth's stomach wet, she couldn't stop herself.

"Aye, maika'i. Maika'i, look at me."

He held her chin up and gave her a smile. She couldn't resist P1. She swore their hearts were in unison and seeing him smile was all she needed before she dried her tears.

"Come on. You came alone?" He questioned as he grabbed her hand.

"'Ae. I told Darcy to stay home. Oh, my goodness, Seth, is this her? I know this is the wrong time to say so, but she is beautiful!"

Keanu lit up bright when her eyes landed on Nas, who hadn't said a peep since the moment Osiris pulled the gun out. She'd finally got her body to stop shaking once Keanu's sweet voice had hit her ears.

"I'm gonna sit by you. Come on, baby."

Nasir smiled when the woman grabbed her hand. She led her to the empty row right in front while everyone got seated. After a moment of silence, the preacher cleared his throat before he began with the opening introduction for Mr. Nawabi Platinum's homecoming. . .

T

"These islands are still as beautiful as I remember them to be when I was a little girl. Going to custom gatherings like our lu'aos, the weekly dance classes and moving these old hips to our custom melodies doing the hula, and how about making the most beautiful leis until the tips of my fingers burned with my mother and sisters.

"It was always worth it though. We'd be making hundreds of them, preparing for May Day to place them on the graves of our fallen soldiers. I swear when time moves it waits on no one... My sweet Nasir," Keanu smiled as she placed a loose orchid over her left ear. "Maika'i."

Nas smiled recognizing the phrase.

"Thank you, Keanu."

"No baby, thank *you*. This flower let's all the men on the island know that you are taken by placing it over your left ear, and I know it's early, but I, Keanu Platinum-Aruba officially welcome you into this family. Now, now I know I'm jumping the gun, but the spirits baby?" Keanu ran her large tooth comb through Nas' beautiful bouncy curls just like she used to do with her daughters. She had an excellent grade of hair.

"They've been messing with an old woman for weeks now. I could feel it the moment Seth came and visited my home in the Bahamas. I knew something was different. Everyone always called me crazy and they all laughed at a girl when she swore God was using her as a vessel. Seth may be stubborn, and he may be an asshole at times because let's just face the facts that all Platinum men were just born with this mean streak.

"I'll be honest, my Akil was different. The sweetest Platinum you'd ever meet. Seth is sweet, don't get me wrong. Keanu loves her P1. With all her heart, but he's often troubled. His baby brother was always the person who kept him level-headed.

"He'd die for Akil. I know that's why he holds his death so close to his heart. He'd rather Akil had been the one to be arrested if he had known that saving him would lead to his departure a year later. It saddens me really to see him so disgruntled, but with you baby?"

She grabbed Nas' chin once again.

"You are, kuikawa. Special. Seth would not have brought you to that homecoming if you weren't, and he wouldn't have brought you to our home-lands if you weren't kuikawa. You scare him. The most he'll probably ever admit to you is a class of intimidation, but he knows with all his heart that you put fear in him. He sees you, Nasir baby, and he wants to do nothing but give the world to you.

"Keanu is not crazy. Time means nothing when it comes to love. True love that is. It means absolutely nothing. The heart wants what the heart wants. I fell for his great grandfather with the snap of a finger. His ole' mean ass. Meeeeeeeean as a junk yard dog I'll tell you."

Nas giggled as Keanu handed her a cup of coffee. It was so fresh, potent, mind stimulating, and pure. They grew it there on the islands, and she'd never tasted anything so refreshing.

"But, he loved me. It's like Akamu knew he was supposed to love and protect me, and that he did. I didn't like the idea of us moving to the states, but we did. We raised our family, he created the Platinum Dynasty, and the rest is just history. I think about him every day. I love my husband don't get me wrong, but the heart never let's go of your first love. Seth reminds me a lot of Akamu. It's frightening."

She handed Nasir an old photograph in black and white of Keanu and her husband when she was eighteen and he was twenty.

"Oh my God!" Nas gasped with a smile.

"Freaky isn't it? It's like, Akamu spit him out. I always knew Seth was the chosen one. Not because he was the oldest, not because he looked like my husband, but because his heart had just said so. My ka mo'opuna nui needs you baby. When a woman brings a man peace and not all that negative drama and heartache like these women nowadays do, that's how you know that the stars have aligned perfectly.

"Don't let his big ass head discourage you. It's a challenge loving a man whose mind is always working, but that's where a woman comes in at. She makes that situation better. My P1 will open up when he's ready, and he *will* open up. He wants to. He just doesn't know how yet. Just watch. I'm sure before you leave this island your heart will truly know where you and Seth stand. You hear me?"

"'Ae," Nas smiled.

Keanu lit up from her response.

"Yes! My great-great grand babies are gonna continue on with the Hawaiian customs! Thank you, Lord!" She kissed Nasir's cheek. "You truly are a blessing, Ms. Nasir. I know it. Now, go on and see what that Seth is up to. Where's my phone? I'm gonna go check on my poor husband who acts like he can't live alone when I'm away." . . .

The warm sand between her toes was soothing as Nas headed over to the hammock where Seth was lying with a blunt up to his lips. The sun was an hour away from setting, and the colors in the sky were beautiful as the wind slightly blew.

Seth placed his eyes upon Nasir as she approached him; her appearance was phenomenal donning the island look. The lei around her neck, the orchid in her hair, the white two-piece bathing suit and mesh coverup skirt with a high split that dragged by her feet suited her snatched waist, flat belly, and thick thighs perfectly.

"Hey."

Nas' voice was soft as she stood beside him whom was looking comfortable as ever with his feet up.

"Wassup my lil' island girl? Keanu was in there talking shit, wasn't she?"

Nas laughed as he stood up.

"Keanu is so dope. How could anyone not love her?"

Seth inhaled from the blunt once more while his hair blew in the wind before he grabbed her by the hand with his free one.

"Let's walk," he instructed... "They call this the Ha'iku Stairs or The Ha'iku Ladder, aka, The Stairway to Heaven."

Nas took in the scenery as he held her in his arms. The high mountains, green plantation, colorful flowers, and the actual stairs that aligned each peak was a sight to see.

"Now the Platinums are from the Hawaiian island, but here in Oahu is where we visited often. We had family that migrated and made home on five of the eight islands, but most of them besides the elders are in the states now...

"I remember back when we were teenagers; I was nineteen, Jediah was seventeen, and Akil had just turned fifteen," Seth chuckled. "That nigga Akil was always wild man. He let Jediah talk him into a bet that we wouldn't climb the stairway to Heaven

for a stack a piece from each of us. He was always a scary ass lil'
nigga, but he'd do anything if a muthafucka bet he wouldn't. It's
illegal to do it. Some people pay a fine, and then most people
trespass.

"Long story short, me, my brothers, and them niggas
Messiah and Prodigy included; my dawgs did everything with us.
They were never left out; my ohana. . . We took all four thousand
steps together, and once we got to the end, we let our feet dangle
over the edge and smoked so much weed I can't even tell you how
we got down. . . Akil was my G. At a certain point you couldn't
separate any of us. The Platinum brothers, we were close. And like
I said, my dawgs were never out of sight."

Seth chuckled again.

"Falcon used to have to drag them niggas home they was
around so much. They peoples ain't sweat it though. They knew
they was in good hands. From a young age, all we swore to was
loyalty. I've had this tattoo since I was fifteen-years-old," he
reminisced while looking down at his hand.

"Falcon was our template. She instilled it in us to love and
protect women, to honor them, and not be biased, sexes, degrading,
and shit like that. She always told us to treat a woman the way
we'd want to see her to be treated.

"A lot of shit just changed over time, mama. Osiris got
dark, so we all got darker. We all were integrated as one, so when
one person went left we all did, and it was like damn. Making
money took over, and it weighed down on his relationship with
moms, on his relationship with us, and it sparked shit that I've
never been able to get back under control.

"Jediah had always been a lil' sketchy. He's always wanted
to stand out so bad that he was willing to do whatever to make it
happen. I could never rock with the fake shit, so the distance
between us grew on sum' tough. He would get all fucked up in the
head about how cool me and Messiah was and about how much
Akil always wanted to be around me too.

"Even when Prodigy joined the crew he felt some type of
way about it. And once we all were put on, shit just really changed.
Any tradition has it that the father passes down the dynasty, the

business, or whatever the fuck it is in the family name, to the first born, and that right there evoked whatever good was left in Jediah.

"Akil wasn't really built for this life. All he wanted to do was go off and play ball for UCLA. Those were his dreams, but JD talked him out of it and promised him that our cartel could give him shit that ball couldn't. Akil respected us both.

"He valued the shit we said, but I'd never push him to not go after what he wanted. This was my dream, this was JD's dream, but not his. In a way, I envied baby bro you know? He was true to himself, but he was easily swayed into some bullshit because he ain't wanna disappoint none of us. And I've hated that..."

His voice trembled.

"... if I would've just followed my first mind and sent him to UCLA when he graduated because I knew Osiris wouldn't, then he never would've gotten caught up in none of this shit and he'd be here. This life wasn't for him, mama. I can't... How can I not stress that shit? But I didn't *see* that shit until the day he was lying in a casket. Si was so selfish and wanted all of his sons to walk in his footsteps so bad that he never paid attention to the love Akil had for ball.

"Kingpin or not, I was at every game with my strap on me. Every honorary awards show; everything. Me and Falcon both. I should've known it was some bullshit when he turned down the scholarship, but we be so caught up in our own shit that we don't consider the welfare of the people around us. And to this day, I still can't place a face with the muthafucka that took my dawg from me. . ."

Seth embraced Nasir with a stronger clutch and buried his face in her neck.

"They took my nigga, ma. And I wasn't there to protect him. I swear to God when I find the nigga that personally did that shit it's nothing but blood. The last time I saw my brother when we were down in Mexico on a power trip, I told him right before he left to promise me that he'd take care of our ohana. He swore a promise, ma, but that same ohana didn't protect him. . ."

Nas turned around and hugged Seth around the neck. Her man had been hurting. His heart had been hurting. His spirit was broken. Seth never had the chance to grieve over Akil's death and being there on the islands where they swore when they were little kids that they'd have million-dollar mansions side by side, toasting to the sky together from their accomplishments, it made him realize that he'd let his little brother down.

He knew it in his heart that some foo-foo shit with Akil's death had gone down. How the fuck was he a target out of everyone? Why not kill or come for Seth? Why not kill Si or Jediah?

What the fuck did getting rid of Akil mean? It didn't settle right with him. A day didn't go by when he didn't try to put the pieces together, but it seemed like he was getting nowhere, and he couldn't stand it.

"So continue to be a good big brother and make him proud," Nas whispered as she held Seth's face in her hands. "Your brother loves you, Seth. He knows that you would've done everything in your power to protect him. You were in prison. People manipulated you, and they used your circumstances against you.

"That's not your fault, and Akil's death isn't your fault either. Remember when we said if we can't control it then let it go? I'm not saying let that tragedy go, but what I am saying is stop blaming yourself for that. Baby, that's a lot on your heart. You're only human too."

Nas was heartbroken to see the tears along his face. Seth was as obstinate as they came, so to see him in this moment showed her why he's been so uneasy. He held her close as she wrapped her arms back around him.

"We'll get through this together. Okay, baby? Do you trust me?" She rubbed the back of his head as he kissed her on the cheek.

"'Ae, mama. I do. . ."

Chapter Twenty-Three

"*How's* Hawaii? It's been the longest four days without you, and how do you still have a job cousin? You stay gone." Riley laughed as she stood in the mirror, brushing up her edges.

"I know right? I put in some FMLA time; plus, Dr. Han wouldn't dare talk that shit to Seth. I don't ask no questions girl, but it's so beautiful here. One of the most beautiful places that I've ever been before."

"That's wassup, boo. I'm glad you're enjoying yourself. Where's Seth?"

Nas moved the camera to show a sleeping Seth on his back with his mouth wide open and the covers down by his waist. When she turned the camera back, she had the goofiest smirk on her face, and they both broke out in laughter.

"Put that ass straight to sleep, Ry."

"Okaaaaay, cousin! I see you girl!"

Nasir giggled.

"Where you finna go, Bookie boo? You looking good over there, Miss Riley *Stuart*."

Her cousin smiled.

"Girl, I'ma get out this house for a minute. I'm going crazy."

"I surely slapped Messiah upside his damn head when I saw him the other day. Fucking idiot."

Riley was quiet. She'd taken the incident from the Jazz club pretty hard and hadn't been able to overcome it just yet.

"It's okay, girl. He wasn't my man."

"Bullshit. He is your fucking man. Ain't no nigga finna be all up under you, introduce you to his baby sister, and not want you. That nigga dun' caught feelings after he swore he wouldn't, and now he's looking stupid. You better check that nigga."

Riley laughed.

"Why you so crazy, Nas?"

"I'm not crazy. You just have to give your man a bit of a reminder sometimes. You see mines over there sleep. Hell, I'm 'bout to wake his ass up for round two. Gon' tap out on me after the first round."

"Nas!"

They shared a laugh.

"I tell you what. My spare key is in the top drawer in my chest of drawers. Take the Rover tonight."

"You sure?"

"Of course, I'm sure. What kind of question is that? Have fun and send me some twerking videos from wherever you go. I know you're going to drink."

"I'm nooooot," she whined. "I got me a pack of Backwoods rolled up already. With my period just days away I can't be getting. . ." Riley's heartbeat felt like it hit a flatline when she looked down at the sink.

"What? Is everything okay? Hello? Riley, say something."

"I'm-I'm good. Tevin's name just popped up and it—took me by surprise," she lied.

"What the fuck does he want? I thought you blocked him?" Nas griped.

"I don't know, and I don't care. Go ahead and get your man's dick back hard. I'm about to head out, okay?"

Nasir turned her lip up in the camera.

"I know your ass is lying, but whatever. Be safe, and don't do nothing I wouldn't do."

"You're the one with the wild past, Nas. Not me."

"Biiiiiiiitch! The shade! You ain't shit! Have fun you little wanch!"

Riley was cracking up.

"I will. Talk to you in a minute. . ."

T

"You have reached the voicemail box of. . . *Riley Stuart.*"

Irritated, Messiah hung up the phone as he pulled his Lamborghini into the parking lot. At first, he was cool with him avoiding her because he was being a dick about their fall out, but now it was irritating him that he couldn't get through to her.

Another week had passed by, and he wasn't putting up with her funky ass little attitude any more. All the ignoring him when he's been trying to apologize to her ass was wearing him thin. If that's not a nigga for ya then I don't know what else is.

Messiah knocked on the door to her apartment impatiently. He looked back at her car, knowing she was home, so he knocked again this time harder, damn near breaking the door down.

"A'ight, since this the fucking game you wanna play," he spat pissed as he put the key in the door and went inside.

"Riley!" he yelled while hopping up the steps.

Messiah looked around all three bedrooms on the top level, and the bathroom in the hall. He could smell the recent burning of weed in the air, and once he saw her bathroom cluttered with hair products and makeup, he knew that she had gone out.

"Yo ass wanna be sneaky, huh? A'ight. Bet." he chuckled as he backed his car out, finally realizing that Nas' truck wasn't there.

He went to the Find My iPhone app and smiled when he pulled up her location. *Down town it is nigga.* Messiah blasted that "No Smoke" by NBA Young Boy as his tires screeched and he headed back to the highway. He was going to get his girl.

$$\mathcal{T}$$

Pow! Pow! Pow! Pow! Pow!

Riley emptied out the clip of the Barretta before she picked up two Uzis and blasted at the targets relentlessly. Mama was relieving some stress. With that classic "Looking Ass Niggas" by Nicki Minaj blaring in the air, she stood with her knees knocked back, ass sitting up high, legs looking good while the five-inch heels on her feet held her up, and her arms out, letting bullets hit the floor. Her mind was racing and the only thing that seemed to calm her was the continuous sounds of the gunshots.

"Baby girl, that's sum' serious right there," one of the ballers who'd rented out the shooting range advised as he pulled the laced blunt from his lips.

Riley pulled the gauge back on the automatic Mossberg before the gun blasted, and she knocked the head off of the police dummy tied to a pole.

"I got this shit," she shot back.

Her tone was sassy yet sexy. It made him grab the dick in his pants, wanting to relieve some of that stress with her fine ass in a different scenery. The man ashed his blunt before he stood to his feet and headed over in her direction. He leaned up against the banister, watching her reload the gun while staring at her slim frame stacked with big titties and a nice round ass.

"What's yo name, ma?"

"What's yours?" she countered, not even looking him in the eye as she pulled the gauge back once again.

"Rome."

Clink-Clack—Bow!

"Wassup."

Riley's voice was dry and uninterested, but that shit did nothing but make his dick hard. The bitches who stunted the most like they weren't feeing him had some fire ass pussy behind it and Rome was destoned to break her back in tonight. It was only a matter of good conversation and persuasion that stood between them.

"Damn, do a nigga stink or sum'? Why you got yo face turned up like I got *fuckboy* written on my forehead or some shit," he joked as he threw his arms up.

This nigga was so corny, and he was trying so damn hard to get her attention that she honestly broke out in laughter from how pathetic he was. Not because he was amusing.

"Damn, so she smiles? You should do that more often. It's sexy as fuck on you. I see I'ma have to keep both my eyes open too. The way you make a gun clap I'ma have to stay strapped."

This dude was so cheesy, and Riley had to admit the blunt she smoked on the way to the range already had her higher than a kite from the moment she got there. The two she'd just ran through like it was nothing had her eyes low, giving her an extra sexy look to match the tattoos gracing her body showing in her crop top and low-rise jeans.

"You gon' tell me yo name, ma, or what? All bullshit aside quit fucking with me like you can't see that I want you."

This Rome had a nice edge in his voice, but she just couldn't take this nigga serious. Riley loved Moneybagg Yo, but she just was not attracted to that nigga by any means necessary and that's exactly who this "Rome" reminded her of. She was flaming his ole' Michael Meyers looking ass in her head and that's why she couldn't stop laughing, not because he was a baller and she had them fake ass giggles tryna win him over. He seemed like he was the type of nigga who paid for pussy the way he was eating her actions up.

Meanwhile, the door to the gun range opened and in walked a drunken Messiah with a bottle of Hennessy up to his lips. He saw red when he got a glimpse of the nigga standing next to Riley tryna spit game. She was smiling too fucking hard. The fuck was funny? He put the bottle down and walked up on them.

"Can I join?"

His sarcasm made them both turn around. Not thinking twice about it, Messiah swung so hard the nigga's slugs came out his mouth when he hit the ground.

"Messiah!" Riley gasped.

He pulled two Desert Eagles out his waist and aimed them high at the niggas surrounding him once their potna had been dropped.

"Yo chill," one guy motioned when he noticed who Messiah was.

They all lowered their guns causing him to chuckle.

"That's what the fuck I thought."

"What are you doing here!"

He cut his eyes back at Riley too pissed off. Messiah tucked one gun away before he bodied her ass, throwing her over his shoulder.

"Messiah, put me down! What the fuck is your problem!"

He slammed the door to his office within the building before he put her down and hemmed her up against the mini bar.

"What the fuck is my problem! The fuck is yo problem! You 'bout to get niggas kilt out here with this bullshit you pulling! Don't disrespect me on my muthafucking set, Riley! You gon' get yo ass fucked up, you hear me!"

"Fuck you, Messiah! I don't wanna hear that shit! I'm not yo bitch! Don't come up in here manhandling me tryna make sum' shake because you feel some type of way for being a dog ass nigga! You would really walk around with another bitch like you ain't been fucking with me the long way! That's the type of bullshit you do for fun! Hurt bitches after all the bullshit you know they've been going through! Some real ass nigga you claim to be!"

Messiah grabbed Riley by the arm and shoved her into the mini pit couch, laying her on her back. He pinned her arms above her head and gave her ass a glare so damn evil her eyes widened.

"Who the fuck yo ass talking to, huh! Who the fuck do you think are, Riley!"

"Yo baby momma, nigga! That's who the fuck I am! And I'm talking to you! Who the fuck else is in here!"

You would've thought she shot his ass the way he shriveled back down to size when those words escaped her lips. He sat up on his knees, still on top of her.

"The fuck you just say to me?" he questioned, aiming the gun at her while biting his bottom lip.

"Shoot me then nigga! Just do it! It'll take me away from all this fucking misery anyway!" she cried before she put her hands over her eyes.

Messiah ran his hands down his face tryna rip his damn skin off. *What the fuck did she just say to me,* he thought with the shake of his head.

"I just found out an hour ago. I still can't wrap my head around it, but I've missed two periods. How the fuck do you think I feel," she sobbed as she wiped her cheeks.

"What?" It was all he could say.

"I am speaking English, right! Why the fuck are you so got-damn appalled! We *never* used a condom, Messiah, and I don't remember yo ass pulling out either, nigga! Ever! You was fucking that bitch raw too, wasn't you? That's why the bitch was so got-damn pressed when she saw me.

"You lucky I felt so damn stupid over your dumb ass that I didn't set that shit off! You sholl right Messiah, but you got a problem with me! You ain't did shit but took advantage of the state that I've been in since my divorce and I fell for it! If anything, the fucking joke is on me!"

Riley tried to sit up, but he pushed her back down, holding her by the neck, and put the gun at her temple. Okay, that nigga might've been acting all crazy and shit, but Riley was turned the fuck on! No if's, and's, nor but's about it! That shit was too sexy. Messiah let go of her neck before he leaned over and kissed her.

"Get off of me," her words were muffled as she threw her head from side to side to keep his mouth from off of hers. "Messiah! I said get off-of meeeee!"

She started kicking and screaming. Riley basically threw a temper tantrum. She felt stupid, she felt used, she felt like every other dumb ass bitch who was still getting played in 2016, but something in her heart was telling her to just relax.

This nigga still sent her money. This nigga was still sending five paragraph essays about how he was gon' eat her pussy when he finally ran into her. He'd been sending "I'm sorry" gifts for the last two weeks now, and she still hadn't given the nigga any play. That's why he was out searching for her ass.

Maybe she was torn because he was the only man alive who made sex feel good for her. Each stroke felt like the end of her fully charged vibrator caressing her walls and it wouldn't stop until she creamed. That shit would make any woman go crazy. Most men didn't know how to fuck. She never had to go through the motions when Messiah had his dick in her.

There wasn't any fake moaning and groaning, no right hand on the bible swearing she'd had an orgasm when she really didn't, or none of that. Messiah rocked her shit every time he got up in her thighs. It felt sinful just thinking about it. Their ability to connect sexually made their vibe stronger. Very contradicting, but it was true.

Messiah couldn't dare sit before her and lie, claiming that he didn't feel something for Riley because she knew that would be some bullshit. If he wasn't really fucking with her then he wouldn't have been acting all crazy and shit. She'd tapped into his feelings, brought a thug down to his knees, and the nigga went nuts. End of story.

"Try to fight me off again, here?" he threatened before he opened his mouth and kissed and sucked all over her neck.

Her skin was smooth, clean, and mesmerizing, and the feeling of his flesh against hers mixed with what the liquor was doing to him, had him ready to dick her down. Messiah wanted to drown in that pussy right now. His lips and tongue kept taunting her soft spot before he trailed kisses along her face until he reached her lips.

Riley gave up. Her pussy was too wet; plus, she was too damn excited about being pregnant to even try to be hateful, knowing that she had every single right to be. She wrapped her arm around his back and they swapped tongues like she's been dying to do for weeks now. She was so overwhelmed about the baby that she couldn't believe she was letting him off the hook like that shit didn't really hurt her.

"I'm having your baby, Messiah. I'm ten weeks along," she whispered as tears fell down her eyes while a smile spread across her face.

She couldn't believe it. That's why she was really letting it loose at the range. She'd tried for seven long years to have a baby then, boom. One nut from Messiah the first time she'd had sex with a man who wasn't Tevin, and she was pregnant. It was blowing her mind.

"How you know?" He smirked.

She laughed a little.

"The pregnancy test told me so. It's in my purse."

"Where yo damn purse at?"

"Upstairs," she sassed while rolling her neck.

Messiah couldn't do anything but laugh.

"I'm too drunk for this shit, man."

He laid down beside her and shook his head at the thought of this whole situation. He was gonna be a father. Riley rolled over on top of him, removing the gun from his hand and held it up to his mouth. She had a vile look on her face as she retracted the chamber.

"I'm getting good at using this muthafucka too, so now, you gotta cut all yo hoes off, or else we really gonna have some problems. Let me find out you out here raw rodding these bitches, Messiah. And that bitch Kema? Cut her the fuck off. Now. Yeah, I know the bitch name, and I don't give a fuck what kinda history y'all got.

"Cut it, and if you think you getting off that easy for that shit you pulled the other week just because I found out I was pregnant, then you really got another thing coming. Do I look like a fucking joke to you? You better ask the last nigga who thought he could fuck with me. I clap back."

She gritted her teeth together as she pressed the gun underneath his chin now.

Messiah pulled it out her hands so fast and dismantled it, her mouth dropped. Riley must've forgotten that she was fucking with a real muthafucking G. He laughed at her before he wrapped his fingers around her throat, pulled her over him, and kissed her shit talking ass; but, she was right. It was clear that he couldn't hide the way he felt about her, and there was no reason to try now. She'd broken him in.

"A nigga owes you an apology, mama."

Riley smiled as she sat up.

"Apology accepted, but don't do that shit again. I got hands."

They shared a laugh.

"Damn man, it's a new fucking day," he sighed.

"You sound so happy." She rolled her eyes.

He glanced up at her with the raise of an eyebrow.

"Come on." He jumped up, wrapping her legs around his waist.

"Where are we going?"

"You talk too fucking much, man. Just shut the fuck up come on."

$\mathcal{T}$

It's only been ten weeks, and no, Riley and Messiah weren't madly in love with each other, but neither of them could deny the feelings that were brewing between them. She knew the connection was there, but she could also be honest and admit that she questioned Messiah's feelings towards her. He was the type of man who shut himself off when he felt like he was getting too close with a woman and it made her mind race, but after tonight he had her seeing him from a different perspective.

Her body was drained from the endless sexual pleasure he'd put on her the moment they boarded the G5 and headed up north to New York City. The skyline was beautiful as she laid in bed, her hair a hot mess, the air hot and sticky from the endless rounds they'd gone, suffocating her, and Messiah's strong arms wrapped around her while their eyes danced along the buildings when they touched down in the Big Apple.

The day was filled with hair dressers, shopping, site-seeing, and photographs that she'd most certainly print out and create a scrap book for versus saving them in her Apple Storage. Photographs were history. They told time. They revealed a happiness and other emotions that word of mouth solely couldn't capture to and describe.

Messiah had taken Riley's world filled with darkness and transformed it into a life with color in just a few months, and she wanted to cherish every last moment.

Was she crazy? Was she gullible? Was she falling into his superman syndrome by helping her walk away from Tevin? Was it real? Was it okay to feel for a man when most women swore that you shouldn't fuck him for the first three months to see if he really fucked with you?

Did his daily calling and texting mean nothing? Were they both caught up in that "new relationship" spell that would eventually break after a while? Was this right? Was doing the unthinkable permissible in 2016?

So many thoughts were captivating her, and her poor heart just couldn't take it, but one thing was for sure. He always kept a smile on her face minus one incident, and she had to admit that she admired that about him.

"Messiah, you are really showing out. That ass is sorry, huh?"

Riley was stunned when he grabbed her hand and walked with her along the roof top of the Mandarin Oriental Hotel. Her eyes lit up when she came across the table set for two, the live jazz band, and the team of servers awaiting them to provide their services.

"What is this? You did all of this! We haven't even been here a whole day!" She beamed with excitement.

It was pretty hard to stay mad when he was throwing shit at her from left and right every time she turned around. He grabbed her by the waist and scanned her from her feet on up. The black Gucci suede sandals with crystals accentuating the red Mugler evening gown that crisscrossed around her neck, and her new body wave, thirty-inch sew-in with the deep side part and the full choppy bang covering her left eye was stunning on her. He couldn't keep his eyes off his woman. That's right. His woman.

Messiah was turning twenty-eight in the winter, and he could either make the decision to keep fucking these hoes, breaking bitches' hearts, and keep sneaking around, which he never really did. He'd fuck a bitch then turn around and take the next one out an hour later even if it was her sister. Messiah was a savage, and even though that life was cool, and it came with no strings attached, shit was different now.

"I got class too, mama. It just took a certain kind of woman to bring it out of me."

Riley smiled as he led her to the table and helped her with her chair.

"Aww, shit, and you got the band playing some Kem? This is sooo dope. I love this song."

She bobbed her head to his "Love Calls" lyrics; the man singing had some vocals on him too.

"And I know you like to eat, so what's on this menu?" She questioned as she unrolled her serviette.

"Aw, you already know I'ma have 'em hook it up," he chuckled as they brought out their first dish.

Everything was so delicious. The creamy cucumber-avocado soup blew Riley's cap back the shit was so good. The mixed green salad with fresh sliced strawberries, feta cheese, glazed walnuts, and a homemade vinaigrette dressing went perfect with the crab and cheddar stuffed mushrooms, lamb chops, grilled jumbo shrimp, mashed potatoes with a garlic sauce, and asparagus. These two were perfect for each other. She could fuck some shit up right along with him, and she wasn't too cute to empty a plate and stack it right on top of his.

Riley was sipping on a glass of sparkling wine, full from their first three courses while taking everything in. Her thoughts were like a pinball bouncing back and forth making her dizzy from the hundreds of different scenarios steadily clouding her mind. It was so overwhelming that she couldn't even make eye contact with the man after a while.

"A'ight ma, it's time to talk on some real shit now. I know the look."

Riley finally looked into his eyes before she laughed.

"What look?"

"That look you get when something's on your mind."

Messiah leaned back in his chair not taking his eyes off her as he sipped the 1787; such a classic branch of wine.

"I pay attention to you more than you think I do, Riley. Like, how you chew on your bottom lip when you're nervous just as you're doing now. Or, how you only take your selfies from the right side of your face to hide the scar on your left jawline that you sometimes forget to cover up when you leave the crib."

Her mouth dropped, causing him to laugh.

"Yeah, shorty, I've noticed. Just like, how you lock every door behind you whether you're in ya room, the bathroom, or how you lock every window and all that shit too. The way you clutch the pillows at night and sleep with ya bat by the side of the bed like a muthafucka gon' come kick the door down and do to you what's been done in the past.

"I hate being up under muthafuckas. Cuddling just ain't never been me, but to see you so fucking shook and frightened; like, mentally etched from what that nigga has done to you, makes me wanna do nothing but protect you. So, I hold you a lil' closer and don't let go until you fall asleep. I don't feel forced to do it; I make the decision to make sure that you feel safe when you're around me.

"A nigga knows that he's earned his title as a 'ho ass nigga' from the way I was moving. I can own up to that. And I'ma be honest, ma, I don't even know where I got my playa' ways from. My pops, he ain't treat my moms like that. He cherished Mina, man. He loved and honored her.

"Good niggas do exist in this world when it seems like side chicks and strippers are the only women who receive glorification these days. How do I know? Because that's who George was. Active, supportive, sympathetic when he needed to be, festive, educated, and all that good shit.

"I just never wanted to be a sap ass nigga. Even we grew up in an era where ballers and shit were glorified, mama, and I got caught up in the hype. Am I a real ass nigga? Hell yeah. Will I ride for my dawgs? Damn right, but along the way, I just ain't gather up the desire to fuck with a female on an intimate level."

He laughed.

"That night you and Nasir showed up at The Flamingo, Seth had to tell a nigga to be nice because he already knows me. I wasn't fronting when I said I would've already fucked you. That's just how I've moved, but because my boy had respect for you and your girl, some shit I ain't neva' seen out that nigga before, I kept my cool and got to know you on a chill level versus sexual and sexual only.

"Real shit, me and bro, since the tenth grade, we did all our dirt together, ma, and Nas already know, so don't be sending no text messages to her ass like biiiiiiitch guess what. Trust me. She already hip."

Their laughter filled the air.

"What I'm saying though, to wrap up this lil' monologue," he flicked his thumb over his nose. "Is, a nigga couldn't control his feelings with you. And it threw me back like damn; I ain't fucked this girl yet? I mean a nigga was tryna hold back when we got to the crib. I ain't even wanna jump all over you like that, but when you took control and broke the ice," he raised his eyebrow causing her to smile.

"Even then though, I ain't fuck you like you was a ho, and trust me you would've known what that felt like, and I never would've fucked with you after that. For a long time with me and Seth, it's just been money over bitches. So, the calling, texting, laying up wit' you, and the dating? I can't lie to you when I say that it's not me.

"Let me correct that; it wasn't me. Yeah, I'll go out on a few dates here and there if I wanted to get out, or just to shut a few hoes up, but everything I did wit' you, ma, was heartfelt. It was genuine. This is genuine. I don't do shit that I don't wanna do. It's not me.

"When my peoples died a couple of years ago it kinda shifted shit around in my head a lil' bit. You know I've been raising my baby sus, Tiri, and just doing that alone? I love baby sus, don't get me wrong. I'll die for her. Don't nobody fuck with Tiri, and you've seen that. That lil' girl is my heart, and after having to raise her and like, really be affectionate with her so she knew that I was being genuine, mama?

"Just keeping her head up and constantly having to tell her she's pretty because she doesn't think it; that shit's a job, but it's made me realize how fucked up in the head I've been because I never really paid attention to my boo like that, or physically showed her how much I loved her until the car accident happened.

"I had to step up and be a man for her, and it kinda broke me in on how I should view women differently. I still moved how I moved once that happened, but I ain't came across no woman that made me wanna show that side of myself until I met you, and that's real shit. So you gotta forgive me if I don't hop on this shit all perfect. I fucked up. I can admit that, and I'm sorry."

Messiah stood up and grabbed Riley by the hand. Her face was flooding with tears and he couldn't help but smile.

"What the fuck I'ma do wit' you man? Cry baby ass."

She laughed as he wiped her tears away.

"Nooooo. I'm not a crybaby," she whined.

"I'm just playing, ma. Don't be so uptight. Come on."

He held her hand inside of his as he pulled her away from the table, then wrapped one arm around her waist. Their bodies began to sway back and forth to "Anniversary" by Tony Toni Tone that played in the air.

"I know you couldn't really read my feelings when you told me that you were pregnant," he continued.

Riley looked up into his eyes.

"Are you happy?" she asked with a quivering bottom lip.

He kissed her.

"I am. More happy for you than I am for myself."

"I don't want you to do this because of me, Messiah. Don't think that just because—"

"Aye," he raised his brow. "This is for *us*, ma. It's my child just as much as it's yours. I knew I was in trouble going up in that shit raw like that. I don't fuck bitches without no glove. So let's clear the air on that. I wouldn't disrespect myself like that, so why would I disrespect you? I'ma be honest though, with your condition—"

"You didn't expect me to pop up pregnant," she dropped her head. "I know, and me either. . .I'm like. . ." she inhaled deeply. "I'm just taking this all in like, God didn't give up on me, Messiah. I can't believe it. . ." she buried her face in his chest.

"That's why you gotta stay faithful, mama. Would you honestly want to bring the child in this world of the man whose got you trembling at the thought of an unlocked door? Karma is real, ma. Don't sweat off what you couldn't do for that nigga because the right one got you now. And I want you to trust me. Messiah got a lot to prove to you; a lot to prove to y'all, mama. A lot to prove to our family because that's what we gon' be.

"I ain't saying a'ight let's go to the altar, let's move in, and all that but I will be true to you and I'ma step up. You've done shit for me mentally and emotionally that you don't even know, and I owe you that. Straight had me acting all crazy and shit last night because you wanted to flirt with other niggas like you ain't know what the fuck it is. Even I was appalled."

Riley laughed so hard she had to let go of him.

"You set yourself up for that shit, Messiah. Gon' have that bitch eyeballing me."

He pulled her back into his arms.

"A'ight, I'll give you that. I'ma fix that though. On me I am—Aww shit this my cut," he bobbed his head as Maxwell's "Ascension" started playing in the air.

"Music. The gateway to the soul," Riley smiled as he spun her around.

"That's the realist shit ever, ma, and don't let them feet tap out on me either because we gotta dance that entre off to make room for dessert. I ain't turning down no key lime pie, so put a pep in yo step," he joked.

If he could make her laugh like this forever she never wanted it to end.

"What am I gonna do with your silly ass, Messiah?" she giggled as she threw her arms around his neck.

"Hold me down. You think you can do that?"

She kissed his lips.

"For sho'."

𝒯

Back in Saint Louis the streets were dark. Niggas were lurking, greed was at an all-time high, and revenge was the only thing being served on the menu. Three cars pulled up in the circular driveway each full of five men loading their M4's ready to shed blood.

"Five minutes tops. Get in and get the fuck out!" The voice barked over the speaker.

"Roger that. . ."

"Trudy...Trudy! Did Messiah leave me some money for my field trip tomorrow! He's always leaving! I told him I was gonna need some money!" Tiri pouted as she ran down the stairs and into the living room where her cousin was smoking weed with her three friends and her man. Her brother had spoiled her so rotten she couldn't help but be a brat.

"You know he left you some money, baby. He even left you a surprise. You like mine?" she teased as she shook her wrist flashing the brand-new Rolex on her arm.

"Awwwwn! This hella fire, Trudy! Yellow diamonds! This Riley got my nigga on his toes! He's been all extra nice and shit!" Tiri beamed as she held her cousin's hand.

"I'm hip. He say he gon' bring her by so we can meet her."

"I've met her. She's so pretty, and she's hella cool. She ain't no stuck-up lil' bitch who's happy she's fucking him because he's a kingpin. She hella real, and my nigga geeked over her. Like, he's stuck y'all."

Laughter filled the air. Tiri was a goof troop.

"Well, shit, I gotta approve of this girl. Anybody to get Messiah on the right path and not wanting to be a ho no more gets a muthafucking hand clap from me. Okay, baby cousin?"

"Okay!"

"You wanna hit this?"

Tiri's heart raced when Trudy passed her the blunt.

"Maybe once."

Everyone laughed.

"Don't act like this yo first time hitting no blunt, lil' momma. You ain't innocent," Trudy's boyfriend, Glock, laughed while he rolled up another Backwoods.

Tiri inhaled like a pro and let the smoke leave her mouth while inhaling it back through her nose.

"Daaaaaamn. You be smoking, girl! Y'all see that shit?"

Tiri laughed.

"Don't tell Messiah. He'll kick my ass. Y'all already know he think he my damn daddy."

"Yo secret safe with me. You finish all yo work and stuff for school?"

Tiri rolled her eyes.

"Man nah. I hate trigonometry. Ain't like I'ma use that shit another day in my life."

"Go do it. I told you to use that app My Mathway. It'll tell you all the answers. That's how I'm getting through college," Trudy shrugged.

"I forgot you told me about that. Thanks cousin."

"You welcome."

Tiri ran up the stairs and went to her brother's room to find the fat wad of money on the dresser along with a small Gucci box next to it.

"Aaaaah! Messiah! Not the Gucci diamond headband like Nicki Minaj! I love it! He's the best big brother ever, I swear to God! Ma and Pops! He takes good care of me. He's always in and out because him and Uncle Seth be so busy running the city, but he's always there for me.

"He does me so good. I'm so glad y'all blessed me with a brother like him. He's really stepped up. Whoever I end up marrying gotta treat me like a princess just like he does. I swear we miss y'all. Every day y'all got me wondering what heaven looks like. It's so surreal."

Tiri held the headband close as she looked at the picture of their folks taped to his dresser. It brought tears to her eyes. A day didn't go by when she didn't think about her parents, but she was so thankful to have her brother. He reminded her a lot of their dad when he wasn't being a ho, and she wouldn't trade him for the world.

The moment she put the money in her pocket she picked her phone up to take a selfie with her new accessory. She also made sure to flash her new full-set that she went to get with Riley and Nas last weekend. After getting the opportunity to only snap one pic that she didn't like, the sound of gunshots ringing in the house frightened her seventeen-year-old soul so much that she couldn't move.

"Tiriiiiiiiii! Tir—"

Tat! Tat! Tat! Tat! Tat!

"Trudy!"

Tiri screamed at the top of her lungs when she heard her cousin's voice being silenced by gunshots. Tiri panicked. She heard the footsteps coming up the stairs and just knew they were coming for her. She locked the door and ran for the window.

"Messiah!" She screamed with tears running down her face.

She reached up and grabbed onto the gutter before she could pull herself up onto the roof. Thank God she was a small framed girl. Her heart was racing. Was this real! Was she dreaming! Tiri crawled on top of the roof until she made it over to the ladder that would get her back to the ground. She could hear voices, but she couldn't see anyone, it was so dark out.

"Hurry the fuck up! The bitch must be hiding or something. Blow the fucking house to pieces! Fuck it!"

Tiri watched the men drop a suitcase next to house and run for the street. Tiri never felt her body work so hard. She jumped down off of the ladder and ran until she made it to the tall wire fence and started to climb. Her body flew in the air when the orange flames rose in the sky and her home exploded into pieces. The sound of dogs barking made her open her eyes and hop up quick. Two large pit bulls came charging at her and she was petrified.

"Messiaaaaaaaaah!"

Her feet ran as fast as she could, but one of the dogs caught her by her pants leg causing her to fall to the ground.

"Help meeeee! Aaaaaah!"

They both were tugging at her sweats, and the first thought was to slide those bitches off and keep running. They charged for her again and by the grace of God she managed to get away and run until she came across a familiar street called Board Walk. She ran until she reached a vacant house with a garage door that could only unlock from the touch of her Apple Watch. She prayed to God that she still had it on before she got in the tub.

Inside was the black Dodge Charger Messiah had shown her a few months ago and kept reminding her about if she'd ever gotten into trouble. Her fingers trembled as she searched through the boxes of newspapers until she found the lock box with the key inside.

He always warned her that this day was going to come, but she always thought he was bluffing. Niggas was scared of Messiah, they knew not to fuck with him, and they'd never come after him. Or so she thought. . .

She unlocked the car and got inside with her heart racing. Tiri had just gotten her permit and had only driven a couple of times around the block, so she didn't know what the fuck to do. Come on now, she's a late bloomer. She couldn't just jump and get a license because she didn't know how to drive. Give the girl a break.

"What do I do!" She panicked.

Tiri couldn't figure out where to put the damn key so she could start the car. She flipped the arm rest open and pulled out the phone that was stowed away inside. Her body shook uncontrollably as it took its time to come on.

"Messiah please pick up! Please, please. . ."

T

"Messiah! Oh my God, baby! Ooooh yesssss, Messiah! Oh, baby don't stop! Ooooh fuck!"

Riley felt possessed. His tongue flicked back and forth over her clit at a speed she couldn't keep up with. She held onto the top of his head and thrust her hips against his face as she felt her rain fall down.

"Stop! Messiah, stop! Ooooh, fuck!"

Her body collapsed on top of the pillows from her previously sitting up, leaning against her elbows, and she couldn't help it when her full-set clutched the sheets. The man wouldn't quit. His mouth slurped on her clit, and his tongue traveled from her slit to her butt while his fingers played with her creamy love button.

He was drunk as fuck and wasn't nothing stopping him from devouring her pussy... until the ringtone that he never should've heard go off on his phone filled the air. Then, he sat up immediately and hopped out of the bed. His heart dropped when he saw the number.

"Messiah! Messiah, please! I can't believe this, Messiah pleaaaaaase!"

"Tiri! What happened!"

His heart dropped as he went over to the duffle bag he'd purchased when they were shopping earlier and slid into some sweats. This mini getaway was over.

"Messiaaaaah!"

"Baby girl, calm down! Quit yelling and tell me what the fuck happened!"

He loaded the Desert Eagle as if he could physically do something in that moment, but that was just off instinct.

"All I heard was gunshots and Trudy screaming! They killed them, Messiah! They killed my Trudy! Then they came for me, but I jumped out the window!"

Her cries filled the phone once again. He sent out a mass text to his mob to head out to Hazelwood County with his other phone before he placed a call to Seth.

"Our house is gone! Mommy and daddy's house is gone, Messiah, they blew it up! Please, I'm so scared! I don't know what to dooooo! I can't even start the car, Messiah, pleaaaaaase! I don't wanna die! I need you!"

Messiah put her on speaker as he went through the phone to find her location. He saw she was still in the area, but he needed her to be safe.

"Tiri, listen to me! Listen to me, bae, a'ight? You hear me! Tiri, answer me!" He panicked.

"I'm listening," she cried, trying her best to be strong.

"You already in the car, bae, so just put yo foot on the brake and push the start button."

She did as she was told and felt the car start up.

"Where am I gonna go, Messiah! I've only drove around the block twice! I can't fucking drive!"

"Tiri, listen to me! Whose baby sister are you, huh? Who you fuck with? Who got yo back?"

"Messiah," she sobbed.

"Who!"

"Messiah!"

"That's right! Muthafucking, Messiah! I don't take no shit from nobody, and you won't from this muthafucking day forward either. Hook the phone up to the Bluetooth. I'ma send you an address to go to. I'ma have Tito meet you at a safe house, alright? You can't be scared, bae. Right now ain't the time for all that shit. I know I gotta stop spoiling you, but right now you gotta know that you can do this shit, ma, a'ight! You hear me?"

"Yes," she cried as she backed the car out, making the vehicle jerk a few times until she pulled out smoothly.

"You get the address?"

"Yes."

"Alright. Stay on the phone. I'ma let you talk to Riley so she can calm you down while I hit up Seth. I'm on my way back in town, alright? I love you."

"Okay. I love you too, Messiah. Just please hurry. . ."

Chapter Twenty-Four

"*Oh* my God! Messiah!"

Tiri wrapped her arms around her brother the moment he busted through the door of their safe house. She instantly started to cry her eyes out; her body soon went limp, and he had no choice but to drop down to his knees. He held her close with his arms around her waist.

Messiah's heart had been racing the whole way back to town while Riley had gotten Tiri to calm down and sleep the fright off after a while, but finally seeing each other had sparked everything she'd just previously been through.

"I'm here, bae. I'm here."

He rubbed the back of her head with his eyes closed trying his damnest not to shed a tear. This shit was really war now. Coming for his baby sister though? Yeah okay. Messiah was about to fuck some shit up. Fuck Seth and that level-headed shit. He was on all that shit, and he wouldn't stop until he got blood.

"You a'ight? You not hurt or nothing are you?"

He pulled her off of him to examine her body. She had abrasion to her jaw line and cheeks, a few bruises, and he peeped the gauze around her ankles from the dog bites.

"What the fuck happened to yo ankles?" He barked.

"The two pit bulls from next door," she sobbed as she held her hand up to her nose.

Messiah stood up and paced the room back and forth. Next thing he knew his fist went through the cement wall, but he didn't feel shit. He was ready to kill somebody.

"Y'all catch anybody in the area?" He hollered as he turned to face Tito.

"As a matter of fact, we did."

Messiah's blood boiled when he noticed Vince, one of Jediah's potnas when the lights on the far end of the room flicked on. He couldn't control himself when he sent a bullet through the nigga's chest while he was strapped down to the revolving wall like Frankenstein.

"Ahhhhhh!"

"Bitch ass nigga don't cry now!"

Messiah's fist wouldn't let up. You would've thought he was training with a punching bag the way his fist kept lighting his face and chest.

"Since you gon' get a nigga all musty and shit, then I'ma make sure this shit worth it, muthafucka!" He yelled as he used a screwdriver and dug it into the man's eye.

Vince's screams filled the air as the end of the tool dug deep into his face while Messiah took his time, wanting this bitch ass nigga to feel every ounce of pain he had to endure upon him.

"Awww, nigga you okay?" Messiah asked sincerely while holding his eye in his hand.

He had a wicked smile across his face as he let it drop to the floor and squished it with his shoe.

"Let me guess? This nigga went back to make sure it wasn't no fucking witnesses huh?" He then smirked. "The fuck you worried about witnesses fo' nigga if y'all dun got shit popping?"

"Aaaah!"

When Messiah's fist merged with his nose, the sound of it breaking could be heard in the air.

"A team was sent by Jediah. They were hoping you'd be home," Tito informed, spilling everything he'd gotten from out of Vince before he arrived.

Before Messiah could respond the door opened, and in walked his partner in crime.

"Damn nigga? Y'all make it in fast enough? I'm just getting the game started with this nigga. You want some?" He laughed throwing his hands up happy to see his dawg before the malice grazed his face once again.

Seth's expression matched the one painted on his potna's face. He wrapped his arms around his Baby T, scanned her body over, taking in all her scrapes and bruises before he kissed her forehead and walked over to their house guest.

"Jediah," Messiah spat. "We on that shit, Seth. Fuck the bullshit. Them niggas want blood, then let's get this shit cracking. I ain't playing with these niggas no more. It's obvious they tryna take us out.

"First the bullshit down in Sycamore, and now this?! If this lil' girl wouldn't be right here standing nigga I'd already be at the palace with them niggas' heads on a platter waiting on yo arrival, bruh!"

Seth rubbed his chin and chuckled at the man screaming with blood dripping along the floor from the hole in his face.

"Baby T," Messiah hollered getting her attention, too amp about this shit.

His sister didn't want to, but she walked over with her hands over her mouth trying to muffle her cries.

"These niggas tried to kill you. They tryna kill yo brother, Uncle Seth, and they killed Trudy," he continued.

Seth dropped his head and said a silent prayer over his potna's family following the pain in his dawg's voice. He hated to see Trudy get caught up in the crossfire of this shit. They'd already lost their folks and now, one of the only other people that he held the closest to him was gone too. Seth felt his potna's pain right now.

When he picked his head up, he saw the two guns from Messiah's waistline in Tiri's hands. She stood before Vince with an evil glare in her eyes before she emptied out the clips. Her fingers worked the triggers until all she heard was clicking. Blood splattered along the floor like she was shooting darts at balloons filled with paint, the hollow points were so swift and powerful.

Tiri dropped the guns down to the ground once the spell of vengeance and retribution wore off her, and she buried her face in her brother's chest. The poor girl had caught her first body at seventeen.

"We gotta get them out of here. I'ma send them to the territory we got in Canada until we get this shit straight. I've already gotten in touch with the school board and got Eloquent closed for all of next week to avoid them tryna come up in there looking for her or Nas.

"I paid off the gym Ry works at to close up shop too. We narrowing it down for these niggas to directly come to us. I even sent Meme Aruba and Darcy out there already. I don't trust them niggas," Seth explained knowing it was time to bring terror to Saint Louis unlike anyone had ever seen before.

"Let's rock these niggas shit to sleep, mane. I don't give a fuck how much blood gon' be shed and who get in the way. No mercy nigga," Messiah countered.

Seth nodded his head in agreement.

"I feel it."

T

"Seth, please be safe."

Nas' lip quivered as she looked into his eyes. He couldn't get her to board the plane for nothing. At first it irritated the fuck out of him that she wouldn't listen and insisted on arguing with him during a time like this, but when he looked into her eyes and saw the pain resting behind them, he realized that this woman was deeply concerned.

Nas loved him. He could feel it. He wrapped his arms around her and held her close. They stood in silence. The wind blew hard. It was almost November, so the fall air was lingering over the city while their hair blew in each other's faces.

"I will, mama," he finally spoke.

"I just want you to be safe, babe," she whispered. "I wouldn't know what to do if something happened to you."

Seth held her tighter before saying, "I'ma be honest. I don't know how long this gon' take."

Nasir looked up into his eyes frightened from his response.

"Could be a day, could be a week. Depending on how hard them niggas clap back we could be making this shit shake for a while."

She let go of him and put her face in her hands.

"Aye, you ain't got shit to be scared of."

"I know you're about this life, Seth. I know what you're capable of, but I'm just concerned about your safety. How many times am I gonna have to stress that!"

"Nas, baby, come on."

She looked back at her mother whom, Seth was sending away with her as well. He knew what it was like to lose a loved one. On more than one occasion, and he didn't want Nas to have to face that hurt. She already didn't have a father. Niggas would come after her in any way, shape, or form to get to him, and he didn't want to jeopardize anything.

"I'm coming," she whispered, forcing herself to calm down.

Catori smiled before she turned around, pulling the shawl over her shoulders and climbed the stairs.

"You love me?" he asked her while lifting her chin and looking into her eyes.

"What kind of stupid ass question is that, Seth?" Nas cried with tears falling down her face, and embarrassed that she'd honestly loved this man when they were only at the three-month mark.

"Answer me," he ordered.

"Yes, I love you. I don't care what anyone says or how brief time has been. I do love you, and I'm not afraid to say it anymore. I just don't wanna see you get hurt."

Seth kissed her lips.

"I love you too."

Nasir felt those words in the depths of her soul. Niggas threw out an "I love you" like wild cards to buy another round in the game, but hearing those words break through Seth's lips did something to her that she never wanted to go away.

"It's crazy, Nas. I trust you more than the people that have been in my life for years and years now. It's like I know I'm supposed to watch over you; like I know I'm supposed to love you. I'm everything short of perfect, mama. Mean as fuck and all that shit but for you," he smirked.

"I can put my alias on hold and give you what you need. I'll keep trying until I perfect the way I'm supposed to do it. We still got a long way to go, but after this we gon' keep going about this shit *together*, a'ight? When me and Siah pop out in Toronto to get y'all, you'll wish that thoughts of doubting me never would've infested yo mind. I can't promise that I'ma make it back in one piece, but I'ma try."

Nasir smiled.

"Keanu said the same thing about Akamu; how he felt that he was supposed to love and protect her from the moment they met too. She told me a lot when we were in Hawaii...I know it sounds crazy Seth and—"

He kissed her lips shutting her up.

"Less talking, more listening. Now get yo ass on that plane."

She smiled as he slapped her butt.

"Okay."

Nas looked over her shoulder and glanced at Seth before she entered the jet. To her surprise, Messiah was still on board with his arms around his sister. Him and his mean ass best friend could be really sweet when they wanted to be.

"I might not answer right away, but text me when y'all make it in, a'ight?"

Tiri nodded her head yes not wanting to let him go.

"Hug Riley. I know I'll see you again," she smiled as she looked up into his eyes.

He kissed her forehead before she finally released him, and he headed over to his woman.

"Don't stress yo' self out, a'ight?"

Messiah's voice was soft as he leaned over with his hands on either side of Riley who was sitting with her legs crossed in one of the personal chairs.

"I won't," she half smiled.

Messiah kissed her lips. Their heads swayed back and forth for a minute before he stood up, said his fellow goodbyes to everyone else, and the door to the jet closed behind him.

The plane soon took off and began to soar through the clouds. Everyone had fallen asleep within an hour except for Riley. Her mind was racing, and she was soon to spazz out if she didn't open her mouth and speak up about what was eating away at her insides. She got up and walked over to Nas who was curled up with her knees inside of Seth's Nike hoodie. She was knocked out with drool all over the leather.

"Hey, sleepy head," Riley nudged her cousin.

"What happened? Are we there?" Nasir panicked as she jumped up.

Riley laughed.

"No silly. Sit up. I wanna cuddle."

Nas smiled as she leaned up against the arm rest, and her older cousin laid between her legs. Catori and Tiri were sleeping in the bedroom, so they had the front to themselves. Riley pulled the plush cover over them as Nas wrapped her arms around her.

"What's on your mind?" she yawned covering her mouth.

"A lot." Ry sighed.

"Like?"

"Liiiiike... how I'm gonna be a mom in seven more months." She looked back at Nas who had the widest smile slapped across her face.

"What! Are you serious!"

"Shhhhhhh! You'll wake everybody up," Riley giggled.

Nas squeezed her with all her might while trying to keep her squeals concealed.

"A baby Messiah! Shut uuuuuuup! I'm soooooo happy for you, Bookie boo!!!!!! Is that what you were talking about the other day when I was in Hawaii?"

"Yes. Girl, my mind has just been fucking blown; like, I can't believe this. One nut girl. I knew I shouldn't have fucked him that night we left the Flamingo, but you always cursing somebody with that 'Let's go be hoes' spell, now look at my ass."

Nasir was cracking up.

"That chant always gets us into some shit, doesn't it?"

"It really does. I'm surprised *you* haven't popped up pregnant yet with all the nuts Seth dun' busted up in your ass."

"Oh my God! Shut up! Don't wish that on me!"

They shared a laugh.

"And girl, I don't know how, but Tevin's been texting me on some, 'Bitch I know you fucking that nigga from the Platinum cartel. You still ain't shit. You still can't have no kids. You gon' be miserable all yo fucking life. Ain't no other nigga gon' do for you what I did—'"

"What?" Nas cut her off after hearing enough. "I thought he was blocked, Ry?"

"He is, but he keeps on texting me from all these different fucking numbers and I just,"

"Get it changed, baby. Fuck him. Break all yo ties with that nigga. The way Messiah's feeling right now, Tevin will be on his list to get popped next."

"Okay? I haven't even told him."

"About the baby or about Tevin?"

"About that shit with Tevin. He knows about the baby. That's how we quote-unquote "made up". I told you about the shooting range, didn't I?"

"Bitch, noooooo, you haven't."

Riley laughed.

"All this happened so unexpectedly it slipped my mind," she sighed, referring to their current situation.

"I went out to the shooting range that night we got off the phone and was fucking some shit up. You should see me now, Nas, a bitch is cold with a thumper. But anyways, this ugly ass Moneybagg Yo looking ass nigga was tryna talk to me. Girl, I was so fucking high I couldn't stop laughing at his ugly ass because I'm flaming him in my head so bad.

"He thought I was actually into him; like nigga, no, you ugly as fuck. Long story short, Messiah pops up, drunk as fuck, knocks the nigga out, throws me over his shoulder, and carries me down to his office.

"Girl, he was tryna go off on me like I was the one who was with another bitch and shit, and he was waving a fucking gun at me, choking me and shit tryna be all zaddish, making my fucking panties wet no matter how pissed off I was."

They shared a laugh.

"Then he gets to talking crazy and says something like, Riley, who the fuck you think you are, because I was going off, and I was like, nigga yo fucking baby momma! That's who the fuck I am!"

"My bitch shut that shit all the way down! Yaaaas best friend. I told you to check that nigga. Even though he was still in control of that situation."

The best thing about their relationship was that they could always count on a laugh from one another.

"So yeah... I told him, he couldn't believe it, I couldn't believe it, and the next thing I know is we ended up in New York City. We shopped, we fucked, we ate, we fucked some more, then he had this cute lil' dinner set up for us on the roof of the hotel we were staying at. There was a live band and the food was so fucking good. Trust me Nas, that nigga was really sorry.

"Then, he got to telling me about why he was the way he was and how after his parents died things changed for him but not completely. He claims meeting me got his act right but he still a lil' rough around the edges. Definitely gotta polish that nigga up for sure."

Nas slapped her forehead.

"Girl, him and Seth both. So, are you gonna say something about Tevin?"

"Man, hell nah. I know not to do that shit. I know how Tevin is and I know Messiah. I don't have time for any mess, and if anything, I'm still kinda on the fence about me and Messiah. I'm happy, don't get me wrong, but it's just like are we moving too fast?"

"Trust me girl. I know all too well. Seth and I told each other I love you today," her voice was soft.

"Really best friend? Do you really love him?"

Nas smiled.

"Yeah... I do. I know, I know... there's no need to get into the time argument. Fuck time. Sometimes that *time* can be your worse fucking enemy. It's like if you love someone, love them. If you feel something, feel it. If you wanna do something, then do it. Tomorrow's not promised.

"Now I'm not saying get out there and just go be stupid, but sometimes you just gotta trust and listen to your heart, Ry. Fuck

Tevin's ole' whack ass. We can pay some niggas in Atlanta to fuck his ass ragged since all he knows how to do is be a bitch anyway."

"I hate you!"

Their laughter filled the air. Moments later both Catori and Tiri came from out the back yawning and wiping their eyes.

"Y'all just won't let us sleep, huh?" Catori yawned again as she took a seat across from them.

"Sorry, mommy."

"It's okay. Is it too early in the morning for wine? I'm about to call the kitchen and pop some Riesling like now. All of this shit has me a bit uneasy. I will say this. I don't know what y'all doing to them niggas, but y'all got some good ones."

"That's the power of the p...ooops."

"Omg, Tiri! Make that two glasses mommy; I can-not! But Riley can't have any," Nas taunted while shaking her head.

"Messiah got you pregnant!" Tiri smiled from ear to ear unable to hold her comment back. "I'm gonna be an auntie! Omg, congrats Ry!" She clapped her hands in excitement.

"You're pregnant, Bookie! My God in heaven! Thank you!" Catori jumped up, got down to her knees, and prayed, causing them all to laugh, but she was right.

It was truly a blessing. How could they not praise Him?

"Now I'm just waiting on Nas so we can have a double baby shower. Seth been digging all up in them cakes auntie," Riley taunted in return.

"Oh, my gosh! Where's the wine! Y'all gotta prepare me for shit like this! Not today Satan!"

Their laughter filled the air. Conversation between the ladies carried on for another hour before they all arrived in Toronto. The women looked like celebrities as they exited the jet in their floor length furs perfect for the 22-degree weather up north while they headed to the limo that awaited them.

The drive for miles taking in the Canadian landscaping was an adventure all in itself. The beauty and obvious differences from there to their home town as the driver entered the Bridle Path area of the city, could be spotted by a blind man. They traveled a total of three miles up a steep hill before they arrived at the 60,000 square foot castle that Nabawi had been hiding for years now.

Nas' mouth was lower than an old lady's saggy ass titties down to her navel as she exited the limo with her hood hanging low over her eyes.

"Oh my God," was all she could say as they followed the driver and henchmen who transported all of their belongings. It was absolutely amazing.

"Shut up! Are we in Genovia!" Tiri shrieked at the odd resemblance that it had to the Princess Diaries castle.

It was similar to the one Seth owned in St. Louis, but this home was ginormous. They all were speechless when the sound of cranks filled the air and a bridge lowered that would allow them all to cross on the Rolls Royce golf carts that awaited them.

"Well I'll be," Catori gasped as they each looked below the bridge at the freezing cold river.

The water was shielded by a thin layer of ice as they made it across to the new section of land.

"This is a fucking dream! Sorry tee-tee Catori, but..." Riley couldn't even finish her sentence.

"Shit, you! There's no way that only running a cartel produced this. Seth and Messiah have to have something else up their sleeves! This is beyond my fucking imagination! Oh, my Lord!"

"Yeah, and next time, can they get golf carts that are like insulated or have a roof and doors! I'm freezing!" Tiri yelled over the winds with her arms crossed over her midsection.

"My dearest apologies ladies. We weren't expecting you to arrive so soon. We didn't have the opportunity to switch out this season's travel vehicles. It's been years since anyone has been here," their driver explained with the sincerest apology.

Once they traveled through a pretty long tunnel, they finally arrived at the front of the home where large French styled doors made of pure gold stood before them. Nas was so blown away she had her phone out recording it like she was on tour.

Of course, she wasn't on social media. Seth didn't cuff a bimbo now. This was going in the video box for sure when she looked back on the past and revisited the journey of their unwritten escapade.

"You ladies have arrived! Hi!"

They all turned around when they heard the sweet voice of Meme Aruba who was accompanied by her husband. They'd pulled up just minutes behind them. They laid over at a hotel not wanting to go to the house until the ladies showed up.

"Hi, Keanu!" Nasir beamed as she held her arms up to embrace her.

"Hello my sweet, Nasir. Oooooh child are you pregnant! I sense some new birth vibes in here now."

Nas laughed.

"I'm not pregnant, but my cousin is. Here, let me introduce you to everyone."

"Are you sure you're not pregnant too? I'll have to do the toothpaste trick in the morning when you have your first pee, and best believe that I will be waiting."

"Really, Meme Aruba!" She gasped.

"You know how I am with the vibes, baby. This old bird still has it. This is my husband Darcy. Darcy this is Seth's future wife, Ms. Nasir," she informed while grabbing her chin, just knowing that they would be wedded in the future.

"Nice to meet you, Ms. Nasir. She hasn't stopped talking about you since your trip in Hawaii."

"Awwwn. It's nice to meet you too Darcy. You too. Everybody, this is Seth's great grandmother Keanu or Meme Aruba, and her husband Darcy. This is my family. My beautiful mother Catori, my best friend and favorite cousin, Riley, whom is the pregnant one Ms. Keanu."

"Oh, it's a girl. I feel it. Child you been sleeping with Messiah's crazy ass? He needs someone to level him out, and his daughter and her mother will surely do it. God bless you baby. You're gonna have to bring her by the islands after you have her, and you're just as beautiful! My God all these tattoos! Do you and Nasir have enough? Y'all some tough ass women, I see."

Riley laughed.

"Thank you, Keanu, so much. I've heard nothing but great things about you."

"And you know Tiri," Nas finished.

"Yes, baby, you've grown up! I heard about the incident with the house; you poor child. Thank the heavens you're alive and well. I've got a remedy for those ankles that will help them heal up in no time."

Tiri looked like she'd just seen a ghost. How could she have possibly known about that? She knew Messiah hadn't spilled specific beans about everything. Tiri had always been convinced the woman was part psychic ever since she was a little girl. Her assumptions were always one hundred percent true, and it was freaky...

T

Nas was unpacking her Gucci luggage bag trying her hardest not to pick up the phone and call Seth again but... *You have reached the voicemail box of...* She threw the phone along the bed and ran her fingers through her hair.

"I've gotta chill," she mumbled as she pulled out the freezer bag filled with lime green and orange buds, then a box of Berry Backwoods.

The rooms in the house were huge; huge like from *The Haunting* huge. They all connected by an adjoining wall with a revolving door in the center. She still couldn't believe that she was here right now, so much was going through her head that she honestly couldn't even think.

"Ms. V! Ms. V! Oh my God! Ms. V!"

"What, baby, what!"

Nas hopped up off of the bed and met her halfway in the middle of the bedroom floor.

"Your video went viral, Ms. V! It's at a million views!"

Nas was so speechless her mouth looked like it was waiting on Seth to shove his dick inside of it.

"What!"

"Ms. V, that's you! Yaaaaass! Sexy as fuuuuuuuuuck! Look at you! I swear something told me this video was gonna blow some smoke!"

There Nas was, one million views later, in a crop top, high waist spankies with the Nasir tattoo on her ass peeking through, and some over the knee, leather 5-inch heels throwing her ass, hips, and wild hair to Trey Songz's "Animal" sexy as can be. She couldn't believe it.

"Is this The Shaderoom?!"

"Yeeeeees, Ms. V! Everybody is begging for another video! What you got girl! I know you have another dance that we can record like, today!"

"Shut up, Tiri!"

They both squealed so loud in excitement that it caused everyone to race in the room.

"Well, that's a big bag of weed!" Keanu gasped with her hands on her face. Nothing got pass her.

Nas doubled over in laughter. She loved that woman honestly.

"What's all of the hollering about? You're pregnant too?"

"Mommy! Why y'all tryna jinx me! Noooo!"

"Her video went viral on social media, Ms. Catori! Look at your daughter!"

"Whaaaaat! Which video?"

"The one to "Animal" by Trey Songz," Tiri showed them the phone.

"Naaaaaaas! Baby, look at you cutting it up! You really about to have Seth out here going nuts now. He's already crazy," Riley joked.

"Have you heard from Mesaiah?" Nas asked softly, not meaning to change the subject.

"No. Not yet," her cousin answered with a half-smile.

Nasir took a deep breath. She'd been trying to keep her cool, but she just knew a bunch of shit was about to unfold, and her heart couldn't handle it.

"Now, now. I know this is a hard time for you ladies. Nobody ever said that it would be easy. Shit, this is only the beginning. If you think this is something, then imagine what else is to unfold the longer you see yourself on Seth's arm?" Keanu's words were the least bit encouraging.

That fast a pin had been stuck in Nas' balloon, and she couldn't control the way tears began to trickle down her face.

"Awww, baby."

Catori sat next to her daughter and wrapped her arms around her. Nas buried her face in her mother's chest. Ever since they made it to Toronto she'd been asking herself if this was something she really wanted. Love and a lavish life came with a price to pay no matter how illegal or legit the road to those riches were. Hell, even celebrities weren't one hundred percent happy with life. Nas would bet any money on it.

Maybe it was just her nerves getting her all worked up. Or maybe being the woman of a kingpin was really too much for her. Nas was an introvert. You take a woman who's used to being alone, you place her in the middle of the limelight, and it's almost like a culture shock for her.

"How about this," Keanu smiled as she grabbed Tiri and Riley by the hands. "We'll have girl-talk later because it's obvious that an old woman does need to school this new generation about love, relationships, and holding on to your sanity, but for right now let's all get washed up and have some fun.

"There's 60,000 square feet of pure paradise at our fingertips right now. Between the bowling alley, dance studio, work out rooms, and the dozen other amenities here, we should keep busy while Darcy figures out what he's gonna fix us to eat."

"Meme Aruba, you got that man cooking? How?" Catori laughed before she kissed her baby's forehead.

"I sure as hell do. He's younger than I am. He just turned eighty, and he still gets down in that kitchen, I'll tell you. But that's just gonna be lunch. I'm sure we can get something more up you lady's alley for dinner. So what do you ladies say? There's a spa here as well. I think we all could use some facials and a mud bath."

"A massage does sound good right now," Riley agreed.

"Mani and pedi?" Tiri questioned while raising her arms and shrugging her shoulders.

"Can I bring my weed?" Nas whined.

"Of course, you can. I'll see if we can get our hands on some wine as well," Catori ensured.

"Well, let's make sure we stop at the cellar first, then!"

"A cellar! Lord have mercy don't tell me that Keanu," Catori placed her hand on her chest. Wine was the key to her heart.

"This is getting ready to be a long seven months without weed. I was pushing it the other day since I was in denial about my pregnancy," Riley sighed.

The marijuana consumption during pregnancy debate was very controversial, and even though she knew a lot of mothers who smoked while carrying, she promised to refrain from doing it. She wasn't taking her chances when it took her seven years to finally get pregnant.

"Well, what about me?"

"What about you?" Keanu questioned as she looked at Tiri. "You out here smoking baby?"

Tiri put her face in her hands, hiding her smile.

"Don't be ashamed. I've been smoking since I was fifteen. Maybe that's what's wrong with me. Hell, I even smoked all of my seven pregnancies, but my kids turned out fine. I didn't use those trashy cigarellos though. Papers only. Judge me all you want."

"Keanu!" Nas gasped letting the laughter escape her lips.

"Well I did. And not those God forsaken cigarettes either. Those damn things are the devil, but yes, I did, and I'm not afraid to say it. You ladies come on. I wanna see some smiles on your faces. Happiness, daily tea and herbs for the body, and moderate exercise will get you to ninety just like me, so let's get to it and make the most out of our time here. A Platinum man may bend, but he won't break. I feel it in my heart that they will be okay. Now come on. Let's have some fun."

T

Falcon's hands shook uncontrollably as she finished the rest of the letter before sealing it and dropping it in the mailbox.

She quickly exited the Post Office and headed to her car before she pulled out of the parking lot and headed back home. She felt like a prisoner in her own life; in her own marriage. Osiris had been out of control and at the rate he was going, there was no telling what the fuck was about to go down.

 No matter how much she loved him, she didn't want to be around to see it. Her Porsche raced down the freeway. The Louboutin bootie on her foot pushed down harder against the gas while switching lanes. All she could think about was the luggage she had packed and the plane ticket she had for the Bahamas.

Falcon had to get away, and if she didn't have anyone else to turn to, she knew that Meme Aruba would welcome her with open arms. She needed some time to breathe, but she also needed to weigh her options on leaving her husband.

Osiris would kill Falcon before he ever granted her the opportunity to walk away from him. She'd known that with every bone in her body, but the man who'd just blacked her eye last night and gave her whip lash once he found out about her evening out at Blush with Nasir, was not her husband.

She couldn't take the pressure any longer. Osiris was so paranoid he was beginning to think that she was secretly communicating with Seth, who was still refusing to talk to her. Everything was just a mess, but she hated that she couldn't get through to her son. She blamed herself. She never should've crossed him.

Falcon should've intervened and got Osiris to do anything other than a crossover, but that was all in the past now. What's done was done, but that didn't mean that she was going to give up. Her son needed her, and no matter what it took she was gonna do whatever she could in her power to get through to him.

Falcon pulled into the garage praying to God, thanking Him that Osiris was still out on business affairs. Jediah's car wasn't there either, so she hurried up and ran inside to make sure she had all she'd need for her vacation. She pulled her wedding ring from around her finger and left it in her pantie drawer knowing it had a tracking device on it.

Your driver is 4 minutes away.

Shit! she panicked once she received the notification from the Uber app. Falcon rummaged around her dressing room making sure she had all her belongings before she grabbed the last suitcase and headed out.

"Where you going?"

Frightened out of her mind, she dropped the luggage when she turned around and saw her son standing behind her.

"Don't scare me like that," she gasped while holding her chest.

"That's not answering my question, Falcon."

"Jediah, I am a grown ass woman; not to mention your fucking mother. I don't know what the hell has gotten into you, but you better calm the fuck down and recognize who the hell I am," she spat, fed up with the way he and Osiris had been treating her because they were all fucked up about the bed they made with Seth.

"Ma, just relax." He changed his tone as he walked towards her.

"I *am* going to relax; just not here. You and your father and all this crossover bullshit is not about to drive me crazy."

"So you're walking out on this family? Is that what you're doing?"

"I'm getting away for a few days to clear my fucking head, Jediah! End of fucking discussion!"

She grabbed the suitcase and turned away from him.

"Where to? Vegas... with Kamikaze?"

Falcon stopped dead in her tracks when his statement hit her ears. Her body trembled so bad she felt little squirts of piss leave from out her bladder.

"What the fuck did you just say to me?" she hissed as she turned around.

Jediah chuckled as he ran his hand down his beard.

"Is that the person you gave Nabawi's necklace to? You know, the one with the key on the end of it? How all of a sudden after your last visit with him, that it ends up missing? And on the

296

same day that Kamikaze was in St. Louis, not to mention, on unmarked territory? Why else would he come out here, Falcon? Huh?"

"Jediah, you watch your fucking mouth. You don't know what the fuck you're talking about," she growled with her eyes now seeing red.

"That's why Osiris beat yo' ass back when he found out you had cheated on him in the 90's. Seth and I swore we'd never talk about the day we saw pops drag you across the bedroom floor and throw you into the wall, through the damn wall before he grabbed you by the throat and refused to let you go until your face turned blue.

"It's funny. You've always had everything at your fingertips: fortune, protection, treatment like royalty whenever you left the house, and a family... yet, you still crossed him. *With the enemy.* Now, just between me and you, he doesn't know that Akil wasn't his son. Yet..."

She dropped everything in her hands as she looked her son in the eye with tears staining her face.

"Si might be all fucked up right now, but that's why he got me. I see and know everything. I give it to you, ma, you keep a few tricks up yo' sleeve. I'll give you that. So I tell you what. You give me the necklace, tell me what it's for, because I know Nabawi told you everything being that you were the only muthafucka who cared about that nigga anyway, and I'll keep yo' secret safe. The last thing you want Osiris to find out is that you've been communicating with Kamikaze."

He chuckled.

"Damn that's fucked up. I didn't wanna believe my men when they told me they saw him on Haven property, but when I saw the tape for myself it fucked me up. And to think Si really thought Akil was his son. Granted, he favored him, but now it all makes sense."

"Jediah..." she whispered, not knowing how to spit her confession out in that moment.

Falcon couldn't believe what she was hearing. How did he know? Falcon thought she'd covered her tracks with her infidelity.

No one knew Kamikaze was Akil's father. No one but Nabawi, and she knew that he would never reveal her secret due to the dangers that lurked behind it, so how did Jediah find out?

"Where's the fucking key, Falcon!"

"What key! Now you're just sitting here talking a bunch of bullshit that you don't even know about! I don't know—"

Pow!

She looked from the gun in his hand, then down at the floor where her blood was spilling. The hole in her stomach made her drop down to her knees while more blood started coming up from out of her mouth.

"You still wanna fuck with me?" His voice was cold as he walked up on her with the gun aimed at her forehead.

A smile spread across Falcon's face as she looked Jediah in the eye. Her son *was* corrupt just like everyone said he was, but little did he know, he'd done her the favor that she couldn't bring herself to do on her own.

"You will reap what you've sewn, Jediah. You hear me?"

Her voice trembled as she coughed up more blood that was spewing from out of her mouth. Jediah pulled the chamber back on the revolver before pressing it against her temple, fed up with the bullshit.

"I'ma ask you one last time. Where is the fucking key?"

Falcon laughed again, as loud as her voice would allow her to before saying, "Seth won't let you and your father get away with this, and that's a promise..."

Pow!

Chapter Twenty-Five
One week later...

Kelani's little bun in the oven had certainly turned life upside down for her. Negativity and spite used to linger within her veins like a dire thirst for blood; however, the thoughts of holding Jediah Junior, or even Jelani Malaysia Platinum in her arms, sent a calm through her body that she never wanted to leave.

Kelani begged her OB/GYN on her hands and knees at her check-up today to do another ultrasound. She couldn't wait until week sixteen for the gender reveal. All Kelani wanted was to see her little baby along the screen and add more ultrasound photographs to the collage she was preparing at home. Reluctantly, the doctor gave in, and no one could slap the smile from off of her face even if they tried to.

"You have reached the voicemail box of, Jediah. To leave a voicemail, please press one ‑ "

Kelani hung up the phone as she pulled up at home.

"I guess daddy's busy right now little person. Let's get in this house and get dinner ready. The pot roast should be nice and tender by now. All mommy has to do is whip up these mashed potatoes and gravy, some asparagus, a simple dessert, and hopefully, he'll be home soon. I told him we were making his favorite tonight, but I know your God mommy will be happy to see how you've been!"

Kelani was filled with nothing but joy as she exited her Beemer while zipping her jacket. The temperature drop was enough to send chills down her spine. The once sunny day had transitioned into a dark, gloomy, and cloudy evening.

The winds blew hard against her small frame, and her pregnancy had kicked her senses into gear unlike anything she'd ever felt before. The woman could smell the rain that wasn't in the day's forecast, and she thanked God that she'd be in for the rest of the night.

Her feet moved quickly as she entered her brand new 10,000 square foot home that her man surprised her with a few weeks ago. She hardly wanted to leave when she was surrounded by such a beautiful palace.

Decorating had become a new hobby of hers since she didn't work. Hell, she needed something to keep her occupied when she had nothing but time on her hands.

Jediah had really showed his ass, and she knew her wedding ring was coming soon. It was only a matter of time before she became the next woman to be married into the Platinum dynasty, and she couldn't wait.

"Baby? Babe, I'm home, and I've got more pictures of our wittle person to share with you!"

Kelani's voice rang like a gracious Sunday church choir as she closed the front door behind her. Between the clean linen plug-ins lingering in the living room and the delightful smells coming from the kitchen, this day kept getting better and better with time.

"Alicia, baby? You sleep?" Kelani wondered as she removed her UGG boots and Nike jacket.

Her relationship with Alicia started out as a malicious plot against Nas as revenge for taking Seth away from them both, but over these past three months, they'd grown to love one another. They fucked like sex addicts, wore matching outfits like Kim K and Kylie Jenner, and their polygamist relationship with Jediah worked out like a charm.

Alicia was lost in this cold world looking for love in all the wrong places just like Kelani was. Who would've known that their hate for Nasir would bring them together? When Jediah wasn't home to hold her, there Alicia was with open arms and a warm smile. Most people might've frowned upon the way they chose to run their relationship and that was okay.

Kelani had a man she didn't have to beg to love her, a woman who may have been a little hot-headed, but her open heart spoke louder than her attitude did, and soon they'd have a child to share that same love and affection with.

Plus, Alicia ended up with the Platinum that she's always wanted, so life was looking up for them. What more could they possibly ask for?

Kelani smiled when she discovered the trail of rose petals along the steps that led to their master bedroom. Alicia was so romantic, and the thoughts of what awaited her made the hairs on her arms stand tall.

"Baby, you did all of this for me—"

Kelani dropped everything she had in hand once she made it to the doorway.

"ALICIA! NOOOOO!"

She dropped down to her knees and cried her eyes out from the sight of her woman lying in a pool of blood that was seeping into their brand new white carpet. Alicia had a gunshot wound to her head with her brains scattered out all along the floor.

A cunning smirk spread across Seth's face as he sipped from the champagne glass he had in hand. His left ankle rested upon his right knee as he watched Kelani break down into a hysterical outburst. He'd been waiting patiently on her arrival.

"What the fuck is wrong with you Seth?! You've already taken everything away from me! Your hateful ass refused to love me! You left me! Almost killed me while I was pregnant! Not to mention you turned around and willingly gave your heart to some bitch like I haven't gone from the fucking moon and back to prove to you that I deserved that spot in your life! And now you do this?! You stupid, selfish, son of a bitch!"

Kelani hopped up to her feet and charged for Seth at full speed, but before she could even attempt to put her hands on him, he grabbed her by the neck and took a stand. Kelani gasped for the air he was cutting off from her lungs while he held her body off of the ground.

Seth's fingers gripped her neck so tight he had to force himself to let up on the pressure. She was no good dead right now. The feeling of a switch blade slowly gliding across her chest made Kelani cry out in agony.

She'd never seen such a deranged look in his eyes. Was he about to chop her up? Hide all of her body parts and force his brother to go on a scavenger hunt to find her remains? Was he really about to take her life before she ever got the chance to hold her unborn child in her arms? He was sick.

When the dizziness subsided for a few seconds, Kelani realized that she was now hanging upside down by one leg, dangling from the ceiling like dead swine waiting on a butcher to finish her up. Little droplets of her blood started trickling along the carpet as Seth pulled up a chair and sat before her.

"It'll take about thirty minutes for you to hemorrhage from the rate you going, ma, so I advise you not to fuck with me," Seth hissed with venom on the tip of his tongue.

"What do you want from me!" she sobbed.

Tears rolled down the sides of Kelani's face as she stared him in his dark, demonic eyes.

"You know what the fuck I want," Seth urged.

"Seth, I don't know anything! I don't!"

Swish!

"Oooooooooouch!"

Kelani cried from the second cut across her chest to match the first one.

"Life span just dropped down to fifteen minutes, ma. You not looking too good from my standpoint."

Seth's voice was calm as he leaned back against the chair and watched her body slightly sway back and forth.

"Seeeeeeeth! I sweeeeear I don't know—"

The gun aimed at her forehead immediately muzzled her screams. Kelani could read his mind. She knew exactly what he wanted. The way she fell into Jediah's arms following his departure made it known that his brother had instilled a trust within her that he had with no one else. Kelani knew all of Jediah's secrets. All of them. But all Seth cared about was the main one. Who killed his brother and why?

"Jediah! It was Jediah!" she confessed with terror.

"Jediah what?"

"He killed Akil! I swear on my life, Seth! I was there when it happened! I'm sorry! I'm so-so sorry! I never would've set Akil up if I had known that he was going to kill him! I swear I thought he was only going to scare him and make him talk Osiris into giving Jediah the dynasty instead of him! He said it wouldn't get ugly, Seth! Jediah promised...he promised..."

𝒯

Three Months Earlier...

Clink-Clink!
Akil loaded the pistol with a full clip and adjusted the chamber before he tucked it away in the back of his jeans. The ringing of his phone made him stop stuffing the duffle bag full of his clothing to see who the caller was.

Osiris

He ran his hand down his head while hitting the side button to cut the ringer off. The face of his wristwatch read 2:00 pm. He was due to meet up with his father in thirty minutes about business affairs, but Akil never planned on attending.

"Fuck this shit, man," he mumbled as he kept shoving his clothes into the Gucci garment bag.

Akil wasn't built for this shit. Never was he soft. The man was a Platinum; power ran through his veins just like any other Platinum breed, but running the dynasty was never in his plans. If Akil had regretted anything, it was allowing Jediah to talk him into declining his basketball scholarship.

The only reason why Akil stuck around was because of Seth. They shared a bond that no one could ever force a wedge through; it was a bond that he never wanted to jeopardize. Seth was there on those long nights when he was up until three in the morning sweating bullets on the court with fears of his scouting game the next day infesting his mind.

Seth was there along his road to recovery when he tore a ligament in his knee back when he thought he'd never make it to the court during his senior year of high school. His older brother pushed him, believed in his dreams, and fought for his happiness no matter what. Not to mention, he saved his life last year when the shit seems like it was just yesterday.

Akil wasn't even supposed to accompany Seth along his trip to MPD, but when he got word that Jediah was sending an army to back him up that didn't include Messiah, Tito, or the normal line-up, Akil hopped on the first plane he could to warn his brother and have his back.

Akil never got the chance to let Seth in on the bullshit that was going on. The moment he made it to the border, a war let loose and the two of them were left running for their lives...

2015
Mexico Border
One Year Ago...

Pow! Pow! Pow! Pow! Pow!
Seth had always been cold with a burner. He could empty, reload, and air out another full clip all in his sleep. Akil was busy hot-wiring a Jeep Wrangler so they could make a successful escape while his brother took on the MPD army with nothing but a pistol and a half-empty AK. Shit had went left and quick.

Seth didn't even get the chance to meet up with Kamikaze's son, Juno, so they could conquer MPD together and gain ownership over their territory. Afterwards they planned on presenting the news to their fathers to end all of their beef and work as a team, but those dreams were short-lived.

It's like somebody had been following Seth's every move. The squad he came with led him right into the arms of the MPD army, and if it wasn't for Akil popping out of thin air to help him escape, he would've been dead.
Vroom! Vroom! Vroom!
"Come on, bruh! Let's get the fuck out of here!" Akil yelled as he hopped in the driver's seat.

Seth took out a few more mobsters before he pulled Akil out of the car and handed him the pistol from his waistline after reloading it.

"The border only half a mile away. You'll be better on foot. Hurry up before the last charter for the night leaves!"

Akil thought he was hearing shit. Did his brother really think he was going to leave him there after all they'd been through? The only reason he was there was to save him in the first place.

"Seth!"

"Listen to me man!"

Rat-at-tat-tat-tat-tat-tat!

Seth hid his brother behind the wall of the garage they were hiding in and let his clip off at the group of four armed men heading in their direction. One ese, two eses, three eses, four... dead and lying in warm blood.

"MPD ain't gon' stop with the search if they don't take no prisoners! Get yo' ass out of here and don't look back! When I pull out, wait until you don't see squad cars and peel the fuck out!"

"But Seth—"

"Akil!"

Akil looked his brother in the eye after Seth slammed the car door behind him. Tears trickled down his face as he and Seth grabbed each other by the shoulders through the open window and pressed their foreheads together.

"I'm not gon' let you lose yo' life for some shit you never wanted, Akil. Promise me from this day on that you'll take care of you, man. Watch over ma and pops and be sure no matter what decision you make, that Jediah don't fuck this dynasty up any more than it already is. Promise me, baby boy."

Seth's voice trembled with fear that this would be the last time that he'd be seeing his baby brother.

*"I promise Malama Pono, bruh. Aloha wau ia 'oe. **Be good. Do Right. I love you.**"*

Seth let his brother go as he shifted gears on the truck.

"Malama Pono, fam. I love you too. Get the fuck out of here."

Akil hid behind a dolly stacked with crates as Seth drove the truck through the wooden wall and took off with MPD on his ass. When the coast was finally clear, he headed out in the opposite direction and followed his brother's instructions. He left for the border and never looked back...

T

The ringing of Akil's cell phone snapped him out of his day dreaming. He started not to answer knowing it was no one other than Osiris with his adamant harassment, but the name Isabella made him take a seat and answer the call.

Akil smiled when the faces of his twin boy and girl appeared along the screen.

"Say hi daddy! Say mommy just gave us a nice, warm bath, and we are waiting on you!" Isabella cooed as she tickled their son's little feet.

"Daddy's on the way, y'all. I promise. I'm headed to my flight now... You do what I say Bella?"

When the camera turned around, Akil was now face to face with his beautiful fiancé. Her mocha skin was glowing in the sunlight that her opened hotel room curtains displayed. Isabella's smile made Akil's departure from Saint Louis worth the risk as he grabbed his car keys.

"Yes. We're at the new hotel. I have a new phone, and I'm spending cash only. Please be safe, baby. We'll be here waiting on you."

Akil smiled.

"I should be there in a few hours, then we can shake to our new spot and start over."

Isabella wiped away the tears falling down her face before she blew him a kiss.

"We love you, Mr. Platinum."

"I love y'all too. I'll see y'all soon. Let me get the fuck out of here. I'm wiring the money to that account as we speak, a'ight? You know what to do if I don't make it out there? Right ma?"

The words burned on the way out his mouth. The man was sure that he'd make it, but he had to prepare himself and his woman for the worst. One thing Akil had always taken pride in was not being too boastful. Every man needed to know their limits.

He wanted his woman to be aware of her surroundings at all times, and to know how to survive without him if he ever left this earth before they'd grown old together. What man wanted to flaunt with a physically beautiful but mentally weak woman who couldn't hold it down, just to be called a man?

"I'm not worried about that, Akil. I know I'll see you soon. Breakfast for dinner tonight as we planned, alright?"

He chuckled.

"A'ight, mama. Bet."

Beep. Beep. Beep.

Akil threw the duffle bag around his neck, grabbed the AR-15 sitting along the bed, and headed for the door. Just as he put his ride in reverse, a BMW hopped the curve and blocked him from leaving. Kelani jumped out of the car with a face full of tears as she ran up to his window.

"Move the fucking car, Kelani, before I do it!" he threatened.

"Akil, please! It's Jediah! He's going crazy! He has Falcon held hostage out in Wentzville with a gun to her head! I swear it, I'm not lying! Look at the video! Akil please!"

Akil's blood boiled when he caught a glimpse of the film. He couldn't tell if it really was his mother because the chair where the crying woman sat was turned backwards, so he couldn't see her face.

"Fuck!" he hollered while slamming his fist along the steering wheel.

A part of him started to run the back of his truck into Kelani's car and not miss his private plane headed for Los Angeles where his family was waiting for him, but he'd never be able to live with his mother's death on his conscious if it were true

Jediah was nuttier than a Christmas fruit cake. The way he beat Kelani's ass, Akil would never put it past him what he'd do to Falcon. The way he'd been popping off at her, not to mention the last few fists fights they'd gotten into due to that same disrespect towards her, Akil knew that his crazy ass had gone off the deep end now.

Twenty minutes later, Akil pulled up behind Kelani at a warehouse they owned right outside of town. He hopped out the car with his AK on his shoulder and yanked Kelani by the elbow once she was in reach.

"Bitch, let this be some bullshit. On my life, I'll chop yo ass up and feed it to yo family tonight," he threatened through gritted teeth.

Screams from inside the warehouse made Akil run for the entrance with Kelani dragging along behind him.

Jediah flashed a wicked smile when his brother appeared in the doorway, but it soon faded when Akil wrapped his arm around Kelani's neck and aimed his gun at him with his free arm. The chair where Falcon was sitting was, again, turned, so he still couldn't see her face. Akil was stuck between a rock and a hard place. His finger along the trigger trembled as he stared his brother in the eyes.

"The fuck is yo' problem, JD!" he screamed in rage.

"Nigga, you my fucking problem! Even after Seth got locked up, O still gon' disrespect my name and choose to hand this shit over to you!"

"That's what this shit is about!"

Akil tightened up his grip around Kelani's throat, feeling himself about to explode.

"Nigga I don't want this shit! You can have this shit! Fuck this dynasty! And fuck y'all! Y'all letting Seth sit in MPD to keep this shit out his hands all because of greed! You and O some fucked up ass niggas, mane! Nigga go 'head! Take over! You ain't never gotta worry about seeing me again! I'll put one in this bitch's head right now if you don't let ma go! What the fuck is wrong with you, nigga!"

Pow!

The grip around Kelani's neck eased up when Akil's arm dropped down to his side. The hole in his chest caused her to scream in fright as Akil fell down to his knees.

"Thanks for saying the magic words nigga. You right. I won't never see yo ass again after today."

Thump! Thump! Thump! Thum-thum-thum-thum-thump!

Akil's body shook back and forth as Jediah emptied out the Uzi in his chest, spilling the blood they once shared all over the ground beneath him.

"Jediaaaaaaaaah! Nooooooo! This wasn't supposed to happen! He agreed to hand it over! You said you wouldn't do this!" Kelani cried as she fell down to the ground with her hands over her eyes.

Jediah laughed as he shot the woman sitting in the chair in her head, causing her body to slump over. Kelani's eyes widened when she laid them upon the dead decoy they had faking to be Falcon in order to lure Akil in.

"Some promises are meant to be broken, ma. Now get the fuck up so we can get his body in the car and get rid of his ride. We gotta make his murder look good."

T

"Seth, please. I'm sorry. I never meant for it to go this far. Jediah—"

Pow!

Kelani's head jerked back when Seth blew a hole right between her eyes. The tears running down his face pushed him further into a deep rage as he emptied out the clip into her stomach, not giving a fuck about the baby or anything else associated with his brother. After all this time he'd been running around slaughtering niggas tryna get somebody from the Kamikazes to come clean about Akil's murder when Jediah's been the culprit all along.

Everything around Seth was dark. He tried to promise himself to remain calm and not lose his mind after his little visit with Kelani, but who was he kidding? He knew that shit was a lie. Seth dialed Messiah's number as the house in his rearview mirror rose in flames.

Two down, two to go, he thought as Messiah's phone went straight to voicemail for the second time around. *I know this nigga ain't on no bullshit. I told him to wait on my call.*

"You have reached the voicemail box of—"

"Fuck!"

Seth made the gas pedal kiss the ground as he hopped on I-64 heading further into the county. He'd bet any money on it that Messiah was headed to Osiris' casino out in Lake Saint Louis, and he prayed to God that he wasn't too late.

Chapter Twenty-Six

"*Where* the fuck do we stand with this Kamikaze invasion? I'm tired of this bullshit. When I say I want this shit done in less than 48 hours, I mean that shit. Enough with these fucking games! And where the fuck is P1?! Out of every CSI agent we got on board, one of them muthafuckas still ain't found him yet?!"

Veins appeared along Osiris' forehead as he flipped the mini bistro table before him over. His anxiety was in overload. Sweat was seeping through his skin making the Armani suit tailored over his frame damp, the stench of musk was lingering from his body as if he hadn't bathed in days, and the cocaine in his blood had his heart racing at a peak that his body almost couldn't withstand.

"I want them muthafuckas dead! Tonight! I want their heads—" Osiris stopped midway through his sentence and pulled out two spears that were hanging along the walls of his office as décor and slammed the flat ends of them against the floor.

"Right…here…And where the fuck is my wife?! Why the fuck does it seem like I haven't seen her in this last week! Her wedding ring says she's home, but all the live feed shows is empty rooms and hallways! I swear if this bitch crossed me I'll mount her fucking head right above her son's!"

Osiris had been so caught up this last week trying to conquer Seth, that Falcon had been the least of his worries until he glanced down at his wedding ring reflecting in the lights. He hadn't physically seen the inside of his home or his wife's face for seven days, and it was about to give him an aneurysm.

Jediah sipped the cognac in his glass trying to come off as unbothered as possible before his father. The sooner they located Seth and Messiah, the better. Once their bodies had been added to his head count, this shit would run smoother, Osiris would calm down, and he'd have it all figured out how he was gonna drop the bomb about Falcon "disappearing" on him.

Claiming victory over the Kamikazes and P1 would be enough of a cushion for Osiris to fall back on once he heard that Falcon had gotten "caught up" in the crossfire of their war, and Jediah's slate would be clean. But he had to keep his cool.

As long as narcotized him remained calm, this shit would be over in the blink of an eye. Then, he and his family could live in peace while rejoicing over his ownership of the Platinum dynasty. It may have cost him a mother and two brothers, but the sacrifice would be well worth it.

Jediah knew once he made a deal with the devil about reigning supreme that he'd have to offer up a number of souls that he called family, and that was fine with him. All his life he'd felt invisible and like an outcast in his own home. Those days were officially over.

"Why the fuck you so damn calm?" Osiris spat as he glanced over at the cocky and unfazed Jediah who wore a smirk along his face.

Usually the cocaine would have his ass bouncing off the damn walls at the speed of light, but he was tranquil. The storm hadn't made its way to its peak just yet, so he thought about his reply with ease, careful not to throw Osiris off. Before Jediah could finally respond, the security alert began to blare in the air around them.

"We've got static coming from the currency chamber. It's Messiah and a squad. Headed this way," the security guard informed as he pulled up the footage along all eight monitors.

"Well, it's about fucking time!" Osiris sniffed up the last line of cocaine on his desk before removing the gun from his waistline. "I want this nigga. I wanna see Seth crumble when I present him with his best friend's head. Unloyal ass muthafucka. It's on now baby!"

"We've got a location on P1. Squad cars spotted him exiting on Highway K. ETA, three minutes."

The CSI agent's comment was Jediah's cue. He hopped up to his feet and took a long swig from the bottle of brandy before he rushed over to his father and placed his hands along his shoulders.

"Looks like Christmas dun' came early, my nigga!" Jediah roared with a wicked smile along his face.

"Bring that nigga to me. Now. I'll handle this. Go ke'iki-ane. *Son.* Go."

Hearing his father call him son in their native language gave Jediah a sense of satisfaction that he'd yearned for all his life. Now he was complete. Now his role as a Platinum felt like his hard work had paid off, and he promised that he wouldn't let his father down.

Seth's Bugatti pulled up in front of the casino the moment Jediah exited the entrance. Seth was surrounded. His brother had an army with him as he exited the vehicle with his gun in hand.

But he didn't sweat it. The nigga he was looking for was already front and center, so his squad just simply blended in with the background.

Jediah's heart raced as Seth slowly approached him. Anger was glazed over Seth's face like he was ready for war, and Jediah was wit' it. He'd waited his entire adult life on this moment, and nothing was going to stop him.

"Move another inch and I'll splatter yo' shit right here and right now! It's over nigga! Where yo' team at now? Where them boys at that supposedly got yo' back now? Where they at Seth? Huh?! But yo' name hold so much muthafucking weight! You siding with the Kamikazes, but you walking around bare ass and unprotected on unmarked territory!

"You ain't learn nothing the first time you thought you was God, nigga? You really must be stupid my nigga! Bow to me! Get on yo' muthafucking knees and show me some got damn respect before I send ma and Akil some company!"

Jediah was so far on a roll that his last statement slapped them both in the face. Seth's eyes flushed red from the sight and the thoughts of Jediah's pussy ass drowning this family for years now. He dismantled his gun and pulled the North Face hoodie over his head before he pulled his hair up.

Seth's actions made Jediah double over in laughter. Did this nigga really wanna bang? Was he on the same shit that had

Jediah strung out, or what? Seth was funny. This nigga deserved an Oscar.

"Believe me nigga. You don't wanna throw hands with a man who's got some snow in his system like it's winter time in Switzerland. You got off with that shit when you got back from the pen. Just know that."

Jediah was no longer amused when Seth removed his wristwatch before balling up his fists. The veins peeking from out his forearms along with his clenched jaw was only the slightest incline of the rage that was brewing inside of him. Jediah might've been right about a few things. Seth *was* alone. He *was* outnumbered. He *was* naked. Solo-dolo. All of that shit.

Yeah, it may have been stupid, but nothing else was on his mind at this hour besides honoring his baby brother with the death of Jediah. Seth knew he was bluffing on Falcon's name, so that didn't spark no heat.

But then again, the disrespect placed upon her soul, no matter where him and his mother stood, was enough to put another barrel in his head once he was finished with his ass.

"I tell you what, Seth."

Jediah dismantled his gun as well and unarmed himself of his other weapons, a signal to his arm to refrain interrupting the brawl that was soon to begin. He stared his brother in the eye as he unbuttoned his suit jacket before removing it.

"You kick my ass?" He threw a blade along the ground as well. "And you carry my head inside to Osiris yourself and my army is your army, but if I'm left standing? I'mma take over your shit, I'mma fuck yo' bitch, Messiah's bitch, and they mommas since you playing Superman and dun' sent them away knowing how I get down. Then, I'mma mount yo' skull on my fireplace for a daily reminder of my accomplishments."

Seth chuckled.

"Me, my wives, and my son gon' sit back and laugh at yo' dumb ass every damn day. Pussy ass nigga, and that's on this dynasty."

"Nigga fuck you and yo' expired ass family. That cheap ass piece of shit ass crib you once had ain't shit but crumbs now. And yo' bitches? A bullet to both of they heads but I showed a lil' favoritism to Lani and lit y'all fetus up with a couple licks too.

" I watched her beg for her life after she told me the nigga responsible for Akil's death was right in my face the whole time… Just to be liked and accepted? You sparked this shit, and killed—"

Seth inhaled deeply before he could finish his sentence.

"You killed Akil over a muthafucking pat on the back because you feel like yo' daddy ain't never loved you, nigga? Huh?! You pathetic! Nigga, the day I kneel before you I'll be six feet under and that's on my life! Fuck you nigga. Come get this work! I'm done talking!"

Jediah's heart almost stopped. Seth had never been the kind of man to tell a lie, and once he realized the blood splattered along his brother's jeans he blacked out. Jediah couldn't respond with words to a fist fight, so he rushed for Seth and they started throwing hands like they always had when they came to a disagreement.

Jediah was correct once again. The crack in his system *did* give his physical strength an advantage, so his fists were swinging rapidly. He and Seth hung tough until Jediah got his brother in a headlock, cutting off Seth's circulation while blood spewed from his busted mouth.

"Get on yo' knees, nigga. On yo' fucking knees and bow to me. Don't make me have to kneel yo' ass in pieces!" Jediah threatened through clenched teeth.

He used all his might to bring his brother down, but Seth wouldn't budge. Sudden images of Akil flashed before his eyes of Jediah gunning him down, and that's all the strength he needed before he removed his brother's arm. With everything in Seth, he twisted JD's wrist, after breaking free, until he heard his bone snap.

"Aaaaaaah! Fuck!"

Wham…Wham…Wham!

Seth threw three heavy blows to Jediah's mouth before he lit him with a nasty ass uppercut that sent his body tumbling into the ground.

"Hwak-twat!"

Seth emptied his mouth of blood before he grabbed Jediah by the shirt with both hands and tossed his body into the nearby Cadillac sedan, smashing the windshield upon impact. He wasn't about to waste the rest of his energy on this nigga when he still had Osiris to go heads up with, but he was gonna make this shit look good.

Jediah groaned as he rolled over on the hood of the car trying to get up, but Seth didn't give him the opportunity to do so. Vile ass niggas had all the strength in the world like they were in the same cult as Jason from the *Friday the 13th* series. They stayed tryna fight back but Seth wasn't the one.

He grabbed his brother by the collar, dragging him down to the ground and positioned him on his knees, now with his gun aimed to his head.

"Nah, nigga, it's time that you bowed down to me. In front of yo' army so that you let these muthafuckas know who always had this dynasty on lock."

Jediah was too weak to respond, too weak to react, and his knees resting along the ground was all the indication the mobsters along the sidewalk observing their brawl needed to see, to ensure that, he had indeed, become the fallen.

Deep chuckles coming from a distance made Seth revert his attention to the casino entrance. His heart raced when Osiris exited the building bloody and wounded from a hard battle with Messiah, but it was his dawg locked up with his father's arm around his neck and a revolver to his head.

"You know what...I gotta give it to you Seth. This lil' nigga right here got heart, but the *audacity* of him to think that he'd conquer me. It's pathetic."

Osiris lead a bloody and severely wounded Messiah down the steps. Even with the arrow from O's spear shoved into his dawg's side and the blood leaking from his wound, he was still standing.

"This a new low for you O. Killing off yo' own fucking son just to uplift the next?" Seth had vengeance in his eyes.

Jediah was now facing their father while Seth's arms laid wrapped around his neck. P1's chest heaved up and down at a rapid pace. Time wasn't on his hands and whatever solution he came up with he needed to act upon it and now.

"Whoever murdered Akil and however it happened was his lost. If Akil would've answered my phone calls that day he was supposed meet up with me instead of running away from this shit like a lil' bitch, then he never would've gotten caught up on Kamikaze territory.

" His body was found in Vegas before it was even shipped out here. Why the fuck you keep on crying over old shit, nigga?! Y'all all have known the consequences of this game before I introduced it to y'all.

"When you took your cocky ass down to MPD you got caught the fuck up and impounded didn't you? I don't give a fuck what you was tryna do with Juno. I wasn't having that shit! Fuck the Kamikazes!

"That's rule number fucking one, bitch. Respect a nigga's set unless you coming hard for that shit like I'm doing now. All your territories, Seth? They're surrounded, waiting on my say to make cease.

"Osiris runs this shit! Like I always told y'all niggas I would. Yeah, bitch, I got people out in Vegas and on the west coast too. You thought it was real cute when you sucked Kamikaze's dick to link up knowing you couldn't fuck with me alone! It's over nigga! Get down and honor me before I put a hole in this nigga's shit right before I off yo' ass too."

The look plastered along Seth's face told it all. Confusion filled him unlike never before.

So Osiris never knew that Jediah murdered Akil either?

Solitarily, that nigga had been stirring shit up, and it all had gotten so far out of whack that no one could piece it together. No wonder why it's been so difficult for Seth to figure this shit out. That nigga had bamboozled them all.

A haunting laughter escaped Jediah's lips following their father's monologue. Seeing that he no longer had anything else to live for, Jediah laid everything out on the table once and for all.

"Akil was murdered in Wentzville at the hands of an empty Uzi clip bitch. I just made that shit look good by sending his body in a bag labeled from Vegas. The lil' nigga got what he deserved. I knew you would hand the crown over to him in Seth's absence, so I took matters into my own hands to officially claim my ownership. Akil wasn't a Platinum anyway, nigga. Falcon pulled the wool over all our eyes. Your beef with Kamikaze?

"Why you think the shit was never squashed? Akil was his son. I would tell you to ask ya' wife about the day King K came in town and met with her at Haven on some sketchy shit while she was seeing Nabawi, but you can't because that bitch six feet under too.

" Checkmate muthafuckas. You always been a sucka ass nigga O, but you trusted this dynasty in the hands of a son who wasn't even yours and then the other son who made a bed with ma's estranged baby daddy?

"I was the only nigga who had yo' back and you shit on me over and over like I ain't been saving yo' ass for years?! Y'all all some fucking bozos, fam! Straight the fuck up! Suck my dick on our way to hell muthafuckas!"

With his free hand, Jediah reached for the gun in close reach, but he was too slow. Gunshots filled the air when Seth lit bullet holes into the back of his head while Osiris emptied out his clip into his chest as well.

Pow!

Seth's body flew back and hit the ground when the last bullet exited Osiris' chamber. O couldn't see anything but red with the thoughts of Jediah's hidden secrets consuming him. While reloading his burner, their father limped across the lot to Seth's body sprawled out after shoving the severely wounded Messiah, who was going in and out of conscious, to the ground.

Osiris stood over Seth with tears cascading down his face, blood saturated his clothes, his body was aching from the three ribs Messiah had broken from the nonstop punches he'd lit to his side, but most of all his heart was dark.

He'd been lied to and deceived after all this time, and since they couldn't run the Platinum reign as one, and his sleezy ass wife had crossed him in the worst way, he'd do this shit alone. Fuck everybody.

"I told you this isn't what you wanted P1."

His voice was low as he continued to stare his son in the eye. If looks could kill Seth would be in a million tiny pieces. Their gaze went on until gunshots filled the air.

Blood seeped out of Osiris' mouth as he dropped down to his knees following the three bullets to his back. Messiah struggled to stand to his feet while holding the smoking gun in his hand.

When he got in reach, he squatted down and helped his dawg stand to his feet. With his arm around Seth's shoulders because he was still so weak himself, Messiah handed him the gun as he got a good balance.

Seth's heart was heavy. There were still so many unanswered questions; he didn't know what was real, what was false, where his mother was, or what was up from down. But none of that had mattered in this moment. It was him and Osiris left.

His father's fate was in his hands. The war had finally come to an end, but Seth could only be honest when he admitted to himself that he wouldn't be one hundred percent satisfied because something was still missing.

Osiris flashed a smile before Seth blew a hole into his head, watching his body collapse on top of his brother's. His face dropped in pity. His mind was blank, everything around him was dark, and he shed two solitary tears. One from each of his eyes.

Seth knew avenging Akil's death wouldn't be a walk in the park, but this? Losing his entire family along the way was a sacrifice that he didn't think he'd have to make to get it. I guess you could say that no matter how out of whack their family was, Seth still had hope, but that outcome was unfortunate, and he was hollow.

Chapter Twenty-Seven

Nas couldn't deny the fact that Toronto was a beautiful city. She honestly looked forward to the frequent vacations she'd be taking there in the future whenever she got tired of the Saint Louis streets. The atmosphere was welcoming, the venues were extraordinary, the food was to die for, and she could only imagine what the city looked like with the change of the weather.

Contrarily, no matter how much she and the ladies were enjoying themselves, her mind couldn't escape the fact that she hadn't heard from Seth in a week. Nasir was drowning in fear. Her anxiety had reached a new peak knowing that she couldn't get in touch with him nor Messiah.

What if her man was severely hurt and needed her help? What if he had been locked up? Did Osiris reign supreme over them? Had his jealous ass brother gotten them caught up? Where was Falcon? So many questions were swarming around in her brain that she just couldn't think straight.

Looking at her phone, Nas saw that it was 4 AM. Seth's face along her lock screen with his arms around her from when they were in Hawaii made her smile. Filled with millions of mixed emotions, she climbed out of bed, changed into a pair of spankies and a crop top, then headed down to the dance studio. She had to clear her mind.

With Justin Timberlake's "I Think She Knows" blaring out the speakers, her body flowed along the dance floor like a professional performer. Modern was her favorite style of dance. She could manipulate it with both ballet and hip-hop, creating the perfect visual for an audience.

"No, I need something upbeat. All this emotional shit is killing me. I'm tired of crying."

Nas wiped the tears away. She changed the track after sliding on a pair of heels to prepare herself for a new ride. Hearing Rihanna's voice instantly made her heart start pumping blood at a faster pace when the beat to that "Nothing Is Promised" had dropped. With the tripod set up and the camera still recording, Nasir's body flowed in a dynamite ass freestyle.

Now she was twirling around the dancing pole stationed in the center of the room, releasing her inner freak until she jumped off and started killing it with some bomb ass moves to every beat. After a few minutes of an acrobatic release, Nasir felt ten times better as the words seeped through her lips while she sang along with the lyrics…

Nasir's chest was heaving up and down as her heels click-clacked on her way to the tripod once the music faded. With her back against the mirrors and the camera in hand she slid down until her butt made one with the floor. She laughed and giggled at her twerking, hitting splits, and moving like an acrobat as if her name was Aliya Janell. Late nights always got the juices flowing.

I'm definitely uploading this bad boy next, she thought proudly as she removed the six-inch heels and headed to her phone.

Before Nas could get her password typed in completely, she received an incoming call. The name along her screen made her lose her breath. She was not expecting to hear from the caller, considering all that's unfolded since Nabawi's funeral.

"Momma Platinum? Is everything okay? Have you heard from Seth? Is it over?"

Nasir didn't mean to bombard her with so many questions, but why else would Falcon be calling her?

"Umm. This isn't Mrs. Platinum. My name is Connie Jenkins. I'm an RN at Ronald Reagan UCLA Medical Center. Is this her daughter, Nasir Valentine?"

Nas damn near had a heart attack.

"Is she okay?!" she screamed at the top of her lungs.

"Before I can reveal any information can you please identify yourself for me, ma'am?"

"Yes, this is Nasir Valentine! What happened?!"

"Oh, thank God. I don't mean to upset you Ms. Valentine. I'll probably lose my job for doing this, but I needed to get in touch with someone. Mrs. Platinum's phone didn't have a lock on it, so I intruded.

"I hated to do so, but the gentleman who dropped her off earlier in the week hasn't been in today and I need permission to do her second blood transfusion or else she won't make it. I saw daughter by your name in her phone and called you.

"Her husband won't answer, none of the contacts that say son are responding, and I almost lost hope. Mrs. Platinum suffered from a gun-shot wound to the abdomen. She was doing great after her first transfusion, but then her health started to decline. She's been in a coma since surgery, so she can't speak on her own behalf, and again the gentleman who dropped her off hasn't been in yet today and I really don't want to risk waiting any longer or else—"

"What gentleman?" Nasir cut the nurse off.

"Are you familiar with a Noel Griffin? You might know him as Prodigy. He's a friend of her son Seth but I can't get in touch with either of them. I don't want you guys to lose her. She's really fighting for—"

"Yes! Go ahead with the transfusion! Do what you have to do to save her! Where are- where is she? Did you say UCLA? How the fuck did she get all the way out to California?!"

"She was transported here from St. John's Mercy Hospital in Saint Louis, Missouri after her first surgery when they removed the bullet and did the first transfusion, ma'am. I was given strict orders by Mr. Griffin not to reach out to anyone, but again, I don't want to lose her, and I can't make the decision to do any further care without family approval."

"Oh my God."

Nas was hyperventilating like crazy. At the speed of light, she ran up to the third floor where the bedrooms they had been sleeping in were located.

"Everybody get up! Put some clothes on! We're going to California!" she yelled while flicking on all of the lights.

They all had fallen asleep in the same room after a long night of junk food, scary movies, and old school music, coining the ultimate pajama party.

"Nasir Valentine! What is going on?" Catori yelled petrified by the pain in her daughter's voice.

"Ms. Valentine?"

Nas reverted her attention back to her phone after she heard the nurse's voice.

"Yes, I'm listening."

"She'll be in the ICU once she makes it back from the transfusion. Her room number is 2108. I'll have your name in her charts for when you arrive. Thank you so much for answering."

"No, thank you for taking a risk and reaching out to me. Please do all that you can to save her. I'm on the way now."

"Yes, ma'am."

"Nasir! What is going on?!" Keanu shrieked once Nas hung up the phone.

"Falcon's been shot and she's going in for a second blood transfusion. She's at a hospital in California and they needed permission to do the surgery because they couldn't get in touch with anyone else."

"Oh my God!" the ladies all gasped in unison.

"What is she doing in California?" Darcy questioned.

"I don't know. She's been there in a coma for the last week. We're all about to find out together as soon as we make it there."

Nas ran her fingers through her hair as she dialed her man's number with her heart steadily beating a mile a minute.

"Seth please answer the phone, baby, please…"

𝒯

Seth opened the door to Nas' apartment to find the entrance flooded with unopened mail. He scrunched his face up while bending over to pick up the letters before him and Messiah entered. After a long eight hours in the hospital and getting patched up, him and his dawg were finally out that bitch against medical advice.

They didn't have time for a few weeks' worth of observation or none of that shit. Once the doctor ensured that their wounds were okay, they bounced the first chance they could.

He and Messiah needed to get out to Vegas and pay a quick visit to Kamikaze before they went to pick up Nas and the gang from Toronto. The war wasn't quite over yet.

Everything had been a blur to Seth since Jediah told him he'd killed their mother. If he could bring that nigga back, chop up his body, and watch his flesh turn to ashes again, he would. In the blink of an eye he'd lost everyone that he once held close to his heart.

The last words Seth had spoken to his mother was during their dispute on the day of Akil's funeral. It felt like his heart had been ripped out of socket and was repeatedly being lit with hollow point bullets...

Seth allowed the hot water from the shower nozzle to run down his back until it ran cold, not giving a fuck about his gunshot wound. He should've been the one dead. Not his queen. If he wasn't already mentally fucked up about Akil and the truth behind it, then he was now.

The Platinum search team had been out looking for clues or anyone possible who would've known about Falcon's remains, but there was no luck. Jediah was as fucked up as they came for murdering and burying Falcon. No matter what she had done, what affair she'd had, or what the case may have been. Her life wasn't worth it.

The sound of Messiah slowly climbing down the stairs caught Seth's attention, forcing him to get himself together before he flicked the lighter on. He held a blunt up to his lips while sitting on the edge of Nas' bed dressed in nothing but a pair of Adidas joggers.

His damp and curly hair hung over his face as he rested his elbows along his knees trying to force himself to refrain from shedding any more tears. Losing Akil was detrimental but losing Falcon took the fucking cake.

"Aloha wau ia 'oe, ma. E 'ike wau ia 'oe. *I love you, ma. I will see you again.*"

The tears ran down his face once again as Seth broke into a nonverbal cry. His heart was damaged... After a few minutes of a brief emotional release, Seth's head rose when he felt Messiah take a seat next to him along the bed.

Messiah held his free hand out before Seth gave him a five and held onto it while tucking his chin into his chest. He owed

Messiah his life. He was truly his dawg. After a brief prayer Seth looked up and noticed that Messiah had a letter in his other hand.

"What's this?" he questioned as Messiah passed it to him in exchange for the blunt.

"I don't know. I noticed it on the kitchen counter with the rest of the mail. I saw mom's name on it and knew it had to be something important. It's addressed to you from her."

Seth inhaled as he removed the papers from the envelope. It was too soon to be taking another L, but at the rate shit had unraveled all in one night, what the fuck else could possibly go wrong?

Seth,

Hello son... My have I missed you so... I never expected the days of a crossover to happen but here we are separated by hate, deceit, miscommunication, and the lack of support on our end. Knowing you and your attitude, Seth, you may never speak to me again. Damn boy you surely are Keanu's ka mo'opuna nui. **Great-grandson.**

Baby, I'm sorry. Momma never meant to hurt you. She never meant to let you down, ignore you, and leave you son. Your father and Jediah have been so obsessed with this dynasty that they've allowed it to destroy them mentally. Unfortunately, my dumb ass just fell in line and allowed things to fall apart without even trying to talk them out of it.

You've always expressed how Jediah wasn't right in the head, baby, and with me loving my son so much, I never could see it. Not until Jediah showed me his true colors and I was physically able to visualize with my own eyes, the point of madness that he'd driven himself to.

I haven't been honest with you all about a few things, Seth, and I can no longer hold it in...

I spoke with Bryan Kamikaze a few days before Nabawi passed away, damn near begging him to throw in the towel so that the Platinums over throwing them would possibly mend things with you and your father. Let's just jump to the important part, Seth.

Akil is not your father's son.

I slept with Bryan a few times a couple of years after Jediah was born...actually it was an affair. I met Bryan on a girl's trip I took to Vegas in '91 when I tried to leave your father for cheating on me with someone who I thought was my friend. Of course, Osiris found out about it, but I convinced him that I was already pregnant before I went out to Vegas.

I lied, claiming that I was planning to get an abortion and that's why he knew nothing about the pregnancy. When Akil was born and the secret DNA test that Kamikaze took came back saying that he indeed was the father, I knew Osiris would kill me if I didn't clean it up.

Nabawi helped me generate a fake test stating that Osiris was the father to keep the secret hidden, and we never spoke of it again. I swore that I would take it to my grave but when Akil died I knew that Kamikaze would act upon his son being killed. It'll be a lie if I said that he didn't love his son but that wouldn't be true.

I've sent him photographs of Akil, I've stayed in touch with him up until his death, and it's killed him that he's had to watch Akil grow up from a distance, let alone settle with the fact that his enemy was raising his own flesh and blood.

I fucked up, baby. I fucked up bad and I wish I could've made things right, but your father never would've allowed that to happen. Momma would've been dead, Akil would've paid a price for my infidelity, and I didn't want to split my boys up. None of you deserved that.

It's a very difficult and messy situation, Seth. This beef with the Kamikazes will probably never end because Bryan wants blood. His love for his son is the only reason why things have been kosher for so long, but a war is coming baby.

I won't tell you what to do or how to do it, but I wanted to warn you. It's the least that I could do after everything has hit the fan. Momma loves you with all of her heart and she doesn't want to see you get hurt.

And another thing. Remember Akil's fiancé Isabella? I'm not sure if you heard about it, but there was a car crash about a week before Akil died. Well, it was fake. He set it all up to send

Isabella away so no one could come after her or your niece and nephew Akil Junior and Akira.

Isabella has been living in LA for the last three months with the kids and Nabawi, and I have been taking care of her. Your brother left her his fortune before he left, but we still have been watching her closely, and we do have a team out there for her safety. That's why I've been visiting LA so much.

Not just to check on our Winery in the city, but to take care of our family and make sure that my daughter-in-law and my grand babies are okay. Osiris doesn't know about this and no, Kamikaze doesn't either. When Isabella is ready she'll reach out to her mother and family, but not until after this beef has been squashed and it's safe for her to come back to Saint Louis.

Your brother missed you dearly when you were locked up, Seth, and a day didn't go by when he didn't pray for you. Akil was the only one in this family who tried his damnest to get Osiris to go after you and bring you home, but your father wouldn't have it...

Akil also told me that you saved him while you two were in MDP, but I just didn't want to believe that Jediah had truly set you up.

With all my heart, Seth, I apologize for turning my back on you. You never deserved that, and I pray that one day you forgive me. You are an extraordinary human being, son. You have always been the chosen one.

We all have known it, and I hate that vanity and greed tore you and your family apart. I know once you get your mind right Mr. Seth P1 Shakur Platinum that you will be UNSTOPPABLE. UNTOUCHABLE. PREEMINENT. A KING.

Believe it or not son, you have something that your father never had, that Jediah never had, and what Akil always possessed, but he didn't have the desire or the strength.

You're humble.

That will get you far in this lifetime son. I want you to run with that. I want you to cherish that and use that quality as a vessel to turn this dynasty around and reunite this family.

It's always been in God's plan for you to be the one, son. I've always known it, and so has your father. Why do you think he *wanted to destroy and break you? You are EXCEPTIONAL, son. So continue to be that man.*

With all of those things being said and taken into consideration, please love Nasir right son. I'm sure she's already told you about us running into each other on her mother's birthday. She loves you. Genuinely.

From the way her eyes glowed every time she heard or said your name I could tell that she had your heart and how you have hers. Don't run from the love that you have to give and also receive in return, Seth.

So what if it's only been three months. Before your father went nuts, I fell in love with him almost instantly and look at us thirty years later. Nasir's a lot stronger than I was though, so I know your journey will be nothing like mine and Osiris'. Just don't turn into your father, Seth.

That's always been my greatest fear for you. You can get so dark and I do not want those demons preying on your soul. You are so much better than your attitude. Don't let that Gemini shit trip you up.

YOU WILL BEAT YOUR EGO! MARK MY WORDS YOUNG MAN!

Don't let greed, hate, and thirst for power turn you into that person. Self-con-trol. Peace. Serenity. Malohia, son. Don't be so uptight. Embrace the love between you and Nasir with all you've got. I believe she is your peace. Nasir is a beauty with a beautiful soul, so you stop being stubborn and you give that woman your heart. You know you want to.

LOL.

And don't worry about me. I'll be fine. I'm headed out to Meme Aruba's and I'm gonna lay low there for about a week until all of this shit with your father blows over. Keanu doesn't know yet, but I'm sure she'll welcome me with open arms. The Platinums are great people.

Nabawi has loved me since I was a little girl and after my mother died from her drug addiction, him, Keanu, and your grandmother, before she died, really stepped in and loved me beyond my imagination. Even if you don't ever speak to me again,

Seth, I pray that you seek forgiveness on my end in your heart. I can't stress that enough.

Sleeping at night knowing that this indifference rests between us makes me feel like I've failed you as your mother, and I've never felt a pain like this. My heart has a weak spot for my boys, so when you guys hurt, I hurt. When you guys are out of line, baby, momma feels that. Y'all are my babies and I just hate that I let the ball drop as a mother because I let my man brainwash me to only serve him...

I love you so much, baby. I think about you and pray for you every day. And before I get too old you better give me a grandchild! You hear me? Put all kinds of babies up in Nasir because I'm ready! One day soon Isabella can come home and hopefully we all can celebrate as one big happy family. Holidays are going to be a blast. I love you, son. Take Care.

Love,
Momma Platinum

Seth threw the letters in the air causing them all to flutter around the room as he stood to his feet, pacing the floor with his hands above his head. Oh, the physical, mental, and emotional pain that consumed him in that moment. He didn't know what to do.

Messiah sat back and bowed his head, knowing how his dawg felt from the inside and out. Losing not one, but both of your parents was a hard punch to take. That shit was hell.

Silence consumed them before Messiah's phone rang. He'd forgotten that he'd cut it back on, let alone had it on him, so the ringtone shocked him when he heard it.

He sighed when he saw Riley's name pop up. Him and Seth honestly didn't even know what their next move was. They knew what they *should've* been doing, but both of their emotions were reigning supreme at the hour and they couldn't focus.

"Riley," he spoke into the phone while rubbing his eyes.

"Oh my God! Messiah, baby, you're okay! I've been so worried about you!"

Her cries ironically brought a smile to his face. Riley did something to him that he couldn't explain, let alone get a hold on, and after all that's happened, he wouldn't know what to do without a woman like her on his side. Without having *her* on his side.

"Don't be getting yourself all worked up, ma. You don't need that kind of stress. It ain't nothing to be all worried about. We alive, mama. How you doing? You and my baby a'ight? How my lil' Tiri?"

When Messiah's facial expression changed, Seth listened closely to Riley talking at the speed of light. All he could make out was the words UCLA, hospital, and Nasir. Hell, that was enough of a formula to make Seth put his frustrations aside and slide a shirt and some shoes on. Wasn't nobody taking Nas away from him.

She was all he had left, and he'd be damned if niggas got to her trying to get to him.

The fuck they doing in Cali? Why the fuck did they leave Toronto anyway? He thought as he motioned for Messiah to stand up before he flipped her mattress over.

Holy assault rifle heaven.

Seth didn't know if he wanted the AR-15, the Scepter M4, the AK-47, the UZI, a Mossberg, or what. He unstrapped all of those bitches and got to applying extendos on each gun that could take one. This was enough heat for them to work with until they re-up'd.

"We on the way."

Messiah hung up the phone before he looked over at his dawg. Seth was war ready, but the nigga was too damn calm. He wasn't sure what all he had heard, but he'd known that whatever info he was hit with had him hot.

"Moms is alive. She's in Cali. Prodigy flew her out there from here. She's in a coma, and Nas just blacked out. They've got them both in the ICU. Let's get the fuck out of here man."

Chapter Twenty-Eight

It was close to 10 AM when Seth and Messiah entered the ICU doors at the UCLA Medical Center. When Tiri saw them strolling through, owning the atmosphere as they always did whenever they made an appearance, she jumped up to her feet and ran for her brother. Messiah held onto his side where his wound was located, due to the pain from laughing at her actions before he wrapped his arm around her.

"Messiah! What the fuck! Look at you!"

Tears rushed to the surface of Tiri's eyes due to the sight of her brother looking like Adonis from a fight scene in *Creed*. He and Seth both wore war wounds that would take weeks to heal but to know that they were alive soothed her aching heart. Messiah and Seth were all she had left to hold on to after losing Trudy, and her spirit couldn't take it to even fathom their departure from this earth. What would she do without them?

"I told you, you was gon' see me again, bae. I don't never make a promise that I can't keep."

Tiri giggled as he placed three kisses to her forehead. She'd always be his spoiled little baby sister no matter how old and mature she was getting.

"Where everybody at?" he questioned as she rested her head along her brother's chest.

"Keanu is sitting with momma Platinum, Ms. Catori is in Nas' room, and Riley just ran off to the bathroom literally two seconds before y'all showed up. We couldn't take being back there any longer. We needed to breathe for a minute. It's a little bit too much right now. I hope they're gonna be okay..."

"How long y'all been here?" Messiah asked.

"Almost five hours now. Uncle Seth, I thought you were too cute to get in a fist fight?" Tiri joked as she released Messiah and wrapped her arms around his waist.

Seth smirked as he placed a kiss to the top of her head.

"Wounds heal, sweetie. At age twenty-seven they're the least of my worries now. You doing alright?"

She nodded her head in agreement.

"I'm okay. Just glad to see y'all. It feels like it's been forever. I hope all of this is over," she prayed in fear.

"Don't be worrying yo' self, Baby T. We gon' take care of it...I'mma go back and see moms and them."

Messiah nodded his head when Seth walked off. As he disappeared behind another set of security doors, Riley came around the corner with her phone in hand speaking to her mother on FaceTime.

She was too cute with her hips naturally switching in her itty-bitty grey shorts that the neon green, long sleeve fitted shirt almost hid completely while she ran her fingers through her hair.

Riley was so busy trying to convince her mother that everything would be okay that she hadn't even noticed Messiah standing there until he started walking towards her.

"Bookie what's wrong? Why you looking like that? Bookie?"

Catrina's voice faded into the background when Riley locked eyes with her man. When he got within her reach, she wrapped her arms around his neck as he grabbed her by the waist with his good arm.

Butterflies were fluttering around in Riley's stomach like a flock of birds heading down south for the winter. Her tears simultaneously managed to squeeze their way between her scrunched-up eyelids.

"Baby you're okay," she whispered as she put her feet flat on the ground so she could look him in the eyes.

They both smiled at one another when Messiah's hand reached down for her ass. Beat up or not that nigga loved him some booty. Messiah would die for the booty. Well, Riley's booty. Rachet hoes got no love.

"What am I gonna do with you, Mr. Stallion? Huh?"

Her voice was soft before her man kissed her lips.

"Have my babies," he whispered as she buried her face in his neck while praying and thanking God that He'd sent him back to her.

"Riley Patrice Stewart! If yo' onion head ass don't answer me right fucking now! What the hell is going on! Do I need to come out to California turning shit up!"

Her mother's screams made her release her arms from around Messiah's neck to bring her phone back to her view. With her head now along her man's chest, Riley laughed when she caught a glimpse of the look painted on her mother's face.

"Well damn girl! I would've said fuck my momma too if my man looked like that! He still fine a lil' banged up. Okay sir!"

"Yooooooo, I can't, ma. Quit playing."

Her daughter was cracking up.

"Okay, all jokes aside. I'm done for the morning. Hello, Mr. Messiah. I've heard so much about you. Thank you for protecting my baby. She's been in need of some real love and affection for a long time now."

He smiled.

"How you doing, Ms. Catrina. You nor her don't have nothing to worry about while she's in my hands. I got her."

Messiah looked down and kissed Riley's lips ensuring her that the words coming out of his mouth were true.

"Yeah, my grandson is gonna be handsome as shit."

"Ma, it's too early to be claiming the sex. I've been pregnant all of two days," Riley joked.

"Weeeell...I've been buying all unisex stuff anyway, so whatever."

"Ma! I just told you like three minutes ago!" Riley shrieked.

"Girl, I'm excited about my first grand baby! I been shopping all fucking week, you better gon' somewhere! Have you been thinking of names because I have?"

"Lord have mercy, this is gonna be a long six months with you, ma. I'mma call you back though. I've gotta see how my man's been doing. He looks like he could use some TLC."

Catrina fake-gagged when her daughter kissed her man.

"Alright, alright. Call me later. I'm about to call your auntie and talk shit with her. Bye."

T

The E Ola Kakou Hawaiian chant known in the Platinum's culture as medicine for the soul, pierced Seth's ears as he opened the door to his mother's hospital room. Keanu's beautiful voice filled the atmosphere at a calm tone while she held onto Falcon's hand. A few candles were burning along with fumes from some of their island herbs as she blessed his mother's road to recovery.

Falcon's second transfusion was a success, and her vitals were now stable. She was still comatose, but Keanu wasn't going to give up hope. She served an almighty God who could make the world stop at the snap of a finger if need be, so her faith in Him and the way He saw things fit no matter how much she didn't understand it, never ran astray.

Seth tried to fight the tears as he gazed at his mother with the breathing tube shoved down her throat. Each time her heart rate beeped along the monitor he felt a fuse coming along like a ticking time bomb just waiting to explode.

"Seth... Come to me."

Keanu's words were low. She was sitting with her back to the door unable to see him just yet, but she knew he'd be there soon. Keanu could feel his dominance, his aura, and his unique presence within the room.

Seth rested his arm around her shoulders while bending down and placing a kiss to her cheek. Tears of joy flooded Keanu's face as she reached back and held onto his head.

"She's fighting baby. Falcon is a solider. She's built tough. This too shall pass..."

Seth dropped down to his knees and cried in his great grandmother's lap. He'd never been the one to release his emotions, and his exterior had never broken in front of her. So Keanu embraced the way he splurged, knowing that the chains around him had finally shattered.

She caressed his head with her hands while also rubbing his back, encouraging him to get it all out. It was exactly what the doctor had ordered.

Seth didn't need to explain the story and how it all ended. She'd already known for a fact that if he was standing then Osiris, Jediah, and their wicked ways had sadly fallen.

Poor Keanu cried just from the sight of Seth's beautiful face all banged up with abrasions, swelling, and bruises. How could the people you called family seek to mentally and physically harm one another when they all were one? The moral of protecting and honoring the family had been disobeyed and used loosely for years now within their dynasty, and it was heartbreaking.

Seth took a few deep breaths before he picked his head up and cleaned himself up. He'd shed too many tears in one day. The shit was making him sick. Keanu held his face in her hands before she leaned over and kissed his forehead.

"Talk to her Seth. Your mother needs you. I keia manawa. *Now.*"

Seth didn't put up a fight. He was so close to her hospital bed already, all he had to do was turn on his knees before he grabbed his mother's hands and lowered his head in prayer. A soft knock from the nurse interrupted Seth just minutes into him asking God for forgiveness and the wellness of his mother.

"Hi. I'm sorry to interrupt. I'm nurse Connie Jenkins. I've been working with Mrs. Platinum since she arrived last week. You must be her son," she greeted with a warm smile.

Seth kissed his mother along the cheek as he rose to his feet. The young nurse was highly impressed to lay her eyes upon the oh so famous Seth Platinum that the hospital staff had gotten her hip about before his arrival. Seth was known in all major cities, and he was just as fine as they said he was.

"Seth," he greeted in a low tone.

"Nice to meet you, Seth. I just wanted to inform you guys that the doctor put in an order to do a Brain MRI to check on her after the transfusion. It usually takes thirty minutes to an hour to get done. I'll be sure to have your mother back safe and sound as soon as possible."

"What room is Nas in?"

Keanu smiled.

"2110, Mr. Cocky. Did you hear what she said?"

Seth nodded his head before he exited the room, letting the hospital staff continue to do their job by taking care of his mother while he headed to see his lady. He needed her energy.

T

The rays of sunshine slithered their way inside of Nas' eyelids, causing her to scrunch up her face and move around in her sleep. When she felt something tugging at her left arm she immediately went into panic mode, causing her heart to race. Nasir blinked at least a thousand times before she saw an image sitting to the left of her, right by the bed.

The blurriness was playing tricks on her. Was she staring at a six-foot-four, peanut butter colored Seth with his hair hanging down his back after a torturing week of his absence? Was his appearance a signal of the end of this stressful ass journey? Oh, how she hoped so.

"Seth..."

Nasir's voice was raspy, causing her to clear her throat before she called out his name again.

"Seth."

This time she was a little louder, snapping him out of his sleep. Seth hadn't realized that he'd dozed off after all of fifteen minutes of sitting next to her once he'd left Falcon's room.

"Nas? You up?" he mumbled as he stretched his arms out before he sat up and met her halfway when she reached for him.

Nasir held her man by the back of his head while their foreheads nestled upon each other. Tears streamed down her face unlike ever before. She'd been unable to get control of her emotions ever since the day she met Seth, and it was driving her up a damn wall.

"Relax mama... Everything's gon' be a'ight."

Nas nodded her head up and down in agreement before he lifted her chin and kissed her. Just one simple kiss rekindled the man's spirit and had him ready to go up against the world again in round two.

"When did you get here?" She softly asked.

"About thirty minutes ago. I went to see Falcon before I came to see you."

"Oh, my God. Is she okay? Is she awake?"

Seth shook his head no.

"Not yet. They just took her back for an MRI."

"Oh, wow. I pray they return telling us something good. When I got the call about them needing to do another transfusion, baby, I just lost it..."

Nas went on to explain everything about the nurse getting in touch with her and how Falcon was transferred out there. All of the hype had triggered her to faint along with being severely dehydrated. That's what had her hooked up to an IV pole.

To her surprise, Seth had already known everything she told him; plus, he informed her of the letter Falcon had written and the contents that still had his head through the roof.

"What the fuck, babe... are you okay? I can only imagine how you feel right now..."

Seth inhaled deeply before saying, "I'll live..."

Nas was blown away. Everything with this crossover just got juicer and juicer as the days went by, and she was trying her best to keep up.

Note to self: if this nigga ever lets the words crossover come out his mouth following this shit, I'll beat his ass myself.

"I'm just so happy to see you, baby. I know this is gonna be tough, but we'll get through it. Together. Just like you told me... and you just had to put that shit out in the universe about you not making it back all in one piece. Look at you, Seth. No offense, but you look like shit."

He chuckled.

"This ain't shit. I'll take surface wounds over no broken bones any day, mama."

"Getting shot is not a surface wound, Mr. Platinum. God, you're gonna give me a heart attack. How long have I been asleep? What time is it?"

"For about five hours. Shit, six now."

"Really? That's the most sleep I've gotten all week."

"I told you not to worry about me."

Nasir mushed him in the head.

"That's like asking if water is wet. Nigga, after all that's happened you still tryna be cocky?"

Seth leaned her head back and kissed her lips, shutting her always right ass up.

"I missed you," he softly confessed.

"I've missed you."

Knock-knock.

"Damn, do people get any privacy around his muthafucka?" He griped with a grimace.

Nas giggled.

"It's the hospital, babe. Stop being such a Krabby Patty. Come in."

Again, it was that nosey ass nurse who kept interrupting him whenever he was tryna spend some alone time with his ladies. Out of all the patients in need she had to be breathing down his family's neck.

"Hello, Ms. Valentine."

"Hey, Connie."

"How are you? You've been out for a minute."

"I feel better." Nasir looked over at Seth and smirked when he looked her in the eye. "A lot better," she finished as their lips met.

"Well, that's great. Physically, you're doing a lot better as well. I'm gonna take this IV out. There's no need to hang another bag; your electrolytes have come back up and your blood pressure is back in a normal range. You should be out of this bed in a couple of hours tops."

"Thank God," Nas sighed.

"I do..." The nurse started back up as she disconnected all of the IV tubing. "Have some information to share with you as well though."

Nasir's heart monitor increased tremendously following the nurse's statement, causing Seth to laugh.

"Calm down," he kissed her lips.

They couldn't get enough of each other. She was lucky nurse cock blocker kept popping up or else he'd give her some dick. He'd bend her over no matter what the circumstance may have been, and his woman knew that.

Playfully rolling her eyes, Nasir did as she was told. She really didn't have much of a choice, did she?

"Well... let me have it."

The nurse smiled before saying, "You are with child, Ms. Valentine. Your pregnancy test came back positive, and your blood test showed high traces of the pregnancy hormone as well. I can transfer you over to a specialist who can take things further from here shortly. Congratulations to you both."

Before Nas could wrap her mind around Connie's words who was now disconnecting the EKG patches from her chest, the loud sound of a trembling voice came on the intercom yelling, "Code Red! UCLA Medical Center Code Red is in full effect! CODE RED! CODE RED! CODE RED! PLEASE PROCEED TOWARDS EACH NEAREST EXIT!"

"Kamikazes put a hit out on the building nigga!"

Messiah's message from his Apple Watch told Seth all he needed to know. He didn't hesitate to cradle Nasir in his arms before he headed for the door, damn near knocking the nurse off of her feet. Messiah met him at the entrance of the ICU after he chirped him.

"It's a bomb threat on the building! You know that nigga dirty! He don't give a fuck about the welfare of these fucking people! He coming for us! Prodigy just hit me up. He got a squad holding it down at the main entrance to buy us some time to get them out of here!" Messiah explained.

An alert from Seth's watch caught his attention when the screen lit up.

Unknown Number: Checkmate

Seth should've saw this shit coming. His emotions had him blindsided when he should've known Kamikaze was gonna react the moment he found out Osiris was dead. They'd fallen right into that nigga's trap.

"Come on!" Messiah urged as he unholstered his strap from his waistline.

Seth followed behind with a terrified Nasir in his arms. When they made it to the main lobby where Tiri, Keanu, Catori, and Riley were all fighting with the hospital staff who tried to escort them to safety, the sound of gun shots filled the air. Everyone in sight started to run even faster and duck for cover.

Nasir's heart jumped out of her chest when Seth hid her behind the receptionist desk. He withdrew a pair of Desert Eagles and got to blasting at the niggas heading in their direction with machine guns.

Him and Messiah were maneuvering like they weren't fresh out the emergency room themselves. Wounded or not, rule number one would always be solid: Don't die.

When Prodigy barged in through the main set of ICU doors with a squad behind him, reluctancy filled Seth, giving him a new burst of energy. Thank God somebody on their team was using their noggin because his brain had been fried for hours.

"Just like back in the day, my nigga!" Prodigy chuckled as he tossed his dawgs two fully loaded AK's.

"Messiah! What are we going to doooo!" Tiri cried as she and the others ran over to them when the gunshots came to a brief halt.

"Follow them! They gon' get y'all out of here!" Messiah responded, pushing her in the direction of the three armed men that came in with Prodigy.

"I got a shuttle waiting around the back for y'all to make it out! Where moms at?!"

"She was getting an MRI! We gotta find her!" Seth answered Prodigy's question as he handed Nas his burner while pulling her into his arms. "Go. I gotta get moms."

"Seth, I'm not—"

"Nasir! Don't fucking argue with me right now! I'm not losing you too! Just go! If we don't make it out in ten minutes then get the fuck out of hcre and don't look back…"

The moment for Seth was like Déjà vu. The last time those words escaped his lips he never saw Akil again. Inside, his heart shattered.

Somebody wasn't making it out alive. He could feel it, but their women and family would. He'd rip his own heart out and hand it over to Kamikaze without hesitating to ensure their safety.

Nas' bottom lip quivered as her mother grabbed her by the arm, pulling her away from her man so they could leave.

"Seth, noooooo!"

Her voice rang above the frenzy as everyone forced her to leave his side. When the ladies were out of sight the trio headed back in search for the rooms where the MRI's were done at. The hospital was chaotic. People were running back and forth racing with patients in wheelchairs and hospital beds screaming at the top of their lungs.

Seth didn't know where the fuck he was going. His adrenaline was at a peak that had his heart racing in irregular beats. This by far had been the most challenging mission he'd ever been on. When he spotted a woman dressed in scrubs, he grabbed her by the elbow and pulled her close.

"Where the fuck they do the MRI's at?!"

"Sir! I have to get—"

"Bitch answer me!" he growled with the barrel of his gun now in her mouth.

Pale skinned Becky burst into tears. Considering all of the excitement and possibly being only a bullet away from heaven, she couldn't control her emotions.

"It's in the west wing! You have to take the elevator down to the lower level to get to the MRI chamber!" she cried when he removed the gun from around her lips.

"Then lead the fucking way!"

Seth shoved her in front of them, but she hesitated to move.

"Bitch you wanna die today!" the trio yelled in unison.

The nurse took off running with the three of them on her tail. Gun shots started ringing behind them in the distance, causing them all to pick up on their speed.

"Aaah! Fuck!"

A shock of excruciating pain radiated in Messiah's side from his previous injuries, causing him to stumble over his feet and drop down to his knees. Prodigy threw Messiah's arm over his shoulder and helped him stand, but he was too weak to continue. Seth rushed over with a nearby wheelchair after taking a quick mental note of the direction the nurse ran in.

"Put this shit on and get him out of here," he instructed as he helped Messiah into the chair.

Prodigy looked at Seth as if he were crazy when he shoved the yellow PPE gown at him that was near on an aid's cart. It was a disguise for him to use to make it out safely.

"Seth," Messiah's voice was low before he roared out in pain from another shock evading his body.

"Y'all get the fuck out! I gotta go for moms even if we don't make it!"

Time stood still. Seth had never been the man to take the easy way out. Yeah, cowards lived, but that wasn't the code he abided by.

Comatose or not, he'd be damned if he left his mother without trying to save her. If it was his time to go then so be it, but he wasn't going without a fight. If he was gonna die, then he was gonna die with honor. Period.

"Malamo Pono, fam, I swear to God the Platinums got you. Ain't shit you did gon' go unnoticed. Get Siah and my family out of here. Now!"

He and Prodigy slapped hands and embraced before he reached down and grabbed Messiah who had his hand out.

"Malamo Pono," were his dawgs' last words before they took off in different directions.

T

Nasir was a nervous wreck, counting down the minutes until she expected to see Seth and his potnas return. Tears stained her face while she tried to ignore everything that was happening around her.

She kept looking at the time on her phone, aggravated with how fast the minutes were flying when it seemed like they'd been in Toronto waiting to hear from them for ages.

"We've gotta go ladies," the driver announced as he shifted the shuttle into gear.

"NO!!" Nas screamed at the top of her lungs while standing to her feet.

"Nasir," Catori tried to console her daughter, but that shit wasn't working.

Nas didn't want to be babied right now when her man was in danger.

"Ma, the building's gonna blow in any minute. Long story short, the Kamikaze mob never puts out a threat that isn't followed through..."

Every woman's heart on board dropped following his response. Tiri wrapped her arms around Riley's neck and cried her eyes out from the thought of losing her brother.

"Messiah! Noooo! God, you've already taken everything away from me! Not my brother, too! Nooooo!"

Riley held Tiri close, rocking her back and forth with tears cascading down her own face as well. Neither of them could believe that after all that's happened, this is how it would end.

"Hold up! Look!" One of the guards shouted while standing to his feet.

Everyone raced for a window to see Prodigy running with Messiah in a wheelchair towards the shuttle.

"Go help them!" Keanu shouted with prayers going out to God.

Nasir stood back stone faced and heartbroken when Prodigy and the guard helped Messiah inside.

"Messiah!" Tiri cried at her brother going in and out of consciousness while they laid him comfortably in two seats.

"Where's Seth?"

Nasir's voice was barely above a whisper.

Prodigy looked her in the eye before explaining, "He made us leave once he realized Messiah was too hurt to continue. He went after moms knowing he might not make it. He wanted y'all to be safe..."

The room started spinning. Nasir ran her fingers with her free hand threw her hair when it dawned on her that she was still holding the gun Seth had given her. When the shuttle doors closed, she inhaled deeply, seconds away from fainting again. The moment the shuttle started moving, Nasir broke for the back of the vehicle and unlatched the back door.

"NAS! NOOOOOOO!!!" Catori screamed at the top of her lungs when her daughter hopped out the door and ran at full speed towards the hospital.

T

Using his instincts, Seth made his way around the building until he found the elevator the nurse told him about. His feet shuffled down the steps until he entered a chamber that looked like a scene from off of *I, Robot.* Large glass windows aligned the halls as he frantically ran, barging in and out of each room until he found the right door.

Falcon was lying inside of a hospital bed hooked up to a transport ventilator. Her heart beat was strong, her breathing was normal, and before Seth made another move he thanked God that she was still alive. But where the fuck was all of the hospital staff? Why the fuck was she alone?

"The difference between you and your father, Seth, is that you have the heart he never had..."

King Kamikaze appeared before Seth's eyes when he made his way from around the MRI machine that he hid behind. A smile rested upon his face that spelled the word *checkmate* out in bold letters.

Two of his goons came up from behind Seth and held him by the arms as they brought him down to his knees. Kamikaze knew Seth would come after his mother. He was the only Platinum who'd honored respect. Hopefully his deed got him into heaven. Hopefully...

"I'll make this brief. You and your mother only have… four minutes and forty-six seconds before you meet the rest of your family in hell. Twenty-three years I've waited on this moment. Twenty-three years I've watched the woman I loved raise my son with the man who took everything away from me. But that's all in the past now. Platinum blood and ownership over all of your territories will be enough compensation."

"Get yo' fucking hands off her!" Seth growled before one of the goons struck him in the mouth, causing his lip to bleed.

Kamikaze rubbed Falcon's hair before he kissed her cheek. Life could've been wonderful for her. If she would've left Osiris like he told her to back in '91 then she wouldn't be lying in a hospital bed by the hands of her own son. The very son who took his dear Akil away from him before they ever got the chance to meet. But she was weak.

Weaker than he ever could've imagined. What woman lies to her husband and allows him to raise a son that wasn't his? What woman could look her own child in the eye and allow him to live that lie no matter what would've unfolded? Kamikaze loved Falcon, but she wasn't fit for this lifestyle, so losing her was bittersweet.

"Fuck 'em. Let's get the hell out of—"

Pow! Pow! Pow!

Kamikaze's body dropped following the bullet piercing him in the head. The guards holding onto Seth dropped as well, for him to turn around and see a teary-eyed Nasir holding the smoking gun in her hands.

Seth let out a deep sigh as he ran for her and grabbed her face with both hands before he kissed her.

"What the fuck is you doing, Nas!" he questioned with mixed emotions. "How the fuck did you know where I was!"

Nasir cried her eyes out as she held him tight with her hands locked onto his shoulders.

"I'll never leave you, Seth…never…"

If he could, he'd sit there and cry in her arms all night, but they were racing a ticking time bomb.

"Come on! We gotta get the fuck out of here!" Seth yelled before he unlocked Falcon's bed and pushed it out into the hall.

Before he left, he removed the switch blade from his pocket and dethatched Kamikaze's ring finger to take as a souvenir. If you didn't possess a piece of your enemy's remains, then the job wasn't done right.

He and Nas rushed down the hall looking for an exit they could get through with that big ass bed. Seth knew they only had seconds to spare before the building exploded, but they weren't having any luck.

"There!"

Nas pointed to the exit door she could see sunlight peeking through since it wasn't closed all the way. It was a struggle getting the bed through the doorway, but they managed to do so, Nanoseconds before the eruption began.

Running full speed, they headed towards the open parking lot. The tires on the shuttle screeched and came to a halt when the driver noticed Seth and Nas heading in their direction. Prodigy hopped out the back door and lowered the transport ramp just in time for them to load Falcon's bed on board.

The UCLA Medical Center crumbled into pieces before the last powerful explosion blew out the rest of the building. Seth held Nas in his arms as they sat along the floor leaned against the wall while the driver got them to safety. He was one hundred percent certain that he'd never see her or his family surrounding him ever again, but God had other plans.

August 2018…

Chapter Twenty-Nine

"Girl I'm way too drunk, I just don't care at all
I just hope you pick up when it's two or three...
And I hope you dooooo
Dooo oooo oooo..."

Nasir made dancing in heels look effortless. Her body swayed back and forth while she tipped the large sun hat on her head low to hide her face from the camera. The screen was her best friend. The director soaked up all of her solo scene before all five women began their routine with Chris Brown, putting the final touches on his "Hope You Do" music video.

Diiiiiiiing!

"Alright! That's a wrap! What the fuck! That was so amazing! Great way to wrap this project up!" The director yelled in excitement.

Nasir removed the hat from her head and fanned herself in excitement as well. What an honor it was to finish her first music video alongside one of the greatest R&B artists in her generation. She just couldn't believe it. After the grand opening of her dance studio gifted to her by her man, so many doors opened for her.

When she received the call back about making the cut, Nas could've sworn that she was dreaming. Not only was she picked to be in the video, but she even assisted with a last-minute routine to meet the director's vision. At a size ten, Nasir was the only plus sized woman amongst the other model framed dancers, and it was like a dream come true.

Excitement filled her to know that her face would be all over YouTube, Vevo, and social media doing what she loved. Her career as a choreographer and a dancer had taken off right before her eyes, and she owed it all to God. She knew He had something great in store for her. All it took was a little time and patience.

"Naaaaaaaas! Baby, you were amazing!" The director, Latif, screeched as she threw her arms around Nas' neck.

"Thank you so much, Tif! I can't believe it!"

"Girl, you better! The first plus sized woman to be in one of Chris Brown's videos?! You better own that shit!"

The ladies shared a laugh before the screams and running of two pairs of tiny little feet caught their attention.

"No, Aerie! Nooo!"

"It's mine, Seth! Give it back!"

Nasir's eyes lit up when her babies ran towards her chasing after one another.

"What are you two doing here!" she shrieked as she squatted down and held her arms open.

"I wanted to give it to mommy!" Aerie whined, folding her little arms and poking her bottom lip out.

"Give mommy what? Come-come. How 'bout you give mommy kisses?"

Her twins ran in her arms and smothered her with their tiny little lips, causing Nasir to giggle. When they made it back to Saint Louis after Nas found out she was pregnant, on her first visit with her OB/GYN, s and Seth discovered that they were having twins.

Just approaching the fifteen month mark, Seth Junior and Ariel Platinum were running around walking and talking like they were toddlers. Nas was reading by the age of two, so to see her babies speaking in full sentences was like seeing a reflection of herself in her baby videos her mother kept of her

"What's this under your shirt, Seth?" Nasir wondered.

"It's from daddy!" Aerie blurted.

Nas laughed before her mouth dropped.

"Oh my God," she lost her breath when she opened the jewelry box and laid eyes on the nickel-sized diamond ring.

When she looked up, Seth was on one knee with their five-month old son, Asim, in his arms.

"Seth..."

Tears ran down Nas' face. She was unable to hold them back.

After Prodigy kissed his girlfriend, Latif, on the lips and handed her their daughter, he grabbed Asim from his dawg so Seth could slide the ring on her finger.

"Why is momma crying, daddy? Don't cry, mommy."

They shared a laugh as Aerie reached up and wiped her mother's tears away.

"She's happy, lil' momma. Mommy's okay." Seth looked into Nas' eyes and smiled. "You up for marrying my mean ass? You ready to be a Platinum on paper?"

Nasir laughed as she wrapped her arms around his neck. She knew he was flying out to LA to pick her up from the video shoot, but this? This was totally unexpected.

"Yes," she whispered, squeezing him even tighter. "I love you, Seth Platinum."

"I love you too, Mrs. Platinum-to be." He looked her in the eye again before saying, "I'm proud of you."

"Thank you, baby."

The ringing of Seth's cell phone caused him to release her as he looked at the screen.

"Seth Shakur Platinum! Where are you? It's almost time for Tiri's party!" Falcon shrieked, damn near busting his eardrum.

"We on our way back. I just picked up Nas," he chuckled.

"Tell my baby I said hiiiiiiii!"

"Heeeey, Momma Platinum!"

"Heeeeey boo! I can't wait to see the video! Don't be late y'all. I'll see y'all when you get back. Bella and I are on the way to the boat to make sure everything looks good for Tiri's arrival."

"A'ight, bet. We'll see you in a minute, ma."

Falcon didn't wake up from her coma until eight months later. She spent another two months afterwards learning how to walk and talk all over again, but she finished out strong. Aside from a nasty scar along her stomach from the gunshot wound, and the removal of her spleen that was hit by the bullet, she was living pretty well. Her hemorrhaging would've cost Falcon her life hadn't she made it to the hospital just in time.

Seeing his mother open her eyes and pull through taught
Seth a valuable lesson about life. Holding a grudge was never
worth it, and as he'd always been taught since he was a child:
honoring, respecting, loving, and protecting the family was key.

"Come on," he whispered before placing one last kiss to
Nasir's lips and helping her up to her feet.

Seth scooped his little rug-rats up in his arms as Nas
grabbed a hold of Asim from Prodigy. He was the savior behind
Falcon's life. Moments before Jediah would've pulled the trigger
again, he knocked him out and rushed Falcon to the emergency
room.

Prodigy had shown up at the mansion looking for his
potnas after he heard about the explosion at Messiah's crib. If it
weren't for him, then Falcon wouldn't be here to this day, and Seth
was indebted to his dawg's loyalty.

When Jediah woke up from being knocked out four hours
later, he had no clue where Falcon had gone or what had happened.
The security tapes in the house had shown him nothing but him
blowing a hole in his mother's stomach, then the video went black.
He threw out the feed and searched high and low for her for as
long as he could until he was just like fuck it.

With everything that was going on, he brushed it off and
would use it as his alibi for her "disappearance". He never
expected things to turn around on him the way they did, but grimy
ass niggas never lived long. Karma always came back around, and
he'd met his match before he could cause their family any further
harm.

𝒯

Riley looked at herself in the mirror, observing her fluffy
face while she adjusted her clothes. She turned around with her
back now to the mirror and saw her eyes widen in her reflection.

"Holy full moon, bih," she laughed as she ran her comb through her long, silky hair before she washed her hands one last time.

"If I pee one more time today, I swear to God," she laughed to herself as she finished drying her hands.

Messiah waked up to her after she exited the bathroom and kissed her lips, knowing where she'd fled off to for the umpteenth time that evening.

"What you complaining about now, mama?" he smiled.

"Your kid's elbow in my bladder. That's what."

Messiah grabbed her hand and kissed her wedding ring before he pulled her close.

"You'll have ya body back soon, Mrs. Stallion. Four more months. I promise to give you a lil' more rest time before the next one."

"Is that so, husband?" she teased with a kiss to his lips.

"It's very much so, ma."

Riley was five months pregnant with their second daughter, Jayla. Everyday it wowed her how God could bless her with all she's ever wanted in life with the snap of a finger. She could admit that she was a bit skeptical about she and Messiah's future together, but he stood by his word and loved her with everything he had in him.

Aside from getting married after a year of dating, he helped her build her own fitness company named Dream Body. From workout tapes to clothing and a shoe line, Riley's career had reached a peak she never could've imagined. She'd made it through the trenches with Tevin to be strong enough for the man who was always meant to place her heart in his hands.

Riley never heard from Tevin once Messiah made it back on his feet after his fight with Osiris. When he saw the messages that nigga had been steadily harassing her with, even after she'd gotten her number changed, saying how he was coming for her and was threatening to kill her and the baby she could never give him, Messiah took care of that shit. Straight like that.

Riley didn't ask any questions. She tried to force herself to believe that they scrapped it out and that was that, but deep down inside she knew the truth. There was no doubt that Tevin would've tried to really kill her.

He was obsessed with her, and the way he locked her in the basement, let her go days without anything to eat or drink, and slapped her around before she finally up and left him, she knew he was serious.

She was thankful that she got out when she did, and how the problem was "resolved" before it had really gotten out of control. It was something she learned to live with, her hardships with Tevin, and all she could do was thank God that those nightmares never had the chance to haunt her anymore.

"Mommy! Mommy!"

The beautiful, chocolate, fifteen-month old Ashanti Stallion ran for her mother at full speed before she jumped into her arms.

"I'm hungry, mommy! Hi, daddy!"

Messiah laughed as he kissed his daughter's cheek.

"Wassup, boo."

"Can I have a snack, mommy?"

"Of course, you can have a snack. Come on princess."

"Shanti! Why'd you run off like that! That baby moves waaaay faster than I ever will!" Falcon shrieked as she ran around the corner.

"You got your hands full, Momma Platinum," Riley laughed.

"Hell, I know! When I asked for grandkids I didn't expect y'all to pop them out like this, now! Y'all giving an old lady a run for her money! Seth, Nas, the kids, and Prodigy's family just made it in, so the captain is ready to take off. Come on."

The entire Platinum family, the Stallions, and a few close friends were enjoying Tiri's graduation/trunk party on this beautiful summer day on their private yacht. Messiah's baby was all grown up and ready for the world with her college adventure.

It brought tears to his eyes to see his baby sister moving on up. They'd never been apart, so to know that he was sending her off in just a few short weeks had him a little uneasy, but he knew that she'd be okay.

"I can't believe y'all did thiiiiiiis! I feel like a queen!" Tiri shrieked as she wrapped her arms around her brother's waist.

"You deserve it, Ms. Valedictorian, class president, and 4.0 graduate! You get that shit from me! I'm proud of you, girl!" Messiah yelled amp.

"Messiah, you wish. But thanks." Tiri joked before her eyes lit up. "Nas! You made it!" she screamed in excitement as they embraced.

"Now you know I wouldn't miss this for the world! Not even Chris Brown could keep me away!"

"You should've brought him with you, giiiiiirl!" Tiri teased, laughing but very fucking serious.

"I know right!"

It didn't take long for the party to get started. Before they all knew it, they were seated and being served the first dish of their five-course meal that awaited their empty stomachs.

"So, which school did you choose, lil' momma?" Isabella questioned as she fed Akil Junior some of the fruit from off of her plate.

The beautiful mother of his babies had moved back home and being around his family turned her life around. Isabella didn't know how she would make it without him, but Falcon welcomed her into her home with opened arms until she got back on her feet.

It was one of the best decisions she'd ever made. Dating was far from her mind right now. She knew Akil would never want her to suffer by holding onto him, but for right now, her kids were all that mattered.

"That's right. I haven't announced what school I was going to," Tiri slapped her forehead.

All the excitement had her mind all over the place.

"Speak a little louder for us at the other end of the table, baby girl!" Catori shouted through her hands.

Tiri giggled as she stood to her feet so everyone could see and hear her as she spoke.

"Yes, Ms. Catori! Thanks everybody for joining me today. I really appreciate it. Also, thanks for all of the gifts and cards, and all of your support. It means the world to me. My parents would've been proud...

"I've been holding on to this secret long enough so here it is. After weighing my options between my last two schools that I narrowed it down to, I chose the HBCU Trinity University in Trinity, California to study medicine and become a doctor."

"Congratulations baby!"

Everyone screamed and applauded Tiri on her endeavor. Messiah never went to college and aside from their mother, Tiri would be the next Stallion with a college degree.

The party went on until nightfall. As everyone danced the night away under the shining stars, Seth, Messiah, and Prodigy all stood back smoking the finest cigars imported from Amsterdam, taking everything in.

After slaughtering the rest of the Kamikaze family, Seth and Messiah were crowned with the keys to the streets in five states, Mexico, Columbia, and parts of Canada. Without hesitating they offered to hand their west coast territories over to Prodigy. Since the early 2000's he'd been thugging with them no matter what direction he chose to go in, and it was the least they could do.

But Prodigy stuck to his word and stayed out of the game. He didn't need to be paid to remain loyal to the niggas who helped him eat when, once upon a time, he didn't have shit. He'd always have their backs just like they'd always have his. It was death before dishonor in his eyes, and that's what he lived by.

His dawgs respected that, but as compensation for stepping in when he didn't have to and helping them come out on top, Seth and Messiah both gave him a brief case filled with a million dollars. Again, it wasn't about the money; it was about respect. With their potna's decline, Tito was appointed to handle their west coast trades.

Other than Prodigy, he was the worthiest of that position and business was looking good. When you added Seth's lending company and Messiah's new men's high fashion clothing line he launched last summer, along with their smaller local businesses, they had more than enough legit clout to make it snow like no one had ever seen with little static.

Life was gravy.

"I never thought Messiah would be the first one married out of us, mane. That shit straight blowing me, dawg," Prodigy laughed.

Seth and Messiah chuckled as well.

"This nigga popped back up in town with a wedding ring on and I thought I was seeing shit. He jumped before I even proposed to Nasir," Seth teased.

Messiah could admit it. Riley had stolen his heart overnight. He never expected to marry her off impulse on her birthday last summer in Barbados, but God just kept telling him that she was the one. The proposal was all planned but holding hands before a preacher and making her Mrs. Stallion along the beach was the beginning of a journey he never wanted to end.

"A man can no longer search when the hunt is over," Messiah responded with the raise of his glass.

His dawgs toasted to his response before Falcon approached them.

"My boys," she smiled with tears in her eyes.

She placed a kiss to Messiah and Prodigy's cheeks before they left her alone to talk with Seth.

Falcon wrapped her arms around her son's waist and cried with her face in his chest. This past, almost two years, have been hard on her. From her recovery to losing Akil, Jediah, and her husband, it was the least bit easy getting through the days without Seth. Their bond was strong before the crossover, but now they were inseparable.

"I love you, son. I'm so proud of you." Falcon flashed a teary-eyed smile as she looked into Seth's eyes. "Thank you for saving this family."

Seth kissed his mother's forehead before giving her smile in return. He looked like the boss he was donning the Alexander Wang white Polo, matching shorts, and Valentino sneakers on his feet with his beautiful curly hair hanging down the sides of his face.

"Aloha wau ia 'oe, makuahine. *I love you too, ma.*"

Falcon smiled like a little girl before she released him.

"Okay. I'm done with my little pity party. Let's enjoy the rest of the night. I'm sure your *fiancé* is looking for you. Congratulations, baby. Excellent choice. Nasir is perfect for you."

Seth took a sip of his drink before saying, "She is, isn't she?" with his infamous crooked grin.

When they made it back up to the high-level, the family was having a good time doing the oh-so famous Cha-Cha Slide. They had Keanu with her hands on her knees and Seth couldn't help but to double over in laughter from the sight of his great grandmother grinding on her husband.

"I see you Keanu! Wooooorld Staaaaaar!" Falcon screamed in excitement.

"Oh my God! Look at Keanu! I see why she had all those kids!" Nasir giggled as she walked up to her man.

Her mother was dancing with Asim in her arms while the kiddos all ran around in their gated off play pin.

"What a day. I'm whooped, Mr. Platinum," Nas smirked as she draped her arms along Seth's neck.

He reached down and grabbed a handful of her ass that the strapless bodycon sundress couldn't hide. Seth looked into Nasir's eyes, never knowing that he'd ever love a woman the way he loved her.

Since the day she walked into his life, things had never been the same. They had their ups, and they surely had their downs. Time and time again Seth wanted to quit; time and time again he'd been ready to leave.

His ego had him on the verge of saying fuck it plenty of times because he was still afraid that he wouldn't be able to live up to or be the man Nasir needed. His mood swings would get the best of him; hell, knowing that he feared hurting her was a lot for a man like him.

It was a lot for a man who's never handed his heart over to a woman before, but Nasir knew just what to do with it.

If she was willing to run inside of a building that was minutes away from exploding for him, how could she not be more than willing to stand by his side when he needed a little push to explore his emotional side?

Seth was everything in a man that she could pray for. He wasn't perfect, but Nas was perfectly blind for Mr. Platinum as he was with her. Together, their imperfections connected all of the dots to everything they both had been deprived of in love. And that was each other.

"Thank you, mama."

Nasir smiled.

"For what?"

"For staying by my side. Believe it or not, you having my back through everything? Not just the hype, but mentally, has taught me how to open up my heart and it's helped mold me into something better. That's love. That's the power of a good woman. God blessed me when he sent you to me, so how could I not love and protect you for life? Thank you for being my rida'."

Nasir kissed Seth's lips until the inside of her legs tingled. She held her man close, knowing from his expression that Seth was truly ready for the next step they were taking in their lives.

"Things won't always be easy, baby, but just know that I'll never let you go. My heart doesn't belong to anyone but you, and since you're promising me forever then, I promise to also love you and continue to be your peace. Until death does us part…"

The End

The move to Trinity, California was a huge step to take for Tiri, and from the day she settles in, her life forever changes...

Heart Up for Ransom
(Love From A Boss Spinoff)

Chapter One

"*I won't say anything…on my life you have my word, but if you don't believe me, then you can just kill me now…*"

-Tiri

1787 Bayside Terrace was a long distance away from St. Louis, Missouri.

Tiri's hair blew in the wind as she held on tight to the large Gucci duffle bag. Her eyes scanned the ocean shore that was only miles away from her dorm room at Spellman hall apartments.

Her chest was heavy. The fall semester came faster than she'd expected it to, and now, she was having second thoughts about being two thousand miles away from home.

"If you scared, sus, we can turn back around right now. I'll go get ya shit like, now."

The sound of her older brother's voice made her smile as she turned around to look at him. Messiah approached her with a smirk before he wrapped his arms around her neck. This was one of the hardest things he'd ever had to do.

Killing a nigga was nothing. That shit came easy but letting his baby girl go was an aspect that was seconds away from bringing him down to his knees.

After their parents died almost four years back, then when their cousin Trudy was murdered at his expense because niggas got to her looking for him, Tiri was all he had family wise.

He was a father and a husband now, and yeah, he loved his wife deeply, but the little girl in his arms right now was his heart. He'd go to war with the devil himself on her behalf.

No words were spoken between them after his comment, so in silence, he followed her back up to her dorm. Messiah helped his baby sister with the rest of her belongings before there just stood the two of them, with the silence taking over once again.

"You know I'm only a phone call away if you need anything, and I mean that, Tiri."

Her eyes watered as she stared at her brother. If it weren't for Messiah, Tiri wouldn't be who she was to this very day. It was unbelievable.

He may have been ten years older than her, but they were like a large Wingstop fry and cheese. You couldn't eat one without the other, so their separation was killing her.

"I miss you already," she cried as she buried her face in his chest.

He wrapped his arms around her back before he kissed her forehead.

"Chin up, champ. You do yo' thing out here, live yo' fucking life, and keep yo' head in them books. You Dr. Stallion in the making, and if you have any second thoughts about anything? Whether it's yo' major, these lil' hot ass, sketchy bitches that you *will* bump into, or if one of these upperclassmen do some shit that you don't like? You already know big bro gon' get shit rocking on a negative or positive note. Long story short though, don't think just because you out here alone that you *are* alone, a'ight?"

She looked up into his eyes.

"Okay. Malama pono, big brother. I love you. Kiss baby Ashanti and Riley for me okay?"

"You can kiss us yourself. You thought I was gone? I had to pee. This baby's elbow is sitting right on my damn bladder, and I couldn't hold it."

Tiri turned around when she heard her brother's wife, Riley, voice. A huge smile appeared on her face when she got a glimpse of her chocolate niece.

"Hey, Shanti Baby! Tee-Tee is gonna miss you soooo much! I promise to be home for Thanksgiving dinner to see you, boo-boo!"

She kissed the baby's cheek, whom was chowing down on her thumb, fighting the hell out her sleep.

"Be safe, lil' bit, but have the time of your life. Seth, Nas, and the kids sends all their wishes, hugs, and kisses too, and you know California ain't ready for you girl, so show out."

Tiri giggled as Riley kissed her forehead.

"Thanks, sis. I really appreciate it. I can't wait to meet my next niece too. Messiah, you gon' let my girl rest before you knock her up again? Gosh."

Her brother chuckled as he ran his hands down the sides of his head. He was still rocking his braided man-bun with a tapered fade.

"Her pussy shouldn't be so damn good, sus. You know how shit go."

"Omg!" She busted out in laughter. "Y'all be safe too. I'mma hold it down here. I promise."

Messiah grabbed her hand and kissed the top of it.

"Malama pono, sus. I love you too…"

The door closing behind them felt like the end of the world, but Tiri soon wiped the tears from the creases of her eyes, startled by the sudden knock right after their departure.

When she opened the door, she was greeted with a warm smile by one of her three roommates, Abby. Abby was your typical white girl who'd flown all the way from Maine to attend school at the HBCU.

"Hi, I'm Abby. We've spoken over Facebook a few times."

"Hey, Tiri. Nice to finally meet you. You can come in."

"Thanks. Damn girl, you've got tons of shit. You're gonna be all day unpacking all of this."

"I know right!" Tiri exclaimed as she thoroughly glanced around her room.

She hadn't realized how much she'd packed until the moving truck arrived. She might've gone a little overboard, so this room arrangement would be one hell of a puzzle to solve.

"Have you checked out campus yet?" she asked after turning her attention back to Abby.

"No, not yet. I was actually a little scared to go by myself. I was wondering, if you don't mind, if you would go with me."

Tiri laughed a lot harder than she should have, causing Abby to laugh as well.

"Why did you choose a HBCU? I have to ask."

Abby smiled.

"I really like black people."

It was quiet before they both busted out into laughter.

"Okay, *Drumline*," Tiri joked.

Abby giggled.

"Seriously, I really do. Y'all are so open and honest about who y'all are and aren't scared of anything. I wish I was that outgoing. Plus, my big sister has mixed kids. Don't worry, I know what you're thinking. I'm not like that. I promise. I got a full-ride here, and I was like well shit. Their medical program is one of the top ten in the country, and I was down."

"That's wassup. You not one of them Vicky from off social media type-chicks, are you? I don't fuck around with the foo-foo shit."

Tiri raised her brow in defense hoping she didn't come off too strong.
"Girl, hell no! I know I'm white! That shit is embarrassing to me, for real. The way she be trying so fucking hard to be "down" is too much. Like, bitch, you gotta wash your hair everyday just like I do, so chill."

Tiri was bugging up.

"Okay. Cool. Where you going on campus? Is it close to Mason Point? I'm starving and some Zaxby's is calling my name."

"Yeah. That's exactly where I'm going, actually. I have to get some things figured out in registration and sign some papers. You're a freshman, right? I know some sophomores live in Spellman Hall too."

"Yup. I am. Just let me shower and get out of these clothes that I flew in, then we can make sum' shake."

"Then we can what?"

Tiri laughed.

"St. Louis lingo for we can go/ to make it happen."

"Oooooh okay. Girl, you gon' have to bear with me until I get hip, but I'll be in my room. The other girls haven't arrived yet, so my door will be open, and you can come right in."

"Wait, you gon' be scared to have it open when they get here?" Tiri raised her brow.

One thing she didn't have time for was sketchy bitches.

"I don't mean to say it like that. They just weren't the friendliest when I reached out to them on Facebook. You were super nice when you responded. One of them just ignored me, and the other... wasn't so nice."

Aw, hell nah. I wonder what the fuck this school year is about to be like, Tiri thought as she unzipped her duffle bag.

"Don't let nobody intimidate you. Fuck them. You here for you and your experience. Not making nobody else happy."

Abby smiled.

"Thank you. That means a lot. I'll be in my room once you're ready. Take your time."

"Okay. I should be about thirty minutes."

"Okay."

T

"Get you a straw nigga, you know this pussy is juicy..."

Tiri stood in the mirror and ran the shade of Silk Indulgent by NYX across her plump lips as that "Motorsport" blared from out of her Beats Pill speaker. It was her favorite song right now even in 2018. She raised her brow as she eyed her appearance following a few squirts of her favorite fragrance, Gloss by Prada.

The high-waist distressed denim walking shorts with creases above her knees, and the white crop top that hung off her shoulders was flawless against her smooth, silky chocolate skin. Everyone who bumped into her swore she looked just like Justine Skye. She was slim with some wide hips and niggas couldn't resist her beauty.

Her jet-black hair with a neon purple ombre was pulled up into a sloppy bun, high on her head while some Gucci Ace kicks rested on her feet. Everywhere she went she was rocking something Gucci.

She was definitely a Gucci Guilty bitch. Of course, Tiri donned Fashion Nova, Gap, and all that good stuff too, but Gucci was the MVP in her book. Her billionaire, drug dealing brother spoiled her rotten with whatever her heart had desired.

Tiri could be a fire cracker when it was needed, but all around she had an innocent soul. When she wasn't checking a bitch for coming at her the wrong way or standing her grounds, she was nothing but a timid lil' cool chick who sat up with her hand in a bag of popcorn while watching Disney movies. She was a kid at heart, and in November she'd be a nineteen-year-old young woman who still had her V-Card.

Tiri wasn't like other girls. Yes, she loved to dress and keep her nails done, and she might have gotten high like Smokey from off of *Friday*, but she wasn't into all the other shit. That's just who she was, but she knew attending a HBCU would come off as a challenge.

366

Trinity College was the most popping school in the region. It blew UCLA out the waters. Her school was always cracking. Their football and basketball teams were the top in the nation, parties were always being uploaded on The Shade Room, and their studies was A1.

She couldn't have asked for a more intense adventure. But one thing she promised herself before she left St. Louis was that she wasn't going to lose who she was by getting caught up in all of the hype. That was a promise that she planned on keeping.

"Okay pretty girl. Time to go."

Tiri cringed a bit when those words came out of her mouth. She pep-talked with her reflection every day and reminded herself that just because she was chocolate, didn't mean that she wasn't beautiful.

The more melanin the better, but it wasn't always that easy until her brother started to drill it into her head that *she* had to love herself first before the world had followed suit. So she did just that.

Tiri was locking the door to her room when two guys entered the hall of their dorm, carrying a big fifty-inch flat screen that no one bothered to cover up or put back in the box. They headed down the hall to the last room on the left.

Them other chicks must be here, she thought as she gave the men that quick little smile you flashed once you made eye contact with a stranger, then went to Abby's room.

"Hey, you ready?"

"Holy shit!" Abby jumped when she heard Tiri's voice over the music. She turned it down and spun around in her computer chair. "You scared the shit out of me, girl. Look at you! You're fine!"

Tiri smiled.

"Thank you. We gon' have to get you blended in here so you ain't so damn shook whenever somebody comes around."

"Ugh, I know right. I'm kinda dreading this walk. I'm gonna stick out like a sore thumb," she panicked as she picked up her large framed and stylish sunglasses.

"Own that shit, Abby. Black niggas love white girls."

Abby was too naive to recognize the shade in her compliment. Tiri didn't mean any harm, and she wasn't racist either. Abby came off like she could be the white girl at the cook out once she loosened up.

It was so funny to Tiri. Abby looked like Hayden Panattier, and seeing her at a HBCU was like watching *Bring it on: All or Nothing…*

Those light but pleasing winds from the sea blew against them as they headed down the block for Mason Point Millennium. It was the temple of campus where the main dining area was located as well as the registration office, the super gym, a library, and all other kinds of amenities.

Niggas were everywhere. Chocolate ones, light-skinned ones, thugs tatted from shoulder to wrist, short ones, fat, handsome ones, niggas with dreads, fades, jocks, lames; just niggas, niggas, niggas!

Tiri was in a fucking candy land, and by the way Abby was secretly pointing them out she could tell she was impressed to. She'd have her a nigga soon. Tiri could feel it.

After grabbing a bite to eat and showing Abby what seasoned chicken tasted like, they headed up the escalator to the registration hall.

"I won't be long. I just gotta sign a few papers then we can go do whatever you want."

"I'm new here just like you, so this gon' be a journey for us both," Tiri laughed as she took a seat. "I've only been here once for the tour. Maybe we can just walk and look around. I think they have a pep rally planned for today on the football field in like an hour."

"Okay. Sounds like a plan. I'll be right back."

Tiri was scrolling through her phone, while Abby took care of her business, when she noticed a woman enter the opened double doors looking bad as fuck! This woman took Tiri's breath away.

Tiri didn't like girls, but when a bad bitch crossed your path with so much poise, attitude, and a vibe that couldn't be ignored, she couldn't help but to stare at her. She had to be someone of importance.

The black, thin strapped bodycon dress hugged her curves like something fierce stopping about calf length. The high split up the side displayed the tattoos along her juicy thigh and the denim red bottoms under her pedicured feet.

Kovu Usher held her head high rocking a blunt cut bob that looked as if God himself had cut it; the red lipstick painted along her lips was all the color she needed.

A tall, light-skinned man rocking a sick ass fade with a man bun high on his head was beside her, along with a mob of five henchmen as they all headed down the left hall and to the back of the office.

Tiri didn't know what had come over her in that moment. The force the unknown woman had brought with her was still in the atmosphere even after she'd disappeared.

Damn, what the fuck just happened? She thought with Kovu's wrath still sitting heavily along her chest.

Though, the ice was broken when she noticed Abby heading back in her direction with a tall, fine ass chocolate brotha' lingering behind her.

He was smiling too wide from the sight of her ass. Abby was slim, but she was stupid thick as if she used to be the volley ball champ back in high school. He licked his lips as he kept walking while eyeing her before he was out of sight.

"Girl, he would not stop staring at me while I was back there," she whispered in disbelief.

"You gave him yo' number, didn't you?" Tiri joked while turning her lip up.

"Shit, I was afraid not to!" she shrieked.

"Shut the fuck up, Abby!" They were cracking the fuck up. "Uh-uh, you can't be giving yo' number to these niggas out of fear. We gotta prepare you for this—"

At the speed of light, a team of men swarmed into the office running with large choppers aimed, cutting Tiri's sentence short. Bullets started blasting from the direction of the bureau that the woman and her guests from earlier had headed to. Tiri grabbed Abby by the hand and they ran behind the nearest counter where they ducked off at to get out of dodge.

Memories from Tiri's first encounter with ringing gun shots flashed in her head, back when she was seventeen, and she couldn't keep up her tough demeanor. That hood shit still didn't sit right with her stomach even after all of her experiences with that lifestyle. Tears trickled down her face as she screamed into her hand that was holding onto her mouth, praying no one could hear her.

The shots were so hollow, so crisp, so close; more men were rolling in, she'd heard too many bullets going off, and her heart couldn't take it. Abby screamed for dear life when the barrel of a Tech was aimed at her. A gunman who'd looked over the counter and discovered them trying to hide charged for her quick. They didn't want any witnesses.

"Tiriiiiiii!"

"Abby!"

The man grabbed her by the arm before another one grabbed poor little Tiri as well and pulled her up to her feet.

"Put her down, nigga!"

The voice startled Tiri. Her eyes searched the smoky room until they fell upon the man holding two Desert Eagles in her direction; it was the guy who was with Kovu from earlier. A foreign dialect with such a heavy accent exited the mobster's mouth who was holding the gun up to her head. His enunciation was so thick that she couldn't understand what he was saying.

The chanting continued, but very briefly before two single rounds were popped from Steelo's guns, then the bullets started blasting again. All Tiri remembered was the man's body hitting the floor who'd had her held up and hers falling on top of his.

She looked over and screamed her head off when she saw Abby laying in cold blood. She'd been shot in the side of the head, and the sight was horrifying.

Tiri scooted on her hands and feet to get far away from the dead bodies when she noticed another armed henchman heading in her direction. Time went slow when she saw his bullet exit the chamber. She could see it flying across the room just before she saw someone jump in front of her.

Steelo leapt forward and threw his body in front of Tiri as a shield with his arms stretched out in the gunman's direction. Bullets exited his chambers, making the gangta's body shake before he hit the ground.

Steelo threw his hand around Tiri's mouth to muffle her screams as he rolled her over and laid on top of her as if he were a dead corpse. They laid there for a minute before the bullets stopped ringing, but he waited a second longer to make sure the coast was clear.

"Steelo!"

Hearing Kovu's voice meant it was time to shake. When he stood to his feet he grabbed the unconscious girl by the hand and threw her over his shoulder. She'd blacked out from all of the excitement.

"What you working with? You get what you needed?" he gasped while going behind his suit jacket and removing the bullet from the Kevlar vest that was in his stomach.

"Yeah, I got it, and I got a full clip. I just reloaded. Here."

Kovu tossed him an M4 as she pulled the chamber back on her own. Sadly, they were the only two left to walk out alive when they'd shown up as a group of seven.

"Who the fuck is that?" Kovu questioned.

She was referring to the girl Steelo had over his shoulder as she stood against the wall while peeping out of the doorway. She could see more men swarming up the escalator. They had to get the fuck out of there and fast.

"Like I fucking know, KD! She was just here!"

"Alright you light skinned, save a ho ass bitch!" Kovu joked as they broke across the hall with their guns blazing while they ran for the nearest exit. It was a good fifty-feet away.

"What's yo' location!" Steelo yelled into his Apple Watch while trying his best to shoot with this left hand, which wasn't his dominant one to handle an M4 with on its own.

"ETA, one minute. Pulling up on the south end of Mason Point's basement," the driver automatically responded
.

"I told you not to let this shit get sloppy, KD!" Steelo laughed as they leapt down the steps rushing for the basement level.

It always wowed the fuck out him how Kovu could manipulate a stiletto as if they were normal tennis shoes.

"I told you that bitch was gon' be on some bullshit! Marius gon' be pissed! We was supposed to be in and out!"

Her heels click-clacked against the gravel until they made it to the sedan with the doors held wide opened awaiting on their arrival. They'd gotten away just seconds before Trinity PD swarmed onto the campus, missing their targets and possible suspects.

T

The obnoxious sound of Tiri's phone ringing interrupted her sleep. She felt like she'd been hit by a damn truck as she sat up along the side of the bed and rubbed her thumping temples. Looking at her phone, she noticed that it was three o'clock in the morning.

Her mind was so hazy, but first things were first; she had to pee. Once her urine had completely exited from out of her body, everything from earlier in the day came rushing back to her mind like a boomerang.

Seeing Abby's eyes rolled to the back of her head made her jump up, clean up, then rush over to her room. It was completely empty: no sheets were on the bed, none of her belongings were there, and even the fresh smell from her Febreeze plug-ins was gone. It was like she was never there.

Tiri ran back to her room and grabbed her phone. She searched all over social media hoping to find something on her roommate. There were posts about the shooting, but no witnesses had been found and there wasn't a single reference made to Abby. Tiri knew she wasn't dreaming.

She knew what she saw! She closed her eyes shut and tried to revisit the madness from earlier once again. Images of the woman in all black flashed in her head, then there was the image of the man holding the two guns in her direction before he jumped in front of her, saving her life.

Did he take a bullet for me? Did he even know me? Why did he save me? How did I get here safely and not raped? What the fuck is going on?!

She panicked as she slid her feet into a pair of Gucci slides before heading for the door. Nothing was making sense to her. This had to be a dream that she was begging God to wake her up from because it wasn't the least bit funny. This couldn't be real!

When she opened the door to her room, she was greeted to a hand around her throat and the barrel of a gun being shoved into her mouth. The man guided her back inside, then quietly closed the door behind him.

He had a ski mask and gloves on, so Tiri couldn't take a mental photograph of who her killer was. She couldn't even make out his skin complexion behind the shield.

All she knew was he smelled of Armani Gio, was well over six feet tall, and he was seconds away from reuniting her with her mother and father whom she'd missed dearly since she was fifteen years old. This moment had to have something to do with the shooting from earlier. There was no other explanation to it.

Steelo looked at the tears streaming down her precious little chocolate face. He'd been waiting on her to wake up all fucking day. The Monstrosity had ordered him to get rid of her body just as they did with the white bitch.

Tiri was supposed to have *been* fed to their pack of hyenas, hours ago, but Steelo couldn't bring himself to do it. He killed people for a living; had been since he was sixteen. He could do the shit in his sleep, blind, deaf, and while physically frail.

After he'd hit one hundred bodies, he'd stopped counting. Nothing else had mattered once he realized that this is who he was: a cold-hearted and restive assassin.

He did the shit and he did it well. After six years of endless, bloody, body sleighing, it had become a fetish.

Now granted, he didn't walk around with his clip blazing just knocking off innocent people, but when it was time to get the game rocking he was down for whatever with whomever. Gender didn't matter, age, sexuality, class, or none of that shit. A target was a target, and the job wasn't done until his animals were fed.

But in this moment, Steelo had a personal mutiny on his hands. Tiri was still alive, and she'd remembered enough to have her life taken away from her. But even now he was hesitating to blow her brains out with the suppressor that was shoved down her throat.

His mind kept telling him to look away from her glowing eyes. The eyes he couldn't break free from while she held onto his wrist without putting up a fight.

She just stood there; almost willingly, no matter how afraid she was. The same astonishment that had filled him earlier when he had her unconscious body laid out along the mortuary table had taken over once again. The machete in his hand was ready to dismantle her every limb and go on about his day *then*. Twice now he stood before her defeated.

Every once in a while, affection and passion could get the best of him. Steelo could sense hatred, negativity, betrayal, evil, and vengeance from a mile away. He didn't know how, and he didn't know why.

It was a trait he'd had honest since he was a child, and he never bothered to question it until scarce moments like this occurred when none of those elements had coined her presence.

Most of his victims were guilty, and some weren't, but nothing had ever stopped him from drawing out an execution. Nor an order like it was doing now. His hand shook as he tightened the grip around her neck, but those eyes… Tiri's dark brown eyes were hypnotizing him, they were turning him into the man that he wasn't: a man of mercy…

Mercy, her flaming eyes kept begging him. *Mercy! Mercy! Mercy!*

Mentally frustrated, he shoved her into the bed and turned to walk away from her.

"I won't-say-any-thing…"

Her cries were barely above a whisper, but they'd gotten his attention. He stopped in his tracks and looked over his shoulder as if he were waiting on her to finish.

"I don't know anything…just please…don't kill me. On my life you have my word, but if you don't believe me then you can just go ahead and kill me now…"

Steelo inhaled deeply before the room door closed behind him and he got the fuck out of dodge. He may have done the devil's dirty work, but when God told him to fall back that's exactly what the fuck he did. It was contracting. It always had been for him, and it always would be.

His actions were sparse tonight, and little Miss Tiri Nyree Stallion better had gotten down on her knees at the very moment. She needed to thank the Lord that the tiny piece of the Holy Spirit concealed within Steelo's tampered heart had, yet again, spared her life.

Coming Soon!

CPSIA information can be obtained
at www.ICGtesting.com
Printed in the USA
LVHW09s0907290918
591716LV00005B/265/P